# The Malleable Blade

To order additional copies, please contact us.
BookSurge, LLC
www.booksurge.com
1-866-308-6235
orders@booksurge.com

# The
# Malleable Blade
## A Jon and Greg Adventure:
## Newport and the Gemstone
## Islands

Dan Whitney

2005

# The Malleable Blade

*Dedicated to*
*Jon and Greg Whitney . . .*
*and the one by whom they came.*


*Special Thanks*
*To my parents, Ray and Vicky, who nourish creativ-*
*ity in me, and continue to believe that I can do almost*
*anything; to all those who have taught me, especially Bill,*
*Rick, Tom, Les, Rhonda, Greg, Carl, Bob, Morris,*
*Wes, and Chuck; to a wonderful extended family that*
*exudes support and encouragement; and to a community*
*of faith that reflects the Creator's love for all people.*
*To those who patiently read the manuscript and made*
*helpful suggestions, and to Jeff for the cover, I offer my*
*humble thanks.*

# PROLOGUE

Dan'l quickly extinguished the lantern on the windowsill. He had been waiting all evening for his father to come back, but the noises outside meant that something more than the anticipated peaceful return was occurring. He needed to see what was happening, and that meant it needed to be dark inside so that he could see outside.

"Mum, something's not right." He spoke urgently, as loudly as he could without allowing his voice to travel beyond the walls of his home. It took a moment for his eyes to adjust.

Ella, his mother, quickly entered the front room from the bedroom, "What da ya' mean? Scootch over an' let me see?"

"I think soldiers are coming this way from the castle. Torches are lit. I think there are eight of them, but," he squinted his eyes, demanding more from them than they could possibly see, "I don't see Father."

Ella gripped her son around the shoulders, squeezing in front of the small window. She quickly confirmed what Dan'l had already suspected. Springing into action, she covered the small window, raced to the hearth, jumped onto a small stool next to the fireplace and reached up to a nearly invisible nook in the stonework. "We can't take any chances. Ya'll have ta go quickly. Take the book an' hide it where yer father described. Don't come back until after nightfall tomorra', an' cast the seein' spell befere ya enter." Drawing a small pendant over her head, she quickly draped it around her son's neck, squeezed him hard and planted a huge kiss on his cheek. "Now go as quick as ya can, and neva make a sound. I love ya, Dan'l."

She didn't say, "Don't be afraid." She knew that would be useless. She was afraid and there was no concealing it. She simply spun him out of her arms and pointed him toward the back room behind the kitchen. She turned to face the door.

The back room was built into the wall of the fortified part of the city, and was completely dark. Dan'l ran through to the back wall, book in hand, grabbing a small knapsack that lay on his pallet. They had prepared for the worst. Several days rations, clothes, and as many coins as they could scrape together were already safely tucked inside.

*Bam, bam, bam!* "Open in the name of the King!" Soldiers were shouting. The banging on the door continued.

Dan'l placed one hand on the wall in front of him and spoke slowly, but clearly, *"Patefacio."* He felt the wall before him grow warm, and then his hand slipped gently through it. Though the visible façade of the wall never disappeared, Dan'l stepped quickly out of the room, through the wall, and onto the ground outside the castle's enclosure. He released the spell, and as he did so, the sound of the shattering of the front door of his home was abruptly cut off.

Dan'l tried to walk slowly—quickly, but slowly. No, he realized that he couldn't do that. He needed to appear calm, but also move as fast as he could. He had to get to the stable, to the horse.

His father had told him that morning that this summons was sooner than expected. Dan'l knew who the enemy was. A powerful sorcerer was corrupting the magic of the land. He had already managed to place himself on the throne of the Ruby Kingdom, and now controlled the three other kingdoms as well.

Eli was Second Mage of the Ruby Kingdom. His superior, Hezekiel, served as First Mage, lived in the palace and attended the King's constant requests. Hez was a wise mage, but was less skilled and less powerful than Eli. Eli found the role of Second Mage perfectly suited to him, for it allowed more time for research and study. It was during his research that he stumbled onto the great treachery.

Records more than two decades old revealed that a previous Ruby King had borrowed jewels and an incredible sum of money from a dragon—the one called the Guardian of the Kingdom. Among the jewels were several Objects of Power—gemstones that were infused with magical abilities. When Eli began to track down these Objects, he was surprised to find them magically locked in a box in the royal crypt. He was amazed to learn that though the Sorcerer King had the Objects in his possession, he didn't know that he had them. The magical locks were the work of a magician from outside the kingdom. Eli suspected that he knew who the mage was, but he couldn't be certain.

The Eye of Ice and the Fire Eye were two of a series of four gems that held extraordinary power. If all four could be joined, they granted the wielder of the Staff of Rufus inconceivable strength and magical ability. Eli was convinced that the King was trying to assemble the entire set, along with almost all the other Objects of Power known in the Gemstone Islands. He was further convinced that this usurper was trying to create a new Sword of Compulsion, a hideous weapon out of legend, which could only be created if all four of the island's kingdoms agreed that it should be made.

Dan'l had trouble believing the Creator would allow such a thing to exist. With his father, Dan'l had studied mage craft and was an advanced apprentice himself. Dan'l knew his father's worries and together they had crafted a plan. The sword must not be created; the Fist of Four must never come together.

The timing had been worked out in intricate detail. Two days ago, just hours after the evil king had embarked on a short journey to visit the Ruling Regent of the Emerald Kingdom, Eli had managed to transport the locked box, among other things, out of the crypt and out of the castle. The king's trip was expected to take three days each way for travel; two days were planned for the visit itself. They had eight days to complete their plans.

The spells were all crafted and carefully written. They couldn't leave anything to chance—there was no margin for error due to haste or nervousness. Eli and Dan'l spent the next two days packing the boxes with all the Objects that had been collected, boxes inside of boxes, spells woven into gems to power the magic, songs sung softly over trunks and treasure. The next step would be to travel slowly to the Island, the "haunted" Island in the center of Lake Aegis. There was a concentration of magical power there, and from there the spell would be cast that would remove all of the Objects, along with Eli, from the world forever.

But this morning, just as they were making their plans to begin their journey, Eli was summoned by the King to return to the palace. Eli couldn't believe the King was back—in fact, he was certain that he was not! Who, then, was summoning him? Hezekiel he could ignore, or at least procrastinate. But this was a royal summons! The king's signet had clearly sealed the scroll. Something was terribly wrong!

Without more than a nod, Eli was taken from his home inside the city wall and removed to the castle. He managed to shout back, "Wait for me till dark."

Now it was dark, and Dan'l's mind was racing. *The Objects need to be removed.* Dan'l knew he was walking too quickly, but he couldn't force himself to slow down. *The King must not get his hands on the kind of power that is concealed in the trunks that are hidden beneath the floor of the stable. But what chance do I have of getting away? There isn't enough time to get to the island in the lake before I'm found. And what will happen to me if I invoke the spell?* knew his father had decided that the spell would banish him from the kingdom, and his father had been willing to pay that price. Dan'l turned onto the small lane where the stable stood. Once around the corner and shielded from general view, he ran. *But how will I survive in a strange and different world? I'm only 14 years old. What will this other world be like? What will happen to my family back here?*

As soon as Dan'l entered the stable, Enoch whinnied. The horse had sensed him—maybe even knew there was trouble. Calming the horse gently, Dan'l was surprised to find him saddled, ready to ride.

"Your father said to have him ready," a shy, small voice spoke from the next stall. "Said you might want a short ride in the moonlight tonight."

Dan'l nearly collapsed in fright against the wall, his illusion of aloneness broken by the sound of the stablehand's explanation. "Elias, you startled me! I didn't know you were here."

"Where else would I be? I still have this mare to brush down"

"I figured you'd be home long before now. Are you always here this late?" Dan'l inquired. The noise of his voice conveniently covered the sounds of the lifting of the loose floor boards in the corner of the stall. Who would have guessed that enormous power lay hidden within the chest that he withdrew?

"Usually I'm finished about now. I'm just a little bit behind tonight. Will you need me to wait for your return later?" Elias asked, politely.

"No, I'll take care of the horse myself. *I don't know how I will do that, but I'll do my best, for Enoch's sake.* There's no need to wait for me." Having extracted the trunk from beneath the floor, and placing the book with the other items inside it, he tied the trunk behind his saddle and began to lead the horse out of the stall.

"Have a good ride, and be careful. Stick to the paths and be gentle. We don't want any accidents in the dark!" Elias chided, gently. He watched Dan'l go, puzzled by the bundle behind the saddle.

Dan'l smiled and waved as he walked the horse out of the stable, mounted and then eased Enoch into a slow trot. Every muscle in his body strained, as he forced himself to go slowly, quietly, when his very being shouted for him to run, fly as swiftly as possible.

He had passed three houses when he heard a banging noise behind him. He turned to see soldiers pounding on the door of a house at the other end of the lane. They were already searching!

His head was throbbing! How could the king have learned about the missing Objects so quickly? How would he ever escape? He needed time. He needed to think. He had to get to the island. If he let Enoch run, they would notice him. He slowed the horse down. He had to relax, to get control of himself. He needed to stay calm!

There were about six houses between him and the house the soldiers were searching. Steeling himself against discovery, he rode straight ahead toward the back of the settlement. He knew he would need to hurry. If the royal heralds were dispatched, he didn't have a chance. But in a moment, the road would turn enough to hide him from the view of the soldiers. Then he would run...but to where?

The thought seemed to jump into his head from no where. The Sacred Grove! The Haunted Island had been their choice for the ritual because it was secluded and provided a concentration of magical power. But the Sacred Grove was much closer, and as far as Dan'l could remember, it was a primary node of magical power as well. Of course, there were all kinds of conventions and procedures associated with entry into the Grove, and he wasn't proficient in the lore. In truth, it didn't much matter. The Grove held the only possibility for success.

Finally past the last house, Dan'l leaned forward and gave the horse his head. Enoch jumped forward, responding to the urgency in Dan'l's voice. A look backwards revealed no obvious pursuit, only the drifting curls of smoke rising from the cluster of cottages that comprised the village outside the fortress walls.

Unwilling to assume that his escape would not be discovered, Dan'l pushed Enoch for several miles, until the homes of the next village came into view. It was as much as he could risk. A rider crashing through the night at breakneck speed would certainly alarm the villagers. He would have to proceed through each settlement slowly, saving the road between towns for maximum speed.

There was a day, not too long past, when this road would have stood unguarded throughout the night. But that day ended when the current monarch ascended to the throne. Banditry was allowed to become commonplace, so long as it wasn't practiced against the interests of His Majesty.

Dan'l knew he would be challenged at the entrance of every village that was beyond sight of the fortress, but there wasn't time to avoid the gates. Slowly he approached the first sentry position, where he was hailed.

"Hold! Who goes there?" a young soldier shouted.

"I'm Dan'l, come to find my father who may be in distress." Dan'l didn't like to lie. He liked even less what he was about to do. "Captain, could you tell me where I might find the home of Severn the trader? I believe my father is there."

"I know of no Severn," the soldier, certainly no captain, responded, walking over to Dan'l. The man was easy to see, the moonlight full on his face. Dan'l fixed the image of the soldier in his mind and muttered the word, "Sleep." Instantly, the man slumped to the ground.

"Hey! What did you do! Stand back from him!" another soldier charged, with sword drawn. Dan'l raised both his hands, backing Enoch away quickly.

"I did nothing. He stumbled and fell. See, my hands are empty," he pleaded, keeping his distance as the second soldier tended his fallen comrade. Dan'l couldn't get a look at the face of the second man, and before any more could be said, the second man was standing and blowing a whistle, raising an alarm.

For a moment, Dan'l froze. But he realized an instant later that he didn't have any choice. He had to go forward, as fast as he could. His only hope was to outrun whatever or whomever responded to the alarm. He kicked Enoch in the flanks and raced toward the small town.

The main road led right through the center of the village, and by the time Dan'l arrived there, three men were saddled and ready to pursue. The advantage was Dan'l's; the full moon was at his back. The thud next to his hip startled him. Looking down, he saw an arrow protruding from the knapsack that rested between him and the trunk on the horse's back. He shivered uncontrollably.

*What was he thinking? He was only a boy, only 14 years old. They were shooting arrows at him—trying to kill him! The world was going crazy!* He tried to think of some kind of spell he could use to slow down the three men who were now following him. *An advanced magical apprentice should be able to think of something!* But Dan'l was too frightened to do anything but hold on to Enoch with all of his strength and will him to go as fast as he could.

The three pursuers seemed to neither gain nor lose distance on him. As Enoch settled into a discernable rhythm, the music of his hooves suggested a course of action to Dan'l.

It took him a minute—it seemed like thirty—to sort out the words he would use. The tune he would borrow. And when he had finally composed it, relying on the pendant his mother had given him, he began to sing:

> *"Strong strides, long strides,*
> *Strength to him who runs and rides.*
> *Safe and steady on the road,*
> *Enoch flies to Sacred Grove."*

Again and again he repeated the lyrics, singing strength into every step the horse took. Enoch responded. Slowly, surely, the horse began to pull away from those following. Unfortunately, though the distance between pursuers and pursued increased, there was no sign of the end of the pursuit. And in just a moment more, the exhilaration that had captured Dan'l's heart at the success of the spell, was replaced by the realization that he was approaching another town, another sentry station.

By now, the moon was high in the sky. Dan'l could see the lanterns of the guard station ahead. It was clear that they were vigilant, ready for a challenge. Dan'l sang the spell one more time, and committed to a course of action that was repulsive to him. Never before had he used magic to frighten or terrorize. He believed that magic was given by the Creator to protect, to encourage, to heal. And now he was doing just the opposite.

Focusing his mind's eye on Enoch, and on his own reflection—seen many times in the surface of the lake—Dan'l whispered the word, "Light." Instantly, he was aglow, and not just him. To the eyes of the soldiers fleeing away from the road, a man of radiant light riding a luminescent white horse thundered past, on toward the town. Certain a demon was attacking them, the soldiers never even saw the three riders follow the monster into the village.

Exhausted, now well beyond the settlement, Dan'l slowed to a walk to allow Enoch to catch his breath. There were no signs of any pursuit. Dan'l dared to believe they had decided to leave him alone. What had happened to the three riders from the previous town, he had no idea. It was well past midnight, and a brief pause to water and tend his mount was long overdue. Dan'l dismounted and walked backwards alongside his horse, humming the tune he had sung previously without speaking the words. His eyes watched the road diligently for any sign of pursuers. None came. He pulled the arrow from his knapsack and discarded it. He didn't need the reminder of his vulnerability.

When he felt that he could delay no longer, Dan'l remounted and started toward the next town. To his surprise, the guards were asleep and he managed to travel quietly through the center of town unmolested. As soon as he was clear of the houses, he resumed his frantic pace. He knew he was pushing Enoch beyond his endurance. But there was nothing else he could do.

Within a few hours, Dan'l realized he had put the last settlement behind him. Because he wasn't sure exactly how far the Sacred Grove was from the Castle, he didn't have the option of slowing down. He had to push until he saw the entrance to the clearing. He had been told the place was unmistakable, that the very air seemed different as one entered the Grove.

The night was less dark that it had been previously. The moon was gone now, and the pitch black was slowly being replaced by a heavy gray. It seemed to Dan'l that there must be woods ahead. If that were true, it wouldn't be much longer. Distracted by his thoughts about what he would have to do in the Grove, he didn't immediately notice the change in Enoch's gait. When it finally caught his attention, it was because the horse was slowing, and then stopping, and then falling. And then it was too late. He jumped sideways off the saddle to keep from being crushed as Enoch collapsed into a frothing, panting mass of flesh. Dan'l couldn't believe how stupid he had been!

He quickly untied the trunk and his pack from the back of the horse. Stroking Enoch's head, he began singing the tune he had sung earlier in the night. Enoch's panting slowed down slightly, and he seemed calmer. But he did not rise, nor would he.

Dan'l strapped on the pack and lifted the trunk to his shoulder. He couldn't afford to wait for his horse—he had to keep moving. He hated himself for leaving Enoch behind, but what else could he do? He said a gentle goodbye, and started walking down the road toward what was definitely forest. The trunk was light, but his legs were jelly, and Dan'l suspected that it wouldn't be too long before he would collapse along the side of the road as well. It was then that he realized he was closer than he thought. The road ahead disappeared into the forest. This was it. He had arrived!

An eerie sense of magic and power permeated the air near the entrance to the Grove. Light was beginning to creep over the horizon behind him, creating long shadows in front of him. Too tired to carry the trunk any longer, he tied it to his waist with a length of rope and dragged it behind him as he stumbled forward through the gauntlet of trees. He remembered that there were rules about when a person could enter the Grove, but he decided it no longer mattered. He was beyond the limit of his endurance. Rational thought had ceased. All that remained was finishing the task—protecting the land—defeating the evil king. He had to believe that if he were about the Creator's business, surely the Creator would not allow him to be harmed!

Once inside the Grove, Dan'l simply fell to his knees. He had never experienced this level of exhaustion and fatigue before. His eyes refused to focus; he had difficulty untying the trunk. He struggled to get back up, to sit on the trunk. He took his pack and placed it nearby on the ground. Opening it, he pulled out the scrolls his father had carefully prepared. But he was too tired to concentrate on the spell-songs written there. It was too dangerous to proceed in this condition. One mistake could mean disaster.

He knew that no one had followed him out of the last town. He would have seen them if they had. Surely he could afford a short rest before attempting to cast this complex spell. Surely he had time…no, he was fooling himself; there wasn't any time. By now, word was already spreading about his late night ride. Soon the king would know where he was. And what if the spell didn't work? If the spell didn't work in this place, he would have to find a way to get to the haunted island. No, there really was no time left.

He remembered a song his mother had sung to him when he was a small boy. He involuntarily began to sing:

*Child of mine, Creator's loan,*
*May His joy to you be shown.*
*Strength for good and words to heal*
*Will form your heart and lend you zeal.*

Dan'l felt his mother's strength as he sang. He wondered how she had fared, but he was convinced she must be safe. She would not easily be captured. She was a mage in her own right, though no one really knew. He hoped that…no, he must not get distracted! He needed to begin the spell.

Unrolling the scrolls, Dan'l reviewed all three parchments before beginning. He carefully practiced the motions. It was light enough now to make out the words. He knew that once he started, he would have to finish, and if he did everything correctly, he would end up in another place and time,—and the trunk would be with him.

Dan'l's knees were shaking. His voice was unsteady as he began to sing. The song was difficult; parts had to be repeated in exact patterns. One phrase answered another. The pendant around his neck began to glow as he dropped the first scroll and sang onto the next. Thirty minutes had passed, but to Dan'l it felt like hours. Sweat was dripping off his forehead, running down the back of his neck. For a moment, he felt cooler, as if the rays of the sun had been temporarily blocked by a passing cloud. He looked up from the page while he was singing and was shocked!

A giant thundercloud was billowing up from the East, obliterating the sun completely. Dan'l had seen many thunderclouds in the past; this one was certainly not natural. Something was happening. Dan'l didn't know if it was the effect of the song he was singing or something else. He wouldn't have to wait long to find out, for in the next moment, a booming voice rang out, "Stop! Stop singing now!"

Dan'l was startled by the voice, but he didn't stop the song— couldn't stop the song.

A breeze was building in the Grove, blowing from the East, seemingly coming right in through the entrance corridor. As the wind grew, fog accompanied it and a malevolent presence rode on the mist, until Dan'l could feel the foulness. His skin began to crawl. His stomach twisted and he fought the urge to vomit. Still, he sang, his song nearing completion.

And then, right in front of him, the fog seemed to gather, to come together, to coalesce into, what was it? What was coming out of the fog?

"Stop!" the voice boomed again. And there standing directly in front of Dan'l was the Evil Sorcerer King. In his right hand was a staff of gold, a brilliant green gem glittered from its golden setting at the pinnacle of it.

Dan'l managed a few final words and stopped, staring at the tyrant standing before him.

"Did you really think you could trick me? Did you think I would let you escape with the Eyes I have been seeking for so long? You fool! I knew that your father had found them, but he would never disclose their location. I figured that if I gave him a chance to move them, he might give himself away. So I planned a little trip." The usurper laughed boisterously and sarcastically at his own cleverness.

Dan'l said nothing.

"Your father is already in the dungeon, alive only because I need him. You I have no use for. Aren't you wondering how I found you?"

Dan'l clapped his palms together, then crossed his arms and clapped the backs of his hands together. Once more, he clapped his hands, palm to palm.

The tyrant's eyes grew wide! "What are you doing?!" he screamed. "Are you still trying to cast that spell?" He lifted his staff, drawing it back as if to use it like a common club. He saw Dan'l's face turn slightly red, then fade to blue. The pendant was glowing red around Dan'l's neck.

"Stoooooooooooooooooop!"

Dan'l couldn't figure out how he was going to complete the spell. The final moment required that a drop of his blood be spilt. He would never reach his dagger to finish the last part. He saw the staff speeding toward his head. He braced himself, stiffened his neck and jaw, for the awful pain he knew must come. He had gotten so close!

He had almost finished! But now he would never...He felt the impact on his cheek, then nothing.

Everything was dark; he tensed against a sudden chill breeze. He couldn't see anything, but there was no pain, either. For a moment he was confused. He expected his jaw to be broken. Touching his cheek, he found a small scratch, slightly moist. He shivered, and realized that he was completely naked. As his eyes adjusted to the darkness of a night lit only by a sliver of moon, he noticed that he was still sitting on the trunk. A wave crashed on the rocks behind him, and turning, he realized that he was on a jagged outcropping of stone, just a few feet from shore. An irregular staircase, hewn out of the cliff face across from him, climbed up from the water's edge and spilled out onto whatever was up there, beyond Dan'l's sight.

There was no time to waste. Hoisting the trunk over his head, Dan'l slipped into the bitterly cold water and crossed the few feet of ocean to the first step of forty. The wind stung his freezing body as he slowly climbed the stairs, sharp rocks cutting into his feet. He stopped abruptly four steps from the top; he couldn't believe his eyes. And then it all made sense. He had been taking the Objects of Power out of his world into a whole new world—and this was it. He had arrived. All that remained was to finish the task, if he survived.

CHAPTER I

# Newport, RI: Twenty-five Years Later

The storm had been unexpectedly violent—two days of driving, unrelenting rain. Great winds left trees torn from the ground, roots pointing accusingly back at the sky. It really had been a terrifying ordeal. But now, everything was calm again. The sun was warm and Jon and Greg were glad to finally be out of the house, free of the storm and the gray melancholy that seemed to soak into everything over the past several days.

First Beach in Newport (or Easton's Beach, as some called it) was a new favorite spot of theirs. For the past six weeks, since their arrival in Rhode Island, Jon and Greg had found every possible excuse to spend as much time here as they could. The beach was a magical place where hours melted into moments, and whole days were lost in a mesmerizing mosaic of surf and sun, critters and seashells, games and adventures. The sand was golden, the ocean, warm and blue, and the song of the waves eased the pain of their recent relocation, pushing it into the recesses of their minds.

Today, the effects of the storm were immediately visible. Sections of the beach had eroded away, exposing rock formations, leaving huge piles of debris scattered over the length of the oceanfront. But the changes in the beach did nothing to dampen their exuberant spirits.

"Hey, check this out!" Jon held up a three-legged starfish.

Greg ran over quickly, "There's tons of cool stuff here! Look at these huge shells!"

"I wonder if...hey, Greg!" Jon had just lifted a large tangled mass of seaweed to uncover a lobster trap washed up with the flotsam. "Think we can get 'em?" "Em" referred to the three lobsters that were currently in the trap and were evidently still alive, though only barely. "I'll hold this open, and you stick your hand in and drag him out."

Greg laughed, "Yeah right. I don't think so. I don't want my fingers pinched off by some monster lobster with 'jaws of life' claws!"

"If you grab them right here on the back, behind the pinchers, they can't get at you."

"Then you do it." Greg held open the webbed entry to the trap. Jon slowly worked his hand into the tangled mass and tried to get in behind the back of one of the large lobsters so he could grab it. Every time he got close to touching one, the critter would move, and Jon would quickly yank his hand away. After the fifth attempt, Greg suggested, "Why don't we try to free this trap and take the whole thing home?"

"Might as well," Jon agreed, a little embarrassed by his lack of success.

Both started pulling at seaweed and ropes. The cable to which the trap was attached was buried deep in the sand and seemed to run toward a small rock that protruded from the beach about three feet in front of them. They gradually cleared the distance between the trap and the rock and began to dig in the sand.

"Try giving the rope a pull." Jon suggested. He already had his hands wrapped up in the yellow plastic braided line, and Greg joined him. "Pull hard!" Feet slipped on disappearing sand, but the rope didn't budge. "Dig some more, Greg,"

Greg began to wonder aloud, "Jon, this trap must belong to someone. What if the person who owns this trap comes along?"

"I think once it washes up on shore it is salvage. Sort of like lost at sea. I bet it is 'finders keepers' after that."

"If anyone will know, Dad will know. We'll ask him when we get home."

And of course, Dad would know. The Curtis family moved to Rhode Island because Dad had been transferred by the Navy to the nearby Naval War College. Captain Curtis was now an instructor. His subject was law. Yes, Dad would know.

Greg found a small, pointed fragment of wood that worked well as a shovel. He began to dig on the far side of the rock, while Jon continued to scrape away at the sand between the rock and the trap.

"I found the rope, but it keeps going around the rock to your side, Greg. I can't pull it free. I'll help you dig over there."

Together, their efforts proved effective, and soon they had bared the rope and traced it down into the sand, where it was lodged between the rock and what seemed to be a piece of buried timber.

"Are you sure this is worth it? Greg whined. "If we get that wood moved, the rope may be caught on something else beneath that...and who knows how long this rope really is? I don't want to spend all day digging for lobsters. I'd rather swim!"

"Well, why don't you go find a way to get some water to pour on those lobsters, while I work just a little longer here. You can get yourself wet while you cool off the lobsters, and if I can't get this rope free by the time you're finished, we'll go somewhere else to explore!"

"Okay," Greg shouted as he ran toward the surf.

Low tide must have been about to arrive, because the distance Greg had to travel from rock to water was substantial. It took a little while, but eventually Greg found an old two liter pop bottle, from which he tore the top. After filling it with salt water, he turned to head back to Jon. But when he looked up the beach, he saw Jon standing, waving frantically at him to come quickly. Greg dropped the bottle and ran.

"Look at this!" Jon gestured. Down in the hole was the outline of a small wooden box. It looked like a chest...a treasure chest! "Help me get it out. Grab that handle and pull!"

Jon was quickly on his knees in the sand, reaching some two and a half feet down into the hole. Greg latched onto the other handle and they began to pull with all their might. By wiggling it back and forth, the chest began to loosen from the grip of the sand. Then, all at once, a hiss and a sucking sound announced the release of the treasure from the grasp of the wet sand. The boys hauled the chest onto the beach and quickly looked around. No one was nearby.

"Should we open it here, or take it to some place private?" Greg wondered.

"Let's open it here. There's no one around, and there probably isn't anything inside it anyway."

The chest was wooden, about 18 inches long, 10 inches wide and 8 inches high. The corners were reinforced with metal of some sort, long blackened with age. There was a metal ring through the latch that kept the trunk closed, but the ring was severely rusted. Jon placed the chest on the rock and tilted it so that the ring lay on the stone. Grabbing a large chunk of pink granite from the beach nearby, Greg pounded on the iron ring until it snapped in half, falling to the beach.

Excitement radiated from the boy's faces! Jon kept thinking about pirate gold. Hadn't he heard some rumors about pirates in these parts? And with a little bit of pirate gold, he could have anything he wanted! He could get a new bike, buy his mom a new car…if there was enough, maybe he could buy his family a house. Then maybe his dad could quit this job that kept them moving all the time, and they could settle down like a normal family.

Greg grasped the latch and tried to lift the lid. No luck. Hinges were rusted tight.

"Hold the box while I try to pry it open," Jon instructed. He quickly found a sharp piece of stone to use as a lever. No sooner had he jammed the stone into the slit beside the latch than the wood around the back hinges gave away and the whole top of the chest flew off.

The chest was certainly not empty, but the contents were not what the boys were expecting. Immediately visible were two jeweled daggers, each about eight inches long. There were no sheaths for the daggers, but the blades were bright and obviously very sharp. Jon and Greg each picked up one of the daggers for inspection.

"Awesome!" squealed Greg. "This is the coolest blade I have ever seen."

"Check out the jewels in the handle," Jon observed. "I bet they are worth a fortune."

"Do you think the red stone could be a ruby? Look, there is a stone just like it on the other side, too." Greg extended the dagger to Jon, twisting it so he could see both stones.

"Mine is the same, or sort of the same. Look, the designs are almost exactly alike, but the two big stones in mine are green. Maybe they're emeralds or something."

Greg was about to reach back into the chest when they heard noises from down the beach. Five kids were headed toward them, running and playing, obviously moving toward the place where Jon and Greg were working. "Hurry," Jon urged, "let's get this stuff home and look at it there. We don't want anyone to find out about this until we know what we have."

Greg nodded and they quickly emptied the chest of the rest of the contents. Each of them grabbed a necklace of multicolored beads and stuffed it into a pocket. They carefully tucked their daggers into their pockets, and Jon grabbed the flat leather pouch that lay on the bottom of the chest. Afraid to run because of the daggers in their pockets, they headed off the beach in a direction away from the kids, a direction that would quickly see them home.

## CHAPTER 2

# Sibling Secrets

All the way home each boy walked with one hand in his pocket, to keep the dagger away from tender skin. But the boys knew that if they were going to get past Mom, they would have to divert her attention. If they entered the house with hands in pockets, Mom would want to know what they had, and then she would make them give the daggers to a museum or something. And they weren't quite ready to part with their new treasures so quickly. After they had rinsed off their feet with the hose out back, they entered the kitchen by the back door, hands at their sides. Mom was at the sink. 'Hi, guys, What'cha been doing?"

"Exploring down at the beach," Greg offered.

"The waves are huge! You can't imagine how much junk washed up on the beach," Jon added.

"Most of it is garbage, but there were some cool shells and stuff. Mostly broken."

"Did you bring any shells home?"

"No shells," Jon replied. "We didn't find any shells worth keeping."

Greg had already slipped through the kitchen and was making his way up the stairs when Mom called out, "Greg, lunch will be ready in about 30 minutes. Why don't you two hang around here until after lunch, and then you can go explore some more if you like."

"Okay, Mom. We're just going to go up to our room to look for some beach buckets and sand tools in the closet."

"Okay, honey. Have fun."

Jon slipped up the stairs to the hallway that led to their room.

Greg's tenth birthday was just a few weeks away. He was asking for a new bike, much like the one Jon had gotten on his birthday a few weeks earlier. The trouble was that Jon's old bike was still in good condition, and since the boys were only two years apart in age, hand-me-downs were a regular part of Greg's existence. He wore Jon's old soccer spikes, Jon's old roller blades, Jon's old winter coats and Jon's old rubber boots. Anything Jon had that didn't wear out under normal use eventually found its way into Greg's closet. Greg didn't mind too much. He knew his folks weren't wealthy, and it wasn't right to waste money. But sometimes, he just wanted something that was only his.

Jon got to do everything first, too. He went to school first, rode a bike first, got to cross the street by himself first, grew tall enough to ride go-carts first. Jon was the oldest, and it seemed that the oldest often got special privileges. Greg wished he had been born first. Then he wouldn't have to work so hard to keep up.

In spite of all that, Greg idolized his older brother. The two of them had invented a thousand games, the rules to which only they knew. They understood what each other liked, and what each disliked. Jon liked carrots, hated peas. Greg liked peas, hated broccoli. Both loved pizza; only Greg ate pepperoni.

And if Greg idolized his older brother, Jon was Greg's protector. Sure, the two of them fought—often! But while Jon reserved the right to sock his own brother, no one else better try it. A boy named Jeremy had tried it once, and it was three days before the swelling in his right eye started to go down.

Actually, though two years apart, Jon and Greg looked a great deal alike. Jon was taller, but only by about three inches. Both had light blonde hair, Jon's wavy and Greg's straight. Since short hair was in style, that difference wasn't noticeable. Blue eyes, pleasant smiles, handsome boys, they were often mistaken for twins. At the moment, Greg's smile was a little amusing, due to some temporary tooth loss. His two front teeth were very prominent, while the teeth to either side had not yet dropped into place. The casual observer might think there was something reminiscent of a beaver about Greg. But that was due to more than just teeth.

Greg was busy! Greg worked hard to do well at everything he tried. He practiced hard, baseball, soccer, basketball. While other kids were watching cartoons, Greg was working—pitching, batting, dribbling. He was creative, often writing stories, imagining what he would be like in different places and in different situations.

As intense as Greg was, Jon was fun. Jon was light-hearted and effervescent. He loved to run, and could run like the wind! Easy going and cheerful, Jon was naturally athletic and a born leader. An All-star on his baseball team in Virginia, Jon was steady under pressure.

Moving as often as Jon and Greg did made the bond between them even stronger. Other friends came and went all too frequently. But brothers were for life. You could count on a brother. Brothers were reliable, stable and understandable. Jon and Greg could pretty much tell what the other was thinking most of the time. And in a world where too many things changed far too often, that was a great comfort.

When Jon opened the door to the bedroom, he knew something was wrong. Greg was waiting just inside the door, and when the door swung open, Greg yanked him inside and quickly, quietly closed the door. "It's gone!" he hissed.

"What's gone?" Jon asked.

"My knife! It disappeared! I had it just before I stepped into the kitchen, but when I reached into my pocket up here, my pocket was empty. We've got to go back down there and…"

Before Greg could finish, Jon felt the outside of his own pocket. Empty. "SShh. Greg. Mine's gone, too. Something funny is going on here."

CHAPTER 3

# Gemstone Island—Ruby Kingdom: Alarm!

Prince Judas heard the alarm and knew the challenge must have happened. Someone was in his closet right now, sorting out clothes, clothes he would probably never wear again. He didn't even want to know who would be unlucky enough to wear them next.

The present crisis began three days ago when the Obsidian King and Queen, along with members of their court, rode up to the city's walls. "We would seek council with our cousins, the Ruby King and Queen," the Obsidian King had demanded.

After an extended delay, which served to make the visiting royal couple all the more irritated, the Obsidian entourage had been admitted to the city and shown to guest quarters on the third floor of the castle. The armsmen, of course, were not permitted into the castle, but were boarded in one end of the garrison's barracks to the west of the castle. It wasn't really that much of a city, after all.

Most of the people lived outside the walls. There was an open patch of ground that was kept clear between the walls and the beginning of the settlement, but beyond that, the homes of the people of the Ruby Kingdom surrounded the central city. Cottages were most abundant on the east side, where the stream that flowed from the spring within the walls of the city broke free and cascaded down across the rocks into a clear pool. The stream that flowed from this pool meandered off to the south and east, watering fields and livestock alike.

At each corner of the city wall, a rounded turret stood to provide a vantage point for the local guard. But even though the turrets stood tall, the castle dwarfed everything else.

The castle stood nearest to the northern wall, facing the south. It was surrounded by a moat that was fed by an underground spring. The moat drained into a small stream that left the city through a carefully constructed, barred and secured hole in the eastern wall.

To the west of the castle stood the garrison's barracks, stables, armory and supply sheds. To the east, behind the stream, selected craftsmen were allowed to ply their trades. These craftsmen were most trusted by the royal family. Of course, any craftsman lucky enough to be allowed to keep shop within the city's walls was guaranteed good fortune and excellent security.

The inside of the front wall of the city hosted a strip of opulent homes built into the walls. These housed relatives, or near relatives, of royalty.

The main gates to the city were made of thick oak reinforced with iron bars and nails. Directly behind them an iron grate on a pulley system reinforced the security of the main entrance.

The castle itself was entered across a draw bridge of wood, which spanned the moat very neatly. Most of the time, the drawbridge was left down. But curiously, when the Obsidian Couple had arrived, the draw bridge had been hastily drawn up, only to be let down again once the entourage was inside the city walls.

The shouting had begun almost as soon as the meeting had started. The Ruby King had received his cousins in the throne room. Judas could hear what was going on because his bedroom was just off the throne room. He heard complaints about mining rights and stolen goods. He heard charges of greed and corruption. He heard threats and promises of war. Then the doors of the throne room had burst open and the raging Obsidian King retreated up the stairs to his rooms on the third floor.

Judas knew sleep would be impossible, so he decided to sneak down into the kitchen to see what the servants knew. If anyone knew anything at all, the servants would be the ones who would know what was going on. His mother wouldn't exactly tell him the truth. And though he hated to admit it, his father was every bit as greedy and treacherous as the Obsidian King had charged. Best to get the news from the servants.

Eli was the butler and chief overseer of the castle staff. He was well over 70 years old, but still had a spring in his step. His white hair framed a warm and kind face, wrinkled yet filled with the joy of life. His wife, Ella, served as the head cook. As calm and joyful as Eli was, Ella was the opposite. Nervous and easily flustered, Ella skittered about here and there, shouting orders, trying to keep everyone and everything in order. Although Eli was technically in charge, in the kitchen, Ella had command.

When Judas entered the kitchen, he ran up to Eli who scooped him up into his arms. Eli was very much the grandfather that Judas had never known.

"What's all this?" Eli asked.

"What's happening? I heard the Black King leave…and was he mad. What's going to happen?"

"I don't know, Judi." Only Eli (and occasionally his wife, Ella) called Prince Judas "Judi." "We'll have to wait to hear the reports. It's too soon to know anything, yet."

"But what do you think will happen?"

Eli thought a moment before answering. "I'd be lying if I said it wasn't serious trouble. Everyone knows the evil nature of that vile king. He's up to no good. But exactly what he has on his mind, only he knows. Of course, now, maybe your father knows, too."

"Maybe," thought Judas, "but that won't help me any. He never tells me anything. Just, 'when you're older, you'll understand.'"

"Well, Judi, there's not much anyone can do tonight, anyway. You might as well head back to bed and try to get some sleep. We'll all know more in the morning. Would you like some hot cocoa to help you fall asleep?"

"I guess so."

"Ella, some hot cocoa for our prince, if you please. Judi, Sam could use a scratch behind the ears, if you don't mind." Sam was an old golden retriever who slept in a corner of the kitchen not too far from the fire. He was curled up on a soft blanket which Judas had given him several years before. Judas wandered over to where Sam was sleeping, sat down next to him, and began to scratch his head. Sam startled briefly when Judas sat down, then he stretched out his head and placed it, along with one paw, on Judas' lap. By the time the hot cocoa was ready, Judas was asleep.

CHAPTER 4

# Newport—Magical Markings

Greg searched the hallway while Jon went back down the steps to the kitchen. It seemed impossible that they could have both lost their knives, in the space of about five minutes. But the knives had to be somewhere, so they could only look where they had been.

"Can I set the table for lunch?" Jon asked Mom.

"Sure, honey. Cream of tomato soup and grilled cheese, so set bowls and paper plates."

"Okay." Jon took his time collecting the bowls and plates, silverware and cups. He dropped a spoon on the floor to give himself a chance to look under the table. The kitchen wasn't that big. By the time he looked under the table he knew the knives were not anywhere here. "How long 'til it's ready, Mom?"

"About 15 minutes. I'll call you."

"Thanks." Jon went back upstairs and found Greg sitting on the bed. The expression on Greg's face told Jon that the knives were still very much lost.

"I can't believe we lost those knives! Where could they have gone?" Jon muttered.

"We couldn't have lost them! One minute they were in our pockets, the next, who knows where they went? It's like they disappeared into thin air!" Greg observed.

"Do you still have the other stuff we found? Jon asked. Jon pulled out the necklace of colored beads and the flat leather pouch. Greg wrestled his necklace out of his pocket at the same time.

"Well, at least this hasn't disappeared. Jon, what's in the pouch?"

"I don't know. Let's find out."

Jon laid the pouch on the bed and knelt down beside it. The necklace he slipped around his neck, under his T-shirt, for safe keeping. Although the pouch was very old, it was not brittle. A leather cord held the opening flap in place, and when Jon unfastened the strap, the flap bent back easily. Inside the pouch was a folded piece of very old, yellowed parchment paper. Jon carefully unfolded the paper and smoothed out the wrinkles on top of the bed. It was obviously a map. The outline of southeastern Rhode Island and southern Massachusetts was obvious. Written across the bottom of the map were the words, "New Yorke and the Gemstone Islands." Neither Jon nor Greg had ever heard of the Gemstone Islands. They knew where New York was, and it wasn't pictured on the map. On each side of the map was the outline of a dagger exactly the size of the missing daggers.

"I wonder if this is a treasure map?" whispered Greg.

"If it is, it is the strangest kind of map I have ever seen," answered Jon. "Look, it says New Yorke, but New York would be down here. Maybe one of these islands off the coast is supposed to be a Gemstone Island, but if this is a treasure map, shouldn't there be something *marked* on the map?"

There wasn't anything marked on the map at all. There was the outline of the land and the islands, the title, and the outline of the two daggers.

"I bet there is a secret here, somewhere. Maybe it's invisible ink, or something written so small you can only see it with a magnifying glass," Greg suggested. "Get the flashlight out of the closet and bring it over here."

Jon got the light and they studied the map carefully. They held the paper up to the window, hoping the sunlight might reveal a hidden clue. They folded and refolded the paper to see if there was a hidden message in the way the paper folded, perhaps revealing a part of an image. They were about to give up when Greg noticed something.

"Do you see the difference between the drawing of the land and the drawing of the knives? I think someone drew the land and then traced the knives we found. See where the line disappears a little, and look here, where the line is doubled up. Doesn't it look just the way your paper does when you trace your hand?"

"You're right, Greg. I bet you are supposed       to place the knife here, and that somehow the knife gives a clue to the map! Aww, I wish I had that knife!"

No sooner had Jon spoken the word, than the knife appeared, right out of nowhere, in his right hand!

"Jon!" Greg gasped.

With a sharp intake of breath, Jon dropped the knife on the bed.

"How'd you do that?" Greg wondered in amazement.

"I didn't do anything! I just said that wished I had the knife, and it popped right into my hand!" He reached down and picked up the knife. "I wonder if it will disappear if I put it in my pocket again?"

"Before you do that, Jon, see if it fits the outline on the map." Jon placed the knife over the drawing on the map. It was a perfect match. Before he could pick up the knife again, Greg held out his hand and said, "I wish I had my knife back." Immediately, the matching dagger appeared in his outstretched hand.

"Amazing!" exclaimed Jon. "Put your knife on the map."

As soon as Greg's dagger hit the map, the paper started to change. What was once old parchment was now a soft and glowing surface. Three purple "X"'s began to glow on the map. In the center of each "X" was a number. The "X" with the number one written inside it marked the spot where the boys had found the chest that morning. But there were two more "X"'s! Two more treasures! One was to the South and East of the first, on the opposite coast of the peninsula, and the other was simply further south, around the bottom of the cliffs. As they were staring at the map, first Jon's, then Greg's dagger blinked out of existence. When the daggers disappeared, so did the markings on the map.

It didn't take the boys long to figure out that whenever the knives left their hands, they would disappear in about two minutes. But it only took wishing them back for them to return immediately to their right hand. In fact, they tried lots of experiments. Greg placed the knife in his closet, then walked down the hall to the bathroom. After carefully locking to door, he wished for his knife to return. Wa-lah! It worked every time!

They were just getting ready to try an outdoors experiment when Mom called them for lunch. They stuffed the map under the bed, along with their knives, and headed downstairs. The soup smelled good, and the excitement of the morning had left them both very hungry.

"Umm, smells great, Mom!" Greg sang out.

"Swiss cheese on the right, Muenster on the left," Mom instructed. Greg loved Swiss; Jon wasn't picky.

Greg grabbed a grilled cheese sandwich to dip into his soup, and before he thought about it, said, "Mom, I wish I had a knife to cut this sandwich." His dagger immediately appeared in his hand! Fortunately, Mom had already turned around to get a knife from the counter. He put his hand down on his lap with lightning speed, and tried to wipe the scared expression off his face. Jon snorted with laughter, but quickly controlled himself.

"What's so funny about wanting a knife, Jon?" Mom asked.

"Uh, I don't know. It's just that he eats those sammiches so fast, it's hardly worth getting the knife dirty."

Mom handed Greg a knife.

Lunch did disappear fast. Afterwards, armed with a leather pouch, two strings of beads hidden under their T-shirts, and a plastic garbage bag for sea treasure, they started back toward the beach. They left their knives under the bed.

CHAPTER 5

# Unwelcome Guests

To the northwest of the Ruby Kingdom lay the foothills of the Severus Mountains. It was in these foothills that the maze of mining tunnels began, and it was from these tunnels that the gems which gave their name to the kingdom were mined. Rubies of every shape and size were found, although most were small. The mines were not as productive as they had been in years gone by. But the truth known by all was that the rubies were not the secret to the stability of the kingdom. Yes, the rubies did provide most of the wealth. And yes, more rubies were traded abroad than any other product of the kingdom. But though ruby production gradually decreased, the kingdom remained strong. The Aegis was the reason.

Every spring, as the snow melted and the rains came, the Great Tirades Mountains, south and east of the Ruby Kingdom emptied themselves of millions of gallons of water. This runoff swelled the rivers and streams that began in the mountains, poured through the foothills and stretched out to the plain south of the kingdom. The Aegis was a giant collecting basin of Great Tirade water. An inland sea of fresh water, the Aegis was full of fish and other edible aquatic life. Because it was fresh water, it provided irrigation for crops on the plain south of the kingdom. So while other kingdoms were forced to sell their manufactured goods to purchase supplemental food for their people, the Ruby Kingdom never ran out of food, nor had the need to buy any. Fish, farm produce, grains, livestock, all were abundant on the Corundum Plain.

And there were more than a few folks who were jealous of the good fortune of the Ruby Kingdom. Three years ago a secret project was begun up in the heights of the Great Tirades. Engineers, builders, craftsman and a couple of squadrons of soldiers from the Obsidian Kingdom stole up into the hills beyond Mount Kyd-juum. Volcanic Kyd-juum, the tallest point in the Tirades, was southwest of the Obsidian Kingdom, and the main source of her mineral production. Once past Kyd-juum, the team began to build a series of dams that would divert the spring rains north and east. By trapping the water in reservoirs, the Obsidian King hoped to return prosperity to his people.

Of course, water that made its way back north past Mount Kyd-juum never reached the Aegis. Within one season of the completion of the dams, water levels fell dangerously low in the Sea, and folks began to wonder what was happening. An exploration team from the Ruby Kingdom discovered the new dams in the mountains. Theft of water was an act of war! It took three months to destroy the dams and return the rivers to their normal courses. It took only three days, once the main dam had been destroyed, for the Obsidian King and Queen to arrive at court. Of course, because of the greater wealth and might of the Ruby Kingdom, no one expected an all out war between the two. But who knew what their dark cousins had in mind?

When Prince Judas awoke, he was in his own bed again. He didn't remember climbing up the stairs to his room, but he assumed that Eli had carried him and tucked him into bed. Judas jumped out of bed and dressed quickly. The room was cold, in spite of the roaring fire in the fireplace. He danced onto the carpet at the foot of his bed until he had pulled on his socks, finally ready to head down to breakfast. When he opened the door to the kitchen, the smoky smell of bacon and sausage filled the air. It was pleasantly the same as any other morning…and the activity of cooks and servants masked the tension that Judas would soon discover.

"Ella, where's Eli?' Judas asked.

"Aye, Prince Judi, what would ya be doin' here? Shouldn't ya be with yer family on a mornin' like this?"

'What do you mean, on a morning like this? Has something happened?" Judas questioned.

"Well it's not fer me ta be sayin'. Here, take this plate back ta yer room and I'll send Eli ta ya. Then you and he can have a talk." Ella filled a platter with scrambled eggs and bacon. Roasted potatoes were on one side, balanced by a goblet of rich, creamy milk. It was pointless to question Ella. Once she had decided not to speak, she took it as a point of honor to say nothing further. Judas would have needed to summon torturers to get any information out of Ella, but there was no guarantee that what Ella thought she knew was the truth to begin with! Judas headed back to his room.

It was night before Judas learned anything at all. He tried for hours to talk to his father, but the king was sequestered with advisors in the library all day long. His mother was complaining of a migraine and had taken to her bed. She would see no one when she was in this condition. The servants all whispered that something was terribly wrong, but no one had any idea what it might be, and Ella wasn't talking. Eli had left early in the morning on a royal errand and wasn't expected back before nightfall. The one thing Judas had managed to discover was that the Obsidian King and Queen were gone!

Somehow, during the previous night, the king, queen, and their entire entourage had escaped from the palace. They were nowhere in the city. Their guards had vanished with them.

When Eli returned, he reported to His Majesty the Ruby King, and then headed to the kitchen. It was in the small room behind the kitchen that Judas finally caught up with him.

"Eli, where have you been?" Judas cried, grasping for Eli.

"Now, now, don't get all upset. I've only been gone the better part of the day. And here I am, all in a piece."

"But where were you?"

"Off on an errand for your Father, His Royal Highness. I can't really say much more than that, can I?"

Judas took Eli's face in both of his hands, gently, so that Eli had to gaze into his eyes. "Tell me," Judas said very slowly, "Please."

Eli sat down on a small wooden three legged stool, and carefully

21

hoisted Judas up onto his lap. He leaned back against the table and began to speak slowly, as warmly and softly as possible...perhaps to counter the seriousness of the words he was about to utter. "There is going to be a challenge, Prince Judas, a challenge according to the laws of the ancient kingdoms."

"What kind of challenge is that, and, uh, what ancient kingdom?" Judas sputtered.

"Be patient, hold your tongue, and I will tell you everything," Eli promised.

"In ancient days, serious disputes were settled by a challenge. One party would challenge the other to a duel, a fight of some sort, to decide who would get their own way. These would inevitably lead to warfare and great loss of life and property. To limit all of this, a special court was invented by a wise magician named Rufus. Rufus created a special Grove, about a day's journey southwest of here. In that Grove, all challenges had to be fought. And they had to be fought fairly, on the Great Board.

"The Great Board?" interrupted Judas.

"The Great Board, the Great Chess Board. Once inside the Grove, the opposing parties would take up positions on the chess board. The king and queen of the kingdom must represent themselves. The bishops were played by priests, the knights by the generals of the army. The rooks were powerful magicians. The two center pawns were for representatives of the king's family, the remaining pawns were powerful warriors from the army. No one else was allowed into the Grove except the players on the board and the field surgeons. Spectators waited beyond the hedges of the Grove to see who emerged first. The first side out had been vanquished. Responsibilities remained for the victor.

"That doesn't sound too scary. You talk like the Great Board is an evil thing. Is it?"

"I guess that depends on how you look at it. The Great Board hasn't been used too many times. In the times that it was used, it did manage to prevent great wars. But there was a great price. You see, the players on the board, they really suffer the consequences of what happens in the game. If a soldier is killed on a battle on the board, he dies, for good."

"Oh," Judas inhaled sharply.

"The reason that wars were averted was that most times the royal family was, umm, eliminated, and one kingdom simply took over the other. So, I guess the people were glad to avoid the war, but if you are in the royal family, it is a lot more frightening."

"Do you think there will actually be a challenge, Eli?" Judas weakly asked.

"Yes, my Prince, I do. In fact, that is where I was. I was spying on the Obsidian King and Queen in their camp. They escaped from the castle by the use of magic and are camped with their army on the Corundum Plain due south. Tomorrow the challenge will appear. Right now they are assembling their challenge team for the Great Board."

"But our armies are mightier than their armies. There is no reason for Father to agree to this challenge!" Judas valiantly affirmed.

"True, Judi, but the strength of our forces doesn't matter much when it comes to the Great Board. Each king has a special amulet around his neck which contains five golden beads. These magical beads contain the challenge spell, and once one bead is cast on the ground in an opponent's castle, the magic begins to take shape. Tomorrow, a magical message will appear in the air above the castle. Everyone in the kingdom will be able to see it. It will challenge your father to a duel on the Great Board. He will have three days to appear at the grove. If, after three full days from the appearance of the message, he has not appeared, his opponent can call him to the Grove magically. This can never be allowed to happen. If called magically, the spell only calls the members of the king's immediate family. They have to take up all the positions themselves, and would be hopelessly overmatched. Also, whichever team arrives at the Grove first gets to choose their position on the board; North always moves first.

"The Obsidian King has already used one of the beads here in the castle. His goal is to move secretly to the Grove tonight and be ready when the sun rises tomorrow. He can't step into the Grove to assume his position until sunset after the message has appeared. The game can't begin until dawn of the next day. He is gambling that by the time your father learns of the challenge, that he won't have enough time to assemble his team and arrive at the grove by sunset. That way, the Obsidian King can have the North side of the Great Board and can attack first."

Judas was visibly upset by all of this news. He was very quiet and was starting to sniffle softly. He held onto Eli very tightly and buried his head in Eli's chest. "What will happen to me? Are my parent's going to die? Will I have to fight on the Great Board? And where will you be?"

Eli stroked Judas' arm gently and spoke in comforting tones. "Don't worry, you won't have to fight. Someone will be dressed in your clothes, a soldier, who will stand in for you. You will wait here in the palace. But I will be there. There is one thing I never told you. I am much more than a butler. This you must never tell another living soul. Disguised as a butler, I am free to go anywhere I choose and am often overlooked in meetings of importance. But I am actually the senior mage of the kingdom, even though Stoneclaw holds the title. Many years ago we decided it was best for us to operate in this way, but tomorrow, we will both be on the Board at sunset."

"Don't go!" Judas pleaded. "I can't afford to lose you! What would I do if something ever happened to you?"

"You will have to go on and rule the kingdom, I suppose," whispered Eli. "Now listen carefully. I will have a special system in place to let you know the outcome of the battle as soon as it is over. If your father and mother win, you need not concern yourself, all will be well. But if they lose, you will need to go into hiding. Winning kings often clean out the palace of the loser, and unwanted heirs to the throne can be a real nuisance. I'm rather sure that the Obsidian king would have you *removed* before the night was over."

"But where would I hide? What would I do?" Judas sniffled.

"Don't worry about all of that yet. There are many secret hiding places and you have more friends than you realize. Even should the dark king win, he would have more trouble holding on to this kingdom than he might imagine. Your job would be to stay safe, be true to what I have taught you, and wait until the right moment. You will know that moment when it comes, and then you will take back what rightfully belongs to you and your family. Will you do that for me, Judi?"

"I don't know if I can."

"It's not about whether you can or not, my boy, you must!" There was a fire in Eli's voice as he continued. "Sometimes things happen that cause a boy to grow up very quickly. One of those things has now happened to you. And your time has come!"

"My time?" Judas queried.

"This is your time, Judi, or at least, it is about to be. You see, no matter what happens tomorrow, this issue has been brewing for a long time. The real problem here is greed. I've tried to warn your father by encouraging him to share the waters that come from the Great Tirades. He will not listen. He claims them as rightfully a part of his ancestral kingdom, but he is afraid to lose this source of our great wealth. If he would share the water, this problem would eventually go away. The Obsidian King is also greedy. He wants the water; his people need the water, so that they can become strong as we are strong. No, as long as a solution to share this water cannot be reached, both kingdoms are in danger. Even if your father wins tomorrow, he will not win forever. And sooner or later, this problem will be your problem."

Judas could say no more. A million questions raced through his mind, and yet he didn't seem to have the strength to put together a sentence to ask one. A great weariness settled over him. Eli was stroking his hair with his hand and humming a tune. He had heard this tune before, many times before he fell asleep. And before he had a chance to wonder if Eli was using some sort of magic to put him to sleep, Judas was asleep.

CHAPTER 6

# Sheep Point Cove

First Beach was only a few blocks due east from the house, but now the two were headed in a different direction altogether. The closest spot marked on the map was due south at what looked like the end of the "Mansion" boulevard, which was Bellevue Avenue. They could have walked down the boulevard, or cut through the campus of Salve Regina, but they were afraid they might get confused and lose their way. The cliff walk was their best bet.

The cliff walk is a rocky walkway cut into the top of the eastern edge of the cliffs that separates the mansions of Newport from the sea. Tourists trek along the famous walkway, peering into the back yards of castles, mansions and other famous buildings. Varied in width and architecture, the pathway, which is ornate in some sections, becomes more and more unrefined the further south you travel. Jon and Greg didn't mind unrefined. In fact, they were willing to sacrifice speed to avoid any unwanted questions or any inconvenient delays. They would simply hide among the tourists.

Once past The Breakers, the largest of the Newport Mansions, the boys thought they ought to check the map again, to get a better idea of exactly where the second "X" was positioned on the map. They looked up and down the cliff walk to see if the coast was clear, and finding no one around, decided to check the map right there on the granite bench at the rest stop. The site really was breathtaking. Behind them was the mansion, obviously named for the breakers that were pounding into the cliff in front of them. The sky was powder blue; the ocean a rich azure. The taste of salt and sea was in the air. Seagulls cried, scouring the surf for their afternoon feast. Others climbed high in the air to drop shellfish onto the rocks below.

The map was spread out carefully, held by the left hand of each. Jon watched north, while Greg looked south. At almost the same time they both said, "I wish I had my knife." Knives appeared from nowhere in their right hands. They placed the knives on the map, and the glowing began. Three "X"'s. And the closest one was slightly to the east of the southernmost tip of the eastern shore of the peninsula.

"It can't be far," Greg observed. "Once we go around this next bend we are in sight of the southern tip. From the look of this map, the treasure could be anywhere along this next section."

"There has to be some kind of shore there, though. We can't dig into a solid cliff wall, any more than they could. Unless," Jon paused to consider, "unless there is a cave somewhere."

"There's no way to tell from the map. The treasure could be underground, buried, in a cave, who knows. I think we may have a really hard time finding this one," Greg lamented.

"Well, all we can do is look. Let's start down around this bend and stop at the first sandy beach we find." Jon led the way.

Past The Breakers, the cliff walk moved closer to sea level and, once around the corner, degenerated into a large levy of rocks, the tops of which had been smoothed for the sake of hikers. Once past those rocks, the boys spied a small section of beach to which they could easily climb. Just beyond them was a dark, overgrown access road back to civilization. Really, it was little more than a trail. Past that, down the coast, they could see clearly to the southern tip of the peninsula, past a small tunnel where the cliff walk ran under a portion of someone's backyard. Though the beach was small and therefore easy to cover, it was immensely frustrating.

."How can we possibly know where to dig? This treasure could be twenty feet down under the sand. Who knows how the storm affected this area?" Jon griped.

"I don't know, Jon, just look around. Look between rocks and stuff. And be patient. It may take us a few days to find it," Greg chided.

Jon walked along the edge of the beach that met the rocks of the cliff walk. Greg ventured out to the water's edge and walked in the surf. From there he scoured the rocks looking for a cave or crevasse that couldn't be seen from the land. They searched the area diligently, but there was no sign of any cave or crack in which a treasure might be hidden, and there was certainly no sign of any treasure. They were about to walk back up onto the pathway when a float from a fishing net caught Jon's eye. Jon walked over to examine the remains of the net imbedded in the sand, and decided that float might make an interesting ornament for the backyard fence. He wished for his knife and began to cut through the plastic netting as soon as it appeared. After a few seconds, he stopped.

"Greg, call for your knife."

"What for? Do you need help?" Greg replied.

"No, just do it. I have a question."

Greg called for his knife, which immediately appeared.

"What does it feel like?" Jon asked.

"I don't know, it feels like a knife. What d'ya mean?"

"Is it cold, or warm? Does it feel tingly?" Jon responded.

"It feels cold, or cool maybe. I don't know. How does yours feel?" Greg asked.

"Mine's warm, and definitely a little tingly. Come over here! Touch mine and compare." Jon ordered.

Greg's eye got wider as he touched Jon's knife. "Yours is the same as mine, Jon. But mine is not the same! From the time I called for my knife 'til now, mine has gotten much warmer. Wait a second, stay here."

Greg walked back to where he was standing when Jon first called to him. The knife was noticeably cooler. As Greg slowly walked toward Jon, his knife grew warmer and warmer. "It's getting hotter the closer I get to you. Start moving around and see if it gets hotter or colder."

Jon walked to the south along the rock wall. The knife cooled down. Greg walked north along the rock wall, his knife cooled down. Both turned back and began walking toward each other. When they met, the knives were the warmest they had been.

"Only two choices left," Jon pointed. "You walk toward the water, I'll climb the rocks." It didn't take three steps to figure out who was moving closer to the treasure. "This way," Jon shouted.

Two-thirds of the way up the rock wall, just over the edge from the walking trail, was a large black rock which supported several of the rocks in the trail above. When Jon reached that spot, he put the knife down. "Man, that knife is hot! This must be the place. But how are we going to move that rock?" All of the rocks were far too heavy to be moved by young boys.

"We're going to have to pry those top rocks off, if we are ever going to get at the black one," said Greg. "Do you see a big branch or a pipe or something?"

Surprisingly, there on the beach was exactly the thing they were looking for. A section of fence from a nearby neighbor had blown away in the storm, only to be deposited right here where it was need- ed. Greg pried off the post with his knife and carried the sturdy piece up to the walkway. Together, the two of them were able to pry three large rocks from the top of the pile, revealing the top surface of the black rock. They inserted the post into a crevasse behind the large black rock and began to push with all their might. Nothing moved. They strained and grunted, pushing with their feet, their hands, their backs. At one point, Greg lost his grip and fell down the rock wall, only to land in the soft sand below.

"It's no use, Jon. We'll never move that rock. We have to get help."

"We can't get help. We don't want anyone to know about this, remember? Besides, who would we tell? There has to be a way to move this thing. We just haven't thought of it yet." Jon sat down on the rock to think while Greg brushed the sand off his back and legs and arms. "What if we slowly pried away the rocks on either side? Maybe we could loosen the smaller rocks and that might make the big rock shift."

"That's gonna be a ton of work!" Greg groaned.

"Yeah, but it's worth a try." Jon grabbed the wooden pry bar they had been using and tried to pull it out of the hole. Unfortunately, the post was now jammed into the opening when Greg had fallen. "The post is stuck. Come up here and help me get it out."

Greg climbed up the rocks and grabbed hold of the post. To-gether the two wiggled and shook the post, trying to loosen it. But the post was really stuck. Jon sat down, exhaling loudly, "I'm exhausted! Maybe we should go home and work on this tomorrow. We could bring back Dad's crow bar, maybe a couple of levers. Then we could move this beast."

Greg knelt down to see if he could determine why the post was stuck, while Jon talked. "That's probably the best idea. We should try this with some real tools before we get any one else involved. If only we could..." Greg stopped mid sentence. His arm was down in the crevasse, up to his shoulder, where the post was stuck. "...Jon, come here. Feel this."

Jon knelt down next to Greg and slowly slid his hand along Greg's arm to the place in the rock where Greg's hand was touching. "Feel that, Jon. Rub your finger around the outline of that hole. That feels like the shape of a..."

"...a dagger!" Jon squealed. "I wish I had my knife!" Jon almost shouted. The knife was instantly present. "Owww! Is this hot?!" He quickly moved to press the knife into the indentation in the rock. The knife clicked into place and began to glow. "There must be another spot on this rock for the other knife."

Greg began to wiggle his hand in the nooks and crannies be-tween the black rock and the rocks surrounding it. It wasn't long before he found what he was looking for. "I found it! I wish I had my knife!" Since his right hand was already touching the hole, it was a simple matter to slide the knife into the correct spot. Light seeped out of the black place between the rocks. Before Jon's eyes, his knife glowed purple, began to darken, and slowly disappeared. But as it did, the black rock itself began to change.

The top section of the rock slowly began to change in color, becoming more and more faint until it was almost clear. Eventually it became possible to look right into the core of the rock. Jon touched the translucent top of the rock and his hand slid right through the rock.

The boys were so amazed they couldn't speak. Jon reached

through the rock to a small brown square that lay about six inches below the surface. It wasn't clear what the square was, but when Jon grasped the end of it, it began to rise through the top of the rock. The brown square was the small end of a long box of some sort, eight inches by eight inches, but maybe a yard or more long. Once the box was halfway out of the rock, it began to tip over. Greg reached out to steady the box and together the boys lifted it clear of the rock.

"Amazing!" Greg whispered. No sooner was the box safely on the ground than the soft glowing light disappeared and the rock returned to normal. "What a hiding place!"

"I can't believe it!" Jon exclaimed. "Who would have thought to look inside of rocks? Let's get it open and look inside."

Before they could even get a good look at the box, however, they heard loud voices from around the bend in the cliff walk. They quickly pulled out the black plastic garbage bag they had brought for sea treasure and hid the box inside. They dashed for the trail that led back to the main street, hoping to be out of sight before anyone came around the corner. And since they never looked back, no one ever had a chance to see the faces of the two kids who were tearing up the cliff walk trail.

CHAPTER 7

# Secret at Risk

The walk home was uneventful. Jon and Greg stuck to the shadows, avoiding friends and intruders, as they wrestled the long box home. The box wasn't exactly heavy, but it wasn't exactly light, either. The main problem was the black plastic bag, which kept slipping and sliding. It was hard to get a good grip on the box because of the bag.

On the way home they decided that their best course of action was to hide the box behind the shed in the backyard until a later time when they could safely open it. That, of course, depended on what time it really was. Dad usually got home about 5:00 PM. Mom was already home, but if they could sneak into the backyard and into the shed without being seen, then they could open it up right now! If it was early enough.

The back yard was surrounded by a fence, solid wooden slats, stained a Cape Cod gray. An old shed stood against the fence at the very back of the yard. To the left of the shed was the outside beach shower, perfect for washing away salt and sand. The back yard gate was on the same side of the yard as the shower enclosure. Behind the back fence, there was a thick hedge row overgrown with wild roses. It was under the hedge, between the hedgerow and the back fence that the boys slipped the box until they could determine the time.

Jon ran around the outside of the house to peek into the kitchen window. The clock over the sink stood at 4:15. It seemed like enough time. Mom wasn't in sight at the moment. Was it worth the risk? If Mom saw them take the box into the house they would have to tell her everything. Jon headed back to the shed where Greg was hiding.

"It's 4:15. We have about 45 minutes 'til Dad gets home. I don't see Mom anywhere."

"Do you think we should give it a try, or wait until later?" Greg asked.

"Let's go for it! You stand up under the kitchen window and watch for Mom. I'll sneak the box into the shed. If you see Mom coming, wave, and I'll head back out. Then head for the shower and pretend like you are washing off the sand. I'll come in, yell for some towels, and then join you in the back."

"Okay, you get the box, Jon and I'll stand watch!"

Greg quietly stole along the wall of the house until he was just under the kitchen window. While he couldn't see the entire kitchen, he could hear everything, and he knew the room was empty. The dining room was obviously empty; that could be determined from anywhere in the back yard. By the time he looked back, the yard was empty.

Suddenly, Greg heard movement inside the house. He was just about to make a dash for the shower when he saw Mom start down the steps from the hallway outside their bedroom. Laundry basket in hand, she made her way down the stairs, turned the corner and started down the steps toward the laundry room. Greg heaved a sigh of relief. When he looked back into the yard, there was Jon peaking in through the gate, waiting for a signal. Greg waved him through. Running back to meet him, Greg held the door to the shed while Jon scurried inside.

"Mom's doing the wash. I think we are safe for now." Greg encouraged.

"Excellent! Let's get this thing open and see what we have." Jon added. Their excitement was almost impossible to contain! Although this box didn't look like a treasure chest, they assumed that what was inside was valuable beyond imagination. Consider how the box was hidden. Think about the locking system, and the maps. Who would go to all that trouble to hide just a few trinkets? No, this was something special, and they couldn't wait to see what it was.

For the first time, Jon and Greg were able to study the box at leisure. They carefully inspected the exterior of the container, examining the grain of the wood, looking for markings. It seemed as if there were no markings at all. The wood was flawless, perfect in every detail. The dovetail joining was masterful—the finish, smooth. The box was fastened with a simple brass, or was it gold, hook and latch. There was no lock. And when Greg slid the hook from the latch, the lid lifted easily without making a sound.

"It's not even locked!" Greg laughed.

"Who needs to lock a box when it is hidden the way this one was?" Jon reasoned.

"Yeah, I guess I didn't think about that. Makes sense. The hiding place was the lock." Inside the box was a roll of something that completely filled it, as if the box was made especially to hold that object. Greg reached in to touch it. "Rough. What do you think it is, a tapestry or something?" They had to turn the box over to dump out the contents.

Out onto the table fell a rolled up, well, it appeared to be, a carpet or weaving of some sort. They placed the box on the floor so that there would be room on the workbench top to unroll the cloth. Slowly, they opened up their treasure. It was a carpet of some sort. Covered with various symbols, shapes, and colors, it wasn't as heavy as it should have been for a carpet of its size. When fully unrolled, it was about 5 feet by 7 feet, although the box that it had come from wasn't five feet long. That was the first sign that something unusual was going on.

But then there were the things that they found in the center of the roll! Tightly bound together by a woven strand of silver were three silver swords. The swords were covered in mysterious writing and carving, and seemed to be of an unusual construction. This was easy to determine because the swords were flexible, well actually, bendable. It didn't look like these swords would be much good in a fight. But by now, Jon and Greg suspected that they must have some unusual power, if they weren't made to stand up to actual combat.

With the swords was a single red gem, the size of a walnut. "Look at this!" Greg gasped, picking up the gem. "It must be worth a fortune!"

"Cool!" Jon responded distractedly. He was already completely immersed in the carpet. "What do you think these markings mean?

"Jon, did you see the size of this gem?! I bet it is worth a million dollars!" Jon looked up, seeing the gem for the first time. His eyes bulged.

"Man, I've never seen a gem that big! I wonder if it's real."

"Has to be. Why put a fake one in a box like this? Naa, this is the real thing for sure. But it may be more than just a gem. Think about everything else we have found. Is there one thing that isn't magical?" Greg observed.

"Well, we don't know about the necklaces yet, but everything else is magic…which means this carpet must have some magical property, too. I wonder if the markings are designed to help figure out what this carpet can do?" Jon wondered out loud.

Greg held the gem up to the light of the window, and shafts of light spattered the walls of the shed. The gem was exquisite, but didn't seem to have any obvious magical powers. He turned his attention to the swords. The three swords were identical, silver in color, and, Greg suspected, silver in composition. He had bought a silver ring as a souvenir earlier in the summer, and he knew how soft silver was as a metal. This stuff felt a lot like the ring he had purchased. "I think these swords might be made of real silver. I wonder why. Silver is too soft to make a good sword. There must be something more here."

By now, Jon had moved the carpet to the floor of the shed and was on his hands and knees studying the markings. "The markings are in pairs. Look here, two red up front, two greens up front—the same in the back."

Greg turned his attention to the carpet and Jon's report of his findings.

"I wonder if you need a key to turn this thing on. I need a knife!" he shouted. As always, his dagger appeared instantly in his hand. "I wonder if the knife will unlock the secrets of this rug." He was just placing the knife on the center of the carpet when they heard a car roll into the driveway.

"Quick! Dad's home! Get into the shower! I'll get the towels!" Greg tore off his shirt and jumped out of the shed and into the shower, dropping the sword on the way. Jon threw the three swords into the center of the carpet, folded it quickly and shoved it under the table. He grabbed the box and stuffed it under the table and threw the black bag on top of it all. Then he raced for the house. "Mom, can I have a couple of towels?" Jon yelled.

"One minute," came Mom's reply from somewhere in the house. Just then Dad walked through the back yard gate.

"Hey, buddy, how was your day?" Dad inquired.

"Great! We spent the whole day on the beach, except for lunch. You should see all the damage the storm did!"

"I saw a good bit of it," Dad replied. "The base was hit pretty hard. There's a lot of clean-up going on all over the place—tree limbs down, a few power lines. I even saw one car completely smashed by a huge branch that fell on it." Mom opened the back door and handed two towels to Jon.

"Hurry and get rinsed off, then set the table for dinner," she said. Jon grabbed the towels and ran back toward the shower stall as Dad and Mom continued into the house.

Jon threw the towel halfway over the door to the shower, then snuck back into the shed to make sure everything was well covered. He was back a few seconds later, as Greg pushed open the shower door, all wrapped up in the towel.

"That was a close one," Jon whispered.

"Too close. We have to be way more careful," Greg agreed.

"See you inside. Mom said you should set the table when you get in."

"It's your turn! I did it last night," Greg protested.

"I guess Mom doesn't remember," Jon grinned as he stepped into the shower.

"That's okay," Greg smiled. "I'll remind her. Don't be too long!" Greg threw his shirt and swimsuit over the clothesline and whistled as he headed into the house.

CHAPTER 8

# Written in the Sky

A deep bell began to toll. The alarm was sounding outside the castle, which awakened Judas to the fact that the challenge must have appeared.

He rolled out of his bed and stumbled over to the opening in the wall which was the only window in the room. Although he knew the message would be there, he was surprised at the size of it, and at the vividness of the colors. "To the Grove—Dawn." A shiver ran through the prince's bones as he read the blood red message stretched across the sky.

He turned away from the window and spied Ephraim in the hallway outside his door. He was dressed in Judas's clothes, in fact, in Judas' best clothes. Ephraim was a boy from the kitchen who helped clear off the tables after meals, gathered and scrubbed the pots and pans, and ran general errands for Eli and Ella. He was the same size as Prince Judas and was probably about the same age, as well.

"Hey, that's my favorite cloak!" Judas protested.

Stoneclaw stepped from out of nowhere, it seemed, to protect the young lad. "Don't let it upset you, Your Highness. Everyone knows this is your favorite cloak, and that is why Ephraim must wear it. He is standing in for you in the Grove tonight, to protect you from harm. No one must know that you are not present until it is too late."

Stoneclaw was an ancient, gray-haired, gray bearded, wrinkle-skinned wizard. He looked just like you'd expect an old wizard to look, from his purple robes to his long staff. He moved slowly, yet there was a fire in his eyes. Rumor had it that he got his nickname from the tight-fisted hold he kept on that staff at all times.

"Oh. Sorry. I didn't understand. Will it be really dangerous?" Judas asked sheepishly.

"Yes," Stoneclaw replied, "really dangerous. But Ephraim understands that, as do all those who will be on the board this evening. We will do everything we can to protect him. Now, quickly, come with us. It is time for the party to depart."

Stoneclaw led Ephraim and Prince Judas to the queen's chambers, only to discover that they were already empty. Stoneclaw was visibly surprised, and stopped a moment to close his eyes and concentrate very hard. "Your Highness, I am afraid that the queen has already joined His Royal Majesty, the king at the head of the procession. They are even now at the door of the castle, waiting for Ephraim and me. Since no one can know that you are not accompanying them, I am afraid you will not be able to bid them farewell. It is vitally important, for the sake of the kingdom, that you stay hidden in your room. An old friend will be by shortly to give you further instructions. Please, Your Highness, go back into your bedchamber, lock the door, and wait as silently as possible. Stay away from the window. And be brave. We will return to you as soon as we are able." With that, Stoneclaw turned Judas back into his bedroom doorway and shut the door.

Prince Judas brushed back tears as he walked through the waiting area and into his bedroom. "They didn't even say goodbye to me!" he thought. "I can't believe that they simply forgot me! I must mean nothing to them." Frightened and unable to understand everything that was happening, Judas grabbed his pillow and jumped back onto bed. He heard the trumpets blaring somewhere far below him, and he knew the entourage was crossing the drawbridge and heading out of the castle toward the main gates. He wanted so badly to stick his head out the window, to wave goodbye, or to at least get one last look at his mother and father. But he knew it was too dangerous. Too much was at stake. He stayed where he was.

About thirty minutes later, he heard a scraping sound in the far corner of his room. He sat up on the bed with a start as a section of the wall of his bedroom slowly opened in toward him. Judas held his breath, his whole body trembling with fear. He didn't know there was a secret passage into his room, but someone else obviously did! Before he could roll off the side of the bed to hide, Eli stepped into the room.

"Eli! It's you!" He shouted. He ran to Eli, almost knocking him back into the passageway behind the open panel.

"SSSShh! Quiet!" Eli whispered. "Remember, you're not here! No loud noises, nothing louder than this." Eli's voice was barely audible. "Now, let's get to work." Eli had a large basket in one hand, which he placed inside the closet in the room.

"What do you mean, 'Get to work?'" Judas questioned.

"We have a great deal of work to do, and only about three hours to get it all done. This is the best time to do it, since most folks are already gone. Come with me, Judi." Eli stepped back into the passageway, holding onto Judas' hand. Eli touched the wall inside the passageway, and the door into Judas' room closed silently, plunging them into complete darkness. Judas followed along behind him, although they stopped after taking only about five steps. Eli brought Judas close beside him. Quietly Eli spoke, "Place your hand on the wall right here." Eli took Judas' hand and positioned it on the wall about four feet off the ground, slightly to the left of a round bump on the wall. "Hold your hand flat against the wall here until the wall grows warm." In just about five seconds, a door Judas hadn't even known was there slid open, away from them. The room on the other side of the door was not lighted, but sunlight from a few windows in that room made it easy to see that they were in the back of the throne room. They stepped inside.

The throne room was a long, rectangular room that covered the whole northern end of the second floor of the castle. The throne itself stood on a raised platform at the eastern end of the room, the point farthest from where Judas now stood. The throne was magnificent! Covered in gold and precious stones, an inlay of rubies began just above the right arm and circled around the entire back of the chair to the left arm, essentially outlining whoever sat there in brilliant red. The effect was stunning. There was a skylight that ran all the way through to the roof that allowed the throne to be bathed in light, even when the rest of the room was dimly lit.

"No one is permitted in the throne room when the king is absent, except by the expressed command of the king. We have such a command, Judi. We need to get something that, for now, belongs to you." Eli placed his arm around Judas' shoulder, and together they approached the throne. Three steps up and then around to the back of it they went. On the back of the throne, inset into the gold, were nine glittering rubies, all of exactly the same size. They were set in a square, three rows of three. Directly above the square was an indentation. It appeared that a stone was missing. The missing stone would have been slightly larger than the ones in the square, and Judas was puzzled.

"Is there a stone missing?" Judas asked.

"Not missing," Eli responded, "simply not here at the present moment. The ruby that rests in that spot is in the possession of your mother. It is hers by right. The nine rubies below belong to the princes and princesses of the realm."

"But there are no other princes or princesses. I don't understand."

"There aren't any others right now, but many kings have had larger families," Eli explained. "In fact, some have even had more than nine children. These rubies belong to the first nine born, when they reach the age of 14 or when crisis threatens. Although you are almost at an age when you would receive this ruby regularly, the crisis has come. It must be in your possession tonight. Stand silently and don't move. This won't hurt." Eli placed one hand firmly on Judas' head and placed three fingers on the first ruby in the square. He closed his eyes and then muttered some words that Judas couldn't understand. "You do wish to be bound to the land, don't you Judi?"

"Of course I do. That is why my family exists, isn't it—to serve kingdom and people?"

"I just had to make sure. No one can be forced to serve," Eli explained. Then he began to hum softly and suddenly, without Judas having any idea how it happened, the ruby was in his closed fist. He hadn't even realized he was making a fist, but when he opened his hand, there it was. Eli removed his hand while Judas inspected the jewel.

The ruby was about the size of a nickel and was somehow plated with gold on one side. Engraved on the gold back was a large letter "R". Judas wondered whether the "R" stood for "Royalty" or "Ruby". Maybe it stood for both. There was a small hole above the "R" that went all the way through the gold and the gemstone as well.

"What is it for?" Judas queried.

"Let's go sit over there and I'll explain everything," Eli pointed over to the side of the room. Along each side of the throne room, almost like risers, there were two raised platforms that served as seats for those waiting for the arrival of the king. Eli lowered himself to the platform; Judas nestled close to him, holding the gem in his open palm.

"Place the ruby in my palm, Judi." Judas did so. "That is the last time you ever do that!" Eli spoke firmly. "Never give this away! This gem can never be taken from you. You can give it away willingly, but if someone tries to steal it from you or take it by force, it will always return to your hand within one minute." Eli reached into his pocket and pulled out a long leather string and threaded it through the hole in the gem. He tied a knot in the cord and placed it over Judas' head, so that it hung around his neck and was hidden by his shirt. Judas looked up expectantly at Eli, beckoning him to continue.

"The ruby is your signet, your identification as royalty. No one will question your identity when shown this gem. But it is also a source of magic."

Judas' eyes grew wide at the word. "Magic?" he whispered with hushed anticipation. "What kind?"

'Nothing very spectacular, but then, magic doesn't have to be spectacular to be very useful. And I think you will find these spells very useful, indeed," Eli grinned.

Eli explained to Judas that the magic in the gem was designed for the use of the royal family, to assist and protect them. Three specific spells were powered by the gem. To use the magic, the gem must be

43

touching the skin of the person casting the spell, namely Judas. Next, Judas would have to think of the person he wanted to affect with the spell. Then he had to speak the word of power. No one other than Judas could use this gem magically. The gem and Judas were bound together by the words Eli had spoken at the back of the throne.

The gem had the power to cast three specific spells. The first was sleep. By holding a specific person in his mind, touching the gem, and saying *"sleep"*, that person would immediately drift into sleep. They might sleep for an hour, they might sleep for eight. That depended on how tired they were when Judas put them to sleep. And more than one person could be put to sleep, Eli clarified. The only restriction was you had to be able to keep the image of everyone you wanted affected in your mind at one time. And of course, the more people you put to sleep, the shorter the duration of the nap they took.

The second spell was *light*. Perhaps 'glow' was a better word. Eli directed Judas to think about the fingernail on the first finger of his right hand. Once he had a picture of it in his mind, Judas said, "Light." When he opened his eyes, his fingernail was glowing brightly. It was amazing! Eli taught him that anything could be made to give off light, and it would continue to do so until Judas released it or the sun set.

The third spell was *truth*, a very useful spell for a king to have. There were other attributes of this most special gem, Eli elucidated. Not only was the gem a signet, it was a means of communication. The gem would grow ice cold if another member of the royal family was in serious trouble and needed help. It would grow warm if a family member wanted to get in touch with you or needed to send you a signal. Eli demonstrated each power of the gem to Judas, so that he would be able to interpret the messages that might come. He also wanted to be sure that Judas could use the gem to full advantage.

"This gem will be of best advantage to you if no one knows it exists. Don't let anyone know it's powers. Keep it hidden; it will serve you well," Eli reassured.

Judas tucked the gem back inside his shirt and wiggled a little as the gem settled into place. It was pleasantly warm at the moment.

He imagined that his mother was sending him an "All is well!" message. But then he realized that although he was wishing she would, the simple truth was that the gem was still warm from his own hand.

Eli stood and lifted Judas to his feet. "We must be off, Judi. There is much yet to see and do." Eli wrapped his arm around the young boy and Judas slipped his hand around Eli's waist. Together they walked the length of the throne room, back towards the opening through which they had come. "Notice, Judi, there is no bump on the inside of the wall. To open a passage from the inside of a room, you must place your hand precisely over the spot where the bump is on the other side of the wall." Eli slid aside the bottom of a small golden sconce that held an oil lamp. Then he took Judas' hand and placed it on the wall. The door slid shut. "Try again," Eli instructed. Judas placed his hand in the same place, and in just a moment, the door swung open again.

Over the next hour Eli took Judas on a tour of all the hidden passageways in the castle. The passages were dark and narrow, and frightened Judas more than a little. He was amazed at how many places he could get to from his room, completely unseen. They started the tour by heading to the top floors of the castle, and ended downstairs in the kitchen. There was a great passageway that linked the kitchen to all of the royal bedrooms, obviously designed by someone who approved of a good late night snack.

Leaving the backdoor of the kitchen took you into a square room, which was a loading dock of sorts for the supplies needed by the castle. In this room were boxes and crates, and several barrels of trash. Everything here was in transit, either headed in or headed out. A small opening in the wall, covered by a thick door and iron grate, led out to the courtyard behind the castle. Behind the door that led from the kitchen into the loading area, another door led down to the cellars that held the provisions for the castle. These cellars were just below the kitchen, and there was, in the far end of the cellar, a small, pulley-driven elevator that was used to lift heavy objects from the cellar straight into the kitchen above. It was over to this elevator that Eli walked.

Judas had seen the elevator work many times before. Kegs of ale or large slabs of mutton or beef were often hauled up to the kitchen by elevator. When no one important was looking, he had even ridden up to the kitchen on the elevator himself, once. But he had never noticed what was under the elevator box. Eli lifted the elevator box by drawing on the ropes that controlled the box. Once the box was off the ground, Judas could see a small, square board on which the box rested. It seemed like a part of the floor, but it wasn't. Eli tapped the board three times and then began to twist it like a lid on a jar. Slowly, the board rose, and after a few seconds, Eli lifted the top off another dark passage.

This passage was little more than a dark hole in the ground. At Eli's prompting, Judas felt inside the rim of the hole until he found the first step carved into the side of the wall. "If worst comes to worst, this is where you must go. There is one who waits below who is always a friend to the kingdom. Don't be fooled by his appearance."

"Who is down there? And why do you need to warn me not to be fooled by his appearance? What does he look like? I'm not..." Eli cut him off.

"The time has come. We must get you back to your room quickly. I must go."

Eli screwed the top back over the hole more rapidly than Judas thought possible and lectured as he did so. "Let no one discover this hole. Only the king knows it exists, and the chief magician. Tell no one that an ally waits below. He may be your only hope."

Judas had millions of questions he wanted to ask. Like—*Why were the kitchens empty at this hour of the day?* And *Who was down in that hole?* And *Why were we in a hurry?* The procession had left hours ago. And then he remembered that Eli was supposed to be in that procession.

Eli was rushing him up through the secret passageways, back towards his room, when Judas suddenly stopped. "Eli, you told me you were going to be on the board. Why are you here? What's really going on?" Judas waited for his answer.

"I promise I will answer all your questions, or at least all that I can answer in the next fifteen minutes, once we get to your room. Now hurry."

After a few more twists and turns, they arrived in the passage outside Judas' room. Eli made Judas open the door for practice, and after entering, shut the door again. "I am in the procession, Judi, or at least everyone thinks I am. Stoneclaw is maintaining an illusion that I am riding on a horse next to his. But he can only maintain that illusion for about three hours. We are getting dangerously close to that time. I will have to transport myself to the horse before the illusion spell quits."

Judas relaxed. For a moment he had been afraid that Eli was hiding things from him, that maybe Eli wasn't the friend he had always believed him to be. The two sat on the edge of the bed, and Eli wrapped his arms around Judas while he explained the most critical part of the plan.

If the Ruby King and Queen were defeated, it was very likely that the Obsidian King would attempt to seize the castle. They would assume that the heir to the throne had perished in the battle, but that there may still be other children with a claim to throne who had been left behind. There was a good chance that the evil king would search the castle looking for rivals. If he found any, they wouldn't be allowed to see the light of the next sunrise. It was important then, if something terrible happened, that Judas escape capture. He would have to flee, and over time build up a resistance movement that could recapture the kingdom and deal justice to the Obsidian King and his family. If Judas were caught and killed, the royal line would end and so would the kingdom. That could not be allowed to happen!

The words that Eli spoke terrified Judas, as Eli knew they would. How could anything like that ever happen? Surely he was just talking about remote possibilities. Things weren't that desperate, really...were they?

As if Eli could read his mind, he said, "Judas, I know this all sounds too horrible to believe possible. I wish it were not true. But it is. Every word is true. There is a good chance that the Dark King could win. And if he does, you will be king. For the sake of the people of the Ruby Kingdom, you must be brave and courageous, no matter how scared you are on the inside!"

Judas started to protest, but Eli hushed him. "Stay in this room, Judi. The basket I brought earlier has enough food for today, and travel rations if you are forced to flee. If you must run, wear dark, sturdy clothes and your warmest cloak. Take your weapon and as much money or jewels as you can get your hands on. I suggest looking in your mother's rooms. Keep your royal ruby in your hands tomorrow. It will be your link to the progress of the challenge. If you feel the gem turn icy cold two times, flee as quickly as you can. If the gem turns warm, rejoice, for we have been victorious!

Eli squeezed Judas affectionately. "Fair well, my child. Be strong! Take courage! And remember, I'll always love you." Eli stood and waved his hand briefly.

"Don't go! Please, don't leave me alone!" Judas panicked and jumped to grab the old man. But it was too late. Where Eli had stood a moment ago, the air shimmered slightly and then was still. Eli was gone.

CHAPTER 9

# Brenton Cove Turmoil

Jon and Greg waited until late that night before they slid out the back door of the house. Their curiosity had been driving them wild all night. Dad and Mom had taken them on a long walk down to Thayer Street for ice cream. Well, actually the trip was an excuse to view the storm damage, and the ice cream was the hook that kept the kids happy to be along. While their parents inspected the wreckage, Jon and Greg discussed their treasure and the task that lay ahead. They considered how they were going to find the third treasure, if that is what it was. There was a third mark on the map. The first two marks had yielded treasure, surely the third would as well.

But the first two marks were relatively close to their home. The third mark was on the other side of the peninsula. From the look of it, the third mark was near Fort Adams State Park. That would be a good hour's walk from their house. And if they found anything, how on earth would they be able to carry it back? Even if they did it at night, they would never be able to transport their loot! And it was risky to leave at night. If Mom or Dad came in to check on them and found them gone, whoa—that would be a mess! They might not even live through an ordeal like that! Well, they'd live through it, but life would be very unpleasant for a very long time. And having to explain their absence—no, too risky to be gone for more than a few minutes at a time.

By the time they arrived at the Newport Creamery, they were hot from the walk and thirsty, to boot. Mom suggested they all have frappes, an idea which met with instant and vigorous support. The cold milkshake, thick with ice cream, would be perfect on a steamy summer night like this one! By the time they were home, the sun was setting and it was time to think about bed.

Mom and Dad usually watched the 10 o'clock news before heading to bed, which meant they were only starting to fall asleep at 11:00 o'clock. It would be too risky to think about sneaking out to the shed before 1:00AM. Jon set his electric alarm clock to 1:00AM and put it under his pillow. Since Mom and Dad's bedroom was at the other end of the house over the kitchen, they would never hear the alarm.

Jon quickly silenced the beeping in his ear as 1:00 rolled around. He placed his hand over Greg's mouth and whispered, "Greg. Wake up! It's time!" The two boys slipped on khaki shorts, T-shirts and slippers and silently made their way toward the back door of the house. In just a moment, they were in the shed, flashlights on, carpet unrolled.

The carpet was a plain pale blue color on one side, but was brightly marked on the other. Circles of red, green, blue and brown were arranged in the various corners and in the center of the carpet. There were six black triangles on the carpet, one in each corner and one on each end. In the very center of the carpet was a blue circle about five inches in diameter, surrounded by a brown circular band about one inch thick. A green square was on one side of the central circular pattern and a red square on the other. There were small black lines radiating from the center of the blue circle. There were beautiful animals woven into the pattern. In each of the four corners, between the black triangle and the group of colored circles at that end of the carpet, four animals were pictured. Always in the same order, they were a rabbit, a snail, then beneath that, a tiger and an eagle.

The carpet was extremely comfortable; its decorated side was soft and cushy. Greg ran his hand over the surface, trying to understand the markings. The boys had the carpet unrolled on the floor of the shed, and were kneeling beside it. Without realizing it, Greg managed to actually crawl onto the carpet in an attempt to touch the patterned markings on the other end. Suddenly the carpet moved, and Greg fell over on his side.

"Cut it out, Jon!' Greg hissed. "I almost whacked my head on the leg of that table!"

"I didn't do anything," Jon protested.

"Yeah, right. Then why did I fall over and the carpet jolt?" Greg inquired sarcastically. "Did the carpet move by itself?" Greg froze. As if saying the words brought the idea into his head, Greg repeated himself. "Did the carpet move by itself?"

"I—I—I—don't know," Jon stammered. "Let's find out. Exactly what were you doing when it jumped?"

"I was reaching over to touch those marking on the far end. I had just touched the green circle when I fell." Greg cautiously reached out and touched the green circle. Nothing happened.

"Was that exactly how you touched it?" Jon asked.

"I think so. I was simply reaching over to feel the spots when the thing lurched."

"Did you have your other hand on the carpet when you were reaching?" Jon wondered aloud.

"I must have, otherwise I couldn't have reached that side of the carpet. But I don't know where my other hand was. I wasn't paying attention to it." Greg explained. Jon placed one hand on the green circle and then began to touch various other markings on the carpet in an attempt to duplicate the previous effect. Nothing at all happened. He was rather frustrated at not being able to figure out the mystery, and his arms were sore from stretching. He spun around and sat down right in the center of the carpet. Slowly, the carpet started to rise! Lifting about 6 inches off the ground, the carpet hovered over the floor of the shed. Jon was startled, but managed to keep his balance by rapidly moving to all fours.

"How'd you do that?" Greg gasped.

"I didn't do anything! I just sat down right here and…hey, maybe you have to be on the carpet for it to work!' Jon guessed.

"Then these circles and squares and arrows, they must be the controls! I think this is a flying carpet!" squealed Greg!

"SSShhh!, keep it down, Greg. If you wake up Mom and Dad, we're dead."

"Okay, I'll try," replied Greg.

Jon crawled off the center markings and sat on one of the two empty spaces on the carpet. Greg scrambled onto the other one. Reaching toward the center, Greg pushed his index finger into the soft pile of the carpet in the center of the blue circle. Slowly, the carpet rose into the air. It continued to rise until Greg removed his finger. The carpet, with Greg and Jon on board, hovered three feet off the ground. Jon reached out a finger and touched the brown band surrounding the blue circle. The carpet slowly sank back down to the ground. From the brown stripe, Jon's fingers roamed to the green circle. The carpet lifted to about six inches off the ground, and began to move very slowly forward. Jon quickly removed his finger to keep from running into the wall. When Greg touched the red circle, nothing happened at all. Touching the green circle at the same time as any of the triangles dispersed around the edge of the carpet caused it to move slowly in the direction of the point of the triangle.

After trying various combinations of circles, squares and arrows, the boys began to get a good grasp on how the carpet operated. Though they were getting sleepy, they decided to give the carpet one last test before they headed back to bed. They opened the door to the shed. Then, as quietly as clouds slipping through an afternoon sky, one hand on green, one on the front arrow, they flew the carpet right out into the night air!

They knew that they couldn't stay out long. Someone might see them, or Mom might check in their room for them. But they simply had to give this carpet a test drive. They soon discovered that speed was controlled by the animal pictures. Touch the snail and you moved very slowly. Top speed was eagle flight. Once you had touched the green and selected the speed, you didn't need to maintain contact with the animal picture. The red circles brought the carpet to a quick halt. The different lines radiating from the center circle all helped you change direction quickly and easily. In truth, the carpet was easier to handle with two drivers working together. Steering often required touching two different directional arrows at the same time, while the altitude also needed to be controlled.

It was thirty minutes that felt like five. Flying high above the town, looping out over the ocean on a clear night was exhilarating beyond anything Jon or Greg had ever imagined. When a clock somewhere struck two, they knew they were long overdue in their beds, and they headed home. Greg handled the directional arrows to steer them back into the shed; Jon lowered the carpet to a foot off the ground, and they glided in to a perfect landing. After rolling the carpet carefully and placing it back in its box, they hid it behind a row of old paint cans on the bottom shelf of a large set of shelves in the shed. Sneaking back into the house, there were relieved to find everything quiet, just as they had left it.

Sleep, after an experience like that, was out of the question. Though snugly tucked into their beds, the boys couldn't help whispering and giggling about the adventure they had just enjoyed, not to mention the promise of all those to come. Greg observed that the carpet was the perfect way to get to the third spot marked on the map, and after endless speculation about what that third X might indicate, the boys finally drifted off to sleep.

Forty-eight hours later, things were set for another late night excursion. After the previous night flight, the boys realized that "wee hours adventures" left one very weary the next day. As much as they hated to wait, two nights in a row really was more than they could do. In any event, they needed to plan this excursion very carefully. While flying on a carpet in the middle of the night was a great way to get around, Newport was a resort town, and folks were on the streets well past midnight. They couldn't afford to be seen by a bunch of loud mouthed tourists. And since they were exploring after dark, they would need to take some source of light, as well as tools for digging. They didn't have any idea where this treasure might be, but they hoped their knives would help them find it.

All of the equipment they would need for the search had been gathered in the shed during the afternoon before the search. They had managed to get a camping lantern that could be shuttered, one flashlight, two shovels, a street map of Newport, and a large mesh bag that could carry a great deal of loot, if they happened to be lucky. They also brought along several plastic garbage bags. You never know what they might find!

Waking again at 1:00AM, Jon roused Greg and then jumped into his all-black attire. Greg was quickly dressed and followed Jon down the hallway, down the steps—skipped the third step, it squeaked—through the dining room and out the back door. Once out back, they felt home free. Because their parent's room was actually a refinished attic room, there were no windows looking out on the backyard. That was mighty convenient! They had the carpet out of its hiding place in no time. They unrolled it outside the door of the shed, and loaded all their supplies into the middle of the carpet. Sitting cross-legged at either end of the carpet, the boys prepared for lift-off.

"Greg, one hand on blue, and hold on," Jon instructed. The carpet began to rise. Jon touched the rabbit and the carpet began to ascend much more quickly. Then he touched the tiger. In the next moment, they were high, high above their house. Jon touched red. Stop. "Okay, Greg, let's go. I'll take care of speed and altitude, you handle the steering."

Very honestly, the boys were surprised that they were not afraid when they were on the carpet. Somehow, there was much more to the carpet than met the eye. When you sat on the carpet while flying, it was as if your body sank down into the carpet a little. It sort of held you in place. While you might not like the heights, there really wasn't any fear of falling…and sudden turns or stops didn't seem to have the power to tumble you off the carpet. All in all, it was a very comfortable ride.

Greg began navigating towards Fort Adams State Park by using the black triangles in front of him. Jon had one hand on green, and had most recently touched the rabbit. They were moving at a comfortable clip, and in about 10 minutes were high above the state park. Jon touched red and the carpet came to a standstill in mid air. He pulled the map pouch out of his back pocket, removed the map, and spread it out on top of their supply bag. "I wish I had my knife," he announced to no one in particular.

"Me, too," said Greg. Jon's knife was already on the map, when Greg added, "I guess you have to actually say the words. 'Me, too,' doesn't cut it. I wish I had a knife!"

Instantly, his knife appeared and was added to Jon's on the surface of the map. The paper turned soft and supple, the three "X"'s glowed out. Comparing the map with the outline of the coast they were viewing first hand, they selected a sheltered cove slightly to the east of the main entry road into the park. There were cliff walls surrounding the cove and just a sliver of beach between cliff and water. A trail led down to the cove from a picnic area above and to the west. At this time of night, the park was closed. But that didn't mean they were free from any wandering eyes. Just slightly outside the cove, in the larger part of the sheltered harbor, hundreds of sailboats were moored. Lights danced on more than a few of these boats, and the docks leading out into the greater harbor were well lighted. Many people sailed to this harbor and then lived on their boats while vacationing in the surrounding towns. And there was sure to be more than one or two folks still awake at this late hour.

Greg decided it would be best if they brought the carpet down near the main entry road, then flew low to the ground, through the picnic area, down the trail and into the cove. There were no houses on this side of the cove, and the darkness would cover their movements. Carefully winding through the banks of wild rosebushes, the boys put the carpet down right on the beach. So far, so good. Opening the bag of supplies, they withdrew the flashlight and the lantern. The lantern was battery operated and Jon completely shuttered it before he turned it on. Then he opened a narrow slot through which light could shine on the shore and the rocks behind. Although the light itself would not be visible to the boaters, the area lit by the lamp might be.

They had decided to allow themselves 30 minutes to search. If they didn't find a clue within thirty minutes, they would try one other area. If they found nothing there, it was back home. After all, they weren't in any hurry. They just had to make sure they didn't get caught.

A quick scan around the cove revealed nothing unusual. There were several large rocks on the beach, obviously pieces broken from the rock wall. Lots of smaller rocks dotted the sand. It only took about five or six minutes to walk around the entire inside of the small cove. They had hoped that their knives might get warm again, leading them to the area of the treasure. No such luck. The moon played on the water in the cove, and the small waves rippled gently onto the beach. It really was a beautiful, warm summer night. But the beauty of the evening was all but lost on these two who were completely absorbed by the prospect of discovery.

After walking the entire beach three times, turning over every loose rock within their power, and sticking their knived hands into as many rock crevasses as they could, it was time to move on. They turned back to cross the distance to the carpet, when Jon stopped. "Look, Greg. Right there in the middle of the cove. What do those rocks about ten feet up look like to you?"

Greg covered his flashlight to keep the glare from blinding his long range vision. The moon had risen further in the sky and was now illuminating more of the cliff face. And now, from this specific angle, a cliff face was exactly what Greg was seeing. "I think it is the head of a man, about four feet tall!" Greg whispered excitedly.

"It's not easy to see, unless you stand right here at the mouth of the cove. And I think the shadow caused by the moon makes the silhouette stand out more clearly," Jon explained. Together, they moved quickly to the large rock that stood just under the roughly shaped face. Climbing up on top of the rock, Jon was just tall enough to touch the rocky chin, above which was the gap for a mouth. "You know," Jon grinned, "if you stuck a knife in this guy's mouth, he would almost look like a pirate!" To demonstrate, he balanced his dagger sideways on the lower lip of the face. It did look a little like a pirate.

Then the mouth slowly opened! A low, chuckling sound came from the wall, and Jon jumped back off the rock in terror. His knife had disappeared, and now, where there was once just a groove where a mouth should have been, there was a deep hole in the rock face about the size of, well, about the size of a basketball. The low laughter continued.

Jon and Greg stood several paces back considering the situation. Although the laughter wasn't loud, noises carried easily across the water in the quiet of the night. They certainly didn't have much time. And although they were scared out of their socks, the other two treasures didn't hurt them...and this was the place indicated on the map for treasure number three. The only thing to do was to reach down into that mouth and see what was in there. And they needed to do it in a hurry. Greg, still visibly shaken by the rumbling laughter quickly volunteered Jon to stick his hand in. After all, Jon was the older brother. It only seemed right that he should protect his baby brother from the possible danger.

In less than a minute, Jon was back on top of the rock, flashlight in hand, peering into the gaping mouth of the laughing pirate. Greg stood terrified on the beach, whispering words of caution. "Hey, it's no big deal. There is a black, metal loop down inside the mouth. But I can't reach it. Come up here and help me."

Greg climbed up on the rock, slightly encouraged by the calm demeanor of his brother. Jon quickly knelt down on all fours on the rock top and told Greg to stand on his back. "See if you can reach it. Try to turn it or twist it or see if you can pull it out."

Standing on tiptoe, Greg managed to get a hand on the iron loop. It twisted right, then left. He pulled with all of his might. But much like barging through a door that is suddenly opened at the last second, Greg's mighty pull met no resistance. Before he knew what was happening, Greg was flying backwards through the air, iron ring in hand, heading straight for the water. Jon jumped off the rock to see if Greg was hurt, and not a moment too soon. For in the very next second, before Jon even had a chance to get his hands on Greg, the entire rock face came crashing down. Instinctively, Jon dove into deeper water to avoid the falling rocks. Though soaked and covered with sand, Greg was already up when the rocks came down and was able to lunge out of the way of all but the smallest fragments. When they looked up, the whole face of the cliff had changed. Where the ragged face had once been, a carefully carved square was inset into the rock. And sitting in the center of that square was a chest, a treasure chest!

Greg and Jon knew they had only moments before folks came to investigate. The noise of the rock slide had been tremendous, and there were guards on patrol at the docks. Climbing up the new pile of fallen stone, they each grabbed one of the handles on the sides of the chest, and prepared to heave. To their amazement, the chest was as light as a feather. More magic! It took no strength at all to remove the chest, so they quickly but carefully scrambled back down off the rock toward their carpet. The moon was their only light, both flashlight and lantern having been lost in the avalanche of stone.

They were nearly at the carpet when a light appeared at the head of the trail that led from the picnic area. "Who goes there?" a voice called out.

Jon and Greg froze in place, held their breath.

"This park is closed! Come out where I can see you!"

Nothing and no one moved. Absolute silence.

"If you don't come out right now and identify yourself, I'm going to arrest you for trespassing, and haul you to the police station." The guard started down the path toward the beach. As if triggered into motion by the guard's first step, Greg and Jon sprinted to the carpet. "Up, up," urged Jon.

They dumped the chest into the center of the carpet. Greg hit blue, Jon hit green and the eagle. With dizzying speed, the carpet shot 500 feet straight into the sky!

The guard heard the boys running and started running down the path himself. But just as he reached the beach, he saw something shoot into the sky. Looking up, he saw a small object reflecting the bright moonlight. Then, before he could react in any way, the rectangle darted off to the east and out of sight. Someone or something had surely been there, the guard thought. But what? And what could fly away like that?

He walked the whole stretch of beach to satisfy himself that the cove was empty. He paused for a moment at the pile of fallen rocks, carefully picking a pathway through them. He never even looked up to see where the rocks had fallen from. In fact, he decided he was better off not reporting the whole incident. He'd simply write that he heard a noise and discovered a small rock slide. That flying thing— probably just too much coffee!

Still trembling from their close encounter with the law, Jon and

Greg headed straight for home. Once there, they stowed the carpet, returned their other supplies, and dried off with some towels Mom always kept in the shed. They would have to hide these wet clothes and dry them when Mom wasn't in the house. The trunk was too large to hide in the shed, even though it was practically weightless. After a few moments of consideration, they decided the best place for it was the old cellar behind the rock.

Jon and Greg lived in a split level house that had three floors. The main floor, which had the living room, dining room and kitchen, rested four steps above and beside the laundry room and the shop. These rooms were actually slightly underground. The steps leading down into the laundry also led to the door to the wood shop. And it was from the wood shop that four more steps led down into the real cellar.

The real cellar housed the furnace, the large oil storage tank, and boxes and boxes of junk. Things that needed to stay dry were stored in the attic, but there were lots of other things, skis, old parts from machinery in the shop, greasy and oily things, these were stored in the dark, dank basement. Even this room was divided into two parts by a cinder block wall. After passing through this junk room, there was a small doorway that took you into the farthest recesses of the house. This room was certainly the most unusual of any in the house, and was situated just under the kitchen and dining room.

When the original builders had been digging the foundation for the house, they hit rock. In fact, the rock they hit was too huge to move, to expensive to blast. So they decided to build it into the foundation of the house. The whole western corner of the house was built solidly on the rock. In fact, the rock formed part of the interior wall of the room and sloped inward for a good eight feet. The majority of this half of the cellar was simply one huge boulder that eventually met with the concrete of the floor. Because of the presence of the rock, this part of the house was basically useless. The unevenness of the rock made it impossible to store things here. And there really wasn't much floor space that wasn't rough hewn rock. No one ever went down here...which was why the place was perfect!

Sneaking into the house carrying the chest, the boys threaded their way through dining room, living room, down steps, through doorways into the wood shop, down steps into the main cellar, across the floor to the far corner, and into the "rock room". They worked their way around the rock and sat the chest in the far corner of the room, out of sight from the entry.

"Should we try to open it now?" Greg asked.

"Let's wait until tomorrow. It's really late and we've been out of our room way too long. We can find a time when no one is home to open it…or we can do it late night, if we have to," Jon reasoned.

"Awww, come on! How can you stand going to bed without opening it?" Greg wondered aloud.

"One close call a night is enough for me. I'm not taking any more chances. Let's get back to bed!" In spite of Greg's protests, Jon pushed Greg toward the door and out of the room. They quietly retraced their steps up into the living room, and were just stepping into the dining room when the silence was shattered! The bathroom door, just about five feet in front of them, clanked shut firmly. The bathroom light clicked on, as evidenced by the sliver of light escaping under the door. Jon and Greg slipped back quickly onto the steps to the laundry room and held their breath. After what seemed like 45 minutes, the toilet flushed, the light clicked off and the door opened. Slowly, they heard, footsteps crossed the hallway and ascended the steps to the bedroom above the kitchen. Whether it was Mom or Dad, they never knew. They waited for an extra ten minutes before risking the last couple of steps to their room. They certainly didn't want to make any noises while whoever had just visited the bathroom was still awake. Stuffing their clothes under their beds, they were under the sheets just in time to see the clock turn 3:00. They never saw 3:15.

CHAPTER 10

# Gateway

The next morning, after breakfast, Mom announced that she had to go to the grocery store to pick up a few items. Planning to be gone for about an hour, she asked the boys if they wanted to go along or if they wanted to stay home together. They knew that if they didn't go along, they would be expected to stay in the house until she returned. Of course that didn't present any problem to them!

As soon as Mom's car was out of the driveway, they ran down into the basement, past foundation rock, and over to their latest find. In reality, this was the first good look at the chest they had had. The box was rectangular and appeared to be made of wood; at least the outside looked like wood. There were dark metal handles on either side of the chest, both of which were very smooth though visibly aged. The top of the chest was flat and carved. Three crossed swords were engraved in the center of the lid, and on either side of the swords was a small dagger. The chest was about four feet wide, two feet high and about two and a half feet deep.

On the front of the chest was a silver latch that didn't seem to lock. The two halves simply came together, but it was clear that the chest was locked. Jon tried to lift the lid, but it wouldn't budge. Of course, by this time, magical means of opening and closing things didn't seem nearly as unusual as it might have a few weeks ago. They began to consider how the trunk might be opened.

Greg studied the carvings on top of the trunk, realizing rather quickly that the daggers carved there looked like the daggers that were in their possession. Without thinking further about the three swords also pictured, the boys called their daggers and set them into place. Instantly, the daggers began to glow and there was an audible click. Jon easily raised the lid of the chest.

Every time Jon had opened a chest, he had been hoping to find gold. This time he did—but not as much as he hoped. Scattered loosely in the bottom of the chest, twenty or thirty large gold pieces winked in the light. On top of the gold, two other items were immediately visible. One was a golden staff, maybe 30 inches long. The staff was covered with carvings and was topped by a small fine-wire cage of sorts. At present, the cage was empty. There were several bands or rings on the staff just below that wire top. And then there was the gem—brilliant blue. One look at it reminded Greg of the other gem already in their possession, the red one they found on the very first day. These gems were obviously related in some way. Both were so unusually round in shape. Their size and cut was identical, only their color differed.

After the staff and gems had been thoroughly inspected, Jon began to remove the gold pieces. They knew by the size of these gold pieces that they were suddenly very wealthy. Gracious, even one of those gems had already made them fabulously wealthy. But if they became greedy and tried to spend any of this too quickly, they would lose it all. If they weren't careful, some museum would claim the whole treasure as some lost artifacts from an ancient civilization, and they would be out of luck.

No, they would have to be patient, and plan very carefully.

As the last gold piece was being lifted out of the chest, Jon ran his finger along the inside corners of the chest to be certain that he had found everything that was in the chest. As his hand reached the back of the chest, he gasped and pulled back his hand very quickly.

"Greg," he gasped, "there's something wrong here. Put your hand in here." Greg moved close to Jon and stared into the chest.

"What do you mean, there's something wrong? What's wrong?" Greg asked.

"I don't think this trunk has a back," Jon responded cautiously.

"No back?" Greg chortled. "Of course it does." He reached his hand forward to touch the inside back of the chest. "It's as plain as...." He stopped mid sentence as his hand passed right through the back of the chest and disappeared from sight. Quickly he pulled it back to make sure it was still there. "Whoa! What is this?" He wondered out loud, happy to find his hand intact.

The chest was standing open now, with the top leaning against the wall of the house. Although the outside of the trunk was solid, it appeared that the whole back of the trunk, at least on the inside, was not. In fact, even the underside of the lid was permeable. They experimented with this startling discovery. First they inserted hands and arms, all the way up to the shoulder. They couldn't feel anything inside. They grabbed a mop from around the corner and stuck that through the blackness. It went all the way in.

"I wonder what is in there." Greg was visibly uncomfortable. "I mean what if there are monsters or creatures from another universe in there. It could be a big mistake opening this door. I don't feel very good about this."

"Well, there really is only one way to find out," Jon rejoined. "One of us has got to take a look. And the only way to look is to stick your head in and see what you can see."

"I'm not sticking my head in there!' Greg stated emphatically. "Something on the other side could be waiting to bite it off for all I know."

"I didn't expect you to volunteer, Mr. Courageous. But hold on to me, in case I have trouble getting back. I don't want to get stuck in there." Jon stepped around to the side of the trunk and placed one hand on the edge of the bottom and one on the side of the lid. Greg wrapped his arms around Jon's waist.

"I'm only going to peek for five seconds. If I'm not out by then, pull me out," Jon instructed.

"Be careful," Greg whispered. Jon was much more nervous than he allowed Greg to see. But Greg could feel the tremors in Jon's body as Jon closed his eyes, and slowly stretched out his neck and pushed his head through the veil of darkness. Five seconds later, Greg was pulling him out. "Come on, Jon!" Greg panted. "Get your head out of there!"

Jon's head bobbed back through the darkness into full view. "Stick your head in, Greg. Nothing to be afraid of. It's just a cave or something." Jon stuck his head back through.

Greg waited. After about three minutes, Jon pulled his head back out, all nervousness gone from his manner. "Don't you want to see this? There's nothing to be afraid of. It's a small cave, maybe five or six feet deep. You can see out the mouth of the cave into the sky on the other side. The cave is completely empty. Come on in." This time Jon not only stuck his head through, he stepped up into the chest and disappeared completely through the back of the chest!

Greg was astonished! Very slowly he stepped to the side of the chest, squeezed his eyes tightly shut, and holding his breath, eased his face through the blackness that was the back of the chest. He waited about three seconds before he had the courage to open them. Once opened, he was amazed at what he saw!

Jon was standing about six feet in front of him on the floor of the cave. The cave was rocky, perhaps about six feet high, six feet wide, and maybe six to eight feet deep. It opened to the sky, and there was nothing other than clouds visible outside the entrance to the cave. Jon was standing at the entrance looking out at the surrounding landscape, all of which was invisible to Greg. "Come on in, Greg," Jon repeated. "There is a whole world in here!"

Greg climbed through the back of the trunk and joined Jon in the cave. Looking out the opening, it was clear that they were in a small cave in the side of the mountain. There was no trail leading up to this cave and there was no apparent way to leave the cave. They were on the edge of a mountain range, and a lush green pine forest skirted the base and sides of the mountain they were in. As they looked past the forest, they could make out patches of land that seemed to be plains, but there wasn't much more they could see from where they were. To really find out what this new place was like, that would require transportation. The whole thing was starting to make sense.

They decided that they better go back and store away their latest treasures and check the time. The back of the cave looked like a regular rock wall, until you placed your hand through it. Jon, then Greg, carefully stepped through the wall, back into the chest, and jumped onto their cellar floor. Jon closed the trunk and threw an old black tarp over it, while Greg gathered up the gold pieces, the staff and the gem. Up the stairs they ran, only to discover that they still had thirty minutes. That's when the idea hit Greg.

"Jon, that cave is the perfect place to store all our stuff. No one can get into the trunk except us, and the cave is large enough for everything. Let's get the carpet, the swords, the gems and everything and store them in the cave."

"But we don't know if the cave is safe from the other side, Greg. Maybe someone else could get into the cave and steal our things," Jon guessed.

"What if we locked the stuff in the trunk? Then anyone in the cave couldn't see what was in the trunk. And after all, who is going to climb that cliff to get into the cave anyway?" Greg challenged.

"That's true. Yeah, let's do it. I'll get the carpet and the swords; you get the gem and the maps. And get a bag for the gold, too," Jon suggested.

They raced though the house, arriving back within five minutes. All the treasures they had collected were with them. They even took the necklaces from around their necks and stowed them in the sack with the gold. While placing the staff back into the chest, Jon bumped the wire cage on the side of the lid, and noticed that it twisted slightly. Looking more closely at the end of the staff, Jon twisted the cage only to discover that the twisting action caused the whole top of the cage to open. But that wasn't his only surprise. Once the top of the small wire cage was open, a red and blue light glowed from the inside of the trunk. Both of the round gems were suddenly dazzling. Looking from the staff to the gems, it seemed obvious to Jon what he needed to do. He selected the red gem and placed it into the opening in the top of the cage. The cage immediately twisted shut, firmly grasping the gem which continued to glow for about 15 more seconds. The other blue gem ceased to glow.

Greg watched the whole process, wonder eyed. "There's something special about that staff. I wish I knew what it was." Jon nodded agreement. Greg paused for a moment and then added, "I grabbed my watch from my room when I was up there. We still have a good 25 minutes before Mom gets back. We could take a short ride in there, if you know what I mean."

"Yeah, let's try it. We can only stay in there for ten minutes, though," Jon cautioned. "We need five minutes to get ready, ten to fly, five minutes to get back out and closed up and out of the basement, and five minutes for any trouble." Jon was already through the back of the chest by the time he finished speaking. Greg was right on his heels.

Jon unrolled the carpet on the floor of the cave. Greg had the staff in his hand as he came through the barrier. "I thought we should bring this along. Maybe we can figure out what it is," Greg said, as he stepped onto the carpet. As soon as he did, the gem in the staff began to glow, and the two small black spots on the carpet began to turn a vivid gold color. Intuitively, Greg touched the base of the staff to the spot on the carpet, only to watch the two fuse together. There was a sudden rush of insight—no, that wasn't it—it was as if there was another presence in his mind. And in another instant, he knew the carpet was alive. The carpet could read his thoughts. The scepter and carpet were designed for each other. And they would serve faithfully whoever brought them together again.

Greg reached up and twisted the first band on the top of the staff.

Jon shouted, obviously startled, "Greg, what happened? Where are you?"

"Right here," Greg replied. In one moment, Greg and the carpet had completely disappeared. In the very next, they were all back again. "This carpet is sort of alive, Jon. It can read my thoughts. We will be able to steer it with the scepter from now on. In fact, there are lots of things it can do. The first band on the scepter is invisibility. When you twist it, no one can see you. The second band is a protective spell of some sort. I can't understand it exactly. The third, at the top, is a weapon."

"How do you know all of this? Is the carpet talking to you?" Jon asked.

"Not exactly. I can't really explain it. It's just like, I just, well, I know. Somehow, I know. Put your hands on the staff and see what it feels like to you."

Jon stepped onto the carpet and placed his hands on the staff. His eyes widened as he experienced what Greg had tried but failed to accurately describe. Yes, the carpet, the staff, they were somehow alive. And there were three functions, invisibility, protection and weapon. And there was no question about how to fly. As long as one hand was on the stick, this thing would be as fast as thought!

Without another word, Jon thought the carpet into the air and out of the cave. Just to be on the safe side, since it was broad daylight in this world, Jon twisted the lowest band on the staff. They both felt, rather than heard, a humming. And while they could plainly see each other, they knew they must be invisible. Out over the forest they flew. Greg checked his watch as they left the cave. It was 10:15. Mom had left at 9:35. They needed to be home by 10:25. Sharp.

The air was cool, but the sky was clear. A few clouds drifted by, slightly higher in elevation than the carpet. Jon flew toward a spot where the forest seemed thinnest, hoping to find out what might be on the other side of the green expanse. In just a minute or two, they were far enough over the forest that they could see the plains on the other side of the forest. Off in the distance, close to the horizon, it appeared that a city of some sort sprawled across the plain. And it was suddenly clear to them that something was coming toward them from that city!

High in the air, approaching at a rapid rate of speed, was a large, something or other. Greg and Jon felt very vulnerable, perched high in the sky, not knowing what was coming. Jon twisted the second band, the protection spell, and convinced Greg to stay where they were. After all, they were protected and invisible. Whatever it was couldn't be coming to see them! It was a coincidence. They would stay put until they got a look at what was coming.

They didn't have to wait long. Moving at incredible speed, the giant red reptile raced toward them, stopping just a few yards in front of the carpet. Greg, sitting behind Jon, had his arms wrapped around Jon, nearly squeezing the breath out of him. Jon had a death grip on the staff. Both were shivering, frozen by fear.

"And who might you be?" the dragon asked in a deep raspy voice.

"You, you c-c-can see us?" Jon stuttered.

"Of course I can see you! Nothing is invisible to the magical eye of a dragon!"

The dragon was a thing of splendor and terror all at the same time. At least forty feet long, his red shimmering scales seemed at once metallic, yet flexible enough to bend and breathe. His head was huge, dripping with fangs and a serpent-like red tongue. His blood red eyes bore into the boys, nearly hypnotizing them. Expansive wings flapped ever so slowly, as the dragon hovered just in front of them.

"Again," the dragon growled, "who are you?"

Jon didn't want to give themselves away to a dragon. He muttered out an answer, stumbling over the words, "We're just some friendly explorers. I think we'll be going now."

This was not the answer the dragon wanted to hear. With a blood-curdling roar, a fireball of immense proportion hurtled through the sky and completely engulfed the carpet and its occupants.

Jon and Greg hadn't seen it coming. They had already turned the carpet around and were headed, at top speed, back to the cave. They heard the growl, and then they felt some unseen force push them along faster from behind. A second later the flames encircled them and passed beyond them.

While they saw the flames, they didn't feel the flames. Greg looked back and the dragon was gone. Then he felt the carpet coming to an abrupt halt. The dragon was now in front of them. "How did you do that?" the dragon asked.

Jon wasn't interested in conversation, only escape. He reached up to the third band on the staff and twisted it. Immediately a bright red, bolt of fire shot out of the gem and hit the dragon squarely in the chest. Taken aback by the attack, the dragon staggered for a moment. Jon darted past the monster and headed straight for the cave.

It was only as they approached the spot where the cave should have been that they realized the problem. From this side, the cave was invisible. The side of the mountain revealed no caves. There were no six foot square holes to be seen. They had never bothered to look back to see if they would be able to find their way home. Before they could figure out what to do, the dragon was on them again, and then past them. He flew to a certain spot near the mountain, and stopped, as if waiting for them. Since the dragon stopped, Jon and Greg followed suit. They stared at each other. Finally, the dragon spoke.

"Why did you attack me?" he asked.

"You attacked us first, remember?" Jon replied coldly.

"But you refused to answer my questions," the dragon accused.

"Why should we? We don't owe you any answers," Jon said.

"Oh yes you do. You are trespassing in my land. I felt you enter it and I came to investigate. You woke me well before my nap was finished," the dragon added, "and I won't get back to sleep very easily now."

Jon moved slightly closer to the dragon, which allowed Greg to get a look at the side of the mountain behind him. While Jon was talking, Greg was thinking. *Nothing is invisible to the dragon. He must know where the cave is. . .he can see it. He is probably blocking our way of escape.* Focusing on the mountain behind the dragon, Greg was finally able to make out some marks that looked familiar. . .dagger-shaped carvings. He instantly understood. To get out of here, he had to get his daggers into those keyholes. It would be tough with a dragon between him and them. But at least they knew now that they were protected from the dragon's fire.

"Now," the dragon continued, "Who are you?"

After a short pause, Jon finally decided on the truth and spoke up. "We are simply two kids from another world. We were curious when we found the entry way and came in to explore. We meant no harm, and we will be happy to leave and never return."

"A wise decision. But not one I think I can afford to allow. You see, if I allow you to leave, you might tell others what you have found. And then who knows what or whom you might bring back with you.

No, for the safety of this world, I cannot permit you to return to yours. In fact, I can't think of a good reason not to destroy you."

"Well, maybe you can't destroy us. Your fire didn't do much harm, as I recall," Jon pointed out.

"True, but you don't seriously think that a dragon's fire is his only means of attack? Remember, I am faster than you and I can see you. That means you can never escape me. And even if my claws or teeth can't reach you, I can bat you around so hard that you will be crushed inside your own defenses."

A plan was forming inside Greg's mind, but he needed to buy some time until he could figure out how to tell Jon to call his dagger. "Uh, Mr. Dragon, do you like jokes?" Greg shouted, his voice shaking with fear.

"Jokes? Like riddles or puzzles? Of course—all dragons love those. Do you know one?" the dragon asked.

"Why do ducks have webbed feet?" Greg meekly asked.

"Why do ducks have webbed feet?" the dragon repeated, questioningly. He paused to think.

Greg whispered to Jon, "Call your knife. The dragon is blocking the cave and the daggers are the key to opening the entrance." In another moment, each had a dagger in hand.

"I don't know," the dragon admitted. "I'm sure the answer you are looking for isn't that it helps them swim."

"No, that's not it, Mr. Dragon," Greg replied. "Ducks have webbed feet to help put out forest fires."

A small puff of smoke rose out of one nostril of the dragon. "Forest fires?" he muttered.

Quickly Greg continued, "And why do elephants have flat feet?"

"Why do elephants have flat feet?" the dragon reiterated.

After a brief pause, the dragon acquiesced, "Tell me."

"To stomp out flaming ducks!" Greg smiled.

An odd smile crept across the dragon's face. At first it was impossible to tell whether the dragon was smiling at a perceived attempt to distract him, or if he was genuinely amused. His next words removed the doubt. "I think there is more to you two than meets the eye. If I let you go, will you promise to keep our secret..."

"Of course", Jon jumped in, interrupting the dragon before he was done.

"...and will you bring back a few more 'jokes' as you call them?" the dragon finished.

"Certainly," Greg smiled.

"Then come again. Perhaps you are here for a reason. Maybe you are the ones who will help save the kingdom. Stranger things have happened." And without another word he wheeled around and flew rapidly back in the direction from which he had originally come.

Jon collapsed back onto the carpet, a huge sigh involuntarily escaping his lips. Greg, relieved, giggled slightly. "And you thought that was a dumb joke!"

With the tension suddenly gone, Greg's comment seemed like the funniest thing Jon had ever heard. He roared in laughter, and in just a moment, both of them were completely consumed by the joy of the moment. They had survived a brush with death. Not that they could tell anyone about it. Still, they felt somehow older, somehow more confident than when they entered this unusual place. That's when Greg remembered the time.

"Jon, we have to get back home, quick." He looked at his watch and his heart sank. The watch read 10:15. That was what it read when they left the cave. They must have been in this world at least 25 minutes, and the time hadn't changed! The watch probably didn't work here. "Put your dagger against the rock over there."

Jon pulled the carpet up to the wall next to the carvings. When both daggers were in place, the rock wall shimmered and disappeared. They quickly entered, deciding to leave everything in the cave in order to get back into the house as rapidly as possible. With no trace of treasure anywhere about them, first Greg and then Jon crossed through the blackness, back into their own cellar.

They listened quietly. They tried to see if they could hear their mother moving around upstairs. The house was still. While Jon closed the chest, Greg checked his watch again. 10:16. Now, that was strange. Had his watch simply started working again since they returned, or did time move differently in the new place?

Jon suggested they sneak upstairs, one at a time. They could pretend they had been in the wood shop looking for glue to fix something. "All clear," Jon yelled down the stairs. "Mom's not home yet." The clock in the kitchen read 10:16.

CHAPTER II

# Javelins

Four well-armed, mounted soldiers led the processional that moved slowly across the Corundum Plain. The road to the Grove began as a well defined highway, but it quickly deteriorated as the last settlements were passed. No one had traveled to the Grove to meet a challenge in decades, and no one would even think of going there for any other reason. Too much magic! Too many strange things rumored to have happened there. No, it was a place best left alone.

Behind the soldiers were the banner men, dressed in gleaming red armor. The king's crest, a scarlet shield on which was set three crossed silver swords, was emblazoned on a large banner carried high on a raised silver lance. On either side of the royal banner were smaller flags representing the members of the royal family. A red rose set on a silver field was the symbol of the queen; a red dragon glistened against a red background, the emblem of the crown prince.

Directly behind the banners rode the knight-generals. Each was in full silver plate armor, shined to a high luster. Their shields were crimson, as were the plumes that radiated from their helms. As dazzling as they appeared, they were inconsiderable compared to the three that followed.

Mounted on a white stallion a head taller than any other mount in the procession, the Ruby King radiated light. His armor was brilliant red, though he wore no helm. A crown of silver adorned his head, with a ruby the size of a silver dollar set in the front of it. Jewels glittered from the crown, from the hilt of his sword, from the trim of his gauntlets, from the saddle of his horse, and from every other place in which a stone could conceivably be set. But the stones themselves were not enough to account for His Majesty's radiant appearance. There was something of wizard light dancing from the facets of the jewels. The casual observer might never question the effect, thinking only that they were witnessing a person of great power and dignity. But this was a magically enhanced appearance. Stoneclaw had done his work well.

The queen was also caught in the glow of the light. She wore a crimson gown, trimmed in white fur at the neck, waist and hem. Woven into her hair was a circlet of silver, studded with rubies, glittering with light. She rode side-saddle on a red trimmed, white horse, just slightly behind and to the left of her husband. To his right, wearing red trimmed in black and Prince Judas' favorite cloak, was Ephraim. The small silver circlet of the crown prince was on his head, though invisible because of the hood drawn tight against the wind, and against unwarranted inspection.

Several flanks of soldiers rode on either side of the royal family, protecting them from any threat of ambush. As hearty as the soldiers appeared, the real defenders of the royals were close behind them. Stoneclaw and Eli rode less than six feet behind the trio, and were followed by the other participants in the challenge. Supply wagons, protected by more soldiers, finished out the caravan.

By the time the royal parade passed the last settlement, it was well past noon. Eli had, in fact, joined the procession just a short time before. And now, as they drew closer to the Grove, tensions began to increase. Eli moved his horse to the right of Ephraim and signaled him to draw close.

"Don't be afraid, Ephraim. Everything will turn out well," he asserted.

"How can you say that? You know the danger. We could all be dead by this time tomorrow." Ephraim spat back.

"Not you, my son," Eli soothed. "I have seen a vision of what may be, and I believe you will be safe."

Ephraim brightened visibly. "Then we will be victorious?"

"Of that I am not certain. I could only see a few faces among those who were leaving the Grove. Yours was among them."

"But whether I was a slave or a free man, you know not?" Ephraim asked.

"No, I do not know. But there are some things you must know, things you must never forget. Now listen carefully. If I should be, shall we say, injured," he paused for the briefest of moments, "or worse, you must get to me right away. Forget the rules of the game; you must get to me, even if just for a second."

"Why?" Ephraim probed.

"That I cannot explain right now, but it will become clear in time. But the second thing is this. If something should happen to us, should heaven decide our cause is not just, then you must remember why you are here."

"I am here because there is a spoiled brat back…"

"Ephraim! How can you speak of your friend like that? He had no…"

"Friend?! What friend would allow someone to take his place in a dangerous situation? What friend would allow someone else to get fried by wizard fire, just so he could watch from a safe distance? No, Judas is no friend of mine!"

"Ephraim, Judas had no choice, don't you know that? This is a decision reached by both the king and by me. If something should happen to us, we must have an heir who can redeem the kingdom. We can't afford to risk both the king and the prince! Judas wanted to be here himself. Don't you understand?"

Still a little confused, Ephraim shook his head and said nothing. He would have to think about this a little longer. But Eli wasn't going to give him any time to think.

"You, young man, are going to have to get over your petty jealousy and think about what is best for the kingdom. You will have an important role to play, but if you allow jealousy to choose your path, you will destroy everything."

"But what about what is best for me? It's not fair to ask me to die before I am even old enough to fight as a soldier!"

"You're right, my son, it is not fair. But little in life is fair. If I were you I would stop trying to keep that score. You will be far better served if you see in each trial you must face an opportunity to grow strong and develop courage and character. In that way, your calamities will bring you growth rather than bitterness."

Ephraim was listening, but he wasn't ready to buy. His mood was still sour, though tempered by the realization that Judas had no part in the switch. He rode on silently, considering. After a few moments, Eli spoke again.

"There's more. Should things go badly tomorrow, remember who you serve. You are the servant of the king. And should we fail in the challenge, there will be a new king, and, listen carefully, you will be in a position to give him aid. Will you do your duty?"

"What do you mean 'I will be in a position to give him aid'?" Ephraim responded.

"Ephraim, will you do your duty?" barked Eli, shortly.

"I don't know. What is my duty?"

"To serve the king to the best of your ability. Will you do it?" Eli's eyes seemed to peer directly down into Ephraim's soul.

"I guess so," Ephraim stammered.

"Not enough, not even close. Here place your hand on my staff. Now say the words, 'I will do my duty to the king of the Ruby Kingdom.'"

Eli guided Ephraim's hand to the staff and held it there as they rode side by side. The stone at the end of the staff felt warm, seemed to pulse under his fingers. Ephraim spoke, "I will do my duty to the king of the Ruby Kingdom." He felt a weight descend on his heart. Somehow he knew this was a promise he would have to keep.

The edge of the forest came slowly into view, along with the sight of a small encampment on the left side of the road approaching the Grove. Black banners waved from the dark tents; the Obsidian King was already in residence. The red army moved into position on the right side of the road, just outside the small opening that led to the Grove. Soon tents were erected and food was prepared. There would be a big feast just before sunset, a last meal for some.

The regulations that governed the challenge stipulated that only those persons who were to be on the board were allowed to enter the

Grove, with the exception of two additional assistants, surgeons. Legends said that once a nineteenth person from one kingdom tried to enter. A mist supposedly enveloped him, and he was never seen again. No one ever tried to sneak extras into the ceremony after that. A full contingent of guards would wait outside the Grove, there to provide protection for whatever remnant emerged from the conflict.

After the feast had been consumed, both processions reformed and began to move towards the opening in the forest wall. When the first part of the sun touched the top of the Severus Mountains, the pace of each quickened. There was no advantage in being first into the Grove, unless the other party arrived after sunset. Since it was obvious that all would be inside the Grove before the sun was fully set, the Ruby King allowed his dark distant cousin to precede him. Once they were inside, a thick fog settled into the opening through which all had passed, and it was clear that no one else would be admitted.

The Grove itself was a round clearing in the center of which was a square, twenty -five yards across. The square was divided like a chess board, eight small squares along each side. Flowering white clover filled alternating boxes, while a dark purple moss covered the rest. The entire perimeter of the "field of conquest" was marked by a border of naked earth, a yard wide, in which no vegetation grew. The earth was sandy, and glittering, as if the dust from many gemstones were mixed into the soil.

Ephraim heard the Obsidian King sneer as soon as the red party entered the Grove. "I see you managed to arrive in time. How clever of you!" His words dripped with sarcasm.

"We need not speak, cousin, the rules of engagement are clear. The challenge is yours, you shall throw first," the Ruby King icily replied. He deftly cleared his stallion and reached for the javelin his knight-general was handing to him.

Since both parties had arrived at sunset, position on the board was determined by a contest. Each king would stand on the south side of the board, outside the dirt pathway that surrounded it. Each would throw a javelin directly north, toward the opposite side of the board. Whichever javelin landed closest to the opposite border, without go-

ing outside the boundary, won for her master the right to choose
board position. North was always chosen; north moved first.

Black plate mail covered the chest of the Obsidian King, and
a large flowing black cape was secured around his neck. The king
removed the cape, and his black helm, and began to heft a sleek black
shaft, pointed on both ends. After a few moments, he stepped to the
center of the southern boundary and paced back six steps. All conversation ceased.

Facing the board, the Obsidian King lifted the javelin in his
right hand, high above his shoulder, and then drew his arm back. A
short sprint forward, a loud grunt, and the javelin was in the air, flying swiftly in a high arc toward the other side of the Grove. Every eye
in the Grove traced the path of that spear. No one breathed. With a
"fffffffthhhtt," the javelin struck the earth, imbedding itself in the
middle of the last rank of squares, less than a yard from the opposite
boundary. The collective groan of the red army was swallowed by the
cheer that rose from the black.

"Hah! Beat that!" the dark king spat, as he swaggered back to
his party.

Without saying a word, lines of concentration etched deeply on
his face, the Ruby King stepped up to the mark. He paced away eight
steps and prepared himself for his throw. Javelin high, he sprang into
action more quickly than anyone expected. His red spear flew straight
and true, so close to his opponent's shaft that it appeared that they
might collide. It stuck into the earth just beyond the dark king's, but
from where everyone was standing, it was impossible to tell whether
the red spear was still within the boundary of the board. Suddenly
everyone was running toward the northern side of the board. Was it
in, or was it out?

The answer came from the board itself. Though the first people
to arrive on the northern side might have seen exactly where the point
of the spear had entered the earth, no one else did. A shower of sparks,
accompanied by a crackling sound arose out of the earthen boundary, and the red javelin melted into a pool of dark liquid, which was
quickly absorbed into the dirt. Only one javelin remained, dark and

foreboding, marking the exact place where the Obsidian King would be standing when the sun arose the next morning.

While the dark army cheered, the red moved dejectedly back to the south side of the Board. It was now safe to enter the playing area, as long as one stayed on his own side of the Board. Sleeping gear was unrolled, and two opposing armies rested together on the Board that would determine their fate. In reality, no one really rested.

Ephraim nestled close to Eli in the darkness. Ephraim had tried to ask Eli a question about what would happen tomorrow, but Eli had made him wait. There was a song that Eli must sing to completion before the night was over. Once sung, Ephraim could ask whatever questions he might have. And so Ephraim waited.

The song had an eerie quality about it. Ephraim had the impression that Eli was singing to someone, but there was no audience that he could see. Thirty, maybe forty minutes had passed since the soft singing had begun, and Ephraim had begun to wonder if this song would last the whole night through. His eyes were glued to Eli's face. As Eli's voice grew softer, perspiration stood out on his forehead. He stopped singing abruptly. Stiffly, he clapped his palms together, then crossed his arms and clapped the backs of his hands together. Once more, he clapped his hands, palm to palm, then sighed. The ruby in the ring on Eli's right hand began to glow brightly. Ephraim watched as a red hue rose on the skin on Eli's face, only to be changed into blue a moment later. Before Ephraim could speak, all was as it had been before, and Eli appeared normal—exhausted, but normal.

"What happened to you?" Ephraim whispered.

"Nothing we should speak about here. But should things go badly tomorrow, we will be ready. Now, what was your question?"

The transition in Eli's appearance had so startled Ephraim that he completely forgot what he wanted to ask. "Uh, I'm feeling a little cold. Would you mind sharing your blanket with me? I only brought along my cloak."

It wasn't quite the truth. The night was warm enough so that the cloak should have been enough. But neither questioned the request. Eli pulled Ephraim close to him and covered them both with his blanket.

"Sleep well, my son, and remember your duty," he whispered into Ephraim's ear. "And remember, I will always love you, my child."

Ephraim held still, hoping he would be able to get some sleep. But it was of no use. His mind was racing to the events of the next day. What would he do if the Ruby King lost? Would his impostor son be eliminated? And what if the battle was lost but he managed to escape? Where would he live? The castle kitchens had always been his home. Would there be a place for him there? And what would his duty be?

Lost in his thoughts, he heard Eli hum a simple quiet tune. A great heaviness entered his mind, and in a moment, all thoughts were gone.

CHAPTER 12

# Out of the Sky

That night after they met the dragon, Jon and Greg decided to try another trip. They needed to test this time theory. It seemed that time passed differently in the two worlds. They needed to know for sure. After waking at one o'clock in the morning, they crept downstairs to the sub basement ready to experiment. Jon wore his watch; Greg left his watch on the floor next to the trunk. They were careful to set their watches to exactly the same time. Calling their knives into their hands, they unlocked the trunk and stepped into another world.

All the items they had left in the cave were still there. From the position of the sun, it seemed to be early morning here, even though it was the middle of the night at home. They unrolled the carpet, attached the staff and grabbed two of the silver swords. Each boy tucked one inside his belt. Necklaces were in place, but everything else was left behind. After a short discussion, they decided to fly straight east for thirty minutes and then return. They were about ten minutes into their flight when they passed over a small clearing on the edge of the forest. Peering out over the edge of the carpet, it looked like there were people in the clearing. They briefly considered dropping down for a closer look. In the very next moment, however, they were falling fast to the ground, still on the carpet, but completely out of their own control! Jon grabbed the staff and hung on, while Greg hugged the carpet as best he could and shut his eyes. In less than two seconds, they were on the ground. No crash, no bang, no thud. They were just there. It was almost as if they had been moved from the sky to the ground by some amazingly powerful force, a force powerful enough to move them at great speed, and yet shield them from damage upon impact. It was frightening! When they opened their eyes, they realized that the force that moved them there wasn't the least of their problems.

CHAPTER 13

# Challenge Enjoined

The sound of a rumbling gong woke Ephraim the next morning. The sky above them was still dark, but dawn was beginning to lighten the eastern edge of the Grove. Blankets were thrown off the board, equipment was checked, and people on both sides of the board began to move to their respective squares. Eli gave Ephraim one last hug. "Don't forget what I told you. Be strong!"

Ephraim moved to his position, one square in front of the queen. To his right was a rugged soldier, to his left, another. The king had carefully dispatched the forces under his command. Hoping to protect his wife's position, he placed his strongest general, Knight-General Zarak, on her side. And although he would have liked to have Eli closer to himself, he sent his first mage to the other side as well. The bishops, he knew, would function dutifully, but he was a man more interested in power and magic than prayer. He kept Stoneclaw and Knight-General Artezes near himself.

The king whispered a few words of encouragement into his wife's ear. Ephraim strained to see the faces of those staring back at him, but it was still too dark to see clearly. He drew his hood over his head, but was careful to keep his short sword free from the folds of the cloak. And then the first ray of the sun cleared the horizon.

Defiantly, the Obsidian King shouted, "King's pawn forward twice!" The Ruby King matched the move.

"Knight-General, take charge at queen's bishop three!" the Black King ordered. Jumping his mount over the soldier crouched in front of him, the knight-general moved effortlessly into position to coordinate the offense.

With a stern voice, Judas' father responded, speaking directly to Ephraim. "Son, take courage; advance one square."

In the next moment, the Dark King called out his other knight-general, and before the Red King could develop any other major players, the Black Queen swept out of the background and moved in to threaten her red counterpart. "You despicable creature! Your greed and your lies will now be found out by all!" she shouted directly at Judas' mother. The Black Queen was carefully guarded by the king's Knight General, but she had not counted on the recklessness of the Ruby Queen. It was, after all, extremely presumptuous to assume that you could move anywhere on this board in complete safety, without regard to the danger the other pieces presented.

Judas' mother understood what the other queen was trying to do—she was trying to intimidate! By moving out boldly into the battle, she was proclaiming that she was not afraid of her opponents. And that was her mistake!

With her staff held low and off to one side, Her Highness, the Ruby Queen, took three quick steps directly toward the Dark Queen. "Foolishness!" she accused, and unleashed a fire-bolt at close range. The charge took the Obsidian Queen in the side, and she was immediately knocked unconscious, removed from the game. "That will teach you to spread treachery and villainy!" the victor crooned. The Red Queen laughed out loud, glared at the black horde, and then turned back to face her own forces, taking a sweeping bow as her loyal subjects cheered. But her cheer was short lived. For though the Knight-General just behind the Dark Queen did catch her as she fell, he quickly handed her off to the surgeons. Before the Red Queen could even turn around to face her opponent, he had drawn, swung, and struck the side of his adversary. His sword bit deep; the queen screamed and fell to the ground, gravely injured.

"Quickly, surgeons, attend to the Queen! Help Her Royal Majesty! Hurry, stop the bleeding. She must not die!" the king implored, despondently. It took every ounce of discipline for the King to stay on his square. He knew that if he stepped off, it would be counted as a move. And one false step could mean the difference between victory and defeat. Ah, why had his wife been so rash?

The history of chess on the Great Board was full of foolish exchanges like this one. Too often, kings were influenced by the flamboyant personality of people, rather than by the strength of their relative pieces. Chess is a game of rational thought, a game where strength is balanced and limited, a game where all are bound by the same rules. Perhaps the reason the Creator designed the Great Board to resolve disputes was that the Board forced kings to think rationally rather than emotionally. And in times of supercharged emotions, that was good. It also forced kings to know first hand every person who fought for them.

It is easy for kings to send young boys they do not know into battle. It is much more difficult to wage war when the people who are at risk are your best friends, advisors and cherished family members. There is a great incentive to compromise when one stands to lose everything they hold dear! But on this day, there would be no compromise.

The Red King sent out his bishop to regain order. And shortly after that, Eli moved onto Ephraim's rank to offer both king and "son" greater protection.

The game developed quickly: A pawn was captured, a bishop killed. A moment later one of the black knight-generals fell to the sword of Red Knight-General Artezes. Another bishop, this time black, was knocked unconscious and removed from the game. And when that bishop fell, the Obsidian King found himself threatened, checked. He moved away quickly.

Now the magicians became more involved. Moving rapidly around the board, chanting incomprehensible phrases, they tried to encourage and strengthen the other players, while threatening their opponents. Unfortunately, the Black Queen's Magician did not pay enough attention to those who threatened him, and in the middle of a curious tune-spell, he was knocked senseless by the flat side of Knight-General Artezes' sword. Wasting no time, the other magician immediately turned and brushed his hand across the general's back. He crumpled into the dust, unconscious, barely alive. Knight-General Zarak quickly retaliated, but was driven away. He retreated far enough to protect himself, but not so far that he couldn't offer protection to other members of his force. His presence in the front line allowed a red bishop to sneak in and attack the Black King. Again, the Black King had to move away.

"Stoneclaw!" the Ruby King commanded next, "Exchange positions with me!"

"An honor, my king." Stoneclaw responded. He was happy to "castle" into action! Distracted by the movement of the magician, the black force missed the bishop moving in to attack again. Once again, the Black King retreated. Soldiers attacked one another, and the remaining Black Knight-General trampled the annoying bishop under the hooves of his stallion.

This was Ephraim's moment. For while the knight-general's horse was finishing the trampling of the bishop, Ephraim plunged his short sword into the rump of the horse. As the horse reared on his hind legs, the knight-general was thrown clear. He hit the ground with great force, and once landed, remained still. Ephraim stepped victoriously onto the knight-general's square! A moment later a black bishop singed Knight-General Zarak, leaving Ephraim surrounded by black forces. A magician, a bishop, two soldiers and the king himself all glared at the boy…as if daring him to try to move any closer to the end of the board.

And, of course, that was exactly where Ephraim wanted to be. For a moment, Ephraim hoped his king would allow him to make a run for it. But before he had a chance, Eli materialized one square in front of him, and to his left. Ephraim was horrified. Eli was completely vulnerable to the black magician standing right next to him. Eli turned to face Ephraim. "Don't forget what I told you. Have courage. Strike back swiftly. Now take my hand."

Ephraim reached out to take Eli's hand, and as he did, the wicked black magician behind Eli struck with full force. Eli's face turned blue then red. A surge of power seemed to flow through Eli right into Ephraim. Ephraim screamed, "Nooooo!" But it was too late. One moment Eli was present, in the next, his cloak floated to the ground, lacking any internal substance to hold its shape. Eli was gone.

The black magician stepped directly onto the cloak and began to chant words that Ephraim did not understand. Ephraim was dizzy with pain, disoriented by grief, but alert enough to remember Eli's words—Strike swiftly! Before the Magician could finish his phrase, Ephraim struck out with his dagger, cutting through the heavy robe of his opponent and into his left side. The wound seemed superficial, but much to Ephraim's surprise, blue sparks flew from his blade the moment the magician's blood touched it. Again, Ephraim felt the surge of power running through his body, and when he looked up, the black magician was also gone. Ephraim felt strange, indeed—somehow different, somehow stronger.

Seeing the imminent danger he was in, the Black King moved directly toward Ephraim. Stoneclaw moved behind Ephraim to protect him, forcing the king to back off.

Triumphantly, Ephraim stepped onto the last rank!

As Ephraim stepped onto the final square, he knew that whatever happened, he would live. Steam began to arise from the dirt in the border beyond his square, and he quickly stepped into it, crossing the border. He knew he could choose whomever he wanted to step back into the game to take his place. But the queen had been so seriously injured by the knight-general's sword. Would she be of any real use? If only Eli were still here. As if thinking of Eli had opened a door in his mind, he heard a voice calling to him, "Look up! Look up! You may choose any creature within the Grove; that is the rule!"

Ephraim looked into the sky as a blue rectangle flew into view, with two heads peering over the side of it.

"I choose you!" he cried, pointing at the airborne anomaly.

Instantly, Jon and Greg were on the ground, in the square that Ephraim had just vacated. No amount of manipulation or persuasion could get the carpet to move from its place. People were yelling everywhere. Wounded players were attempting to rise to their feet. Screams of defiance filled the Grove. The Obsidian King was enraged and began to raise his staff to attack. Jon instinctively grabbed the scepter and launched a fire bolt directly into the king's chest. He crumbled to the ground. In almost the same instant, Stoneclaw was shouting, "Behind you! Off the board! Look out!"

Jon turned just in time to see the Obsidian Queen raise her staff high above her head, releasing a black spray of death over both of them. The fire bolt that Jon unleashed cut through the center of the mist, engulfed the Obsidian Queen, reducing her to ashes. The mist released by her staff would have certainly meant the end of both boys had not the shield been in place. Unfortunately, while the shield protected them, it reflected the force of the blast. Stoneclaw, standing directly behind them, was overwhelmed. While Jon and Greg watched in horror, he slowly melted away. Ephraim ran to him immediately, but a final touch was all that Ephraim could offer. There was no time for anything more.

"What is going on?" Jon shouted. "We're in the middle of a war here!"

"Stay on the carpet, whatever you do!" Greg yelled back. "They can see us, but I don't think they can hurt us as long as the shield holds."

"Stand behind me and watch the other direction. If anyone comes near us, grab the scepter and blast them," Jon instructed. But no one was moving. In fact, the whole Grove was eerily silent.

With the Obsidian King dead, the challenge was officially over. All that remained of his force was three pawns and one bishop, an ancient priest with an evil glint in his eyes. Standing as tall as his weary old frame would allow, the priest, Marfessol, announced in a bone chilling voice, "Today we acknowledge your victory. But time will judge whether the rules have been broken and whether the Grove can ever be used again. We depart in peace." Gathering the surgeons, a few horses, and a few wounded comrades, the Obsidian force was gone within minutes.

As soon as the enemy was out of sight, the red camp erupted in high celebration! Soldiers cheered as Knight-General Zarak saluted them, in spite of his wounds. Men were running back and forth across the Grove! Ephraim didn't know how to feel. He was excited at the victory but devastated by the loss of Eli. In the end, the internal conflict was too much for him, and he simply collapsed to the ground where he stood, weeping softly. In a moment, he realized he wasn't the only one weeping. Off to his right, on the western side of the board, was a surgeon, kneeling on the ground, sobbing. "I did everything I could," he was saying. "The wound was too deep. There must have been poison on the blade."

On the ground in front of him lay the still form of the Ruby Queen. Kneeling by her side, speechless, holding one of her hands, was her husband. The look on his face was odd. He had a far-away kind of look, like he was thinking of something else. Then he placed her hand back across her abdomen and stood to his feet. "Onto the board, all of them!" he shouted. Then he looked at Jon and Greg. "Join me, friends, at camp tonight. I have a reward for you."

Jon and Greg found they were free to move, and quickly made themselves invisible and took the carpet to the sky. They would find the king later. For now, they simply wanted out of this clearing in the woods.

The king moved to his stallion and mounted while the remaining soldiers carried the bodies of all those who had fallen back onto the board. Those who were simply wounded, Knight-General Artezes among them, moved toward the opening in the trees, which was now clear.

It was the task of the victors to place the bodies of all those who had died in the challenge, both friend and foe, back onto the board on the square from which they had started the match. Once the task was completed, the remaining company moved to join the king. Jumping from his horse, the king went to one knee. He was followed by every member of his party. With his hand over his chest, he bowed his head for a brief moment. Raising his head again, he shouted, "We salute you!"

A flash of lightning, followed by the crash of its thunder, split the sky, striking the center of the board. Flames shot up from every square, consuming foliage and fallen comrades alike. When the smoke subsided, all that remained was scorched earth, surrounded by a dirt boundary, in a perfect, glittering square.

# Sacred Grove Chess Match

| Obsidian | Ruby | Obsidian | Ruby (con't) |
|----------|------|----------|--------------|
| 1)P-K4 | P-K4 | 19)R-N2 | P-KR4 |
| 2)N-QB3 | P-Q3 | 20)N-QR4 | B-QN5 |
| 3)N-KR3 | N-QB3 | 21)K-QB1 | N-KB6 |
| 4)Q-KN4 | P-QR3 | 22)KR-K2 | NXR |
| 5)Q-KN5 | QXQ | 23)RXN | N-KB7 |
| 6)NXQ | B-KN5 | 24)R-K2 | N-K5 |
| 7)P-QN3 | R-Q1 | 25)B-N2 | BXPch |
| 8)B-QR3 | N-KB3 | 26)K-N1 | P-QB4 |
| 9)P-KR3 | B-KR4 | 27)B-KR1 | P-QN3 |
| 10)P-KN4 | B-KN3 | 28)K-N2 | O-O |
| 11)B-QB4 | BXKP | 29)P-QB3 | BXPch |
| 12)N@N5XB | NXN | 30)K-N1 | P-Q5 |
| 13)P-KR4 | P-Q4 | 31)P-QR3 | P-QN4 |
| 14)B-KB1 | N-Q5 | 32)NXB | PXN |
| 15)O-O | BXBch | 33)BXN | R-Q7 |
| 16)K-N1 | N@K5XBP+ | 34)RXR | PXR |
| 17)R-K1 | P-KB3 | 35)K-B2 | R-Q1 |
| 18)R-R2 | left NXNP | 36)K-N1 | P-converts |

CHAPTER 14

# Confusion

It was halfway to noon when Judas felt the first change in the stone. He had slept fitfully and had awakened with the sun's first rays. He knew the match would be beginning. He hungrily gnawed on a chunk of cheese and followed that with yesterday's bread. The water in the pitcher was room temperature. It wasn't the kind of breakfast he was used to, but then he figured no one would be eating the usual breakfast today. In fact, there would be nothing usual about this day at all.

Bored with sitting around in his room, Judas decided to explore the passageways he had only recently discovered. He placed his hand on the wall where he knew the secret device was hidden, and waited a few seconds for the wall to grow warm. When it did, the door slid silently open. Stepping into the darkness, Judas closed the door. Then, with one hand on his royal ruby, he visualized a light glowing from the end of his finger. He whispered, "Light." Instantly, his index finger, from the first knuckle forward, began to glow. Inwardly, Judas was elated. Even without Eli, the magic still worked! He had half expected that once Eli was gone, the magic would be gone with him. But it was all still here. The royal ruby was still hanging by a leather strap, but for the moment, rather than being around his neck, it was wrapped around his wrist so that the stone could be held in his hand.

He was in the passageway outside the throne room when he heard voices. At first he couldn't tell where the voices were coming from. Things tended to echo in an unusual way inside the stone castle. But it was soon evident that someone was inside the throne room.

That surprised Judas, because Eli has specifically said that no one was admitted to the throne room when the king was not in residence. Judas thought about going in to find out who it might be, but then he realized that wouldn't be smart. He didn't know who might be in there—but more importantly, he remembered that he was not allowed to be seen. He walked down the full length of the corridor, hoping to get closer to the end of the room where the voices were coming from. As he walked down toward the eastern end of the corridor, he saw steps leading upwards, straight into a stone wall. He wondered why steps would lead no where, as he began to climb slowly to the top. With one hand holding on to the ruby, and the other offering the light needed to see, he kept his shoulder in contact with the wall in order to maintain balance.

At the top of the stairs, a landing of sorts, maybe a half yard square, completed the incline. It wasn't until Judas turned around to see where he had come from, that he realized what he had found. Built into the wall of the throne room was a stone that was lighter in color than the rest. When Judas reached out to touch it, the color began to change, and then to disappear. The stone was still there, but it was transparent. Judas could look directly into the throne room. Because of the dimensions of the room and the position of the stone, he could really only see what was in the front third of the room. And he had almost no view of what might be close to the wall where he was standing. But the throne itself was clearly visible, as were the two men standing behind it. Because the throne room was dimly lit, it was hard to make out the actual identity of the men, although they were clearly dressed as servants. One stood directly behind the throne on the raised platform, the other was standing on the floor level. The one closest to the throne had a knife in his hand.

"Try to get one of those rubies out," the servant on the floor commanded.

"But I thought only someone with royal blood could touch these gems. That means you have to do it." The other commented.

"Figures. I should have to do all the work. Give me the knife."

The men traded places. Just as he was about to touch the knife to the throne, he gasped. "What's this? The missing stone is back!"

At the same moment, the ruby in Judas' hand turned an icy cold. Judas wanted to drop the stone. He didn't want to feel the burning cold sensation in his hand. He knew it could mean only one thing. Someone was injured, or worse. When he looked back in the throne room, the two servants were headed toward the door, making an escape. Judas wanted to stop them, but he was too confused to know what to do. He could clearly see the back of the throne itself. His mother's stone filled the spot that had been empty just a moment ago. Choking back tears, Judas ran through the passageway and headed for his room. In a minute more he was on his own bed, sobbing into his pillow. He wondered what could have happened. What could have gone wrong? Would he ever see his mother again? Should he start to run now?

He hadn't been in his room very long when the ruby began to change again. This time, however, it grew warm rather than cold. Judas was confused. He tried to remember what Eli had said. If the stone grew warm, all was well. If the stone grew cold, run. But what to do if the stone turned both cold and warm? Perplexed, Judas slowly changed out of his clothes and skipped into his bed. His head hurt and he was cold. And suddenly he felt very tired. He knew he was going to have to run. After all, if he didn't run, and it turned out he should have, all would be lost. But if he did run, and it turned out that all was fine, well, that was more easily dealt with. Since the contest was just finishing, it would be impossible for anyone to be back at the castle before nightfall. That meant Judas could sleep for now, and start his journey late in the afternoon. As long as he was gone before dark, he should be safe. Snuggling into his blankets, Judas fixed a picture of himself in his mind. He gripped the ruby in one hand, and whispered, "Sleep." And he did.

CHAPTER 15

# Encampment

The king and the red honor guard quickly struck camp and prepared for the journey home. They knew that they couldn't make it all the way back to the castle before they lost the light, but they decided it would be better to make camp among the settlements than to risk spending another night out here in the wild.

The Black entourage was already leaving when the king emerged from the Grove. Without enough men to carry all the provisions they had brought, much was left behind. In addition to a few wounded comrades, three soldiers and a priest were all that was left of the challenge team, and together with a score of armed guards, they moved rapidly away from the forest.

When they were far enough away, the Ruby King ordered the remains of the black camp plundered. When every valuable thing had been taken, including the abandoned food rations, the rest was set aflame. The king wanted no reminder of the presence of the Obsidians in his kingdom.

By the time the sun began to set, the red delegation was more than halfway home, and well within the security of the kingdom. They set up camp in a field and began the process of preparing the evening meal. Although the stores they had brought from the castle were more than adequate, the king ordered a nearby farmer to donate a steer for the celebration feast. After all, the king had just saved the entire kingdom. Didn't his farmers owe him at least that much?

While dinner was being prepared, Jon and Greg spotted the encampment and flew down to check out the scene. They decided to go invisibly, so that they could learn as much as possible before joining the crowd. They were able to see how many men were in the company, and figured out that this wasn't a whole army. They also were surprised to discover that the boy who had gotten them involved in this whole thing wasn't anywhere around, at least not that they could see. Landing the carpet behind several tents, they rolled it, folded it in half and strapped it to Jon's back. Greg carried the staff in his hand. Each had one of the silver swords strapped to his side, as they strolled into the center of the camp.

A cheer rose up as the soldiers recognized them. The king walked toward them, eyeing them suspiciously. "You did not travel with us, and yet you are already here. How did you make such a good pace?"

"We have magical ways of movement, Your Majesty, that are best left unspecified." Jon answered, without a hint of a smile on his face. "But you did invite us to join you tonight, and we thought it best not to ignore a royal summons." Then the smile crept onto his face.

"Indeed, I did summon you! And grateful we are for the help you rendered to us today in the Grove. Zarak, bring me the leather pouch from my tent, quickly. Come here, you two. What are you called?"

Jon and Greg walked to the king's side of the fire, standing directly in front of him. Both went to one knee before answering. "I am called Gregory of Newport," Greg responded.

"And I am Jonathan of Newport," Jon added.

"And are you brothers as well as being both from the same kingdom?" the king asked.

"Yes, we are, Your Majesty." Jon answered quickly.

"And where might I find the Kingdom of Newport?" the king quizzed.

"Newport isn't exactly a kingdom. It is more like a city. It is hard to explain, really. You see Newport isn't anywhere around here. It's far away from New Yorke and the Gemstone Islands," Greg explained.

"Aahhh," the king sighed knowingly, "then you must be sorcerers of great strength and power. It is good that you have come at a time like this. I have great need of a sorcerer just now. As you may know, the one who was secretly my first Mage for many years perished on the board this morning. Someone will need to replace him."

"I'm afraid we can't be staying, Your Majesty. Duty calls us to return to our city very quickly. But with your invitation, we would like to visit your kingdom as often as we are able," Greg managed to add.

Before the king could reply, Knight-General Zarak returned with the pouch from the king's tent. The king withdrew two silver medallions, each hanging on a leather strap. "You are, of course, always welcome in our realm—more than welcome. I am presenting you with the sigil of my house. When you next return, join me in my throne room, where I will make your adoption into the royal family official!"

The crowd cheered as the king slipped the medallions around the necks of the still kneeling boys. "Rise, my sons. The kingdom is in your debt this day."

"Long live Prince Gregory! Long live Prince Jonathan!" the crowd cheered.

When the revelry had died down, everyone gathered at the center of the camp to enjoy the feast. Jon and Greg couldn't believe what was happening to them. Princes! Who would have ever thought this could happen to them? They had never been popular at school. Too much moving from place to place. In fact, they had started to dread even the prospect of making friends back home. After all, why make friends when you have to say goodbye so soon? It was all too painful. They had gotten used to relying on each other. And even though they didn't always get along with one another, they at least knew the two of them would always be together. Yes, they would rely on each other. It would be enough. It would have to be.

As the people settled down to eat, the king departed to his tent with Zarak. Once they were inside, the king began to speak very rapidly. "Don't let those two out of your sight! We must get them back to the kingdom so that they can be bound into the royal family. We cannot afford to lose them. With Eli gone, we are weak. If these two should form an alliance with another kingdom, all could be lost. Find a way to make them stay."

Jon and Greg looked over the feast to see what was available for dinner. The contents of the bubbling pot of stew were a mystery, and the butchered steer, roasting over a huge fire was less than appetizing. In fact, the word *disgusting* came to their minds. It didn't take but a moment for them to decide to wait until they got home to eat.

"We really should get back home, Jon." Greg whispered in Jon's ear.

"You're right. But how are we going to sneak away?" Jon questioned. "We don't want them to see how we travel, if we can help it."

Seeing a man come from behind a tent, Greg jabbed the soldier next to him in the ribs to get his attention. "Where do you go if you have to...you know, uhh, if you have to...if you have to go?"

The soldier looked confused, until Greg crossed his legs and danced on one foot, continuing to say, "...you know, if you have to go?"

A grin of recognition crossed the soldier's face and he laughed out loud. "Over behind those tents—where that soldier just came out."

"Thanks. See you later!" Greg grinned.

"I think I'll join him. Save me a piece of meat," Jon yelled back over his shoulder, as he headed for the tents. As soon as they were behind the tents, they unrolled the carpet, joined the staff to it, and switched on the invisibility.

Zarak emerged from the king's tent just in time to see Jon disappear behind the tents at the opposite side of the encampment. He ran quickly to follow them. As he rounded the corner to where the boys had gone, he stopped cold. He saw Jon reach his hand into the air to the top of the staff, and in the very next instant, the boys vanished. Both had been sitting there on the ground, or on something. It was hard to tell. Now he would have to tell the king he had failed. It wasn't a task he would relish.

## CHAPTER 16

# Flight!

In spite of the catastrophe at hand, Prince Judas slept soundly through the rest of that day and night, under the influence of his own magic. In fact, he slept so soundly that the sun was full in the sky before he awoke. Lurching awake with a start, Judas wondered what time it was, and how he could have slept so well. Then he remembered the stone and the spell, and the cold and the hot, and he realized, contrary to his wishes, it wasn't just a dream. It was all frighteningly real, and the worst was about to begin.

Judas jumped out of bed and began to prepare quickly. The food Eli had left included travel rations. He stuffed one change of clothes, all the food he could, and a heavy blanket into his knapsack. He strapped on a short sword and draped his heaviest cloak over his shoulders. Using the secret passage into his mother's room, he moved to her jewelry chest. He collected an assortment of small gems and stones, nothing too large, for fear of robbers. He also found a few gold pieces on her dressing table. Back into the passageway, he headed for the kitchen.

Judas followed the secret passageway down toward the kitchen, finally finding an exit into the entry room that connected the kitchen to the service entrance. Close to the secret door, Judas found another block that he could make transparent. Someone had thought the need to escape might one day be important. Unfortunately, the room was not empty. Sitting on top of one of the garbage barrels was a serving boy, waiting for some sort of delivery. Without a second thought, Judas fixed the boy's face in his mind, then said, "Sleep." In a few seconds, the boy was snoring loudly.

Judas placed his hand by the bump on the wall and the door swung into the room. He jumped down onto the floor, and moved quickly to the cellar entrance. He was in the basement in less than 20 seconds. Not knowing when someone might need to enter this part of the kitchen complex, Judas wasted no time. He tied off the elevator at a height of about a yard above the ground. Tapping on the base three times, he unscrewed the cover to the passageway that only Eli knew existed. He dropped his pack down the dark hole, reversed his position, and began to climb into the darkness. Wedging his body across the opening, he slid the cover back into position, and using the handle on the bottom of the base, he screwed the top back on. Folks might wonder why the elevator was tied as it was...hopefully no one would wonder enough to look for a secret passage.

Once safely inside, Judas said aloud, "Light." His index finger glowed, lighting up the tunnel. It was only a couple of yards down to a landing, and then the tunnels seemed to travel to the northwest. Judas picked up his pack and moved rapidly away from everything he knew and loved.

The tunnel was dark and rough hewn, but Judas was surprised that it wasn't damp. He knew that a spring entered the city near the front of the moat. The stream that flowed from the moat and out through the city wall was proof enough of that. And he had never seen the dungeons that were rumored to exist under the front towers. In his mind he pictured mold, damp, cold. This was not that. Cobwebs, yes—dusty, dry dirt.

After walking for what seemed to Judas like several hours—how does one tell time without the sun?—Judas stopped to rest and to eat. He chewed on some of the bread and drank from a skin of water. He was surprised at how tired he was. And how quiet things were. And how alone he felt. Back in the palace there were always people around. Even without brothers and sisters, there were more than enough people to entertain him. His parents didn't have much time for him, but the other adults paid attention to him. He was, after all, the prince, heir to the throne. Here, he felt like no one. There was no one to talk to, no one to follow. And of course, he had no idea who waited for him at the end of this journey, nor how long this journey would last. He didn't know which was worse, the loneliness or the fear of what was to come. As the temperature in the tunnel began to rise, Judas rolled up his cloak and tied it on top of his knapsack.

He was certain that he was beyond the walls of the city by now. Even though the going was slow due to the unevenness of the tunnel floor, he must be approaching...he couldn't quite figure what he might be approaching. The many twists and turns in the tunnel confused his sense of direction. And though he wasn't sure why, he had the sensation that he was going deeper into the earth. Who would be living down here, he wondered?

He rested for about 30 minutes after eating, and then started up again. He was anxious to find the help at the end of the tunnel. He was hoping that whoever it was had a nice comfortable bed, and maybe even some fresh bread. He would be tired tonight! After another hour of walking, Judas noticed that there seemed to be a glow coming from someplace ahead in the tunnel. He let his finger light dispel, so that his eyes could adjust to the ambient light in the tunnel. Yes, there was something ahead! He could see the orange glow bending around rock corners. Judas slowly moved forward. Gradually he could make out a soft rasping sound. The tunnel was visibly narrower at this point, perhaps only two yards high and a yard or so wide. But nothing prepared him for what he would see next!

The intensity of the reddish-orange light, and the extreme heat in the tunnel should have given Judas a clue as to what lay around the corner. They didn't. Judas stepped slowly around the corner to face a doorway a yard wide and a yard and a half high. There was no door, but the other side of the doorway was completely covered by a shiny red, metallic substance. In the center of the shimmering red blanket was a black line, slightly curved, about half a yard long. Judas stepped to the doorway quietly, not understanding what he was seeing. He stared at the red tapestry, trying to decide if he could go through it, or if there was a way to move it aside. It was then that he discovered that this red thing was moving! Ever so slightly, he could detect a slow rising and falling, along with that annoying rasping sound. He was only an arm's length away from it, when the black line trembled slightly, and opened! It was an eye, a huge eye, bright fiery red! And it was staring straight at him!

Judas leaped back in fright. He cowered against the far wall of the tunnel. He wanted to run, but he was paralyzed by his fear. The huge eye blinked once, slowly. And before Judas even had time to think, the voice filled the cavern. "Go back, Judas, go back. The time has not come."

Then the eye shut.

After a few moments of terror, Judas realized he had stopped breathing. He willed himself to inhale, trying to regain control. A moment before he had been pinned to the far wall of the tunnel, now he simply collapsed to the ground, his legs no longer able to bear his weight. He sat there for a moment, dazed. Whatever that monster was, he wasn't coming after Judas. That was a good thing, because Judas certainly didn't have the strength to run away. Several minutes passed before Judas had recovered enough to replay the message in his head. "Go back. The time hasn't come yet?" What might that mean? Whatever it meant, Judas knew he was headed back. He couldn't go forward, that was obvious.

Judas waited until the pounding of his heart subsided before he tried to stand to his feet. He managed to get up, walked about 25 yards, and decided he was too tired to go on. Noting a smooth spot on the tunnel floor, Judas unrolled his blanket and wadded his cloak into a pillow.

While drifting off to sleep, Judas thought of his older brother, dead these past seven years. His brother had died alone, somewhere in the Primeval Forest. Having wandered away from a hunting party, Jervis encountered a wild boar. Thinking himself invulnerable, he attacked it, only to end up gored and severely wounded. When the hunting party finally found him, he was curled up in a ball at the base of a tree, his life's blood soaking the dirt around him, dead. He never saw his fifteenth birthday. Judas remembered his parent's grief and his own sense of loss, even though he was but a small child when it happened.

Judas wondered what it must have been like for his wounded brother to sit by that tree, all alone in the forest, desperately fighting the pain, hoping help would reach him in time. And Judas wondered what was in store for him when he returned to the castle. Would someone seize him and eliminate him? Would he spend years in a dark dungeon? Judas didn't want to die, and he especially didn't want to die alone. But going back was his only option. Was there any way he could figure out what had happened and escape before someone grabbed him?

While he was ruminating over his options, his emotional and physical stamina ran out, and he fell into a fitful sleep, deep in the bowels of the earth.

CHAPTER 17

# Next Door Neighbors

When Greg and Jon stepped back into their basement, they checked their watches. The time was 1:30 AM. Amazingly, only thirty minutes had passed in Newport, while the better part of a day had elapsed inside. Now they knew time passed differently in this new place, but they also knew they were more than thirty minutes worth of tired. Straight to bed they went, exhausted, though once they were safely under their blankets, conversation began again, slowly. Greg started.

"Jon, I'm afraid. I think we could have been killed in that battle," he said nervously.

"Maybe, but I think we were pretty well protected. I don't think anything can hurt us inside the magic shell of the carpet," Jon guessed.

"But what about the other people? That Black Queen just disintegrated into ashes. And the Black King...." Greg was too overwhelmed to continue.

"It's okay, Greg. There was nothing we could do. The king attacked us; I had to fire. And the queen would have dissolved us just like she did that guy behind us. Everything we did was in self defense," Jon rationalized.

"But I've never even seen a dead body before," Greg protested. "I'm not sure I want any more adventures like that. I think we should tell Mom and Dad everything and forget about this place."

Jon was silent, thinking.

"What do you think they were fighting about back there?" Greg wondered.

"I don't know." Long pause. Jon continued, "I wonder if the good guys won?"

"We probably changed the outcome of the battle, and we don't even know what the battle was about. We should have been more careful," Greg observed.

"We should have been more careful, but we didn't have any choices to make. Someone had the power to force us to get involved. Someone set us down in a game where we were immediately attacked. All we really did was defend ourselves. The fact that it happened to benefit the red guys was pure luck," Jon explained, again.

"Yeah, you're right. But what if the black fighters were the good guys? We might have helped mess things up in that world. Maybe we should go back there and find out what is really happening," said Greg.

"I guess so. But there must be lots of other places to explore in this new world. I don't want to get too involved in anything. After all, it's not our world," Jon pointed out, beginning to tire of the conversation.

"Yeah, but if we messed things up, we probably have to help straighten them out again, right?" Greg questioned.

"Hey, they're the ones who forced us to get involved. It's not our responsibility," Jon insisted.

"I'm just worried…"

"Greg, you can worry about this in the morning. I am going to sleep," Jon pronounced, ending the conversation.

"Maybe tomorrow night we can go back, invisibly, and just scout around. We could listen at the camp fire, or fly around the towns and figure out what is going on. Then we would understand what's happening. Maybe they even have a library or something where we could borrow a book about this place, who knows? What do you think?"

Silence.

"Jon, what do you think about that?" Greg added impatiently.

Without saying a word, Jon pulled the sheet over his head. Greg heard the noise and sighed. Then he rolled over, too.

The next morning the boys were awakened by noises in the yard next door to them. A white truck was parked in front of the neighboring house, and two guys wearing white were removing equipment from the back of it. They appeared to be craftsmen of some sort. Jumping out of bed, the boys bounded down the stairs to the kitchen to find out what was going on.

"Morning, sleepyheads!" Mom sang out. "I can't believe you slept this long."

"What time is it?" Greg inquired.

"9:00," Mom replied, "and you're usually up by 7:30—especially on a Saturday!"

Saturday! Cartoons! They were missing them. After giving Mom hugs, they grabbed cereal bowls, milk, cereal boxes and scrambled to the table. There were strict rules about eating anywhere in the house, except in the kitchen. No cereal in front of the TV for them.

"What's going on next door?" Greg finally asked, chewing a mouthful of Honey Nut Chex.

"Someone bought the house. I guess we are going to get some new neighbors soon," answered Mom

"Do they have any kids?" Jon asked.

"I don't know. I do know that they are military folks, because your Dad heard something at the base yesterday. They should be here sometime this week."

Dad had apparently just left to go to the gas station. The red gas can was empty, and it was lawn mowing day. Jon was relieved, at least for the time being. Dad thought Jon was old enough to mow the lawn, but Mom wasn't ready to let Jon handle a power mower just yet. She had argued for one more summer, until Jon was a teen. Jon knew there would be no escape this time next year.

"What are you guys planning to do today?" Mom continued.

"I don't know—watch some cartoons and then, something outside. It's beautiful out there!" Jon said as he scanned the sky beyond the back door.

"Why don't we plan to go to the ocean together at about 12:00?

Dad will be done with the lawn by then, I'll pack us a lunch, and we can all head down to the beach," Mom suggested.

Mom wasn't much of a swimmer, but she loved the beach and was good for a variety of beach games. Of course her favorite beach activity was a good book, a good chair, waves at her feet, and sleep just a few minutes away.

"Sounds great, Mom! We'll be ready!" Slurping up the last of the cereal, they headed into the living room, planted themselves in front of the television, and contentedly allowed their minds to be turned to jelly.

At noon, after cartoons had fuzzied out their vision, Mom called in, "Guys, let's leave in about 15 minutes. Get any stuff you want at the beach and don't forget your boogie boards." The boys raced upstairs to change into swimming suits, and to gather the things necessary for an afternoon at the beach.

They loaded all their stuff into the trunk of the car, and then headed off. Dad would drive the car down to the beach while the rest of them walked. It was only a short walk, but even a short walk was uncomfortable when loaded down with beach chairs, baskets, towels, boogie boards, and all the other necessary beach junk. Dad was waiting for them when they arrived, unloading the car. Once empty, Dad drove the car back home. He wasn't about to pay the $10 fee charged to park a car at the beach for the day!

Dad had selected a spot right in front of the carousel, centered on the beach. The waves were great, the sun was hot, and Greg even managed to win a game of beach tennis against Dad!

A minute later, Jon got mad at Greg because he thought he was cheating at tennis. Grabbing a handful of wet sand, Jon hucked it at Greg and yelled, "Hit that, Mr. Cheater!" Dad saw the sand toss, yelled at Jon for throwing sand, who promptly quit the game, grabbed his boogie board, and ran out into the ocean.

Greg stomped back to Mom. "Why is he such a jerk sometimes?" He sat on a towel beside her beach chair.

"Who, honey?" Mom had missed the whole exchange, lost in her book.

"Jon. He called me a cheater, threw sand at me, and then quit."

"Were you cheating?" Mom asked.

"No! He just thought the ball was in. I didn't try to hit it because it was out," Greg explained.

"Oh, I see. Maybe you should think of something to play by yourself for a while." Mom suggested.

"I'm going to walk down the beach and look for some shells," he moped.

"Okay, but stay in sight."

Greg stumbled slowly down to the water's edge, and then headed west. He ambled along, kicking over seaweed, sticks, assorted drift wood, whatever happened to be in his path. In about fifteen minutes he found himself at the end of the beach, the same end where they had found the first trunk. He hadn't been paying attention to his surroundings. He had been watching his feet. So he was surprised when a voice said, "Hello."

He looked up, and there sitting on the very rock by which they had made their discovery, was an old, old man. Greg was so shocked he couldn't think of anything to say. He just stared at the man. The man looked vaguely familiar—familiar, but exceedingly odd. After all, no one came to the beach wearing the kind of clothes this man wore. A long tunic covered a pair of breeches of some sort. The fabric was wrinkled and faded. The man himself was as wrinkled as his clothing, with gray hair unkempt and a great fatigue in his eyes.

"I said, Hello, young man."

"H-hhelllo," Greg managed to get out.

"My name is Eli. And what would your name happen to be?" the man asked.

Greg, still not completely recovered from the shock, began to respond, "My name is...uh...I don't talk to strangers. Bye." He turned on his heels and began to run back to where the rest of his family was gathered. Although he could hear the man call after him, he never looked back. When he finally got back to Mom, he looked back down the beach to explain, only to find that the man was gone.

He hesitated. He couldn't decide whether to tell Mom what had just happened. Was he dreaming it? Where could the man have gone so quickly? But if the man was dangerous…. In the end, he decided not to tell Mom. Jon was a better choice. He waded out into the water where Jon was riding the waves. It was hard to get his attention, so he tried to judge where the boogie board would land, and waited in the water at that point. A few waves later, Jon came cruising by, howling with delight at the joy of the ride. The waves really were good today!

"Jon, I just saw something strange." Greg started.

"What?" Jon asked absently, heading back out to sea, consumed with thoughts of the next big wave.

"Stop for a minute and talk to me!" Greg insisted.

"Get your board and come out and float with me," suggested Jon, as he headed out to sea.

Greg saw the wisdom of this strategy, even though Jon didn't realize how good of an idea it was. In less than a minute, Greg had his board and was out bobbing in the waves near Jon. "Jon, I just saw someone on the beach."

"So, what's the big deal?"

"Well, it wasn't normal. This guy was old, and he was dressed in a robe of some sort…nothing like the stuff that regular people wear." Greg stopped, then he added, "And he tried to talk to me."

"What did he say?" Jon inquired, more attentive now.

"He said that his name was Eli, and he asked me what my name was."

"Eli? Do we know any Eli? Did you tell him your name?"

"No and no," Greg answered. "But I had the strangest feeling that I knew him from somewhere. I didn't hang around to find out any more. I ran back down the beach to Mom, and when I got there and turned around, he was completely gone!"

"Gone?!" Jon exclaimed. "Where did he go?"

"Who knows? But there wasn't enough time for an old man to get very far away. And the strangest thing was this. He was sitting on the rock where we found the first treasure!"

The boys floated a little while thinking about what this could mean. Was this just some odd tourist on the beach? Or was this a visitor from another place? After all, if they could get into another world, it only made sense that those folks could get back into this one. There may have been any number of doorways between Newport and, well, between Newport and wherever they had been.

"We better hang together for the rest of the day, just in case that guy comes back. If you see him, yell. I want to get a good look at him," Jon instructed.

Unfortunately, the old man did not show himself again. Lunch was eaten, and afterwards, Dad and the boys built sand castles and sand forts along the water's edge.

"Dad, I was wondering. If one of us dug up a pirate treasure right here, would it belong to us, or would we have to give it to a museum or something?" Greg asked innocently.

"Well, that would depend. Technically, something lost at sea as part of a ship wreck is considered salvage. If it is recovered within a certain amount of time, it belongs to the original owners. But after that time has expired, it belongs to whoever found it. Treasure or artifacts found on public land belong to the government who owns the land, if that treasure is a part of the history or heritage of that country. But I imagine if someone just buried a pot of gold in the sand, it would be very hard for the government to seize it. Things that are lost or mislaid belong to the person who finds them. Are you expecting to dig something up here?" Dad grinned.

"Absolutely!" Greg bantered. "I know that there must be pirate gold here somewhere, and who better to find it than me?"

"What would you do with it if you did find it?" Dad wondered aloud.

"I don't know. I would probably put some away for college, get us a new car. If I found enough, I would buy us a house so you could retire right now."

Dad understood immediately. His plan was to retire from the military in 8 years, once he had his twenty years of service in. But in eight years, he could easily be required to move his family two more times, maybe even three. This move had been hard on both Jon and Greg. And he knew they didn't want to move again. "That would be nice, Greg. What about you, Jon? What would you do with your treasure?"

"I don't know. Maybe it would be fun to live near Grandpa and Grandma. If we had a house near that community swimming pool, we could swim all summer!"

Dad laughed out loud. "You guys crack me up! Here we are, living four blocks from the beach, and you want to live near a swimming pool!"

"This place still seems like vacation to me. I keep thinking we are going to pack up any minute and move back to Virginia. Sometimes it's hard to believe we really live here," Jon explained. "Especially since we don't have any friends, yet."

"That will change once school starts," Dad observed, "And when that family moves in next door."

"Do you know who is moving in? Do they have kids?" Jon asked hurriedly.

"I don't know for sure, but the house is a four bedroom house. I don't think a family without kids would buy a house so large, do you?" Dad reasoned.

"Excellent!" Jon said.

The chatter continued through the afternoon, as Jon, Greg and Dad built castle after castle, linking them with canals, passageways, and roadways covered with shells. By the time the tide threatened to undo their masterpiece, it was time to head home for dinner.

Gathering up boogie boards, sand toys, beach chairs and assorted paraphernalia, the family moved toward the side of the road, while Dad sprinted for the car. While the three of them waited for Dad to arrive, Greg poked Jon in the side, whispering, "Jon. Look. He's there."

Jon discreetly pivoted toward the far end of the beach. There sitting on exactly the same stone was the old man Greg has seen previously. He stared, trying to see if he recognized the old man. The man was clearly watching them. Mom didn't seem to notice, and in a moment, Dad drove up. As they stepped across the sidewalk to load the car, the man dropped out of view. Neither Greg nor Jon spoke a word on the trip home.

Once they were home, everyone headed into the back yard to clean up. Greg and Jon showered first, were wrapped up in towels, and herded into the house. Up in their room, they quickly dressed. "That guy gives me the creeps." Greg finally confided. "I think we should tell Mom and Dad about him."

"Maybe you're right, Greg. But if we tell them about him, we might have to tell them the whole story. I mean, one of the reasons this is so strange is because of where he was sitting!"

Greg agreed that they might have to tell. But since they were safely home, there was no reason to rush. They decided to talk about it tonight, and then if they chose to tell, they would do it in the morning.

Running down the stairs to the kitchen, Jon heard the front door shut. He assumed that Mom or Dad had just left, so he headed into the back yard. Mom was there picking up towels and putting beach things away in the shed. Dad was not in sight.

"Where'd Dad go?" Jon asked Mom.

"He's changing his clothes. Then he is off to the store to get some hamburger rolls. I think we will grill some burgers tonight," Mom answered.

Inside the house, Dad had finished changing, and was just coming down from his bedroom when Greg emerged from his own. "Want to go to the store with me, Greg?" he asked.

"Sure, where're we going?"

"Stop 'n Shop," Dad replied. "Maybe they will have some fresh corn!"

Dad and Greg went out the back door, through the yard and into the driveway to get the car. Jon, although puzzled for a moment, shook the uneasiness off. He thought Dad had already left. Maybe Dad had done something in the front yard first. He put the image of the closing front door out of his mind, and helped Mom finish putting away the beach umbrella.

Dinner was delicious, and although it was too early in the summer for the corn to be local, it was still rather tasty. Greg talked Dad into another walk to an ice cream store, and so the four of them strolled down Bellevue Avenue to their favorite place. When they passed the Tennis Hall of Fame, they realized that some one famous was present. The place was full, and they could see several players in tennis whites battling on the grass courts just on the other side of the entry corridor. They tried to figure out who might be in there, but they couldn't see enough to make any identification. Time flew by, and at the first mosquito bite, they all headed for home.

That night, after Dad tucked them into their beds and said their prayers with them, he paused for just a minute. He stood staring at them, then finally sat down on the foot of Jon's bed, and began to speak. "I know it has been hard for you to move so often. It's not easy having to make new friends and start over. And I know you guys really loved Virginia. I'm sorry we had to move. I didn't tell you this sooner, because I was afraid to get your hopes up, but there is one important reason why I applied for this job and accepted it when it was offered. I'm hoping that a professor's job might just be a little more stable than many others. I am gambling that we might be able to stay here for the full eight years."

'But Dad," Greg interjected, "if you had quit the military while we were in Virginia, we could have stayed there. Then we could have lived there forever."

"You're right, Greg. But I am not ready to quit yet. And I honestly believe this is what is best for our family. You know, Newport wasn't my first choice when I considered this move." Dad sighed.

"What do you mean?" Greg questioned.

"I don't talk much about my childhood. You know that. I lost my parents when I was a young teen and had to live in an orphanage for a while. Eventually, I was placed in a foster home. My new parents were great, but I never got over the feeling of being all alone in the world. One thing I never told you—the orphanage and the foster family—they were in Middletown, just on the other side of

First Beach. It's not easy coming back here. Brings up old memories," Dad trailed off.

Neither Jon nor Greg knew what to say. They never realized that this place had a history. The room had suddenly grown very quiet.

After what seemed like an eternal pause, Dad continued. "Ah, well. This isn't easy on any of us, but I really think you'll grow to love this area. It really is beautiful. And in the meantime, if there is anything I can do to make this more pleasant for you guys, speak up, okay?"

Jon spoke up immediately, "Would you try to find out who is moving in next door when you get to work Monday?"

"I'll do that; now get some sleep. I love you." And Dad kissed them each on the forehead and slipped quietly out of the room.

Jon wondered about what Dad had said. He wondered what it would be like to lose his parents. He decided he didn't want to think about that. It was too frightening to consider. And yet, it must, from time to time, happen. Jon lay there, very still, feeling sorry for his Dad.

Greg's slow, steady breathing meant he was already asleep. Jon listened to his brother's breathing for a few minutes. It was a good feeling to have a brother nearby. And a Mom and a Dad. He was glad that he was not alone in the world. As the warmth of that thought spread through his body, Jon found himself relaxing, breathing deeply. In a moment more, he joined Greg, already deep in sleep.

Jon and Greg never heard the door to their closet slide gently open. They never saw the figure of the old man walk over to the bedside; in fact they never even knew he was there until his hand was firmly over Jon's mouth. The old man's head was close to Jon's ear.

"Jon. Wake up. SSShhhh. Be very quiet."

Jon came fully and immediately awake. Panic stretched his eyes wide, as he saw the old man. He tried to reach out to knock the man's hand away, but the man was sitting on the sheets, effectively trapping Jon's arms. He had no choice but to listen.

"Jon, my name is Eli. I am from the other world. And I am your friend. Please, I need to talk to you. I'm sorry to scare you like this, but the need is urgent. We don't have much time." He slowly removed his hand, gesturing Jon to be quiet.

"How do I know you won't hurt us?" Jon whispered.

"If I wanted to hurt you, I could have done that already, couldn't I?" Eli reassured him. "And I know all about the places you've been. I would think you'd have lots of questions for me." Jon paused for a minute. Before he could speak, Eli continued, "Why don't you gently wake up Greg, so that he won't be startled like this? Then I can explain everything to both of you."

In spite of the fact that Jon was terrified, there was a tenderness and gentleness about this man that was unmistakable. Jon quickly roused Greg, who sat up in his bed.

"Whattdya want?" Greg mumbled.

"Greg, be quiet. But wake up. Now." Jon tried to stay calm. "We have a visitor."

"A what?" Greg asked, still not completely awake.

"A visitor. From the other place."

Greg sat up quickly and turned toward Jon. He instinctively backed up against the wall, away from the others in the room, pulling the covers up to his neck, eyes widened in terror. He was unable to speak.

"Greg, don't be afraid. I will not hurt you in any way. Please believe me. I am here to ask for your help, but I will not make you do anything you do not want to do." Eli spoke calmly, quietly and confidently, and yet the sense of urgency in his voice was unmistakable.

"What do you want?" Jon asked timidly.

"First let me tell you who I really am," Eli suggested. "My name is Eli Rocquefist and I was, until recently, the first mage, and also chief butler, of the Ruby Kingdom. I know that you were recently involved in a game of chess, a game played between my kingdom and the Obsidian Kingdom. I also know that you were present at exactly the right time. How that happened, I have some idea, although I do not know all the specifics." Eli paused for a moment, allowing the boys to mentally catch up.

"I wish I had time to explain every detail to you, but let me say this as simply as I can. I was also on the chessboard. I traded my existence in my homeland in order to come here. The tools that will save my land are here. And because I still have a magical link to the Ruby Kingdom, I know when the tools will be needed there."

"What tools are you talking about?" Greg asked sheepishly.

Eli grinned, "In one respect, the carpet, the staff, and the gems of power are what I am referring to. And yet in a greater way, the tools my homeland needs more than any other, I believe, are you!"

Greg looked confused and Jon mirrored that expression. "How can we be tools for you?" Jon asked. "We're just kids. We don't have any special talents or abilities. Really, we're just regular kids!"

"Hardly regular!" Eli assured them. "You are the bearers of incredible power. You have found ways to master complex mysteries. You have traveled between worlds. And you have fulfilled the dream of the Creator. I would not call that regular!"

"What are you talking about?" Greg asked, more than a little perplexed. "Most of what happened to us was just dumb luck!"

Eli laughed. "Do you honestly believe that this has all been simply luck or fate? Not so. I barely believe in those concepts myself. I do believe in courage, discipline, sacrifice, providence, initiative, compassion...but luck, I don't think so. Someone has arranged the opportunity for you to be involved. You followed through on that opportunity. Now one opportunity leads to many more."

"I'm lost, I think," Jon spoke slowly. "I'm not really sure I understand what you are trying to say. All I know is that we found some magic stuff. And now look where it has gotten us!"

"Exactly, uh—not completely exactly right." Eli struggled, "It's true that your discoveries have brought you to this moment. It is not true that you have found magic stuff. You see, the Creator set up a system of devices that were endowed with special powers. He entrusted these articles to men and women of great integrity. The ancient books give the reason for this choice.

"When the land of the Gemstone Islands was created, the inhabitants were given freedom to make real choices for themselves.

These people were not created as slaves; they were created to be companions. Of course, the Creator knew that giving folks the ability to make real choices meant that some would make poor, or even wicked, choices. The Objects of Power were created to restore balance, should evil ever get out of hand. Knowledge of the Objects was hidden with the mages. In the Gemstone Islands, mages weren't taught magic, they were instructed in wisdom and morality and integrity.

"Eventually, evil did get out of hand, people being what they are. Unfortunately, a haughty mage was among those who were corrupted. Soon the articles of power were being warped from their original purpose. The Creator was reluctant to intervene, hoping that people would choose voluntarily to follow the path of justice and harmony. But finally, in order to keep the Islands from sinking into complete ruin, the Creator found a way to hide most of the Objects of Power. He left in their place, four Guardians—one for each of the kingdoms on the Islands.

"Jon, Gregory, some of these Objects of Power are under your control. I can only believe that is by the Creator's design. But the Creator usually limits his intervention to the opening of doors. We must still walk through doorways."

When Eli finished speaking, the room was silent. Jon and Greg were both staring into Eli's face. They had trouble believing that there was anything special about them. And neither was sure they were ready to accept what they had just heard. But before they could even form a question to ask, Eli continued.

"Tonight, I am here because I have chosen a new role to protect the land that I love. Through the eyes of a boy in the Ruby Kingdom, I have access to what is happening there. My knowledge is limited to what he knows or believes, and therefore it may not always be either perfect or complete. But my eyes and ears believe with complete sincerity that you are desperately needed in my homeland. Immediately!"

"Immediately?" Jon echoed.

"Yes. Right now. I must encourage you to depart for the Ruby Kingdom within the next fifteen minutes, or all could be lost," Eli urged.

"But how do we even know if the Ruby Kingdom is, well, I mean, how do we know you are the good guys?" Greg inquired carefully.

"You don't," Eli said simply. "But I believe the Creator will help you sort that out. It is the land that I want to see saved, and I will trust you to do what you must, because I believe the Creator has already trusted you."

"Oh, great," Jon sighed. "That's not a whole lot of help."

"More than you may think, Jon. I believe the reason I could not be as much help as you can is that I was not impartial. I was bound to the Ruby Kingdom. You, however, must serve the land. Whatever you do, don't allow anyone to bind you to any kingdom, or you will lose your freedom to be yourselves!"

"How can we keep that from happening?" Greg asked.

"Binding requires willingness and a ritual. It involves gemstones particular to the Kingdom of binding. Do not participate in any rituals or oaths. Your words are very important. Be careful. Now, you must go, or it will be too late. Look for the prince. He will be needing you."

Greg and Jon quickly threw on sweats, T-shirts, and sneakers. Noticing that the time was 12:30, they slipped down to the basement, opened the trunk, and stepped through it into the cave.

CHAPTER 18

# Deep Beneath

Judas was aware of the heat before he was fully awake. He was sweating where he lay, on the floor of a cave. His muscles ached from sleeping on stone. The corridor was dark, and so Judas pictured the end of his finger and spoke softly, "Light." The finger glowed. He didn't need to think hard to remember what had happened before he slept. It was all there in the front of his mind. He knew he had to get back, and so he stuffed his cloak into his pack, and hurried back from whence he had come. He chewed on stale bread as he climbed gradually uphill.

Judas had no way of reckoning time, and really had lost all track of it. He had no way of knowing how long it had taken him to reach the tunnel back up to the underbelly of the castle. He also knew it would be dangerous to simply pop up into the castle cellar. Eli had told him that this tunnel must always be a secret. He couldn't afford to have anyone find out about it by accident. Sitting at the bottom of the passageway, Judas thought about reentry. What kind of precautions should he take? Who would he find when he got back upstairs? If Eli were in the castle, surely he would know where Judas had gone. He would protect the area in case of Judas' return. But what if the message from below was wrong? What if things were not right? He strongly suspected that his mother was dead. Why else would her jewel have returned to the throne? And who were those two spies? They could be anywhere.

After thinking for what seemed like another hour, Judas decided that all he could really do was listen. If he heard nothing, then he might proceed. If he heard something, then—suddenly it dawned on him. Win or lose, there would be a feast. If his father won, there would be a celebration. If the other king won, his enemy would celebrate. If he simply waited until the feast preparation had begun, he would hear the wine casks being drawn up into the kitchen. They always lifted enough wine for the entire celebration at one time. No one wanted to keep a noble waiting for more wine! That meant, once the noises stopped, if he waited about an hour, everyone would be upstairs serving. That would be his chance. And if he got lucky, they would leave the third cask on the elevator in the kitchen, on the chance that it would not be needed and could be taken back down to the cellar.

Judas waited a very long time. How long, he couldn't be sure, but it seemed several hours at least. A heavy dragging sound, followed by a thump directly overhead signaled that something was happening upstairs. After about ten minutes, there was a loud bump, followed by a repetition of the previous noises. This happened twice more. Four casks of wine! Judas had never seen that many casks in the kitchen at one time. He couldn't figure out what it might mean, but he decided that thinking about it was a luxury he couldn't afford. He began to track time. "One and two and three and…" Judas counted to sixty and began again. Carefully, methodically, Judas marked the minutes in the dirt of the floor. After sixty minutes had passed, he climbed up the tunnel, released his light, placed both hands on the plate that covered the hole, and began to turn it.

Judas was relieved that the cover turned easily. He was also relieved that, once the cover was removed, the room was completely dark, except for a small shaft of light coming in from the open door on the other side of the room. He jumped out of the tunnel, replaced the cover, and moved into the shadows behind the open door. Peering out into the room of garbage, he tried to decide where to go first. Should he just head into the kitchen to see what Ella knew? What if things weren't as they should be? No, an open entry was too risky. Best to be sure. Better to stick to the passageways.

The garbage room was empty just now. There was a guard posted at the back door to the room, but he was looking the other way. It would be risky, but it was necessary. Holding his gem in one hand, he pictured the guard in his mind and spoke the word, "Sleep." Instantly, the guard leaned back against the wall and slid down into a sitting position. Judas didn't wait a moment. He jumped into the room, and onto the top of a barrel. He landed in front of the wall where he knew the secret passageway was located and placed his hand on the proper spot. It took just a second or two, but the wait seemed an eternity. The door slid open, Judas jumped in, and the door shut behind him. Judas sighed loudly. To be certain he hadn't been seen, he activated the spying block and looked into the room where he had just been standing. The guard was still very much asleep, and the room was empty. As he stood watching, a cook's helper stepped out the back door of the kitchen carrying a heaping mound of garbage. She hastily threw it into a barrel, never noticing the sleeping guard. Or if she did notice, she decided to ignore him.

Judas turned and climbed the hidden stairs up to the second floor of the castle. The corridor was dark; Judas recalled his finger-light. As he approached the secret entrance to his room, he could hear voices in the surrounding hallways. There were lots of people around and the throne room was not empty. He decided it would be best to reemerge from his room, so he triggered the mechanism to open the door, and stepped in. There, sleeping on his bed, was Ephraim!

"What are you doing in here?" Judas hissed, surprised to find his room occupied.

Ephraim startled to his feet, and shook the sleep out of his eyes. "Oh, it's you."

"Of course it is me! What are you doing here?" Judas demanded.

"I'm still pretending to be you," Ephraim replied, with a hint of condescension in his voice. "Would you like your job back, now that the danger is gone?"

"You can't talk to me like that. I'm the crown prince. Don't you value your life?" Judas angrily shouted.

"Don't try that stuff on me, Your Greatness. I know the secret. And there are others in the castle who know as well. If you so much as threaten me, I'll tell the world what I know and you will never sit on the throne of the Ruby Kingdom."

Judas reached a hand under his shirt. He closed his eyes for a moment, then said, "Sleep!" Ephraim fell immediately asleep, slumping to the floor. In the next minute, Judas tied Ephraim's hands behind his back with a belt. He leaned Ephraim's unconscious body up against the bed, then pulled out his dagger. After placing the dagger against Ephraim's throat, Judas released the sleep spell.

Ephraim's eyes opened, and then opened even farther. He saw the blade at his throat. Confusion registered on his face. "What happened? How did you do that?" Ephraim asked cautiously.

"There is more to being crown prince than you might suspect. I know that you are slightly older than me and physically bigger than me. But that doesn't mean so very much at the moment, does it?" Judas slowly said. But even as he said it, he remembered what Ephraim had done for him, and he felt funny inside. This wasn't quite right, was it? And actually, he realized, he should have some measure of gratitude for the service rendered by this boy. In fact, Ephraim deserved a reward. But since the nature of the deed could never be made public, neither could the reward. And now here he was, threatening the very person he should be thanking! But Ephraim was so arrogant! How could he reward that kind of attitude?

Judas started again, slowly. "You shouldn't threaten me—ever. I am able to do far more than you suspect. If I thought you would really tell the secret, I could end your life right now. No one would question me, if I killed you in my room. I could simply say you were attempting to kill me."

Ephraim was holding his body very still, not wanting to test the steel of the knife that was poised at his throat. On one level, he was listening carefully to what Judas was saying, but at the same time, on another level, something was happening deep inside his head. It had never happened before. And it was very unsettling. Somewhere, deep in the recesses of his mind, he could hear another voice speaking. At first he couldn't make out either the words or the identity of the speaker. But in just a few moments, both became crystal clear.

*"Remember your promise! You promised to serve! You must keep your promise!"* It was Eli! Somehow, Eli was speaking to him. Eli knew what was going on, and he was inside Ephraim's head! It didn't make any sense. It wasn't as if Ephraim was just remembering what Eli had said to him some days ago. Eli was speaking, now, present tense! It was all too overwhelming.

Judas sensed that for some unimaginable reason, Ephraim had lost focus and was no longer listening to him. He was sure of it when Ephraim gasped, "Eli!" Judas spun around fully expecting to see Eli behind him, but the room was empty.

"What do you mean, Eli?" Judas spat out.

"I heard him! In my head!" Ephraim responded.

"I didn't hear anything," Judas said, "except for what I was saying. And I think you are trying to distract me. Don't forget…" Judas stopped. He was getting angry again, and he knew that wasn't where he ought to be going. "Did you hear anything I said at all?"

"Yes, I did. I admit that I don't know how you got me into this position. And you are right, you could easily kill me right this moment, and no one would think twice about it."

Judas sighed, realizing his point had been made. "Except you," Ephraim added.

"What do you mean, 'except me'?" Judas asked.

"If you killed me like this, you would know what you had done. And I think it would haunt you for a very long time. And it might even determine the kind of king you would one day be," Ephraim calmly added.

Judas hadn't considered all of this. And yet, he knew what Ephraim said was true. Not only was it true, it was where he had been headed himself.

"You're right," Judas said, lowering his knife. "I had started to figure that out myself when you started talking about Eli. But you keep confusing me and I never get a chance to finish a thought. I think we really need each other; perhaps we can start over."

"Perhaps," Ephraim replied, "though it will be hard with my hands tied behind my back."

Judas sheathed the dagger, and untied Ephraim's hands. In an explosion of motion, Ephraim rushed Judas, pushed him back against the wall and began to choke him with both hands. Their faces were inches a part. "Don't you ever threaten me again," Ephraim leered, "or I will kill you, I promise! See how easy it would be for me?"

With the ruby pressing against the flesh of his chest, Judas could have put Ephraim back to sleep. But as afraid as he was, he didn't believe Ephraim was going to kill him. And he was right. A second later, Ephraim's grip loosened; then he threw him by the scruff of his shirt onto the bed. Ephraim reached for the door to leave, but before he could escape, Eli's voice was back. *"You promised to serve!"* Ephraim froze.

"What?" Judas asked.

"Nothing," Ephraim responded, the anger still evident in his voice.

"Something is keeping you from leaving, and it certainly isn't me," Judas said, evenly..

"It's Eli. He keeps reminding me."

"Reminding you of what?" Judas asked.

"Never mind." Ephraim turned back toward the door to leave, but Judas stopped him.

"Wait, please." Ephraim stopped and faced Judas. "I hate to ask this, but I really do need your help."

"That's no surprise. All I've been doing lately is helping you." Ephraim smirked.

"Are you loyal to the Ruby Kingdom?" Judas asked.

The question surprised Ephraim. He had been asking himself the very same question. He had promised Eli he would serve. He had always considered himself an honorable individual, loyal to his king. But when the kingdom wore the face of Judas, he wasn't so sure. He paused a moment to consider, and as his thoughts crystallized, he realized that though he may not personally like this new face, he would defend his king and kingdom with his very life. "I am loyal," Ephraim answered, "to my king and to my kingdom."

"Do you mean by your king and your kingdom, the Ruby King and Kingdom?" Judas continued.

"Yes, that is what I mean," Ephraim finished.

Pressing the ruby against the flesh of his chest, Judas said softly, "Truth." He knew immediately that the boy facing him was honest and reliable. He was loyal, and would always be so. He might not like Judas very much, but he would serve his kingdom.

"You need to know some things. Please do not feel that I am challenging you or threatening you. What I am about to tell you, you must never repeat. Do I have your word that you will always keep this confidence?" Judas paused.

"You have it."

"I was never in any danger from you. Even when your hands were around my neck, I could have put you to sleep in a moment. Because I am of the royal family, I wear a gem." Judas lifted his shirt to display the jewel. "This gem gives me limited magical power, and it also provides some significant protection." Ephraim started to speak, but Judas cut him off.

"I don't say this to shame you or belittle you. I say this to help you understand. I am not as helpless as I appear, but neither am I as strong as I should be. I am grateful for what you did for me in the Grove. I didn't wish you to do it. I would have gone myself if I had been allowed. But I was not consulted. The choice was made for me. Even so, I am grateful for what you have done." Judas paused for a moment, as Ephraim considered the implication of his words.

"Further, I am still in the dark about a great many things. I do not yet know what happened in the Grove. I assume that since you are here, our kingdom prevailed. But the communication has been incomplete; I do not know where things stand. Would you please tell me what happened?"

In that moment, an incredible sinking feeling sucked all the energy out of Ephraim. Ephraim was an orphan. With both parents dead, Eli had brought him to the castle and raised him, with Ella, as a grandson. He knew what it felt like to lose a parent. But Judas didn't even know that his mother was dead. And now he would have to tell him. Pity overwhelmed him, both for Judas and for himself. Judas had lost a mother; he had lost his grandfather.

Slowly, gently, Ephraim recounted the events of the Grove. He told of the javelin toss, the losses of Eli and Stoneclaw, the arrogance of the Obsidian Queen, and then he told of the heroic death of Judas' mother. Judas cried out, then began to sob softly. Ephraim felt like he should try to comfort him somehow, but their recent conflict, along with the fact that they were both adolescent boys, kept them in their separate corners. After a few long moments, Judas recovered enough to ask Ephraim to continue. The appearance of two magical warriors from the sky was related, along with the death of the Obsidian King. This brought a sigh of relief from Judas. Finally, Ephraim described the closing rituals and the journey home.

"Thank you for telling me," Judas sniffed. "I'm sorry you had to stand in for me, but I am glad you did such an honorable and commendable job. Although there is no way we can reward you publicly, I promise that my father and I will find a way to reward you privately."

"Thanks," Ephraim muttered.

"I can't believe Eli is gone," Judas whispered, and began to sob silently again. When he looked up, he saw tears forming in Ephraim's eyes. Ephraim quickly looked away.

"I can't, either." Ephraim agreed.

*Who said I was gone?*—a voice inside of Ephraim's head asked rather tersely.

"Eli? Is that you?" Ephraim said out loud.

"Who are you talking to?" Judas asked.

*Of course it is me! Tell Judas to wait a minute, and I'll explain everything.*

"Be quiet a minute!" Ephraim hastily cut him off. "Give me a second to sort this out."

Judas waited impatiently, listening to one side of a conversation:

"Where are you?" Ephraim asked out loud.

*Do you remember the spell I cast the night before the battle?*

128

"Do you mean the song you sang, when your face turned different colors, and then you clapped your hands, and all that?"

*Yes, exactly. I was preparing for what I expected the next day.*

"What were you expecting?

*This conflict we are in was not going to be solved on a chess board in the Grove. The two kings were greedy, and though I am sworn to protect the Ruby Kingdom, only a grand compromise between them could have benefited our kingdom in the long term. I believed that I had to bring in some outside help if we were ever to truly resolve this current crisis, and so after I had discharged my duty to protect the king, I planned to leave the Gemstone Islands so that I could send reinforcements. This is what I have done.*

"Are you really still alive?"

*Yes, I am very much alive.*

"But how is that possible? I saw you die!"

*You saw me attacked, and you saw me disappear. You did not see me die. The attack triggered the spell I had previously cast. I simply moved from one world to another.*

"Then where are you? How can I get to where you are?"

*I am in a far away place, and you cannot get here. I have banished myself here for a very important reason. The key to our success is here. I must convince those who are able to help us that they must do so. But I cannot ever return, nor can you come here.*

"Why not? I don't want to lose you. You are all the family I have left!" Ephraim was sobbing now, and was clearly very agitated.

*I am not all the family you have left. You still have Ella, and now you have Judas. They are your family. And one more thing, you will always have me. In the same way that we are now talking, we will always be able to talk. I am a part of you and you a part of me. I am able to see through your eyes when you allow it. I will teach you how it is done.*

"I don't understand."

*You have an important job to do. Do you remember the sudden rush of energy you felt as I was leaving?*

"Yes."

*In that moment, I transferred almost all of my power to you. I do not need it where I am. You will become the second mage, and will be trained by Stoneclaw.*

"But Stoneclaw is dead!"

*Oh my! I hadn't counted on that. Did you feel anything when he died?*

"Yes, I did. It felt just like when I thought you had died."

*Amazing! Stoneclaw must have transferred power as well. Actually, that won't help you very much. No one person can effectively handle all the functions entrusted to a mage. You are going to have to choose a person you trust to give that power and responsibility to. They will need to. . .I am sorry, Ephraim, too much too soon. There will be time for all of this later. For now, you are the first mage. You must tell the king what has happened. Tell Judas as well.*

Eli's voice stopped. Ephraim waited for him to continue, but the silence stretched until it was obvious that the conversation was finished. Sensing that things had changed, Judas jumped in. "What happened? What did he say?"

Ephraim recounted as best as he could everything that Eli had told him. He was tempted to keep back the first mage stuff, but decided that since Judas had told him about the royal jewel, it was only fair to share this secret as well. And after all, Eli had specifically told him to tell Judas. "I think Eli is sending us reinforcements of some kind, but I don't understand why we need them. I thought this battle was over."

"I'm not surprised. While everyone was gone, I did a little exploring. I discovered two spies in the throne room trying to steal some of the gems from the back of the throne. I couldn't see their faces, and I was supposed to be in hiding, so I couldn't confront them. They are still in the castle somewhere. I think there is more unpleasantness coming, probably very soon. We will have to be careful."

Somehow, in the last fifteen minutes, the nature of their relationship had changed. Antagonism had been replaced by a cautious trust, and that had given way to a growing sense of their need of one another. It would be too much to say that they were friends, but they were, at least, headed in the same direction. Their futures were inextricably linked; that certainty had dawned on both of them.

"It's time I made an appearance!" Judas announced. "And I think Ella would like to know your latest news. Where is my father just now?"

"I think he must be in the banquet hall by now. He was finishing up court just a short while ago, and the plans were for a grand celebration banquet immediately afterwards. I'd dress for dinner if I were you!" Ephraim suggested.

"That I will do. And once you have seen to Ella, I invite you to join me at my table for dinner. You can keep the clothes you are wearing, or select new ones from my closet if you wish," Judas offered.

"I think it is best that I keep my secret for a little while longer," Ephraim explained. "Perhaps His Majesty will have a suggestion as to how we should proceed. Don't forget, even if I am first mage already, I don't know how to act like a first mage. Nor do I know how to use his powers. This is going to take some time!"

"You are wise, Ephraim. You will make an excellent first mage. I will see you after breakfast tomorrow. Meet me in the kitchen, and we will go from there." Then Judas embraced Ephraim, forearm to forearm, left hand to right shoulder The grasp was firm and sure, and in that grasp an alliance was formed, an alliance stronger than iron.

CHAPTER 19

# Coercion

The grand banquet hall was on the first floor of the castle, comprising the whole eastern side of that level. The kitchen ran behind the head of the hall, with two entrances for servants on either side of the raised platform upon which the head table stood. Two rows of tables ran perpendicular from the head table down either side of the room. The hall was filled with nobles and guests, all assembled to welcome home a victorious king.

Proceeding directly from the Throne room, the king and his entourage swept down the grand staircase and turned left into the hall. All who were in the room turned to face the king; those seated stood in order to bow. Those already standing there bowed in the king's direction. Four royal body guards led the procession, two of which crossed the dais and stationed themselves at the far side of the head table. The other two guards remained in place, as the rest of the group moved past them.

As soon as the king was seated in the center of the table, the other honored guests found their places. To the king's right was an empty chair, presumably in honor of the absent queen. To the king's left was General Artezes, followed by four decorated warriors. General Zarak occupied the place past the empty seat, with three more soldiers to his left. Everyone on the platform was a veteran of the Grove, and each sported a new star, red trimmed in gold, on the breast of their uniform coats.

As the guests were settling, someone from the crowd shouted, "Long live the king!" The rest of the group roared back, "Long live the king!" The Ruby King grinned and waved for silence. "Thank you, thank you," the king responded. "Today we honor those who risked all to defend our kingdom. As the leader of the brave squad who faced death squarely without flinching, I speak for us all. We are proud to have served you. Now let the feasting begin!"

The slamming of the king's goblet on the table sounded like a shot from a starter's pistol. Musicians began playing in the center of the room, while servants poured wine and brought steaming dishes to the tables. Servants were scurrying in every corner of the room, as folks began the job of getting royal food onto their plates and into their mouths. This may have been a banquet in honor of someone, but it was first and foremost about eating. And this crowd was accomplished at that art. It was at this moment of high energy that Judas stepped into the room.

Judas was all but lost in the roar of the feast, but he ran up the side of the room to where his father was seated. His father saw him as he stepped onto the platform. Evidently everyone else in the room noticed him for the first time at the same moment. From a loud roar, the room became quickly silent. The musicians, confused about what to play, considering a member of royalty had just entered the room, stuttered to a stop. Judas froze in the silence. His father fixed an icy stare at Judas, saying "How good of you to join us, my son. Please take your seat."

Judas crossed the remaining distance to his seat, the insincere smile on his father's face warning him that all was not right. "Musicians, play!" the king commanded. The music primed the pumps of conversation, and soon the room was contentedly noisy again. But contentment was in short supply at the head table.

"How could you embarrass me like this?" the king spoke through a forced smile pasted on his lips for the sake of his guests. "First, you are not here to appear with me when I return victoriously. I am forced to make excuses about an illness that overtook you. Then, you are not present for the Royal Remembrance Ritual for your dear departed mother. And now, late to a state dinner! How can I ever imagine that you could someday become king of this land? If only your brother were still alive. I have a good mind to…"

A trumpet sounded out in the main hall, and every eye turned toward the doorway.

\*\*\*

Jon and Greg flew straight towards the castle, once through the cave. Although they had never seen the castle before, they could figure out where it must be from the direction the king had headed when leaving the Grove. Given their vantage point, 1000 feet up in the air, they didn't have any trouble seeing the largest architectural structure in this part of the world.

The castle itself was made of stone; a small moat spanned by a drawbridge encircled it. Guards were posted at the main door, and though the drawbridge was down, the doors were shut. Jon took note of the carvings on the castle door—three swords crossed.

Above the doorway to the castle, about 30 feet off the ground, there was a large circular opening which allowed fresh air to circulate into the building. The opening was about 5 feet across, and flying invisibly, Jon and Greg easily entered the main hallway. Looking for a secluded spot to land, Greg noticed that the second floor was vacant. They stopped the carpet in the hallway outside the throne room, then quickly rolled it up, strapped it to Jon's back, and moved silently down the steps. Each boy had a silver sword tied at his waist, two long cords around his neck, and was dressed in black. Jon held the golden scepter in his hand. As they got to the bottom of the steps, they were challenged by the guards at the door to the banquet hall. Because they were already in the castle, the guards were more concerned about social standing then about security. The clothes the boys were wearing were not the clothes a noble would wear to a royal banquet.

"Who are you and where do you think you are going?" the first guard barked.

'My name is Sir Jonathan and this is Sir Gregory. We have been invited by the king and wish to be shown to him." As he said this, Jon slowly pulled the king's medallion out from under his shirt, holding it out for the guard's inspection.

Cupping the medallion in one hand to be certain of its genuineness, the guard immediately relented, signaled a herald who blew a short, three note fanfare, to announce more royal guests. The doors were opened, and Jon and Greg stepped into the once again quiet room. Over a hundred pairs of eyes stared at them as the guard led the two boys to the king's table.

"Ah, excellent!" the king shouted. "I am so pleased that you could come. Friends, these two are honored guests, who did combat on the Great Board in our defense, and who did, in fact, slay the murdering king of Obsidia! Quickly, two more chairs, one on my right and one on my left!"

Servants scurried to fulfill the king's demands, and Judas, while glad to have his father's attention diverted, was a little miffed to be moved aside for some strangers he had never met before. After all, he was the crown prince! Who were these intruders? And did they really fight in the Grove? How could they have, when he had never seen them anywhere in the kingdom before?

Once the crowd returned to their eating, and the musicians began playing, the king turned his full attention to the newcomers. "I was afraid we had lost you when you did not accompany us directly to the castle."

"We hadn't expected to be delayed in this place. We did have some matters to conclude before we were free to return." Jon fielded the king's questions, while Greg questioned the boy next to whom he was now seated.

"Hello, my name is Greg. What is your name?" Greg asked pleasantly.

"What is my name?" spat Judas. "Everyone knows my name. In fact I have never been asked such a stupid question in all my life."

Although Greg was normally rather shy socially, the events of the last several days had bred the beginning of a backbone into him. Without betraying his surprise at the caustic answer, he simply replied, "Well, not everyone knows your name, since I, for one, do not. And I am certainly not stupid. Will you be so kind to tell me your name, or shall I ask the king who the ill-mannered boy to my left is?"

If Greg had been surprised by Judas' answer, Judas was doubly surprised by Greg's. A second's reflection allowed Judas to realize that he certainly didn't want Greg saying anything like that to his father, especially right now. Who knows, his Father might disown him and adopt these boys as heirs instead! *Ever since his older brother had mysteriously died, Judas felt very vulnerable. His Father had never quite recovered from it, his disposition sour, critical, and unpredictable.*

Surprised at his own quick fuse, Judas laughed to himself, and smiled. "Sorry. We haven't even met and I'm already acting like a fool. My name is Judas, Prince Judas."

"You're the prince?!" Greg gasped.

"Of course, who would you expect to be sitting next to the king…or almost next to the king," Judas remarked.

Greg felt immediately uncomfortable, noting that he was sitting in a precarious place. It was inappropriate to separate father and son, and yet how could he have defied the king's command? "We need to talk. Eli told us to find you," Greg whispered.

"Eli! You've seen him?" asked Judas

"Yes. But we must talk later, in private." Greg said quietly. Then in a louder voice he added, "And what might this meat be?"

"Oh, that's quail," Judas grinned, understanding the misdirection.

"Quail? What's a quail?"

"Oh, you will love it! They crunch ever so nicely!" and Judas bit right into the roasted morsel. Greg grimaced but gave it a go.

Through further questioning, the king attempted to figure our exactly where Jon and Greg had come from. Jon insisted that they were from a different country, far away, but that they were no threat to the king or his kingdom. They were just traveling for pleasure when they happened upon the incidents at the Grove. Expressing his gratitude profusely, the king made Jon promise to attend him in the throne room at the conclusion of the banquet. There were royal presentations to be made, gifts and honors that could not be bestowed in a simple banqueting hall. The king referenced the special red and gold stars that all those at the head table wore (with the exception of Judas), and hinted at other honors as well. "Besides," the king added," I promised to exchange those silver medallions for something of real value when I got to my castle, and I mean to keep my word."

The banquet proceeded wearyingly. Although Greg did manage to stuff down a few sweet pastries, most of the food was unidentifiable, and consequently, inedible, to him. Jon, somewhat braver, managed to eat a little mutton, some roasted fish, and some sweet smelling, mashed root, before deciding to limit his intake to pastries as well. After about two hours the king stood, an action which demanded silence from the room.

Excusing himself from his guests, the king once again lauded the accomplishments of those who had saved the kingdom. He was happy to include himself as leader of the group. He bid the banqueters stay as long as they would, but departed with Greg, Jon and Judas, citing pressing kingdom business. The four honor guards traveled with them, as they made their way out of the hall, up the stairs toward the throne room.

The king stationed the guards at the door of the room, then motioned for the three boys to join him alone at the front. Inside, the hall was dim, but the throne itself blazed with reflected red light. The magic of the skylight was very effective. Seating himself on his throne, the king began to speak very directly to Judas. "I see you have come into possession of an important artifact in my absence." Judas nodded, afraid to speak. "I was opposed to awarding it myself; I did not think you ready. Eli insisted, for fear of the worst, though now he has been proved wrong." Judas hung his head. "I still do not believe you are ready to bear any responsibility at all. You disappoint me."

'But you, Sir Jonathan and Sir Gregory, you do not disappoint," the king continued. "Your acts of bravery have earned you an important place in this kingdom. I would begin by making you honorary knights of the realm, and awarding you the Champion's Star." The king pinned a star, identical to the ones worn by the honored guests at the banquet, to each of their black T-shirts. "But there is more I would like to do for you. Let me show you."

Standing, the king walked around the throne to the back of the dais and invited the three to join him. He gestured to the gems that were imbedded in the material on the back of the throne itself. "These gems are the exclusive possession of the royal family of the Ruby Kingdom. They are powerful and verify our status and identity. Only actual members of the royal family may wear them, and they serve to strengthen and protect our family. I would like to invite you into our family. With my wife gone, it will be many years before Judas may have brothers or sisters. I would that he had two brothers, so that if something happened to him, uh, what I mean is…umm…so that he would not have to be lonely as he learns how to be a monarch. Will you accept these gems?"

Gregory spoke up, sheepishly, but clearly. "I hope you will not think us ungrateful for questioning your gifts. But you have done us a great honor, and we do not want to become a disappointment or an embarrassment to you. While it is true that we are able to do many things, we do not know what the requirements of a knight might be in this kingdom. For example, if a Knight is expected to marry, we are not quite ready for that yet," Greg grinned.

"That I can see," the king smiled. "But since you are simply an honorary Knight, there is no duty attached to the title. Honorary Knights carry two privileges with them always, a safe haven here in the castle for the asking, and the right to an audience with the king in the event of any crisis. There is no service required in return, for the honor results from the services already performed."

"Thank you, Your Majesty. But I would suspect that becoming a member of the royal family might have some rather significant requirements," Greg added with an arched eyebrow.

"Yes, that is true. Becoming a member of the royal family does carry significant requirements. And I can see that you might not be ready for all of that yet. Perhaps it would be best if I gave you time to consider this part further. In the meantime, I would like to exchange your medallions for the gems I promised you. If you will both stand over here by the back of the throne…"

The king already had his hand firmly on Greg's arm and was

moving him toward the throne. Caught somewhat off guard, Greg resisted momentarily, stepping backward away from the king. "Come closer, Sir Gregory. I must place my hand on your head so that the gem will know you as its owner. This will prevent anyone from stealing the gem from you, ever. You do want the gem, don't you?"

Eli's words of warning flashed through Greg's head. No oaths, no promises. Don't be bound to any one kingdom. Jon was obviously thinking the same thing, his wide eyes giving him away. The expression wasn't lost on the king.

"What is the matter? Don't you want to be a part of this kingdom?" the king asked, a little irritated.

"Your Majesty, it isn't that we don't want to be a part of your kingdom. It's just that we don't know what is expected of us or what is involved yet. We don't even know what was going on in that Grove."

In a flash, the irritation that had appeared briefly on the face of the king was replaced by a calm smile. "I'm sorry. Forgive me for moving too quickly." He took a step toward Greg, and gently wrapped his large strong hand around Greg's bicep. "Let me explain more specifically." Greg winced as the king's grip turned to iron, jerking him toward the throne. In the same motion, the singing sound of a sword being drawn filled the room. "Now listen carefully." Acid dripped from the king's voice. "You will either accept this stone willingly, now, or you will die, now. Those are the only two choices. Sir Gregory, you will be first. Sir Jonathan, if you move, your brother will die. Judas, get the ropes from those tapestries over there and tie their hands. Quickly, now, move!"

Jon thought about trying to blast the king with the scepter, but Greg was too close. Any fire-bolt from the scepter would surely get them both. In the end, there wasn't enough time to come up with a better plan, so Jon allowed Judas to tie his hands. Greg was tied next, forced onto his knees behind the throne.

The hand that held the king's sword was placed on the back of the throne over one of the gems, while his other hand was on Greg's head. The king began to mumble some words softly.

As soon as Judas had begun tying Greg, Jon had softly called for his knife. Since his hands were behind his back, neither Judas nor the king could see Jon slice quickly through his bonds. Though his hands were free, and though he was now armed, he needed some kind of plan before he could act. He had to think fast; he couldn't allow Greg to be bound to this land. He didn't know for sure what exactly that meant, or how that might harm them, but Eli's words had been enough to warn them that this could not be permitted. The king's voice shattered his thoughts.

"Sir Gregory, you must repeat after me. Say, 'I accept the gem'". Greg said nothing. Anger exploded from the king! Pulling Greg's hair harshly and shaking him, the king roared, "Accept the gem now, or die!"

Jonathan, fearing for Greg's life, sprang toward the king, knife in front of him, hoping to at least knock the king off balance. Maybe then he could get a shot at him with the scepter. Unfortunately, the king still had his sword in hand, and instinctively swung the sword toward Jon to protect himself from the charge. Jon realized he was too late. The sword would easily hit him long before he ever reached the king. It had been a stupid mistake, and now he was going to pay, maybe even with his life. No one even heard the word Judas spoke.

The next thing Jon knew, he was on the floor, being shaken awake by someone. It was Judas, and there was terror in his voice. A quick glance around the room revealed Greg lying on the floor behind the throne and the king lying next to him. Jon's first thought was that Greg had been seriously hurt, and his heart sank in his chest. Judas spoke again, "Jon, wake up!"

All in one motion, Jon pushed Judas aside, leaped to where Greg lay, and called for his knife. "You, stay away from us!" Jon demanded. He reached down to touch Greg's head, afraid of what he might find.

"It's okay, Sir Jonathan. He's only sleeping. I put you all to sleep," Judas said, with obvious trembling in his voice.

"You did what?" Jon asked

"I put you all to sleep. It was the only thing I could think of to keep anyone from getting killed."

Jon turned his attention to Greg, who was slowly coming around.

"I released Greg from sleep. Now we will have to act quickly. My father will probably only sleep for about 10 minutes more." Judas explained.

"Why did you put your father to sleep? You could have protected him by just putting us to sleep," Jon observed.

"Eventually, he would have killed you or forced you to be bound by the gem. For some reason, Eli sent you to me. That is reason enough for me to want you alive. And since you didn't want to be bound, what other choice did I have?" Judas reasoned.

Greg sat up, rubbing his forehead, obviously disoriented. He had only been asleep a few minutes, but he was soaked in perspiration, as if emerging from a hideous nightmare. He looked around and suddenly remembered where he was and what had been happening. "Jon, what's going on?" he nervously asked, hands trembling in fear.

"Don't worry, Greg. We're fine for the moment. But it is time to get out of here." Turning he asked, "What will you do, Prince Judas? How will you explain this?"

"You guys really do need to get out of here. Are you able to do so?" Judas asked.

"Yes, that won't be any problem. But what about you? Your father may kill you when he finds out what happened," Jon guessed.

"I think I have an idea that may work. As soon as you are gone, I am going to lay down and pretend to be asleep. I will be certain to stay asleep longer than my father. When he awakens, I will suggest that you must be powerful mages and that you must have cast a spell on both of us in order to escape. He won't say too much, because he will be embarrassed by your escape." Judas added one other question, hesitantly. "I'm sorry to have to ask this, but I really must know. Why wouldn't you accept the gem? Are you already pledged to another kingdom? Are you spies?"

Greg grinned as he answered Judas. Jon was already unrolling the carpet to prepare for departure. "We couldn't accept the gems because Eli told us not to. He said that if we were really going to help the land, we must be free from allegiances to any one kingdom. We are not spies, of that you can be sure!"

"Thanks," said Judas, visibly relieved. "I was afraid I had rescued a couple of traitors!"

Jon and Greg chuckled, then Greg continued, "Thanks for protecting us from your father. I'm not certain, but I'm pretty sure we will be back soon. I think Eli wants something done by us, and I don't think we have accomplished it yet."

"I'll look forward to your return. My room is on the second floor of the castle, third window from the front. If you can't slip into my room to meet me, leave a white pebble on the window ledge. I will meet you in the royal stables as soon as I find the pebble, second to last stall."

By the time Judas was finished speaking, Jon had unrolled the carpet, affixed the staff, and Greg had joined him. "See ya later," Jon waved, and with a flick of his finger, they were gone. At least, Judas couldn't see them any more. Jon and Greg flew invisibly toward the door of the throne room. They watched until Judas lay down on the floor, pretending to be asleep. If Judas had been watching the door, he would have seen a small hand appear out of thin air for a brief second, open the door, and then disappear again. There was no other noise, as Greg and Jon sped across the sky, headed for home.

CHAPTER 20

# Whispered Voices (Earlier)

In the kitchen, the clamor was deafening. Servants flew hither and yon, while cook's assistants loaded food onto trays, each of which was inspected by Ella for presentation. Crude though it was, Ella's sense of how food should look was partially responsible for her enormous reputation as the finest cook in the kingdom. Ella spied Ephraim enter the room, and before he could even approach her, she warned him away. "Not now, no time for tears right now. Come back when the banquet is over," she scolded. She moved on to inspect another dish, while Ephraim grabbed the end crust from a loaf of bread.

He sauntered toward the back door of the kitchen, pausing to allow Sam to catch up with him. The dog had joined him upon his entrance, and Ephraim snatched a bone out of the "soup" pile for him, "accidentally" dropping it on the floor. Sam had the bone in his mouth in a matter of seconds, but he still didn't move too quickly. Arthritic joints slowed his pace, but he did manage to catch up by the time Ephraim reached the door. Ephraim sat down against the wall, just outside the kitchen, ignoring the stench that emanated from all the garbage in the room. He had spent enough time in this place that the smell didn't really bother him that much. And if you wanted to be left alone, there was no better indoor spot. Sam curled up about three paces away, contentedly gnawing on his meaty treasure.

Ephraim couldn't get the images from the Grove out of his mind. He replayed Eli's last moments again and again—the brave move made to protect Ephraim, the attack from the rival mage, Eli's hand in his, the strange feelings, the empty clothes lying on the Great Board. It didn't make any sense. Oh, how he wished he had Eli back again! He needed him. He wished....

*Ephraim, don't be afraid.*

It was Eli's voice! He was back again. Well, not exactly back, but back inside his head. "Where are you?"

*I am far away, as you know. But I am well. I am sending someone to help you.*

"Who? Who are you sending? And how will they help me?"

*I am sending two boys about your age. Sir Jonathan and Sir Gregory. They are already on their way and should arrive shortly. Treat them well.*

"I will if I ever get to see them. How will I know who they are?"

*They are dressed all in black, and you will remember them from the battle on the Great Board. They took your place. Do you remember?*

That wasn't something Ephraim could ever forget. "Yes, I remember them. In fact I will always remember them. How did you find them? And how do you know they will help me? Are they friendly?"

*Ephraim, relax and take a deep breath. So many questions. You must slow down and get control of your mind. What I need you to do for a few minutes is just listen. The boys will be there soon, and you must be certain to guide them to complete the task I will describe for you.*

"I'll do my best, but it isn't easy. I miss you so much. Hearing your voice gives me hope that you are not dead, if only I could see you one more time!" The grief welled up inside Ephraim again, threatening to overwhelm him. Eli's steady, reassuring voice brought quiet and calm, and helped him focus again.

*I know this is difficult, but you are strong and brave. More than that, your task is very important. You will need to concentrate very carefully if you are going to complete it. Tell me, Ephraim, do you know where my staff is?*

"No, I don't remember seeing your staff since we were in the Grove."

*That's what I suspected. When I was attacked, I had already placed the staff under my feet, so that when my cloak floated to the ground it would be covered. I couldn't afford the staff to end up in the wrong hands. It is very important that you recover the staff, Ephraim. You must get the staff.*

"Why is the staff so important?"

*As I told you, before I left I transferred to you all of my powers. While that is true in one sense, in another sense it is misleading. I do not have any special powers, no one does. People can't have unusual powers, people are just people. But people can have wisdom and knowledge. What I passed to you was all the wisdom and knowledge that naturally passes to the first mage, but in condensed form. Without the staff, you will never understand what was passed to you. And, without the staff, you will never be able to use the wisdom and knowledge you have received. All the power resides in the staff. It is the combination of what is in you, with what is in the staff that creates what others think of as magic.*

""But what if I can't find the staff?""

*Prepare for a lifetime of working in the kitchens. The staff must be found and it must be put to use. You are one of the protectors of the kingdom now. Your weapon is the staff and the wisdom to use it wisely.*

"But Eli, I can't even go into most of the castle. You have to be a noble just to climb the stairs, or a member of the royal family's personal staff. How can I find this staff?"

*If you can find a way to make the king believe you are the first mage, then he will willingly give you the staff. Believe me, he wants to have that staff in the hands of a loyal first mage! He needs all the allies he can get. In fact, I would be very surprised if the king doesn't already have the staff under lock and key in his personal armory. The problem is that he will be very unlikely to believe that you are the first mage. First of all, you are a commoner; second, you are a young boy. He will be looking for someone with natural wisdom, and some measure of experience and education. He will be looking among those in training to become mages. He will not be looking at folks like you.*

"Then why did you pick me? If I am so unsuited to being first mage, why put me in such grave danger?" For a moment, Ephraim felt slighted, then a little confused.

*You are not unsuited, Ephraim. More important than training, more important than knowledge, is loyalty. Much can be taught, but love, respect, trust, those things are earned slowly over time. Ephraim, you are like a son to me. Who could I trust more than you?*

Ephraim relaxed a little, his confidence increased. He was grateful for Eli's words of encouragement.

*But you must now prove that my trust in you is not misplaced. I know that you will not fail me through lack of effort or through unfaithfulness. But there is every chance that others will seek to get the staff before you can get your hands on it. The staff could be twisted and used by a mage from another kingdom, and that would dismantle the balance of power that is already so fragile. There are spies within the castle, I am sure. And if they can get the staff, the Ruby Kingdom is in grave danger. You must not allow anything to keep you from getting your hands on that staff!*

"Where should I look for this staff, then?"

*In the room where the king sleeps there is a private armory where the king's weapons are locked. Swords of magical power were once kept there, but no longer. If I were the king, I would lock the staff in there. The armory can only be opened by someone linked to a royal gem, or in the possession of one of those swords.*

"But I don't have either. How will I ever get it open, even if I could get into the king's dressing room?"

*Sir Jonathan and Sir Gregory should be able to get you into the room. Judas has the gem. You will all have to work together to get the staff. Now see if you can find those you will need to complete this task. They should all be present by now, I would venture.*

"Eli, how can I call you if I need you?"

*If you simply think of me and then call me, I will come if I am able. I cannot come if I am sleeping, unless you step into my dream to get my attention. That you should only attempt in the case of a rare emergency, and then only after you have the staff. I also cannot come if I am speaking with someone here. In order to be present in your mind, I must be silent here. In order to see through your eyes, I must be blind here. I am vulnerable when I am present with you, and I must be certain to protect myself in this place.*

'But Eli, I am afraid. I don't want to do this thing. If I am caught, I will be killed."

*It is okay to be afraid, my boy. You would be foolish not to be afraid. But if you are not successful, the kingdom will fall and you will be killed anyway. To be very honest with you, Ephraim, I am also afraid. I am afraid that no matter how hard you try, you will be unable to succeed. But I am trusting that Providence has sent you the help you need, and that in a very short time, all will be well and in balance again.*

"Don't go, Eli. It feels like you are getting ready to leave."

*I must, my boy. If I do not go, you will never get started. And nothing is more important than that. Farewell. Know I always love you!*

"I love you, too," Ephraim thought. But it was too late. Once again, Eli was gone.

Sam was still chewing on his bone and hardly noticed Ephraim struggle to his feet. Passing quickly through the kitchen, he lined his eye up with the crack in one of the doors that led to the banquet hall. He could see many of the people in the room, but from his vantage point, he couldn't tell who was at the head table. He stepped back not a moment too soon, as two servants came barging through the doors.

"Two more places at the head table, quickly!" they shouted. Chairs, plates, goblets were quickly assembled and a team of servants ran back in to accommodate the king's latest wish.

When they returned, Ephraim asked the servants who the places were for.

"No idea," the servant said. "Never saw these kids before in my life. They must be important, though. The king placed one on each side of him!"

Ephraim's heart leaped! His help had arrived! And they were in the good graces of the king. Maybe this task wouldn't be as hard as he had hoped.

Approaching Ella, Ephraim tried to ask if he could serve at the royal table, but Ella was still too busy to listen. When he finally got his chance, Ella quickly dismissed him, citing his inexperience and lack of training. He tried to explain that Eli had ordered him to get in touch with these new guests, but the mere mention of Eli's name started tears in Ella's eyes and a sharp rebuke. "I told ya, not now. Later. Now get out o' my kitchen!"

Crestfallen, Ephraim headed out the back door into the mud room. He couldn't afford to head up to the servant's rooms, or he might miss his opportunity to confront his helpers. And though he could walk through the main entryway, he could never loiter out there. Anything more than a quick pass through, and he would be booted out of the castle quick as a flash—especially when there was nobility in the hall. He had to think of some way to get the attention of Sir Jonathan and Sir Gregory!

Quickly, he called out for Eli. He waited, and in a moment, Eli was present.

*Haven't you started yet?*

"I can't get started. Ella won't let me in the banquet hall and now she has booted me out of the kitchen. I can't wait for them in the main entryway; there is a formal event in progress. Anyplace else, and I'll never see them. I need your advice."

*Is there anyone in the garbage room?*

"Other than me, no. There is a guard standing outside the back door, and Sam is here."

*There are some secret passages in the castle that very few know of. You must never tell anyone they exist. The doors are activated by placing your hand in a certain spot on the wall. One door opens about seven hands off the ground, above a barrel along the back wall. You must measure the spot for your hand very carefully. Do this before you climb the barrel, and be prepared to jump away should anyone enter the room. You must close the door behind you immediately. Once inside, I will explain the other details. From the corner of the room, count in fifteen hands. From the floor, count up ten hands. Once you are on the barrel, and you have listened carefully to be sure no one is coming, place your hand flat against the wall at exactly that spot. If nothing happens, move your hand slightly left or slightly right until you find the right spot. You will know you have found the spot when the spot begins to warm just a little. Then the door will swing open. Step inside and then reach for the bump on the inside of the wall in exactly the same place. A simple touch will shut the door. Go to it.*

Ephraim grabbed Sam's bone, much to Sam's amazement. When the bone skidded across the kitchen floor, Sam simply stood up and shuffled off to retrieve it. By the time Sam was back, Ephraim was nowhere in sight.

"Eli, it's dark in here. How will I find my way?"

*I'm sorry it's dark, but there is nothing I can do about it. Now listen carefully. You are going to have to find your way along by feel, but you must also be careful about what you touch. You must only contact the walls with your fingertips. Otherwise, you might accidentally open another secret door. That might be disastrous. Now walk toward the banquet hall, down the stairs, and over the entrance to the kitchen.*

Eli waited for Ephraim to carry out the instructions. Ephraim concentrated on moving quietly without losing his balance. Eli couldn't see where Ephraim was because even Ephraim couldn't see where he was.

*Once you have passed the steep stairs up and then down, move very slowly. In just a few steps you will encounter a solid stone wall. There will be iron handles embedded in the stone, but you will not need them. Place your hand on the fourth bar then turn slowly to your right. Drag you hand from the bar, along that wall to the wall that is now in front of you. You are facing a wall that looks into the Grand Banquet Room. Somewhere in front of you is an observation stone. If you place your hand on it, it will become transparent, and you will be able to look into the room. You do not need to worry, it does not work in reverse. No one will know you are watching.*

The stone worked exactly as Eli predicted. Ephraim had an excellent view of the entire room, with the exception of the head table. Not that he couldn't see the head table. He was just at an odd angle to it, and he could see more backs of heads than anything else. In addition, the people on the far side of that table began to overlap a little. Still, he was very relieved to be in visual contact with his targets. He stood watching for a very long time. While he could see, he had trouble hearing because the noise in the room was so loud most of the time.

When the king finally stood to announce the end of the banquet, Ephraim was more than ready. He felt like he had been standing there for at least two hours, and he was anxious for his opportunity to prove himself. He watched as the guards led the king, with Prince Judas, Sir Jonathan and Sir Gregory, out of the main doors into the main entryway. But now where were they going? How would he get to them? "Eli, help!" he called in his mind. "They're moving! How do I get out of here?"

*Where are they going?*

"I don't know." I can't see…

*Ephraim! Be Quiet. Listen! If they go up the stairs, you will be able to hear that. If they move to the royal quarters, you will hear their steps fade away. If they go into the throne room, you should hear the doors open and close. Now be quiet and listen.*

Ephraim froze in place, listening as hard as he could. He placed his head against the stone wall under where he guessed the stairs might be. Sure enough, he could hear the steps, ever so faintly. They were headed up the stairs! As the party climbed higher, the steps grew louder. Then, suddenly, the steps seemed to stop. Ephraim held his breath. The he heard the dull thud of the closing of the door. They were in the Throne Room!

"Eli, they are in the throne room!"

*Then you must go back the way you came. There is a very narrow passageway with stairs leading up to the second floor. Take those stairs. There is another observation stone looking into the throne room, but it is located at the other end of the corridor. Go quickly, but do not make a sound. Look into the throne room to see who is present. If the king is in there alone with Judi and the boys, open a secret door into the room and announce yourself. Explain my instructions, and have the king get you the staff. But if anything unusual is happening, or if anyone else is present, wait until you can be sure of what is going on.*

Ephraim moved as quickly as he dared. With no light to guide him, the going was slow. It took him about ten minutes to reach the observation stone, even though the distance was fairly short. Standing on the steps at the end of the passageway, Ephraim activated the stone.

What Ephraim saw made no sense at all. The king was lying on the raised platform behind the throne. He seemed to be sleeping or something. Prince Judas was talking to Sir Jonathan and Sir Gregory, as Gregory stepped onto a colorful square on the floor. A golden staff sprouted from the center of the square. With a simple touch of the staff, the two boys simply disappeared! Prince Judas moved back towards his father, laid down on the floor, and went to sleep!

"Eli, my helpers have vanished into thin air! Eli, Eli, what should I do next?" But Eli was gone. And Ephraim was alone. More alone than he had ever felt in his life. He slowly sunk down to the floor, resisting the urge to cry. He was too old for that, he told himself. He would simply have to find another way to get the staff.

CHAPTER 21

# Powers Concealed

The trip back to Newport had been a quiet one. Neither Greg nor Jon had very much to say. Both were rather frightened at what had happened in the throne room. And contrary to what Eli had predicted, Judas didn't seem to need their help at all. Or if he did, they didn't think they had really helped him. But all of that was of little concern to them. Greg gently massaged his sore neck, the muscles of which had been strained when the king jerked his head. And his scalp was sore. And very honestly, he was angry. Why had Eli sent them on so dangerous a mission? That king had threatened to kill them, and for no reason, as far as Greg could tell. He couldn't wait to hear Eli's explanation when they returned home.

But when they got back into their room, they were surprised to find Eli gone. It was 1:20AM; where could Eli have gotten to? They weren't going to find out, apparently, since there was no one to ask.

"Where do you think Eli went?" Greg wondered aloud, breaking the silence.

"I don't know," Jon replied, "but I wish he was here. I, for one, would like to have some answers."

"Yeah, what was that all about? And why did the king threaten us? I thought he wanted us for friends. I thought we were supposed to get rewarded. You would have thought we were the enemy!" Greg griped.

"Something happened that turned us from friend to enemy, but I am not sure what it was. I'll tell you one thing, I'm glad I am not Judas when the king wakes up!"

"Do you think the king will know that Judas put us all asleep?" Greg asked thoughtfully.

"I don't know. I think that the king will probably suspect that we did it somehow. What I am afraid about is whether the king has some magical way to make Judas tell the truth," Jon added. "That might end up getting Judas into huge trouble."

"I hope he doesn't get into too much trouble. He was cool, and I think we could be friends. Who knows, maybe we are already," said Greg, wondering.

"He took a big risk helping us. He could have just let his father do what he wanted to do. I think we owe him, but I am not anxious to go back there any time soon. What about you?" Jon asked.

"Not tonight, anyway. I'm going to sleep. Tomorrow let's talk Mom into letting us have a lock on our bedroom door!" Greg insisted.

"Fat chance. It will never happen. She would be afraid we were doing drugs in here or something. I wonder how Eli got in here. Magic, maybe?"

"Who knows," Greg answered, "we'll talk about it tomorrow. I'm dead."

"Me, too. G'night, Greg."

"G'night, Jon."

***

Ephraim, very confused, worked his way back down to the garbage room outside the backdoor of the kitchen. Using an observation block, he was able to jump out into the room while it was empty, quickly shutting the door behind him. The kitchens were still bustling. Though the crowd in the banquet hall had thinned out considerably once the king left, they were still loud, and somewhat inebriated, noblemen calling for more food. While the servants carried out the last of the sweetmeats and then the pastries, Ella sat on a stool in the corner supervising the final phase of the banquet. She was obviously exhausted and was sweating profusely. She had a serving towel in her hand and was mopping her brow. With her other hand, she grabbed the apron of a servant scurrying by with a tray of pastries.

"Give one and then move on. These folks have had plenty ta eat, now, and we want everyone ta have at least one o' these wonderful delights befere we run out o' them," she instructed. "Off ya go!" she said as she gave the servant a slight push toward the exit. She spied Ephraim walking into the kitchen, and waved him over to her. "Now what were ya so all fired up ta tell me befere, my boy?" She pulled him close to her right side.

"I don't know how to tell you this, mum, but..." he paused.

"Best way is ta just spit it out," Ella blurted. "We can sort out the details as they come."

"Well, I don't know exactly how to describe it, but I can hear Eli talking to me in my head." Ephraim explained gently.

Tears welled up in Ella's eyes as she gazed into the boy's face. "I understand exactly. I keep thinkin' I am hearin' his voice, too. I can't believe he is gone. It feels like he is still here with me. I don't know what I'm gonna do."

"It's not like that, mum. This is different. I can actually talk to him. And he talks to me. It's not like I think I am hearing him. He is saying stuff in my head that I can understand."

Ella stopped and stared. "What are ya talkin' about? Ya sound like yer mad."

"Mum, I know this is hard to believe, but even though Eli is gone, he's not dead."

"What do ya mean, not dead? The king himself told me that Eli was gone. How can he be not dead?" Ella's voice was filled with tension. She wanted to believe Ephraim, but there was too much pain in taking the chance. What if Ephraim was wrong? It would be like losing Eli all over again. Ella jumped off the stool and forcefully grabbed Ephraim by the arm, leading him out of the kitchen and up the stairs toward their quarters. As soon as they were out of earshot of the rest of the servants, they sat down on the stairs. "Tell me everythin'," Ella commanded.

Ephraim told how Eli had spoken to him in his head, where Eli had gone and why. He told Ella that he knew for sure that Eli was alive, but he really didn't understand where. He also said he didn't think Eli could get back to where they were. He explained about the transfer of powers. At that, Ella's tears began again, but only briefly.

Ella explained that if Eli had given up his powers, there must be some great reason for it. It probably meant that he couldn't come back, but Ella told Ephraim to never give up hope. Then she made Ephraim try to call Eli. When Ephraim was unsuccessful, Ella made him promise to come get her the next time Eli contacted him. There were things she needed to know. With that, she gently cradled Ephraim's head into her bosom, giving him a great hug. "There are great things in store for ya, my boy. Ya have been given a great trust, and ya must always do yer duty, ta the king and ta the land! And neva forget, I always love ya." Ella held him for a minute more, then released him. "I've got ta get back ta the clean-up, now. If I am gone, the servants will disappear and leave my kitchen in a shambles! When the cat's away, ya know…" and she disappeared out the door.

Ephraim sat there on the steps thinking about the staff and about Eli and about what Ella had said. "A great trust"—those had been her words. If Eli's powers really were in his body, he had been given a great trust indeed. Why didn't he feel powerful, then? Mostly he was scared and confused. He climbed the back stairs to his room, changed into his nightshirt, and jumped into bed.

CHAPTER 22

# Spy Search

The king stirred once, then stretched, and then as if suddenly realizing what had happened, jumped to his feet and looked around. The throne room was empty, except for his son, sleeping on the floor about six feet away from him. As soon as he saw him, he shouted him awake. "Judas. Where are they?"

Judas jumped, genuinely startled by the loud voice of his father. He rubbed his eyes and got slowly to his feet. "What happened?" he asked.

"Where are those two spies?" the king insisted, as he ran to check the door to the throne room. The door was shut, and it was clear that the entire room was empty.

"I don't know,' Judas hesitated. "One minute they were here and I was tying up Sir Gregory, and next moment I heard you waking me up. What happened?"

"They must have enchanted us. I knew they were powerful, but I underestimated their power. We must find them right away. If they fall into the hands of our enemies, we are doomed!" the king boomed.

"What do you mean, 'we are doomed', Father?" Judas asked sheepishly.

"Stupid child, don't you realize that this kingdom lost both mages in the Grove? At the present moment, the only magical power we hold is the power I have as king, and that is very limited. I can't believe that Eli was so reckless on the Board! Now we are in very great danger, indeed. If one of our enemies would attack us right now, we would be very vulnerable. We need those two boys, desperately. And we need them bound to our kingdom!"

Judas finally understood what his father had been trying to do. By binding the boys to the Ruby kingdom, he was trying to prevent them from assisting any enemy of the kingdom. For a moment he was ashamed of his actions. But as ashamed as he was, he certainly wasn't stupid. He wasn't about to tell his father what he had done. That would have been treason, and he knew the punishment for that. In spite of the sense that his father's actions now made, Judas was still uneasy about what had happened. He needed time to think.

"How about I search the castle, while you organize a search outside the castle walls? Now that I have my gem, I can contact you if I find anything inside, and you can let me know if you run into anything," Judas suggested.

The king paused for a moment and looked at Judas. "That's the first intelligent thing I have heard you say. You get busy. I'll call Zarak and organize the search. And if you find them, put them to sleep until I arrive. Use the gem." No sooner had the king spoken, then he realized what he had said. He scratched his head for a moment, considering something, and then shook the thought away. Judas bolted out of the room, not waiting for the king to fully consider the possible sources of his previous nap.

CHAPTER 23

# Moving Day

It was the smell of bacon frying that brought Jon out of a deep sleep. Ah, Sunday morning! Full breakfast and no time to lose! He jumped out of bed and ran down the hallway and stairs to where Dad stood, spatula in hand, in front of the stove.

"Morning, buddy. How did you sleep?" Dad asked.

"Great!" Jon yawned.

"Hungry?"

"You bet!" Jon really was hungry. And he could almost taste breakfast already.

"Go get your brother and holler up to your mom. Then set the table. It will be ready in one minute," Dad instructed, stirring up the eggs that were scrambling on the stovetop.

Jon ran back up the steps and yelled for Greg, adding a second word for his mother. Back down he came, collecting plates and silverware from the counter between the kitchen and dining room area. In no time, the table was set, the food was ready, and all four were seated around the table.

"Isn't this nice!" Mom exclaimed. "Honey, you do a great job!"

"Thank you, my dear," Dad smiled back. Mom was already dressed for church, and once the eggs and bacon and toast and orange juice were gone, she would be helping the kids get ready while Dad dressed. It was the same every Sunday morning. Sunday was a "No T.V." day in their house, so cartoons were out of the question. They would be dressed up and in church by 9:30, and then back home by 12:30, unless they went out to a restaurant for dinner. That happened about half of the time. They liked the routine, and today was no different—until they drove into their driveway after church. There, parked in front of the house next door, was a huge truck, orange with black letters on the side: "ALLIED VAN LINES."

The back doors of the truck were open and a metal ramp descended to the level of the street. Two men were struggling with a large couch when the Curtises finally arrived on the scene. Mom and Dad knocked on the front door of the neighbor's house and were invited in by a lady who seemed to be about the same age as Mom. Jon and Greg stayed outside. In another moment, Dad stuck his head back out and yelled for the boys, "Jon and Greg, come in here a minute." Dad held open the door for them as they ducked inside.

Inside, there were six people standing in the middle of an empty room. Mom, Dad, two other grown-ups, and a small child of about two in diapers, and right in the middle...their hearts sank...a girl. She was about as tall as Jon, maybe even a little taller. She took one look at the boys, then looked down at her feet.

"Jon, Greg, I would like you to meet Annie Monagul. Annie, this is Jon, this is Greg. Annie is in the sixth grade, so she is a year younger than you, Jon, but a year older than Greg," Dad gestured. "Why don't you take Annie over to our house and show her your things?"

Annie grabbed her mother's waist, as if to say, 'I'd rather stay here.' Her mom spoke up quickly, "Why don't you show them your new room, Annie. I bet they would like to see it."

"Okay," Annie responded rather quietly, without very much enthusiasm. "This way." She slumped out of the room toward the stairs in the hallway. Greg and Jon followed. At the top of the stairs, Annie turned left and moved down a further hallway to the last room. She pushed open the door. "Come on," she muttered.

"Where are you moving from?" Greg asked politely.

"San Francisco," Annie grumbled, "and I wish we could have stayed there. I hate moving."

"So do we," added Jon. "This is my fourth move, Greg's third. I can't really remember the first one, but I remember the last two."

Annie looked more sympathetic now. "Is your dad in the Navy, too?" she asked.

"Yeah," Greg answered. "And we are hoping that we never have to move again. Well, actually, we'd like to go back to where we just moved from, but I don't think that is going to happen."

"How long ago did you move here?" Annie inquired.

"Just a few months ago. We moved near the end of the school year. We didn't bother to start school here for just the last few weeks of the year. We don't know anybody here." Jon observed.

"Well, then I guess I'm not the only newcomer," she sighed.

"Nah, there are probably more like us, too. Once we get to school we'll find out. I bet other Navy kids moved here this summer," Greg surmised. "Hey, we're heading to the beach after we change our clothes and eat. Do you want to join us?" Jon shot Greg an evil look.

"I don't think so. I doubt I can find a bathing suit, yet. And I think my mom will need help watching my baby brother while the movers are still here. Maybe I'll catch you tomorrow," said Annie.

"Okay. See you later!" quipped Jon, who was out of the door, down the stairs and out of the house in a flash. Greg followed along more slowly. When they got downstairs, the adults were outside walking around the lawn, viewing the exterior of the house.

"Where are you guys going?" Mom yelled to them.

"Home to change, "Jon yelled back.

"Set the table for eight, and get the old high chair out of the basement. We are having guests for dinner," Mrs. Curtis instructed.

"Okay," Jon said, his heart sinking. He had been hoping for a few boys next door. Now he was stuck with a girl, and she was coming to dinner. He knew the afternoon would stretch on forever. Usually when they were finished eating, Jon could ask to be "excused," but when company came, you had to stay and make "conversation." This was going to cut into his beach time.

Greg started to set the table, while Jon went downstairs to get the high chair. The only reason they still had it was in the event of a visit from their cousins. It was rarely used, and was sequestered in the basement beyond the wood shop. When Jon reached the bottom of the basement stairs, he suddenly realized that he wasn't alone. There, off to one side, stood Eli.

"Jon, relax," Eli spoke softly. "You don't need to be afraid of me."

"How can you say that, when I never know where you are going to show up? And the last thing you sent us to do nearly got us killed, by the way!"

"I know you were unsuccessful in your task, but I didn't know the details of your journey. I'm sorry it turned out to be so dangerous," Eli apologized.

"I'll bet you're sorry. But it was our necks on the line, not yours. I think you should leave us alone!" Jon demanded.

"I can't do that. I'm sorry that I have to intrude on your lives, but the future of my world and of many people that I love rests in your hands. From that I cannot walk away. Neither can you," Eli said, his voice slow and measured.

"Of course we can walk away. We can do whatever we want. You said you wouldn't force us to do anything. And if we want out..."

Eli raised his hand, silencing Jon. "Your parents will be here in less than a minute. I must be gone when they arrive. Listen carefully. We can talk this all out tonight, late tonight. I will be back to hear the full story. But there is something I must tell you immediately, so that you can find a way to act. You are needed again in the kingdom, and not you only. Annie is also chosen. You must find a way to get her here, so I can explain everything to her."

"Annie is chosen!?! What do you mean? You want us to tell her the secrets? We don't even know her! There's no way we are going to..." Jon was cut off by Eli's voice.

"Your Father is entering the house and will come directly down here if the high chair is not upstairs. Quickly, carry this up. We will finish our conversation later." Eli thrust the high chair into Jon's hands and moved him toward the stairs. "Later, my son, we will discuss it all later, but very soon indeed. There isn't much time."

CHAPTER 24

# Maxim One

Away from his father's presence, Judas began to organize the search of the castle. At first he considered using the household guard, but quickly thought better of that. He didn't want to scare Sir Jonathan and Sir Gregory away. He really needed to talk to them. He settled on a compromise plan. He called together eight members of the guard and gave them the assignment to search in all the very public and visible places. He also posted a guard at the main entrance to each floor. Once the guard was dispatched, he headed to the kitchens to find Ella.

Ella was immersed in the clean-up from the banquet. Prince Judas pulled her aside for a moment to make his request, and was surprised to find her so quickly agreeable. He borrowed four servants, giving each a small note with the royal seal on it. These four he sent to search all the back hallways, visitors' rooms, and all the out of the way places. They were to finish their assigned tasks and report to his room personally in one hour's time.

Judas himself returned to his room to wait for his servants to complete their tasks. Once inside his room, however, he locked his door and then activated the secret entrance into the hidden passageways to begin his own investigation. Judas inspected the castle, top to bottom, from the inside out. Using light he generated himself, he found his way quickly and quietly. From what he could see, Jon and Greg were nowhere to be found. He wasn't surprised when the others reported the same news. Posting a double guard at each entrance, and a single guard at every window, Judas decided to head for bed. There was no telling how long his father would be away. And if his father was as unsuccessful as Judas had been, he really didn't want to be present when his father got home. It wouldn't be a pleasant thing.

The next morning Ephraim woke with the light of the sun. Ella had been up for several hours, preparing breakfast. But even before Ephraim could get out of bed, Ella was back from the kitchen, bread in hand, nagging at him to get ready.

"Here's somethin' fer yer stomach. Now we have a task ta begin today, and a difficult task it is. It will have ta be added ta yer chores, and I'll not have a word o' grumblin' from ya about it. Ta grumble is ta prove yerself unworthy fer the task," Ella lectured. Ella sat down on the small cot opposite Ephraim's pallet.

"Bein' first mage is not about havin' power. A first mage is known by his wisdom and trainin'. Sorry ta say, Eli is not here ta train ya. But I will do my best ta begin the trainin' and Eli will help as he can from the inside, I guess."

Ella continued as Ephraim sat uncomfortably on his bed. "The father of all mages was a great man named Rufus. It was he who first explained the systems that keep our lives in balance. Workin' with the Creator's blessin', he catalogued the Objects o' Power and trained mages in their use. The Objects were given ta restore balance wheneva the choices o' citizens allowed evil ta flourish. But more important than the Objects was the teachin' that allowed the Objects ta be used properly. It is that teachin' that makes a true mage. For once the teachin' is mastered, the mechanics o' manipulation will be understood and properly wielded."

*Pay close attention, Ephraim. What Ella is telling you is of first importance. The lives of everyone in the kingdom may depend on you learning this well—and quickly.*

Ephraim suddenly snapped to attention, sitting rigidly straight.

"What is it?" Ella asked inquisitively.

"He's here. Eli's here."

"Tell him I love him, Ephraim, and ask if he has any advice fer me," Ella instructed.

*Tell her she's doing perfectly. You must take possession of the book. And I miss her, too.*

"He says you're doing perfectly, that I must take possession of a book." He paused before adding, "And he misses you, too."

A tear slipped down Ella's cheek. "Ask him if there is any way that he can return ta..."

Ephraim was already nodding his head "no" by the time Ella finished the sentence. "He says that there will be time to explore that later, if we survive the present crisis. For now, the teaching is most important. Start at the back, work toward the front." Ephraim relayed Eli's instructions.

Ella sighed, taking a small square booklet from the pocket of her apron. The cover was divided into four squares, each a different color, red, green, black, gold. In the very center of the cover was a white circle in which stood the letters "B R". "This is the Book o' Rufus," Ella explained. "Everything ya need ta learn is here. But ya must more than learn it, ya must master it. These teachin's must become a part o' ya. They must shape who ya are. If they do not, every attempt ta use the power o' yer staff will be warped.

"If Eli says start at the back, start at the back we will." Ella opened the book to the final page, and began to read, slowly, carefully:

**The land is the Creator's gift;**
**People are the Creator's treasure.**
**Justice is yer duty, mercy is sweet, forgiveness sublime.**
**Arrogance reveals ignorance, selfishness despoils, pride kills.**
**Strength is a trust, talent an obligation,**
 **Wisdom is the crown o' virtue."**

Phrase by phrase, Ella made Ephraim repeat the words. Again and again, she read, explained, and asked for recitation. The sentences seemed strange to Ephraim, yet there was something of power to them.

**"Neva in defense o' self, unless self-defense**
**Is defense o' others."**

Ella explained that the first section of the book was filled with stories that served as examples of the virtues described. These stories were to be studied carefully, so that their lessons could continually unfold over time. The second section described the relationship between virtue and power, as well as describing the Objects of Power that had been created. The third section, the maxims, summed up the truth embodied in the stories. This section was to be completely memorized.

Ephraim gave the first maxim a try, "The land is the Creator's gift; the people are the Creator's pleasure, uh, treasure."

"Good," Ella encouraged him.

"Justice is your duty, mercy is sweet, forgiveness sublime. Arrogance reveals..."Ephraim paused.

*"Ignorance—"*

"...ignorance, selfishness..."

*"despoils, pride kills."*

"...despoils, pride kills."

"Excellent, Ephraim. Ya are doin' very well!" Ella enthusiastically cheered. "Can ya finish?"

"Actually, Eli was helping me," Ephraim admitted sheepishly.

"Eli, stop that this minute! Ya won't be helpin' him by givin' him the answers. He'll need them on his own soon enough," Ella chided, then remembered that Eli probably couldn't hear her. "Tell him I said that," she added. Ephraim passed the message along.

"Strength..." Ella prompted.

After a few seconds, Ephraim resigned. "I can't remember any more. I'm sorry, Ella."

"No need fer that. I only ask that ya do yer best. Now take the book. Treasure it above yer life. Read it every chance ya get, but show it only ta those who know yer secret." Ella stood.

Ephraim took the book from Ella's hands, and then wrapped his arms around her. "Thank you," he whispered in her ear. "I won't disappoint you."

"See that ya don't. And Ephraim, if ya don't disappoint Rufus, ya won't disappoint me." She winked, gave him a kiss on the cheek, and pushed him back onto his bed. "Read the first story. We'll talk later." With that, she turned and was gone.

Ephraim flipped through the pages of the book. Inside the back cover, he saw handwritten in small letters, "Ella Pebbler, Green of the Emerald". He wondered what that meant, and decided to ask Ella about it later. Turning back to the front of the slim volume, Ephraim began to read the story of Tom Turnavil, a hero from before the time of Rufus. Time slipped away as he become lost in the story.

\*\*\*

Judas had spent the better part of the morning looking for Ephraim. He had checked the main castle and the area outside surrounding the structure. None of the servants had seen him, and since the royal family traditionally stayed out of the servant's quarters, it never occurred to him to look for Ephraim in Ephraim's room. Ephraim didn't have a room by himself. He shared the male servant's quarters that were located behind the kitchen and about half a flight of stairs above it. Beneath that room, the female servants slept. Eli and Ella's room was above all of them, actually on the third floor of the castle, with connecting passageways to all the other servant quarters. When it finally occurred to Judas that Ephraim must be hidden somewhere, he decided to check the servant's quarters. Sneaking up the back stairs, Judas entered the room where Ephraim was reading.

Ephraim jumped to his feet when Judas entered. "What are you doing in here?" Ephraim asked, somewhat startled.

"And good morning to you, too," Judas sarcastically replied.

"Umm, sorry, Prince Judas. Good morning. Can I help you with something?" Ephraim quickly changed his tone.

"Something is not right, Ephraim, and I don't know exactly what it is. Right now the whole castle is searching for Sir Jonathan and Sir Gregory. My father is searching the surrounding lands; I have organized a search inside the palace. But I am certain they have escaped. I'm certain, because, I helped them." Judas' eyes were on the ground as he finished.

"Ah, that explains what I saw," Ephraim surmised.

"What did you see?" Judas asked quizzically.

"Eli showed me some secret passages in the castle. Last night I watched some of what happened in the throne room from inside the

wall. When I arrived, you were talking to Sir Jonathan, Sir Gregory
was standing to the side, and your father was lying on his side. At first
I thought your father was injured, but then I saw he was only sleeping.
Watching the two magicians disappear was very spooky, don't you
think?"

Judas began slowly, "At first I thought I was doing the right
thing by letting them escape. My father was trying to bind them to
the kingdom, and they certainly didn't want to be bound. After they
escaped, my father explained that as long as we don't have any active
mages, we need their magic to help protect us from enemies. Then I
didn't know what to say...or think."

"Does your father know you helped them escape?" Ephraim
asked cautiously.

"I don't think so," Judas guessed. "If he thought I had assisted
them, I would probably be in the dungeon right now. Maybe that is
where I belong."

"No, I think you did the right thing. Oaths and promises must
be freely given to have any value or meaning. It's not right to force
people to do things against their will. But I think we have a different
problem," Ephraim explained. "I think Sirs Jonathan and Gregory
were here to help me get my staff." Ephraim told Judas about his conversation with Eli and the instructions he had received. He described
how important it was for the staff of the first mage to be in his hands,
for any power he might wield would have to come through that staff.

"Do you know where the staff is?" Judas wondered.

"Eli said it would have been gathered from the Great Board after
the battle. It should be in your Father's possession. He thinks your
Father would have it in a secret armory in his room."

"Now that presents some problems. Even I can't get into the
king's room without his permission. Unless there is a secret passage
into his bedroom, I don't think we have much of a chance," observed
Judas.

"Eli doesn't seem to think we should have any trouble on that
account. He thinks the king will want me to have the staff. After all,

the sooner I have control over Eli's powers, the sooner I can start to protect the kingdom," explained Ephraim.

Trumpets sounded at the front entrance of the castle; the king was returning.

"Let's go find out," suggested Judas. "He's going to be in a bad mood, but maybe this will improve his attitude." When Judas turned toward the door, Ephraim grabbed his book from under his pillow and stuffed it inside his pants. He followed Judas quickly, as the two of them made their way toward the king's chambers.

CHAPTER 25

# Friends for Dinner

Dinner at the Curtis home, at least on Sunday, was a somewhat formal affair. The only thing that rescued this event was that the Monaguls hadn't even unpacked all their clothes yet. They washed their hands, in a token attempt to get presentable for dinner, but a simple hand washing didn't have a chance of getting the job done. Everyone was hot and sweaty, and being crowded around the table wouldn't help, either. Mom had placed a roast in the crock pot before leaving for church that morning, and now she was busy in the kitchen stretching the meal she had planned for four to feed eight. Mrs. Monagul was helping her, washing vegetables, preparing a salad. Annie was occupying the baby in the living room.

"I think we are ready," Mom announced. "Let's find seats at the table."

The high chair occupied one end of the table, while Capt. Curtis sat enthroned at the other end. Three Curtises sat across from three Monaguls, Annie in the middle of them. After a short grace, Mr. Monagul spoke up. "It sure is nice of you to have us over to dinner today. We really appreciate your kindness."

"It's our pleasure," Mrs. Curtis replied. "We hope you really like it here. And I suspect that this is just the first of many times we will share together!" Conversation continued amiably around the table, until every bite of pot roast was consumed, every crust of bread eaten, and every drop of milk disappeared. When the question of dessert was raised (by Jon, of course) Mom apologized, and suggested a walk later that night to the local creamery. Mrs. Monagul agreed, but only tentatively, contingent upon the successful assembly of their beds.

Captain Curtis volunteered to assist in the assembly, and Mrs. Curtis suggested that she might help get the kitchen organized, and why didn't they all just plan to come back for pizza later that night? Then they could consider whether ice cream really was a good option. Mom was very persuasive and the Monaguls finally agreed. Jon and Greg, along with their parents, changed out of their Sunday clothes, and headed over to help their new neighbors.

By the time they all got next door, the movers had completely unpacked the truck. Boxes were piled everywhere, and there was very little room to move. Mrs. Monagul wasn't quite ready to have Annie unpack upstairs boxes without being present herself, and she really wanted to focus on the kitchen. And the upstairs really was very hot.

"Why don't you three go outside to play this afternoon? There isn't that much you can do right now until we get things a little more organized. Boys, I'd be grateful to you if you could keep Annie occupied while we get things straightened around in here," Mrs. Monagul suggested.

"If you don't mind," Jon spoke up, "Maybe we could go over to our house. By now the air-conditioner will have cooled the upstairs. We could play some games and stuff."

Mrs. Curtis agreed with the plan, and the three were off to the house next door.

They were no sooner out of Annie's yard and into their own, when Jon started talking. "Annie, can you keep a secret?"

Greg looked at Jon oddly, as if to question what he was doing.

"What do you mean?" Annie asked. "What kind of secret?"

"Nothing bad, nothing wrong. But first, you have to promise not to tell anyone," Jon pressed.

"Jon, what are you doing?" Greg asked. "I don't think this is a good idea. I mean…"

"I talked to Eli just before dinner," Jon explained, frustrated. "He told me she has to know."

"She has to know?!" Greg exclaimed.

"Know what?" Annie injected. "What is going on here? And what is this secret?"

They were in the house now, and Jon had led them down the stairs into the first basement. He stopped there, Greg nervously bringing up the rear.

"I'm going to tell you an incredible story, one you will not be able to believe. And I am asking you to promise not to tell anyone else this story unless the three of us agree. Okay?" Jon waited.

Annie hesitated, then sheepishly said, "Okay. Tell me."

Greg inhaled sharply. "Jon, are you sure we should do this?"

"We have to. Eli said," Jon answered.

"Who is Eli?" Annie asked impatiently.

"Sit on the steps," Jon said. . "It's a long story, and we might as well start at the beginning." Jon started from the lobster trap on First beach and walked through all of their adventures. He covered the carpet, the daggers, the swords, the jewels, the necklaces. He described the Grove and the Great Board, the castle and the king. He even told Annie about the dragon. Annie looked confused throughout the whole story. Jon was obviously serious, but who could believe a story like this? It was utterly impossible! Greg didn't utter a word. And when Jon was finished, the room was completely silent.

Finally, Jon broke the silence. "Annie, would you like to see it?"

"See what?" she asked.

"The Ruby Kingdom," Jon responded, evenly.

"You're kidding, right?" Annie joked.

"I've never been more serious in my life," Jon said. "Tell her, Greg."

Greg still hadn't said a word. And when Annie looked at him, all he could do was nod his head up and down. He still couldn't believe Jon had told the story. And hearing it himself, he had to admit, it was pretty hard to believe!

"Annie, if you will promise to keep our secret, I will show you the entrance into this other world. Would you like to see it?" Jon inquired.

"Show me. I promise," Annie announced, solemnly. "I'll have to see this to believe it anyway!"

"Follow me," Jon said, as he walked to the back of the room, and turned the corner into the rock room. Annie followed Jon, who in turn was followed by Greg.

Removing the cover from the chest, Jon called for his knife and beckoned Greg to do the same. In a moment, the chest was open, and the three of them were staring into it.

"It looks like the back of this chest is solid, but it isn't." Jon demonstrated by putting his hand through the back of the chest. Annie gasped. "This is the way into the other world. Show her Greg."

Greg stepped into the chest and walked right through the back of the chest and disappeared. Annie's breath caught in her chest! "Amazing! How do you do it? I didn't know you guys were magicians!" she bubbled. "Now make him come back!"

Jon stuck his head through the back of the chest and called for Greg to come back, which he promptly did. "You try it, Annie. Put your hand through like this." Jon stuck his hand through, demonstrating.

Annie was extremely apprehensive, unsure of exactly what was going on. Tentatively, she reached out her hand, but when her hand got to the back of the chest, it struck wood. Her hand didn't go through. "Am I supposed to say some magic words or something?" she asked, turning to look at Jon.

Jon was bewildered. His hand was halfway through the back of the chest, but Annie plainly could not get her hand through.

"It's not that easy," came a voice from behind them in the room. All three kids jumped out of their skins! Jon smashed his hand on the front of the trunk as he wheeled around, and Greg instinctively hit the deck beside the trunk. Annie just stood there staring, too afraid to breathe.

"Eli, don't scare us like that!" Jon shouted. "Give us a warning when you are going to appear from nowhere!"

"I'm sorry," Eli apologized, "but I forget that you can't sense it when I am nearby. Most mages can do that. And I think of you as mages. Forgive me, please."

Annie still had not moved, and Jon was nursing his sore hand. "Annie, this is Eli, the man I mentioned before. He is from the Ruby

Kingdom. He won't hurt you. He is the one who told me I had to tell you. It seems that you are to be a part of our little adventure."

Annie exhaled, but was still clearly uncomfortable.

"Don't be alarmed, Mistress Annie. I am very pleased to meet you. And I can see you are having trouble understanding everything that is going on. Please don't worry; that is to be expected. But it is important that we help you understand very quickly, for you three need to be on your way shortly."

Jon looked at Eli, his expression asking for an explanation.

"Matters are somewhat worse," Eli explained. "The staff of the first mage is missing. You must find it. I fear there are spies within the castle, which means that both Prince Judas and Ephraim are in great danger. Ephraim is especially fragile, for without the staff, he can never access his powers. I need you to return to my land very quickly."

"But Annie is unable to enter. I tried to show her…"

Eli cut Jon off, "My fault, Sir Jonathan. I never fully explained how it is that you can enter. Because you are bound to the dagger, you are able to move through the veil into the other world. But without an *Object of Power* from that world, no one can cross the veil. And not any *Object* will do. It must be one of the Objects identified by the veil itself."

"But we don't have anymore daggers," Greg observed. "How can we get Annie in?"

"The top of the trunk pictures more than daggers, Sir Gregory. The silver swords are also Objects of great power. Give Mistress Annie one of those, and she will slide through just as easily as you do."

Greg jumped into the trunk and entered the cave, returning with one of the silver swords. Placing the handle in Annie's hand, Greg invited her to try the trunk again. With the sword in her left hand, Annie reached out her right to the back of the trunk. To her amazement, her hand slipped right through. Where once the wood had been solid, now there was only air. Annie's eyes were wide with amazement.

"Mistress Annie, everything the boys told you is true. The only thing they didn't mention is that the dangers are real. You must be very careful when you enter my world. Not everyone will be your friend. But the good that you can do will far outweigh any dangers you face. Have courage, and may the Creator protect you as you go!" Eli gestured toward the trunk.

"Where do you think I am going?" Annie asked. "You put a silver sword in my hand and you expect me to jump right into another world? Even if I believed there was another world, why would I want to go there?"

Jon put a hand on Annie's sword hand. "Annie, I can't explain to you what I feel. But something about what we are doing is very right. It is dangerous. And I get pretty confused from time to time. But on the other side of this veil is a place where we can make a difference—a huge difference. And I'm afraid that if we don't make that difference, things will get very bad for a whole lot of people. On the other side of this veil there is a small cave. In that cave are the objects that we have stored there, including our carpet and staff. I'd like to ask you to take a ride with us to visit the castle. We will meet the crown prince and his first mage, and then, you can decide whether we stay and help, or whether we bring you right home. Just check it out with us, okay?"

Annie thought for a moment; the others were silent. "If I don't want to stay, you'll bring me straight home?" Annie questioned.

"Yep, that's the deal," Jon reassured her.

"Well, how can I refuse a magic carpet ride?" "*I must be an idiot,*" Annie thought to herself.

"Sir Jonathan, I am very worried about Ephraim. If you could check on him first, I would be most grateful. Warn him again of the importance of finding the staff. And if he cannot find it alone, help him all you can. Bon voyage, my friends."

Jonathan gave Annie a hand as she stepped into the trunk. Greg had already jumped through and was unrolling the carpet, when Annie stepped into the cave for the first time. Her heart pounding in her chest, Annie couldn't begin to describe the excitement she was feeling. This was the adventure of a lifetime! And she thought that tiny Rhode Island would be boring!

By the time Annie stepped into the cave, Greg had already unrolled the carpet and was seated on the back of it, staff in hand. Jon quickly grabbed the pouch that held their necklaces, tossing one to Greg and placing one around his neck. He gave two gold coins to each of them, pocketing two himself. He invited Annie to sit on the front end of the carpet, while he sat in the center, legs wrapped around the staff.

"Annie, this is a magical carpet. I know it is hard to believe, but it is true. We will be flying out of this cave in just a second. We will be invisible to everyone except certain magical creatures. There won't be any need to hold on, you will be completely safe. Just stay seated on the carpet and relax. We will be protected by an invisible shield, and we have significant weapons with us." Jon tried to sound reassuring, but he remembered how frightening his first ride on the carpet had been. "Here we go," he added as the carpet lifted off and slowly glided out of the cave into the afternoon sky.

Annie was impressed with the beauty of the land, and mentioned that it reminded her of the mountains out west. Greg told the story of the chess match as they passed over the Grove, and pointed out other features of the land they were beginning to know. Before long they were flying over houses and fields, settlements and villages, all subjects of the Ruby King. Soon the city and the castle came into view. The boys took turns adding details to the story, so that Annie would know who the main players were, and what Jon and Greg thought of each of them.

Once at the castle, they flew directly to Prince Judas' window. They considered leaving a pebble, but then decided it was easier to wait, invisibly, in the room itself. Once they were inside, however, they decided that they didn't want to sit on the floor, and so the carpet was rolled up and stowed on Jon's back. Lounging in the room of a prince was something Annie hadn't quite pictured herself doing today. A noise outside the room alerted them to the presence of others, and they quickly scrambled to a spot behind the door, just in case someone other than Judas stuck his head through the door.

CHAPTER 26

# Earlier

Jeremias had been busier in the last two days than in his whole life. And he was worried. Things were changing rapidly, and the latest word from his brother was that there would be war in the land. But before the attack could come, things must be made ready on the inside, the inside of the castle. And that was Jeremias' job.

Jeremias was one of three priests that served the royal chapel that was housed within the castle, on the eastern side of the third floor. He was the newest of the three, and though few in the royal household knew this, Jeremias wasn't a full fledged priest yet. He was actually a fourth stage novice, who would only take his final vows when he reached his eighteenth birthday. He had been training for the priesthood since he was twelve, five long years. If he were young for an assignment like this, that could be overlooked considering his incredible abilities. Jeremias spoke several languages and was well-trained in political protocol and statesmanship. He understood how the castle worked. He seemed wiser than his years could allow, and he was also very ambitious. He had only been in the Ruby Kingdom for five months, coming from the Rufinian Monastery, high in the hills of the Great Tirades. Already he had the ear of the prince, in part, because their age difference was relatively small.

All the major responsibilities of the chapel were shouldered by the two veteran priests; Jeremias functioned much like an assistant in training for royal service. This gave him more free time than the others, time he was able to put to good use.

As kind as Jeremias appeared, there was much more that lurked beneath the surface. In fact, no one associated with the monastery knew the true reason Jeremias had joined. That knowledge would have made Jeremias a security risk.

While it was good for a king to have many children to insure the succession, the very children that bring stability to the kingdom can also cause problems down the road. Younger children can become rivals for their older siblings when the throne becomes vacant. And once younger children reached an age where they posed a threat, they were often moved out of proximity to the court.

By the time Jeremias reached twelve years old, his oldest brother had already been killed in a hunting accident. The official story was that he was knocked off his horse by a low branch while chasing a deer through the woods. No one believed that. Many thought that the second brother in line had masterminded the "accident". Others thought that two powerful nobles of the kingdom had orchestrated the plot, in order to replace a headstrong prince with one they thought would be more agreeable to their personal plans.

Jeremias didn't know what to believe, but his father acted quickly to remove Jeremias from the kingdom. One month after his brother's death, Jeremias was in the Rufinian monastery. And now he was a priest in training in the Ruby Kingdom. No one in that castle knew that he was both priest and second in line to the Obsidian throne!

Under his priestly robes, a small circle of obsidian hung from a leather thong around his neck. His Royal Obsidian was the mark of his deepest secret. Through it, he was in contact with his family, to the extent that the stone allowed. Through it, he had felt the cold pulses that marked the death of his mother and father, just a few days ago. He had hoped to be invited to the Grove, but his superiors had been on the Board instead. He couldn't believe that both his parents were gone! He had just seen them two nights before. In fact, he was the one who had aided their escape from the castle, through the tower window at the rear of the chapel area. And now he would never see them again.

He wasn't sure what he thought about that. On the one hand, he resented deeply being sent away from his family. He had been angry at both his father and his mother for a very long time after he entered the monastery. He understood why he had been sent, but he was angry nevertheless. He felt like an orphan during his years with the Rufinians, his mother only allowed to visit him once a year. But as angry as he was, there was a difference between feeling like an orphan, and actually being one. True, he had brothers and sisters, but how far could he really trust them? No, being alone in the world was not a pleasant thing to be.

Still, there were some prospects worth considering. His brother, the crown prince of Obsidia, had just contacted him through a special messenger. A raven, assumed to be simply another bird, had deposited a capsule in Jeremias' hand while he was standing out on the tower lookout. Jeremias immediately went inside to his quarters, and opened the capsule. Inside was written, "When alone, say "Sum familia obsidium." Jeremias followed the instructions, and within moments, his head began to swim. He sat down on his bed, only to hear the voice of his older brother say, *"Listen carefully, we only have a few moments. Don't answer me out loud if any one is around. Destroy the message after memorizing the words. This communication will work only one time daily, and only if I am able to respond. I will attack the Ruby Kingdom when I get the signal from you. You will signal when the First Mage's staff is in your keeping, and we are safe from its power. You must get the staff before a new mage is chosen. If you succeed, I will place you on the throne of the Ruby Kingdom, to rule as my imperial governor. Do you understand?"*

"I understand," Jeremias replied.

*"Good. Goodbye."*

There was a grin on his face. Maybe he would never need to take those final vows. Perhaps there was a throne in his future after all.

Jeremias hadn't been idle during the time the castle was empty. He had attempted to get a royal ruby from the back of the throne. He knew the words of binding for his kingdom, and he had hoped that perhaps he could bind a servant of his to a royal ruby from this one. It didn't work.

He also introduced a young boy, 11 years old, to Ella in the kitchens. Juvenal, a very distant cousin of his, was presented as a destitute boy willing to work in place of Ephraim while he was gone.

Jeremias hoped the assignment would become permanent. He needed a set of ears among the servants and kitchen staff. He was gratified to learn just this morning that Ephraim had been replaced and that Juvenal was the replacement.

And now, Jeremias knew exactly where to look for the staff. While inspecting the tower that stood behind the chapel, next to the priest's quarters, Jeremias had found the secret passageway that connected the king's quarters to the tower. Well, actually, it wasn't that he found it, it found him. One day while he had been out in the tower meditating, the king had come through the door right next to where Jeremias was standing. Startled, Jeremias had jumped, shouted and banged his head on the wall next to him. The king apologized, and swore Jeremias to secrecy. Apparently, the windows that opened from the second floor tower level were very narrow for security reasons. The king far preferred the view from the third floor, and chose this vista frequently. And since no one but the three priests were permitted on the third level of the tower anyway, it didn't seem like much of a security risk.

The next time the king was out of the castle, Jeremias began to explore. He figured out how to open the door, and traced the passageways. He had managed to get down to the king's room, and found the passageway that led to the queen's room. That particular passage ended at her room. He also found passageways from the Southeastern Tower to the Northeastern tower, and several into the third floor guest rooms. That's as far as he had gotten. It was watching the king in his room the day he left for the Grove that yielded the information he needed.

After the senior priests had departed, Jeremias entered the secret passage and moved quietly down toward the king's quarters, to see if he could hear what was going on. While watching through one of the observation blocks, Jeremias saw the king reach his hand to the wall, opening a way into a hidden closet. From that closet, the king returned with his sword. Jeremias knew his own father had a secret armory where Objects of Power could be stored, along with his crown. This must be where the king hid his own valuables.

If the staff were in the king's possession, that is where it would be! A plan quickly came to him while he considered his options. He would need some help, but he thought it best to move as rapidly as possible.

He sent a messenger to get Juvenal from the kitchen for a special task. While Juvenal was coming, he changed into black, nondescript clothes, over which he donned his priestly robes. Lunch would be served within the hour; it was important that everything be in place before then.

Juvenal entered the chapel and was quickly escorted behind the altar curtains. "We must work quickly, Juvenal," Jeremias whispered. "Today is the day you become a hero." Juvenal's eyes widened and a grin appeared on his face.

"Today the king will be served lunch in his quarters as soon as he returns. You need to be the person serving him that lunch," Jeremias smiled.

"But Ella will never choose me to serve the king. Only experienced waiters are allowed to…" Jeremias cut him off.

"Ella doesn't have to choose you. I already have. You must be behind the doorway to the third floor when the waiter approaches the royal apartments. Simply step through the door and beckon him to step in with you for one second. I will be there with you, and will allow you to change places with him. You take the food to the king. I will instruct you as to how to serve the food, where to stand, and what to say. But most of all, you must keep the king out of his bedroom! While you are serving him lunch, I will be elsewhere on important business. You don't need to know what I will be doing. But if the king moves to enter his bedroom, you must delay him by whatever means necessary. Pour a bowl of soup on his head if you must, but I will need at least one minute from the time you give warning to the time the king enters his room. Do you understand?"

"What is in the bedroom?" Juvenal asked.

"That is not your business, Juvenal. But this I promise you. If all goes as planned, you will move from servant in the kitchen to a member of the court in less than one month's time. Don't fail me.

Keep the king out of his bedroom! Now get in place. The king could return any second," Jeremias said, dismissively.

Juvenal was gone in a flash. Jeremias turned and headed straight for the secret passageway. With his contingency plan in place, he could begin to explore the king's room. Jeremias entered the king's bedroom and went straight to the wall where he had seen the closet door mysteriously appear. He began to search the wall for some sign of the secret door, but was amazed at how seamlessly the entrance was hidden. He reached for his royal obsidian, and began to run his hand over the wall in front of him. The wall grew warm to his touch. He spoke the words that would have opened his father's armory, had he been back home in his own castle, but nothing happened. Well, almost nothing happened. For just an instant, a shape shimmered in the center of the wall. Jeremias smiled. He knew how to open this door. And he had exactly what he would need!

As he made his way back up the secret passageway to his own quarters, he heard the trumpet sound. The king had returned! There wasn't much time! Jeremias' stomach twisted inside him and his heart began to pound. Too many things could go wrong! This was too dangerous! And yet, it had to be done, and he was the only one who could do it.

Racing to his quarters, he extracted from under his sleeping pad the last thing his father had given him before he left for the Grove. It was a magical dagger. His father had handed him the wooden case, telling him not to touch it unless all was lost. His father hadn't told him not to open it. As soon as his father had gone, Jeremias looked inside the case and saw the beautiful knife. A royal obsidian was set in each side of the handle. It was obviously an Object of Power.

It wasn't until he saw the shape on the wall that Jeremias understood the true nature of the dagger. Placed at exactly the right spot on the king's bedroom wall, this would open the armory! He was almost sure it would!

Before he could go back, however, he had to help Juvenal make the switch. Running down the steps from the third floor, he saw Juvenal crouching behind the door that opened to the second floor. There would be guards just a few feet away on the other side of the door. He could not afford to be seen by them, or it would be impossible to deflect suspicion later.

From the noise in the hallway outside the door, it was obvious that the king was ascending the front staircase and moving rapidly toward his rooms. He was yelling various orders, and servants seemed to be scurrying to comply. Jeremias heard the door to the royal apartments shut with a bang. The food would not be far behind. Having been out searching all night long, the king would want food right away. And just as Jeremias had predicted, not two minutes passed before Juvenal saw the cart being wheeled toward the king's door. Pushing the door open slightly, Juvenal gestured to the servant pushing the cart to join him for one second. As the servant passed through the door, Jeremias spoke silently, "Sleep!" The servant slid to the floor. Jeremias hid the body behind a curtain in the chapel, while Juvenal quickly manned the food cart, wheeling it to the door of the king.

Once the sleeping servant had been hidden, Jeremias discarded his robes in his room and rushed to the secret passageway behind the king's room. By the time he arrived, the king had already stripped out of his dirty riding clothes and was putting on a comfortable, yet lavish tunic over trousers. Jeremias watched through the observation stone, until finally the king left his bedroom, shutting the door behind him.

In a few moments, Jeremias was in the king's room. He heard the king speaking to Juvenal on the other side of the door, and then the room next door grew quiet. He didn't have any time to waste! Withdrawing the dagger from its case, he held the knife against the wall. Nothing happened. He frowned. Then he remembered what he had done before. Placing one hand on his royal obsidian and the other on the wall, he concentrated on locating the secret passage. The shape shimmered briefly. Placing the dagger directly on that spot, which was a few inches lower than he had remembered, he was amazed to feel the dagger simply melt away under his hand. He was more amazed, when three seconds later, a crack appeared in the wall, and a door slid open to reveal the king's secret armory.

Stepping inside, Jeremias called for light, (one of the three royal tricks he knew), and began to examine what he saw inside. On the shelf in front of him was a small golden crown set with a single ruby, beneath which hung a beautiful silver horn. Next to it a beautiful set of polished plate armor was mounted on a stand. A row of swords hung on a rack against the back wall, with larger weapons beyond that. He looked around at the assortment of objects, frustrated that a mage's staff was not among them.

The horn was compelling. He picked it up to examine it. It was obviously some object of power and he felt the urge to take it as well as the staff, once he found it. But not knowing exactly what this horn was, he felt it was better to leave it here. He would ask his brother what it might be. After all, he could always come back and get it later!

He returned the horn to the spot where it hung, and then reached up to examine the crown. As he did, two things happened at the same time. First, the crown rolled slightly, revealing something lying on the shelf beneath it. Second, there was a crash just outside the bedroom door of the king!

Jeremias knew he had only seconds. Lifting the crown, Jeremias spied the thing he had come for, the mage's staff. It was easy to identify; the red ruby in the top a dead give-away. Grabbing the staff, he put the crown down, stepped out of the armory and shut the door. In less than ten seconds, he was across the room, into the secret passageway back to his quarters, the door shut behind him. He didn't dare wait to see what would happen. The king knew this passageway existed. He had to get rid of this staff as quickly as possible. The whole castle would be searched. He had to get Juvenal out of the castle, and maybe it would be best to get himself out as well.

Ditching the now empty case to his dagger under his sleeping pad, he tucked the staff inside his priestly robes, and grabbed the sleeping waiter. Dragging him down the stairs, Jeremias waited until Juvenal emerged from the king's apartment. According to their plan, Juvenal ducked behind the door for a moment, as Jeremias woke the servant and gave him strict orders to take the cart directly to the kitchen. "Tell Ella that the king was not pleased with you. You did nothing wrong, but because of his foul mood, he was angry. Someone else must be sent to serve the king tonight," Jeremias instructed the drowsy waiter. As the waiter walked away, Jeremias stepped back through the door.

Juvenal was behind the door, tense as a frightened kitten. Jeremias placed a hand on his shoulder, and spoke softly, "Everything went well. Now we must get you out of here."

"Jeremias," Juvenal began, "I heard what the boys were telling the king. I think it is important."

"What was that?" Jeremias responded patronizingly.

"They said that Ephraim was the new first mage."

Jeremias stopped suddenly. "They said what?"

"They told the king that Ephraim was the first mage. They were headed somewhere to get something he needed," Juvenal explained.

"Then we are luckier than I imagined," Jeremias said. "Juvenal, I need you to purchase some horses outside the city walls. Go to the stables marked with a black Pegasus. Find the owner, a man named Cyrus. Tell him the plan "Darkwing" is on for tonight. Get four horses and hire a guard from Cyrus' stables to watch them outside the postern gate of the city at dusk. You must be within the city walls at that time, watching the walls of the castle. A white cloth hanging from a window will be the sign. As soon as you see it, cross the rear bridge and wait under that window. Bring whoever Cyrus appoints with you. We will have some precious cargo to move. Now go, quickly." Jeremias handed Juvenal several gold coins from inside his robe. Ascending the stairs to the third floor, Juvenal turned toward the servant quarters, Jeremias back toward the chapel. Juvenal barely had time to get down the back stairs and through the kitchen, before the castle came to life. People were yelling everywhere. Juvenal bolted out the back door and across the small bridge just before it was raised. He knew he had to get those horses, and he didn't have much time.

## CHAPTER 27

# Several Hours Earlier

When Judas and Ephraim emerged from the kitchen, they were immediately spied by General Zarak, who was waiting in the front entryway. "Judas, your father wants to see you right away." He stared at Ephraim. "I'm certain he meant alone. He's in his chambers."

Both Judas and Ephraim climbed the stairs to the king's rooms. Zarak wasn't about to yield easily. He directed his deep voice toward Ephraim, "Boy, where do you think you are going?"

"He has information the king must hear. He is with me. I promise you, you will not want the king to wait for what he has to say," Judas responded with as much authority as he could muster. While it was true that as crown prince he did have certain authority, his youth meant that most senior officials felt as though they outranked him. That wouldn't last too much longer, Judas thought to himself.

Two guards blocked the doorway that opened onto the hallway from which the king's suite of rooms were entered. A nod from Judas gained them entrance, but he noticed that one of the guards looked over the banister to where Zarak stood before stepping aside. Apparently General Zarak decided not to call Judas' bluff. After all, the only information Ephraim had was the story of Eli's transfer of power. And in reality, they had no way to prove that the story was true. Getting the staff depended on convincing the king that Ephraim really was the first mage.

The first door past the royal dining room was the king's study. They knocked on the door and were admitted by one of the king's personal servants. Judas sat himself in a comfortable chair near the door; Ephraim stood behind him.

"Did *you* find anything, Judas?" the king asked bitingly as he entered the room, chewing on a large drumstick.

"No, sir. No one has seen anything and they left no trail at all. We even had Sam try to follow a scent, but that didn't work either," Judas explained.

"Sam wouldn't be much help, I expect. Those two seemed to fly into the Grove, as I recall. They probably didn't even leave any trail at all." The king seemed dejected and irritated at the same time. "We must find those two at any cost. If they get linked up with Obsidia, we will never survive." As if noticing Ephraim for the first time, the king continued, "What are you doing here? And who are you?" he asked.

"This is Ephraim, father. I have brought him with me because he has an incredible story that I think you must hear. You remember him, I think, from the Grove. He is the boy who stood in my place," Judas said, instructively.

"Ah, yes. Well, be quick about it, I have more to do today than ever I can remember." The king quietly shut the door behind him as Ephraim spoke. Behind that door was a short hallway which led just a few steps to the king's personal lounge. He must have been taking lunch in there today.

Ephraim began to explain his relationship to Eli. When the king hurried him along again, he jumped to the part about the spell that Eli cast in the Grove, about the transfer of power before Eli died…or left…or whatever he did, and about the voices in his head. He explained that he had been told by Eli to get the staff and begin to train to become first mage.

From the moment that Ephraim mentioned the transfer of power, the king stood silently. When Ephraim was finished, the room was silent.

"Who are your parents, lad?" the king questioned.

"I don't know, Your Majesty. They died years ago. Eli brought me to the castle, where he and Ella have looked after me, while I worked in the kitchens."

"I see. Is there any way you can prove to me that this story is true and not just some treasonous plot to get the staff of power into your hands?" the king asked pointedly.

Ephraim paused, silent. "No, Your Majesty. I have been thinking about how I might prove this story to you, but there is no possible way to do it. In my defense, I can say that Ella believes me. Beyond that there is nothing I can say." Ephraim stopped speaking.

The king mumbled something, not more than a word or two. His eyes bore into Ephraim, and Ephraim had the feeling that his very soul was being examined. Five, six, seven seconds of complete silence followed, while the king stared. Suddenly, Judas blurted into the silence, "Father, use your..."

"Judas! Quiet! Don't speak another word! Will you never learn?" the king asked harshly.

Judas' face fell. He had stood to his feet when his father entered the room, now he slumped into the chair behind him, deflated.

"Ephraim," the king began, "I can see your story is true. I certainly do not understand why Eli chose to desert us at a time like this. But if he has chosen you as his replacement, that is good enough for me. Let us go and get the staff. Follow me."

The king turned quickly around and headed through the doors toward his private apartment. Ephraim followed Judas, who followed the king. Tossing the bone he had been chewing onto the serving tray, the king reached out to grab another as he walked passed the young boy who was tending the meal. As his hand latched onto the turkey leg, the whole tray came out of the hands of the boy, crashed down onto the floor and showered the king with turkey parts and pieces. "Fool!" the king shouted. "Clumsy fool! Get this cleaned up immediately and report back to the kitchen. Tell Ella you are never to serve in my quarters again. And not at any state occasion, either. You're lucky I don't put you out of the castle for good."

The king wiped off his shirt while the boy quickly gathered the food that had spilled in front of the doorway to the king's bedroom. "Stand out of the way. We can't afford to wait for you." The king pushed open the door and entered the room, with Judas and Ephraim right on his heels. This wasn't a place that Judas had been very often.

"Judas, shut the door," the king ordered. "It is time for you two to know things that must not be shared with anyone else. I am about to show you the secrets of the royal armory, as well as uncover some of the mysteries of the kingdom. Once you know these things, you are a potential threat to the kingdom. An enemy that successfully kidnapped you could gain critical information about our security, our strength, and other things that will be soon apparent. That can never happen. From today, until the day that you are able to begin using your powers, you may not leave the second level of the castle, Ephraim. You may, of course, travel to the chapel on the third floor. I would install you in Eli's rooms immediately, but Ella still inhabits them. Until tomorrow, you will stay in Judas' room with him.

"Judas, when Eli gave you the royal ruby, you were magically bound to the Ruby Kingdom. From that point on, if you ever tried to willingly betray the kingdom, the ruby itself would begin to throb in your head, eventually driving you mad. That doesn't mean you can't do something stupid that would destroy the kingdom, it only means that if you INTEND to harm the kingdom, the ruby would try to prevent you. Ephraim, the same will be true for you when you accept this staff. The ruby in the staff acts in a similar manner. In addition to harboring all the manipulative power of the mage, the staff binds mage to kingdom. And although the binding will take place quickly, you will not be able to unleash any of the power of the staff until you master at least some of the training that is required of all mages.

"Ephraim, are you willing to be bound to this kingdom? Are you willing to serve both the land and the king?" the king asked regally.

Ephraim's head was bowed. He never dreamed he would ever be in a place like this! Imagine! Standing before the king, about to be bound to the kingdom! He was shaking with nervousness, as he slowly lifted his head and met the king's gaze. "I am willing, Your Majesty. I will serve as best as I can."

For the first time since they entered the king's chambers, a smile crossed the king's face. "So you shall, Ephraim. So you shall." The king turned and walked quickly over to the wall opposite the tower entrance. Placing his hand on his chest, and one hand on the wall,

he closed his eyes and paused. In a moment, a crack appeared verti-
cally in the wall. As the king withdrew his hand, a section of the wall
opened into the room. The king stepped inside. "Join me," he said,
without looking back.

Judas stepped into the closet, Ephraim on his heels. The room
was dark, except for where the light of the bedroom spilled into it.
Suddenly, the entire closet was bright. Ephraim turned to see the
hand of the king glowing brightly. It was an odd sight, seeing a glowing hand. Ephraim didn't know that the king was a mage as well. He
was just thinking that there was more to this king than he ever suspected, when the king gasped. "It's gone! Impossible! No one could
have gotten in here except me." He paused. "Or another member of
the royal family." He glared at Judas. "Judas, did you enter this room
while I was gone?" a second later he added, "Truth!"

Judas recognized the spell. "No, Father, I did not enter this
room. Before today, I did not even know it existed."

The king relaxed slightly, but he was still highly agitated. "Someone has attacked us, here, in the very heart of our defenses. This is
more serious than I can ever begin to describe." The king shouted to
his servants, "Call for Zarak. Get him in here at once! Seal the castle!
Judas, you and Ephraim wait in your room."

Judas had been staring at an unusual horn that was hanging on
the wall of the armory before the king addressed him. As the king
strode out of the room, his attention was drawn back to the horn.
It was silver, polished to a high luster, with a scarlet cord wrapped
around the mouthpiece and tied to the tubing. It was beautifully
wrought, and seemed to call to Judas.

"Judas, Ephraim, get moving!" the king shouted. The shout
broke the trance Judas was in, and the two boys moved quickly out of
the king's chambers, being careful to stay out of the king's way. By the
time they reached the doorway out of the king's apartments, Zarak
was on his way in.

Zarak glared at the boys, assuming that they had upset the king,
but there was no time to explain otherwise. The boys walked down
the hallway at the top of the stairs and headed straight to Judas' room.

This hallway was open on one side to the main entryway into the castle, so the boys could see the front door as they passed back toward their destination. Guards were already shutting the doors. The drawbridge was on its way up. The castle was being sealed.

Judas and Ephraim stepped through the door into the small alcove that separated the main hallway from Judas' bedroom. Reaching out a hand, Judas stopped Ephraim and signaled for silence. Gesturing, he indicated that he thought someone was in his room. The door to the room was ever so slightly ajar. Judas inched up to the crack by the door hinges and peeked into his own room. His suspicions had been right. They were waiting for him inside!

## CHAPTER 28

# Juvenal

Finding the Black Pegasus was easy compared with getting out of the castle. When Juvenal got near the door, Ella appeared. And after the return of the servant who had served the king lunch, she was in a foul mood, too. The poor servant couldn't remember anything about the afternoon, and Ella couldn't decide what to do about it. Exasperated, she sent the servant to work in the basement, while she began preparation of an extra-special evening meal, designed to win over an antagonistic king. When Ella went down into the cellar to select wines for the evening meal, Juvenal slipped out the back door.

He exited the city by way of the postern gate, and found the stables he was seeking about 100 yards north west of the walls. Cyrus was a crusty old man, but when Juvenal mentioned "Darkwing", he seemed to come to life.

"How many horses did you say, youngster?" he barked.

"We need four. Whatever you need should be added to that," Juvenal answered, trying to sound as if he really understood what he was talking about.

"Then we'll need six horses altogether. Where is the coin that will purchase these steeds?" Cyrus asked.

Juvenal pulled out the coins that Jeremias had given him. Gold coins. Large coins so valuable that Cyrus had only rarely seen them. Juvenal pressed three coins into Cyrus' hand, which closed upon them quickly.

"Done. We meet you when?" Cyrus questioned.

"You're to have a man waiting with the horses outside the postern gate at nightfall. I will be with him. The other man comes with me inside the city walls to help remove the parcels." Juvenal instructed.

"There is the problem of guards," Cyrus observed.

"Inside the castle, that is our problem. Outside the castle, that is yours. Would you like to earn an extra coin against some additional labor?" Juvenal inquired.

"It depends on the size of the labor and the weight of the coin," Cyrus clipped.

"Same coin. We need supplies sent to, you know where. Two weeks for six people. The supplies should be sent as soon as they are ready, well ahead of us." Juvenal waited while Cyrus did some figuring.

"The supply horse is mine on the other side of this venture?" haggled Cyrus.

"Yes," Juvenal answered, hoping it was the right answer.

"Again, done," Cyrus said crisply. "A pleasure doing business with you, lad," as he held out his hand. Juvenal pressed the last gold coin into Cyrus' greedy hand.

"Tonight at the wall," Juvenal repeated, as he walked out of the Black Pegasus.

CHAPTER 29

# Stealthy Slumber

Judas thought about calling for guards, but then decided it might be best for him to solve this problem himself. Peeking through the crack in the door, Judas could clearly make out the back of one head. He had no way of knowing how many people were in his room, but he knew he could put at least one of them to sleep. Just maybe, if one were to suddenly fall asleep, he could seize that moment of distraction to enter the room and face the remainder. If there weren't more than two or three others, Judas would be able to quickly subdue them as well. Judas motioned for Ephraim to stand aside, while he touched his ruby, and spoke the word of power, "Sleep!" He waited two seconds, then opened the door quickly and jumped into the room facing the group behind the door. "Sleep!" he shouted.

And sleep they did, all three of them. He had been surprised to see the faces of Sirs Jonathan and Gregory staring back at him when he leaped into the room, but he was already committed to his course of action, and he wasn't able to stop himself from putting them to sleep. But the sleeping young lady that now lay on his bedroom floor was completely unfamiliar to him. He called for Ephraim to enter and shut the door behind him.

"Ah, I see you have caught the escaping mages. Your father will be very pleased," Ephraim observed.

"I think it would be better if I found out what their intentions are before I announce that they are in my custody. I am still uneasy about what happened in the throne room yesterday," Judas explained. "I believe I will awaken the youngest of them, and see what I can learn."

"Sir Gregory, wake up!" Prince Judas said, releasing the spell.

Gregory came slowly awake, rubbing a spot on his head that must have hit the floor when he fell. "Put me to sleep again, did you? I hope you know I don't like middle of the day naps."

"I'm sorry about that, but I had no way of knowing who was in my room. Usually it is empty when I return to it," Judas replied.

"Okay. Next time we will leave the pebble and wait outside. Now, will you wake up Jon and Annie, please?" Greg asked patiently.

"In a moment," Judas responded, "but first I'd like to ask you a few questions. Do you remem..."

"Is something wrong, Prince Judas," Greg interrupted, "that you don't trust us? Has something changed since the last time we were here?"

"I don't understand. Why would you ask that?" Judas dissembled.

"Well, last time we were here, you were saving our lives. Now you are questioning us individually...and I'm not really all that comfortable with my brother laying here asleep, along with a friend on her first visit to the castle...a friend, I might add, that Eli personally sent here." Greg finished and waited for a response.

"Eli sent her here?" Ephraim gushed, powerless to suppress his surprise.

"That's what I said," Greg added, distantly.

Judas looked puzzled for a moment, then a light dawned on his face. Squinching up his eyes, he said, "Truth," and stared at Greg.

Greg looked away, suddenly uncomfortable. Ephraim stared at Judas. "What did you do, Prince Judas?" he asked.

"Later," he whispered. "Sir Gregory, I am sorry. Forgive my suspicious nature, but much has happened in your absence. Sir Jonathan, please wake up. And you, young lady, please awaken as well."

Jon and Annie slowly worked their way to consciousness, while Judas gestured for Greg to sit on the bed. Ephraim chose to stand near the window, and Greg assisted Annie to her feet, before sitting beside her on Judas' mattress. Jon sat on the floor, leaning against the bed. "What was that all about, O Prince?" Jon inquired.

"We scared him," Greg injected. "He didn't know who was in here, so he put us all to sleep. We covered this while you were napping. The prince is about to bring us up to speed on what has happened since we left."

"Oh," was the sum total of Jon's response.

"Forgive me, Annie. This is Prince Judas, crown prince of the Ruby Kingdom. This is Ephraim, if I remember correctly, the guy who got us involved in this whole mess in the first place. Gentlemen, this is Annie Monagul, sixth grader from the Kingdom of Newport."

"Actually, I am going into seventh grade this fall," Annie corrected.

"Excuse me," Greg corrected, bowing slightly toward Annie, "Seventh grader from the Kingdom of Newport in Rhode Island."

"At your service, milady," Prince Judas replied, reaching for her hand.

Annie quickly pulled her hand back from him before he had the chance to kiss it. "None of that. Just call me Annie. What shall I call you two?"

"Prince Judas," and "Ephraim," sounded at the same moment, followed by an, "I'm sorry," from Ephraim. Judas grinned.

"I'm glad that Eli sent you, but I would like to know why. Do you have any idea what you are supposed to do here?" Judas asked, warmly.

"No idea at all," Annie replied. "I didn't even know there was a Ruby Kingdom until a few moments ago. I am about as baffled as I have ever been in my life. I have no idea where I really am!"

"Well, let me see if I can help," Judas suggested. He began by explaining a little of the story of the conflict between the kingdoms, and gradually brought the situation up to date. He explained about the search for Jon and Greg, and then added the details of the search for the missing staff. The very idea of spies in the castle was terribly scary, and the fact that one had penetrated the king's bedroom meant that nothing was safe. The castle was in a high state of alarm, and as the nature of the danger became known, things would only get worse.

Judas explained how important the staff was, and then, against his better judgment, decided to let Jon and Greg know Ephraim's secret. "If my father knows that I told you that Ephraim is First Mage, he will be very angry. Please keep our secret. He is afraid someone will try to harm him to keep the kingdom weak. That is why we have been sent to this room. There will be two guards outside our door by now. We will not be allowed out until the entire castle is searched. In fact, you should probably leave soon. It is quite possible that the king might even assign a guard to stay with us inside our room!"

Jon spoke up when Judas had finished. "Perhaps we can help where others cannot. Searching for a spy is a difficult thing, for the spy knows he is being sought. Of course, it is most likely that the spy is someone known to you, just unsuspected of treason. He will only give himself away when no one is watching him. If we followed suspects within the castle while invisible, we might be able to catch someone doing something unusual, someone who thought they were unobserved."

Judas recognized the sense of the plan. "We would want to watch the actions of individuals who thought they were alone, to see if they did anything suspicious. But how would we choose who to follow?" Judas wondered.

"I think the best plan is for Judas and I to go on an invisible ride through the castle. We can follow an individual for as long as we need, until we are certain they are not compromised. That way we can check out several people and no one will be aware that they are being watched," Jon suggested. "Judas, you'll have to choose who we follow. But don't forget, the spy may be someone you trust. We need to think about people who had an opportunity to steal the staff."

"I think you guys better get started," Greg remarked. "The longer you wait, the more likely the thief will escape, if he hasn't already. Time is wasting."

"You three stay here. Don't leave this room for any reason. We will be back as soon as we can," Jon instructed.

"Uh, one detail we have overlooked, I think," Judas interrupted. "How are we going to take this invisible ride?" After the events in the

Throne room, he suspected that Jon and Greg had a way of getting around invisibly, but he certainly didn't know what it was.

"Well, it is an afternoon for trading secrets," Jon explained. Taking the carpet off his back, he quickly unrolled it. Greg held the staff while Jon smoothed out the wrinkles. Taking the staff in his hands, Jon fastened it to the carpet. Ephraim and Judas simply stared. Already standing on the carpet, Jon invited Judas to join him: "Hop on, Prince Judas. If there are guards at our door, we better find another window to enter." Pulling on the staff, the carpet rose into the air about a foot. Then with the twist of a switch, the whole thing disappeared!

Ephraim gasped! And even though Annie knew what was happening, she gasped, too! When she was on the carpet, she had been able to see the other boys, even though they were all invisible to everyone else. But she had never seen anything simply vanish into thin air before!

"Now make sure you stay here," Judas' voice spoke out of nothingness.

"We'll be back as soon as we can," Jon added. Then there was silence.

After a few seconds, Annie sighed. "Incredible!" she said. "I've never seen anything like it!"

"Me, either!" Ephraim exclaimed. "You guys must be powerful mages to have magical items of such ability!"

"No, we're not mages," Greg explained, while Ephraim stared at the place Jon and Judas had just been. "We're just kids who have gotten tangled up in some big mess. Eli seems to think there is some purpose in it, but it is hard for me to understand," Greg explained.

Annie sank back into the bed, while Greg sat on a trunk against the wall. Ephraim had wandered over to the window, trying to see where Jon and Judas had gone. Once he realized that there was nothing to see, he turned and sat against the wall, under the window.

Their conversation drifted from Eli, to magic, to the present crisis, and continued on. Other than a sense of being lost in a greater struggle, these three didn't have much in common. Greg and Annie talked about how their world was different from this one. Ephraim helped them understand a little of the history of the Gemstone Islands. From national history, they made their way to personal history. After Annie told of her fear that she wouldn't make any friends in her new home town, Greg confessed to the same feelings. Although it was good to have an older brother, every kid wanted a best buddy, right? Ephraim barely understood the conversation. He had no true friends, other than Eli and Ella. His life amounted to work, work and more work. He had been a servant all his life. He dreamed of a day when he might have a family of his own, if the king allowed him to take a wife. He had hoped for a chance to become a squire, so that he might improve his station in life. But that hadn't happened. Until a week ago, he had been afraid it was too late for him. Now that he was the First Mage, he wasn't sure what was possible.

Without knowing it, the sharing of their stories created a trust among them. Subconscious defenses tumbled as the hours passed by. Night would soon fall. They began to wonder what was taking Judas and Jon so long, when finally they heard someone coming into the vestibule outside the room. They hoped Jon and Judas had remembered to bring them some dinner!

CHAPTER 30

# Reconnaissance

Judas' first inclination was to seek out General Zarak. It wasn't that he didn't trust the general; it was just that the general was always around his father and certainly had opportunity. And Judas was certain his father would never suspect Zarak. The general was his father's right hand man, and he was more than a little ambitious, it seemed to Judas. Artezes, the senior general, was significantly older than Zarak. Though revered by the soldiers, Artezes was outclassed by the vigor, prowess and tactical ability of his junior partner. Technically, Zarak was in charge of foot soldiers, while Artezes marshaled the cavalry. Together, they were the military.

Judas indicated that Jon should fly in through the open round window in the peak of the front facade of the castle. This placed them high above the main entryway and in view of traffic on two floors of the castle. Fortunately, Zarak was just emerging from the king's apartments, and was easily followed.

After speaking to the guards by the royal apartments, Zarak cut through the kitchen and headed out the back door of the castle, making his way toward the garrison. Jon couldn't follow through the kitchen door, and so he cut back through the front window and picked up Zarak outside. The garrison was along the western wall of the city, flanked by the stables. Zarak walked straight into the main building, and it was obvious that his presence generated significant movement. In a matter of moments, soldiers were running in several different directions, off to take up protective positions around the castle and at strategic points within the city as well. A few minutes more saw groups of two soldiers each meandering through the shops and businesses inside the wall, plying businessmen with questions, seeking information. Zarak remained inside the garrison.

Flying close to an open window, the boys could see that Zarak was now alone inside the building, except for one other soldier. The front door was shut, then locked. Once the door had been secured, the soldier returned to the table at which Zarak sat. The two began to talk.

"Anthony, there is going to be war," Zarak confessed, "and I don't like our chances. The staff of the first mage has been stolen from the king's private armory. I don't know how that is even possible. I can't bring myself to believe that the king would lie about something like that. But I know he is itching to wipe the Obsidian Kingdom off the face of the earth. Part of me wonders if this is an excuse to mobilize our forces to attack them while they are weak. Perhaps he can scare us into believing we must attack first. I don't know. The other possibility is worse.

"If the staff really has been stolen, then an enemy knows we are without a first mage. If they were responsible for its removal, then they know our weakness. We would be very vulnerable to any magical attack right now. Candidly, we don't have a second mage, either. The Obsidian Kingdom knows both our mages were killed. But they also lost mages on the Great Board. What if their strategy included keeping their strongest mages back in the kingdom, while lesser mages fought on the board? What if the Obsidian King was goaded by his countrymen into a challenge he didn't really want to make? In that case, we could be facing a full scale invasion of armed and magical forces. We would be sitting ducks." Zarak stopped.

Judas was amazed that Zarak would talk so candidly to a subordinate officer. Judas didn't really know who Anthony was, but the kind of information Zarak was sharing was highly confidential. He began to wonder where this conversation was going.

"I think you should consider leaving, Anthony," Zarak continued.

"But father, that would be desertion!" Anthony protested. "I would never desert—especially when my kingdom needs me!"

"Retreat isn't desertion, my son," Zarak countered. "You are the most able young officer I have. You make good choices consistently. You are a valuable asset to this kingdom." He paused. "And you are much more likely to survive an all out assault, should one come, if you were not around here. Besides, there is another reason why you must survive this fight. Should the king perish, an usurper would likely steal the throne for a time. There must be a remnant in hiding, slowly gathering support, to vindicate us. I would expect the king to send Judas into exile, should the fighting get bleak. You would need to ally yourself with him, so that together you could one day reclaim the throne."

"With Judas?" Anthony said disgustedly. "That little weasel has never done anything worthy of nobility. He hides from the Grove and shirks his duty."

"Do you really believe he had a choice concerning the Grove? As long as his father is king, Judas also is a subject. One who obeys orders."

"But Father, if the king had been confident of Judas' abilities, he would not have had to give the order for him to stay behind. He shirks his duty by not preparing for it," Anthony explained, with frustration in his voice.

By this time, Judas was not only embarrassed, he was angry. He was ready to get involved in this discussion, but Jon had a hand on his arm and managed to control him. He mouthed the word, "Later" to Judas. Judas understood. Sometimes the mission was more important than the details.

"I believe that you will find there is more to Judas once you get to know him, should you ever get that opportunity. Next year he will begin training with the guard. Maybe then you can get a better measure of the man," Zarak advised.

"I would gladly spar with him. I'm certain I could teach him a few things," Anthony grinned.

"As could any soldier worth his salt, who had a ten year advantage on his opponent." The grin left Anthony's face. "Son, you must look beyond your own reputation and abilities to the character that dwells within you. Unless you are willing to sacrifice personal fame for the cause of the kingdom, you are not truly qualified to serve at all. You may achieve fame, but if that is your goal, it will come at a horrible price."

Anthony was a little confused. His father was a famous general. Everyone knew he was the most gifted military man in the kingdom, even superior to the king. That was why the king so heavily relied on him. But he had never considered why his father served as he did. "Father, if this king ordered you to betray the kingdom, would you obey his orders?" Anthony asked.

Zarak responded slowly and cautiously. "The king would not order me to betray the kingdom. He cannot because he is bound to serve the kingdom, just as I am. My bonds are moral and internal, his are physical and magical. But they are both equally powerful. Now should the king order me to do something foolish that would amount to betrayal of the kingdom, I would argue with him mightily in private. And then I would have to make a decision. I would either have to follow his order, or surrender to his justice. Perhaps he would allow me to go into exile. I would not want to be in a position like that."

"But it could happen. This king isn't exactly wise, is he?" Anthony tentatively inquired.

"He may not be kind or gracious, but I believe he is shrewd. And I have no doubt about this loyalty to the kingdom. I'm not sure how much more you can ask. But, Anthony, this discussion is not about the king, it is about you. Who are you? Where do your commitments lie?" Zarak pressed.

"I am loyal to the king and to my superior officers. I will do as I am commanded. And if the day comes, no matter how much it galls me, I will serve Judas loyally."

His father smiled. "That is all anyone can ask. Now, hide a horse outside of town to the north. Pack supplies for a week long excursion. If you ever see me with a green cloth tied around my neck, depart immediately. In fact, if you ever see me holding anything green at all, get out of town."

"As you wish, General," Anthony saluted.

"I'm proud of you, my son," and Zarak saluted back.

Judas was seething as Jon pulled away. He couldn't believe anyone would say about him the things he had just heard. Those things weren't true. And no one had the right to say them. He would show them. He would get even. He would...

Jon interrupted his thoughts, taking the carpet about five hundred feet up into the air. It was instantly cold. "Judas, don't be embarrassed. People don't know you yet. Soon you..."

"But he had no right to accuse me of cowardice. I am not shirking my responsibility. I train with weapons every day. I ride and shoot the bow. I am an excellent swordsman for my age. It isn't fair that..."

"Judas, cool down. You are letting your pride get in the way of what you can learn here. Anthony's observations are based on rumors and on limited information. But you have learned a great deal today. First of all, you know who is loyal. That is a gift beyond measure. You now know two men who will serve faithfully. And you also know what you will have to do to earn the respect of the future captain of your guard. Knowing what you need to do is the first step in getting there. If you learn from this, rather than getting offended, you will be on your way to proving who you really are."

Judas thought about his words. The more he thought about it, the more he could see Anthony's perspective. Yes, he would have a great deal of work to do in order to earn the respect of his people, if he ever could. And if he wasn't on the throne at the time, that respect would be all the more important!

"I think we can rule out Zarak as a spy. Who else might we consider?" Jon asked Judas.

'I don't know. Let's go back into the castle and sit in the main entry way. If we hover high above the floor invisibly, maybe we will see something suspicious," Judas suggested. Flying high across the southwestern turret, they did exactly that.

Servants ran hither and yon inside the castle, but most were familiar to Judas. They followed several to see where they were going and what they were doing. Now that the castle doors were sealed, there was no traffic in or out. Dinner was served to the king in his room as evening began to fall. Judas was about to give up, but Jon insisted they continue a little longer.

"If I were going to escape from the castle, I would do it at night. What time does the guard change?" Jon asked.

"Midnight," Judas replied. "That would be the time of greatest confusion."

"Then let's do this. Let's head down to the kitchen and get ourselves some food. After that, let's check in on Greg, Ephraim and Anne. They will have eaten by then. After dinner, we should post one lookout at each window on every side of the castle. I think we should watch until one hour after midnight. If someone is trying to escape, they will attempt to distract the guard. But if we are watching from above, perhaps we can catch something that they might miss."

Judas thought the plan made sense, and so off to the kitchen they flew. Making their way into the garbage room, they waited for an opportune moment for Judas to get off the carpet. Jon remained hidden, but Judas strolled in and grabbed a huge plateful of food. Ella was no where to be seen, and there was no one else in the kitchen who would dare challenge him. He stepped back into the garbage room, shutting the door behind him. Alone again, he got back onto the carpet where Jon waited. They ate in silence, eight feet off the ground. The temptation to shoot chicken bones into the garbage barrel on the other side of the room was more than they could resist. The contest came to an abrupt halt, however, when the door suddenly swung open and a serving girl entered carrying a bucket of slop. She thought she saw something fly through the sky toward the far corner, and she definitely heard a thump. She completely froze, and looked carefully around the room. Seeing nothing, she put the bucket down on the floor where she stood, and bolted back into the kitchen, slamming the door behind her.

Jon giggled, but knew it was time to get back. Unfortunately, the door to the kitchen was shut, and the exit to the outside was sealed. Getting back without being seen was going to be a problem. Jon mentioned as much to Judas, who told him to fly over toward the back wall. Reaching out his hand, Judas touched the wall at exactly the spot that corresponded with the bump on the opposite side of the same wall. In a few seconds, a secret door slid open, and the boys flew in, careful to shut the door behind them. Landing the carpet on the floor, it was quickly rolled and tied to Jon's back.

"You're full of surprises!" Jon whispered to Judas once they were safely inside.

"I do my best," he replied, obviously pleased with himself. "Follow me. We'll be back in the room in just a moment." Judas made his finger glow, which earned him ever greater respect from Jon, whom he led around the corner and up the narrow, secret stairs.

When they arrived at the room, Judas decided to peek before entering. Unfortunately, the room was dark. He couldn't see anything. He thought that was odd, but decided to enter anyway. Stepping through the secret entrance, Judas found the room completely empty. This didn't make any sense at all. Jon was right behind him.

"Greg, Ephraim, Annie, where are you?" Jon half-whispered. There was a sense of urgency in his voice that was unmistakable. There was a rustling from under the bed. Jon called for his knife, and Judas drew a small dagger that was strapped under the leg of his trousers.

"Who ever is under that bed...come out slowly," Judas announced sternly, jumping up onto the bed himself.

"Don't hurt me," a small voice crackled from under the bed. "I'm coming out."

As soon as the first tuft of hair protruded out from under the bed frame, Judas had his dagger poised to strike, just inches away. As the head emerged, Judas stared down into the eyes of...Greg, who looked up to see the blade of a knife, two inches from his face.

"Greg, what are you doing under there? Where is everyone else?" Judas asked all in a rush.

"They're gone! They've been taken—kidnapped!" he cried, despondently.

## CHAPTER 31

# Jeremias' Subterfuge

Jeremias had quite a few things to take care of before departing. And he knew that the next few hours would likely be the most dangerous of his life. Getting into the prince's apartments wouldn't be all that hard. It was the getting out that would be hairy.

The very idea of taking Ephraim out one of the two exits from the castle was preposterous. With security tight as a drum, he would have a hard enough time escaping on his own. But with an extra bundle? Not likely. The only way out was through a window, and that would only be possible at night. Midnight was the obvious time for his escape, since the changing of the guard would create confusion. But Jeremias believed that the king was looking for someone to escape, and so it made sense to assume that the king would know his own weaknesses. No, the king would expect an escape around midnight.

After a good deal of consideration, Jeremias worked out a plan: As soon as the "packages" (Ephraim, and Judas, if he was present) were ready to be transported, a large jar of combustible oil would be pushed out a third floor window on the eastern side of the castle. A wick in the jar would insure a rapid fire that would spread quickly. A flaming arrow shot into the roof of the shop across from the castle would assure two fires and plenty of diversion. Fire on both sides of the moat would cause the back bridge to be let down. While the guard was fighting the fire, they would quickly lower the bundles by rope, exiting the castle through the windows of the prince's room. If all went as planned, they could be across the back bridge and out of the city inside of five minutes. Of course, it was hard to believe that all would go as planned. A large portion of this plan rested on the success of a young boy. Would Juvenal really be able to make all the necessary arrangements? In time?

Jeremias realized that the best he could do was be ready, and wait. And perhaps there was some time to create a little more mischief before he left. Part of his training in the monastery included herbology. He understood the effects that various plants could have on the human body. He also had a good collection of herbs and spices in his room. Knowing that *sparkweed* would make a person nauseous and ineffective in battle, Jeremias decided to improve his army's chances by "seasoning" the food in the kitchen pantry.

He would be able to send his brother the message to attack in the morning. If by evening folks were starting to get sick, the level of panic in the castle would rise dramatically. When the king saw his troops unable to fight, he might even decide to surrender, though that was unlikely. The most Jeremias could really hope to achieve was to swing the odds further in his brother's favor.

Taking his full stock of sparkweed into his robe, Jeremias entered the kitchen just before the mad rush to prepare the evening meal. The stew that was boiling in the pot smelled delicious; Jeremias dumped half the contents of his package into the large caldron. Glancing across the counter, he saw a vat of fat, and several other barrels of ingredients waiting to be turned into various delectables for the staff and guard. He walked casually past them, keeping his face on the two servants in the room. His hands worked behind him, carefully sowing the sparkweed into several containers. Not surprisingly, he felt a little guilty about the servants and helpers who would suffer the effects of his spices. Their only crime was that they served a selfish, arrogant king. But only for a little longer, Jeremias thought to himself.

As he turned to leave the kitchen, a growling noise began directly below his left knee. He was surprised to see an old dog, obviously very tense, threatening him with bared teeth. At just that moment, Ella entered the kitchen from the side storage room.

"Sam, ya cut that out." she barked. "Shameless dog, barks at anythin'. Is there somethin' ya'd be wantin', Father?"

Startled at the sudden appearance of another person, Jeremias stuttered for a second, and backed away from Sam. "I was just looking for a crust of bread, kind woman. I'm on a fast of anything more substantial than bread and water right now, and I was hoping to find a small loaf I could take to my room. I'd like to spend tomorrow undisturbed." He smiled piously.

"O' course, Father," she nodded as she spoke. "And I'll tell the servants not ta bother ya in the mornin', if that is yer wish." She opened a small cabinet and pulled out a large crusty roll which she gave to the priest.

"I appreciate your kindness. And you should consider fasting yourself. It is good for your soul," he added, hoping she might take him seriously.

"Thank ya, Father. But after all, I must keep up appearances. Who'd want ta eat the food of a thin cook?" she laughed, as he hurried out the door.

One last trip back to his room was all that was necessary. He gathered everything he needed for the trip, set up the incendiary device in the eastern window, and double checked his inventory. He would not have an assistant in the castle, so he would have to do everything himself.

Jeremias descended the steps from the third floor, pushed through the door that led to the second floor hallway, and proceeded around the balcony overlooking the main entry to the door of the prince's room. A guard was posted there, and Jeremias spoke with him quietly.

"The king has instructed me to come to Prince Judas' room to offer my support and counsel. Would you please go in with me and announce my arrival to the prince?" Jeremias asked kindly.

"Certainly, Father. Come with me."

As soon as the door was open and the guard was inside, Jeremias put him to sleep, catching him before he hit the floor. He leaned the body behind the door, and moved toward the inner door to the prince's room. He could hear movement inside and knew he would have to hurry.

"Prince Judas, did you bring us anything to eat?" a voice from inside was saying as they opened the door to the entry corridor. As the door swung open, Ephraim saw the priest, curiosity showing in his face. Before he could speak, however, he, too, was falling asleep. Jeremias caught him and gently laid him down on the floor. From somewhere back in the room, Jeremias heard another voice, and when he turned and looked through the door, a young girl was approaching.

She managed to say, "Ephraim, what's the matter?" before Jeremias spoke the word "*sleep*" for the third time. The flickering candlelight revealed the rest of the room to be empty. Jeremias knew he had to work quickly. First, he placed a white cloth on the windowsill, praying Juvenal would immediately recognize the sign. Then he slid the bodies to the window and maneuvered them into burlap bags, covering their heads with pillow cases. He got one rope out from under his robes, secured it to the door, preparing it to be thrown from the window. He moved the guard into the queen's room, and then, shutting the external door, made his way back to the third floor room where the oil pot was waiting. He lit the arrow first, then shot it across the moat into the roof of the shop straight before him. Then he knocked the pot out the window. It smashed and the wick did its job. Flames were roaring in just seconds, and even the oil that slipped into the moat was burning. Jeremias turned and ran down the steps.

Slowing his steps as he passed out the doorway into the second floor hallway, he suppressed the urge to run and gracefully walked toward the prince's room. There was no guard, of course, and he casually let himself in.

Once at the window, he strained his eyes towards the ground, looking for Juvenal. No one was there. He cursed his luck and began to think about what he should do. If Juvenal did not show up, all he could do was escape himself. He couldn't be certain that Ephraim would not remember his face. His cover would be blown. As he watched out the window, he heard an alarm raised, and saw the garrison empty, soldiers running around the back side of the castle. He watched, wondering how much time he could afford to wait for his accomplices. He didn't have to wait long. While the guard was still emptying out of the barracks, Jeremias saw a shadowy figure slide around the back corner of the castle, inside the moat. There was a thin strip of land between castle and moat, and it was on this land that first one, then two people approached the window at which Jeremias stood. Juvenal! And he had help!

Jeremias tied one bag shut with one of the ropes, and lowered the bundle through the window. The men below caught the package gently. A second bundle was quickly lowered and was followed by a man half climbing, half sliding down the face of the wall. There was no time to be concerned about ropes; they were left hanging. Juvenal ran ahead, while Jeremias carried one bundle, his new accomplice the other. They crossed the small bridge at the back of the castle, among guards carrying buckets from the kitchen toward the fire. The general pandemonium on the other side of the castle effectively kept folks from noticing what was plainly before their eyes. Lots of folks saw the three men leave the area. But what they saw were two men trying to rescue possessions from a fire. No one even gave a second thought to what might be in the bundles. Not until it was too late!

CHAPTER 32

# Kidnapped!

Sliding out from under the bed, Greg barely had enough energy to stand. He slouched onto the bed, visibly shaken. The light from Judas' finger was disconcerting, and Jon asked if some candles could be lit, so that they could see what they were doing. Judas lit the candles, while Jon sat next to Greg on the bed and asked what had happened. Judas proceeded to examine the rope that was tied to the bedroom door and led out the window, down to the ground below.

"We waited for a long time for you to come back. Finally, we heard you entering the outside corridor, so Ephraim opened the door to let you in. I was sitting here, on this side of the bed, when I heard you. I stood to walk over to the door, but Ephraim collapsed as soon as the door opened. Annie was right behind him. She started to say something, when I heard someone on the outside say, "Sleep!" I immediately hit the floor, here behind the bed. I stayed as still as I could. I was able to see a little of what was happening by looking under the bed. Someone wearing a long robe, I think a priest's robe, came in and tied up Ephraim and Annie, then slipped them into a bag. He blew out the candles. He left for a few minutes, and—I should have gotten up, but I was afraid. I didn't know who this was."

"Don't worry, Sir Gregory. You were wise to protect yourself," Judas reassured him. "Please, continue."

"Whoever it was, he did something at the window. I could hear him moving, but the room was dark. I don't really know what happened after that. I heard more scraping sounds at the window, and then the room was very quiet for a very long time."

Once again, the room was quiet while the enormity of what had happened sunk in. Judas spoke first, highly agitated. "Someone has kidnapped Ephraim and Annie. We've got to get them back! And we don't have much time!"

## CHAPTER 33

# Desert-driven

Traveling at night was difficult, but Jeremias didn't think they had any option. In the darkness it would be easy to camouflage the bundles they were carrying, but once the sun rose, it would be much harder. The place to which they were traveling was less than a day's journey, but there were many dangers involved. Passing through the maze of small villages and towns that surrounded the castle was effortless. His position as a priest of the castle guaranteed him clearance through every check point. Of course, it also meant that it would be very easy to track where they had gone. Still, the first part of this night's long journey would be easy compared to what was ahead.

As soon as the band left the cover of the towns, Jeremias became skittish. Juvenal and Cyrus had performed competently so far, and their other accomplice, Crustus, had proven his worth. But it wasn't the skill of his companions that made Jeremias nervous, it was the terrain. Settlement north of the castle was much sparser than any other place in the kingdom. The reason was simple, desert. Between the last town and the foothills of the Severus Mountains, sand was the most plenteous resource. And, of course, sand did not provide much cover.

Jeremias was headed toward an abandoned ruby mine that had been purchased by his father's agents, just in case a spy had to run for cover someday. He knew roughly where it would be located, even though he had never been there himself. The mine itself would be completely empty, except for some basic equipment that had been hidden there against a future need. He could expect a pot or two, provisions to make a fire, probably a blanket. There would be a small amount of coin hidden somewhere, anything more than that would be a surprise. Most important of all, the place would be defensible and hard for an enemy to find.

The six had been traveling all night long. Ephraim and Annie had been freed from their sacks about an hour earlier, and although still bound, were grateful to be able to see where they were going. There was no point in yelling for help, no one could possibly hear their cries. The mountains loomed in front of them; the nearest village was miles behind. Annie was terrified. She couldn't believe what was happening to her! One minute she was standing in the bedroom of a prince, the very next, she was waking up tied over the back of a horse. And though she was now riding behind a large man, she still had no idea where she was going or who was taking her there. She tried asking the man in front of her some questions; he acted as if she didn't exist.

Annie could see that Ephraim was riding behind another man, one who was leading the band. He was some twenty yards ahead of her, and there was no way to get his attention. Tears were running down her cheeks. When she looked up, she noticed the first rays of sunshine peeking over the horizon to the right. Annie wondered when they would stop.

"Hurry!" the lead man shouted. "We must get behind that hill as soon as possible. Once we are out of sight of the plain, we can take our time. It won't be long now." Off the horses dashed, and in another thirty minutes, they rounded the hill and slowed to a trot, then stopped altogether.

Hands were untied, and everyone dismounted. Loud groans involuntarily filled the air as cramped muscles were tested and stretched. Ephraim had recognized the lead captor by this time, and decided it was time for some answers.

"Father, what is going on? Why have you kidnapped us? This doesn't make any sense!" he asked, his voice filled with disappointment and confusion.

"Ephraim, it is very important that you do as you are told. There is a war going on, and I am afraid you are a prisoner of it. I know who and what you are, and I am afraid it has become my job to make sure that you do not get injured in the conflict that is about to erupt," Jeremias explained calmly.

"There is no war," Ephraim sputtered. "And besides, what could I possibly do to assist anyone? If you really know who and what I am, you will also know that I am powerless."

"That is true in only one respect," Jeremias explained. "You may not have access to your magical power yet, but you still have the power to inspire. Your armies will fight bravely if they have the confidence that the first mage will help them. With the first mage absent, they will quickly lose confidence and collapse. So you see, you are a threat even though you are powerless."

Ephraim grunted, knowing he had lost this argument. Having nothing further to say, he simply shut up.

"Now if you will cooperate, we will try to make this as painless as possible," Ephraim spoke to the two captives. "This way."

As the group stepped into the mine shaft, the priest's hand began to glow brightly. It took a moment for their eyes to adjust to low light, but the shape of a room came quickly into focus. Having taken a short walk into the mine, they stopped in what appeared to be an old staging area of the mine. The space was cavernous with old shelves cut right into one of the walls. The shelves were full of things: picks, shovels, broken pieces of tools, spikes, ropes, broken and unbroken lanterns, even some iron bars. As their eyes adjusted, the group found the room to be dimly lighted by light from the outside.

Two further mine shafts branched out from the back of the room they were now occupying. The trails leading up from these shafts merged, then divided, cutting the large room in half. One side of the room contained a few thin mats for sleeping, an iron pot, some wood stacked against a wall, and some coarsely woven bags. The kidnappers unloaded all their remaining supplies in this area. The other side of the room, the side of the shelves, was littered with broken things, a small work bench, an anvil fastened to an old stump, more things than Ephraim could take stock of in the brief glimpse he got. While the kidnappers were unloading, the priest was securing his unhappy guests.

Leading Ephraim and Annie into the right mine shaft, Jeremias spoke softly. "There really is no reason for you to attempt to escape. You don't know the way back to the castle, and there is no one within many miles who can help you. The war that is about to begin will be over shortly, for a variety of reasons. The sparkweed I flavored the castle stores with is only one of the many reasons that this siege will be short. Once the Ruby Kingdom is in the hands of the Obsidian Rulers, you will be freed from captivity. Of course, you will need to pledge yourself to the new rulers of the kingdom, if you are to enjoy your freedom for any length of time."

Ephraim was growing angry by this time, but decided it was best not to talk. No need to anger the priest anymore than necessary. Annie, however, was still rather disoriented.

"Sir, why have you kidnapped me? I am just a young girl. I have no power, no special ability, no rank. I was simply visiting friends…"

"Unfortunately, you were visiting powerful friends. And since you now know more than you should, you will be forced to endure the same captivity as your friend. Your fates are tied together, it seems. For better or worse, there is nothing I can do about that now," Jeremias concluded.

Around the corner, out of sight of the main room, there was a small alcove in the mining shaft. Within the alcove, a small mat lay against the wall, just underneath two manacles that were chained to iron fixtures deeply rooted in the rock wall.

"Sit," Jeremias ordered them both. He carefully locked one manacle around Ephraim's right leg, the other manacle around Annie's left. "Make the best of it, and don't give us any trouble. You should be able to sleep. We'll feed you as long as the food holds out." And then he was gone.

Walking back to the main cavern, Jeremias stumbled slightly. He had never been so tired in his whole life. Riding hard the entire night, after a tension filled day of subterfuge, he was emotionally and physically spent. He gave quick instructions to his crew to secure the mouth of the cave, and then he curled up on a small mat near the wall of the cave. He was asleep in moments. And no one was anxious to awaken him.

Annie and Ephraim were not quite as sleepy, however. Though bruised and battered from riding tied to horses, the spell that had effected their capture did in fact provide actual rest. Now they were rested and in pain; the combination kept them wide awake—and afraid, uncertain, and very curious. It wasn't the darkness or the cave that frightened Annie. She had been in caves twice before, when she was rock climbing with her father. Annie's father, a military man, enjoyed climbing and often took Annie along. She started climbing when she was eight years old, so she had several years of experience under her belt. She didn't know any other girls who enjoyed climbing, but that didn't bother her one bit. She liked it and really didn't care what anyone else thought.

Annie had a myriad of questions about the Gemstone Islands. Ephraim told her as many stories and legends as he could remember. Then, when he started to talk about Rufus, he remembered that he still had the book Ella had given him. He pulled it out wishing there was enough light to read, but there wasn't. He remembered the story about Tom Turnavil, and had just begun to tell it, when he heard another voice speaking.

*Ephraim, don't forget. Work from the back to the front!*

"Eli!" Ephraim exclaimed. "Where have you been?" Annie jumped when Ephraim shouted.

"Who are you talking to?" Annie asked, twisting around to see if anyone else was present.

*I'm here where I have always been, since that day in the Grove. But where are you? You've been asleep for a long time, it seems to me.*

"I have been," Ephraim explained out loud. "Oh, wait a second. I have to explain to someone who is here what is going on."

*Do you really think you should? I can come back a little later.*

"Trust me, she'll still be here. And I don't think you will mind her knowing the situation." To Annie he said, "Annie, a man who was like a grandfather to me left this world and went to your world. I don't completely understand all the details, but sometimes he can still speak to me, inside my head. When this is happening, he can also see this world through my eyes."

"Is it Eli?" Annie guessed.

"Yeah. How did you know? Oh, I'm sorry. I guess you already know who he is. You told me when we first met that Eli had sent you. I forgot that you two had already met. It's Eli who is speaking to me right now in my head."

"Amazing!" Annie whispered.

"I need to concentrate to hear what he has to say. I will tell you all about it when we are finished. I will need a little quiet until we are done, okay?" he asked.

Annie nodded and went silent. Ephraim turned away.

"Okay, I'm ready," Ephraim spoke into the darkness.

*Where are you, and why are you and Annie sitting in the dark?*

Ephraim explained that they had been kidnapped, and they were now prisoners in an abandoned ruby mine. They had been asleep during most of the ride, so they weren't exactly sure which way they had traveled. They assumed that they had come north, since that was where the mines were located. And Ephraim was able to report that they were in a mine on the edge of the mountains, one whose entrance was on the back side of the first major hill they had come upon.

*Who brought you here? Agents of the Obsidian Kingdom?*

"Yes," Ephraim answered, and went on to identify Jeremias the priest. "There were four men altogether, although one was more a boy than a man." He had seen the boy at work in the palace, though only recently. He had heard some names: Juvenal, Cyrus.

*And how are you? Are you injured? Have you been fed?*

"We are bruised but nothing broken. We are chained to the wall by one leg. We are on sleeping mats. We are hungry, but we have been promised food."

*Good. It will be best to use this time for study. I will guide you as I am able. And Annie can help you memorize the axioms you must know by heart.*

"We cannot read. There is not enough light. I have my book, but..." Eli cut him off.

*Light, I believe, we can produce. You are in an abandoned Ruby mine, right?*

"Yes."

*Do you remember anything that Ella taught you?*

"Yes, I think I do. 'The Land is the Creator's gift; people are the Creator's treasure,'" Ephraim recited.

*Excellent. You are in the mine given by the Creator to the Ruby Kingdom. It was from these mines that the rubies for the Objects of Power were unearthed. The Creator charged those rubies with power to achieve His purpose. And I believe it will serve His purpose to grant to the dust of those stones the power to shed light on your studies. We will ask the Creator to do that. And once we have both made our requests, here is what you must do: place your hand on the floor of the cave. Hold your other hand in front of your face and concentrate on your index finger. Annie will have to hold the book. Then close your eyes and imagine in your mind what your finger would look like if it were to glow. Once you have a firm picture in your mind, say softly the word, "Glow." If the Creator has heard your request, your finger will be glowing when you open your eyes. To turn off the light, simply wish it away. And Ephraim, don't let anyone else see you do this.*

"Eli, I'm going to explain to Annie what we've been discussing, then we'll give it a try."

*Take your time. Don't rush. Once you have light, start at the back of the book. Work together to learn all that you can. Memorize as much of the back section as you can. The more you learn, the stronger you will be. And I think you will need to be very strong very quickly. I have some other things to attend to. I will return later.*

And Eli was gone. Ephraim explained to Annie what had been said and prepared for the experiment. Annie held the book, and secretly asked the Creator of this odd land to give them a little light. Ephraim and Eli must have done the same, for a second later Ephraim's face was shining from light reflected from his index finger. He stood up and lifted his finger high into the air, to get a better look at his surroundings. There wasn't much to see. He and Annie were in a hall-like tunnel just around the corner from the main entrance. The tunnel sloped down away from them on one end. Some broken timbers and other debris littered the corridor. They could see the mouth of a second tunnel that branched out from the main cavern, but they couldn't see into the main cavern at all.

"We might as well do what Eli asked," Ephraim suggested. "It doesn't look like there is anything else to do."

Annie agreed and they settled back onto their mats, getting as comfortable as possible. Ephraim began to read. "The Axioms according to Rufus. The land is the Creator's gift; people are the Creator's treasure..."

## CHAPTER 34

# Search

It was decided that Judas would search inside the castle for clues to the disappearance, while Jon and Greg searched from the air. Outside, it would be a difficult search, for darkness had settled across the land. Still, there wouldn't be that much traffic moving across the roadways at night. Any movement at all would be suspicious.

In no time at all, Jon and Greg were on their carpet, invisible, flying in ever-widening circles around the city. They flew at eagle speed, and covered a great deal of territory. But there was so much to cover, and after two hours of searching they had not found anything suspicious.

Judas was more fortunate. Trying to delay telling his father what had happened, he stopped first at the kitchen. When he entered, preparations for the serving of dinner were in full swing. Dinner was late due to the disturbance caused by a small fire outside the castle wall. Fire control was always the first order of business in a city like this! The evening meal was just now being carried to the castle staff and members of the royal family. Ella was busy trying to get back into the good graces of the king, and Sam was lying on his side near the door that led to the garbage room. Judas stopped for a moment, and then realized what was wrong. Sam never slept at this time of the day. This was the time Sam was most active. He would usually be running around the kitchen, scavenging for food dropped from a tray or crumbs swept from the counter. He wasn't above jumping up on a servant in an attempt to jar something loose. Normally, Ella's patience would wear thin, and she would put Sam out in the garbage room until the rush was over.

Judas knelt down beside Sam and rubbed his back. Sam rolled over and moaned. It was a loud sick moan. And Sam was shaking, his legs twitching. And the smell! It wasn't pleasant.

"Ella," Judas shouted, "something's wrong with Sam. Come over here."

"Now's not the time to be worrin' about a dog, my prince. He's just eaten more than he should." Ella shouted from across the room.

"No, I think it is more than that. I never saw a dog shake from eating too much. Sleep, yes. Shake, never," Judas responded.

Ella finished giving a servant orders and crossed the room to where Sam and Judas were huddled. She no sooner bent over Sam, when she disgustedly exclaimed, "AAAHH, the smell. Somethin's wrong with that..." She stopped suddenly. "Judas, go get the priest. Quick," she yelled, "bring back all o' the food. Take the spoons from their mouths. We may have been poisoned!" She herself ran straight for the king's quarters, while other servants scurried in every direction.

Ella pushed past the guards at the door of the royal apartment, shouting as she went, "Stop eatin', Yer Majesty. Don't take another bite." She continued to yell until she stood face to face with the king himself.

"Ella, what is all this commotion?" he demanded angrily.

"Don't eat another bite," she barked, grabbing the bowl of stew from the tray in front of him. "Somethin' happened in the kitchen, and I don't like it. Sam is sick, and I think he's been poisoned. If I'm right, someone added somethin' extra ta some part o' this meal. I don't know what yet, but it isn't safe ta eat any o' it until we're sure."

The king looked blue in the face. "Ella, I already ate half of that bowl of stew. What should I do now?"

"Get the priest ta give ya some o' that potion that makes ya bring up the contents o' yer stomach. It isn't pleasant, but it's fer the best. I'll be in the kitchen, and I'll have Artezes with me."

The king didn't say another word. Walking quickly past Ella, he exited his apartments, pushed past his own guard, turned the corner and started up the stairs to the third floor. Crossing through the chapel, he came to the door to the priests' chamber. It stood slightly ajar. Without knocking, he entered and was surprised to find Judas standing in the center of the room, candle in hand. "Judas," he barked, "what are you doing here?"

Judas jumped, startled by his father's appearance. "Ella sent me to look for the priest. Sam is sick, and she is afraid someone has poisoned the evening meal. But the priest is gone. This place is empty. Where could Father Jeremias be?" Judas asked, with uncertainty.

"I don't know. But I have already eaten some of dinner, and I think I need a priestly remedy. Do you know where he would keep his medicinals?" the king inquired.

"No, but why don't we try to find out," Judas suggested. The king began to search the small chamber directly off the chapel, while Judas went into the priests' sleeping quarters. Of the three personal cells, it was obvious that one had been recently vacated. The first two were neatly ordered, just as they had been left by the two priests who had served the kingdom in the Grove. They had never returned and their rooms had not been disturbed. The third room, obviously Father Jeremias', was disheveled and disorganized. Someone had been in a terrible hurry to leave!

Judas found a small chest on the floor of the small closet in the room. It contained various spices and herbs. He called his father. Though the spices were labeled, the words were in a language that neither could understand. The king picked up the chest to take it to the kitchen, hoping that Ella's nose could identify what their reading skills could not. As he passed by the bed, he stopped. Judas had ruffled the room rather thoroughly, and in the process had unearthed a variety of small objects. The king put the chest down and picked up the small case that now lay on top of the sleeping mat.

Opening the case, he announced to Judas, "I believe we have found our traitor."

"Father Jeremias?" Judas asked, stunned.

"I'm afraid so," the king replied, frustrated. "We won't find him around here, I suspect. He must be long gone."

"Why would he do such a thing, Father? I mean, he was a priest, an honored member of our household and..."

The king silenced Judas by holding up the case. "This case is finely carved and exquisitely executed. The wood is rosewood, very rare. It once held an object of power, a special dagger. Unless I miss my guess, it had two obsidians set into its handle. If Jeremias had this dagger in his possession, he was either the chief spy of the Obsidian Kingdom, or he was a member of the royal family himself. I would bet on the latter. I can't believe any king would willingly give this particular dagger to anyone outside the family. The dagger is a key, of sorts. In fact, it is the only way I know that someone might have been able to get into my room and open the secret armory. I can't believe we allowed him to get this close!" By the time the king finished, he was furious. He grabbed up the chest, and moved quickly out the door, across the chapel and down the steps toward the kitchen. Judas ran to keep up with him.

In the kitchen, Ella was busy supervising the disposal of the remains of dinner. Every pot had to be scoured, every surface thoroughly cleansed. Seals were being checked on the stores, and anything found open was discarded. Into this chaos, the king descended. A tense hush fell over the staff at his entrance. "Yer Majesty," Ella whispered.

"Here are the priest's herbs, but I am afraid our priest is gone, long gone" the king announced, placing the chest on the long center counter.

"The priest gone?" Ella asked. "He told me himself this afternoon that he would be in his room fastin' tonight and tomorra'. I thought..."

"Where did he tell you this?" the king questioned.

"Right here in this kitchen. Just this afternoon." Ella stopped, hearing what she had said. Her tone changed quickly, she spoke slowly as she put two and two together. "He was right here in this kitchen, and Sam was growlin' at him when I entered. He said he was just lookin' for a crust o' bread. A crust o' bread, that's what he said, the scoundrel."

Ella noticed that one compartment in the chest was completely empty, with the exception of a few broken leaves in the corner. Extracting these leaves, Ella knew exactly what the poison was. Sparkweed had a distinctive aroma. Every cook knew the smell because sparkweed and parsley looked so much alike. Since they grew in similar areas, it was important not to mix the two.

"Yer Majesty, it seems that no one has eaten as much as you. Ya were served first, and were only half way through yer first bowl o' stew. At the most, only a few other bites have been taken. Except by me. I have been tastin' the stew ta season it all afternoon. Now I know why it was so hard ta get it ta taste right. I must admit that I have already begun ta feel poorly." Ella began to work while she spoke. She had taken some leaves from the chest and was grinding them finely. These she mixed with some hot liquid.

"Ya will be relieved ta know that this poison is not fatal. You and I will probably be violently ill tomorra' and maybe the next day. After the first two days, the worst will have passed. But our stomachs will be sensitive and will not tolerate any food. We will not be able ta eat anythin' fer several days, maybe more. We will drink lots o' milk and thin broth. After that we can start ta rebuild our strength. I'd say we will be back ta normal in about three weeks. But here's ta good fortune and the blessin' o' the Creator."

Ella handed the king a cup of the warm liquid that she had prepared. She poured another for herself, holding it high as if toasting.

"What is this?" the king demanded.

"It is the medicine we need. It will cause the return o' everythin' presently in our stomachs. The effects will be immediate, so go quickly ta yer rooms and prepare ta feel quite sick. I shall do the same. If we are able ta get rid o' most o' what is in us, we may greatly reduce the time that we are ill. And be grateful that Prince Judas uncovered this treachery, or this whole castle, includin' yer officers and armsmen, would be in the same shape as us!" Ella bowed slightly, turned and ran up the back stairs toward her room. "Go, yer Majesty, don't waste a second."

The king looked at Judas. "You'll tell me the details tomorrow.

First things first." The king, cup in hand, was through the kitchen door in a flash, moving rapidly toward the stairs to his apartments. Judas stepped after him, but then changed his mind. He hadn't told his father about Ephraim's disappearance. Maybe he wouldn't need to. If he could find Ephraim by tomorrow night, things would look different when it came time to explain. And that was worth hoping for.

Judas took the remnants of the liquid that Ella had left behind and mixed them with the water in Sam's dish. It was going to be a job to get the dog to drink this!

CHAPTER 35

# Search Extended

The aerial search was not as productive as Jon and Greg had hoped. Darkness was a major frustration. The other was a lack of landmarks. Once you passed the outer rim of settlements that surrounded the castle, it was hard to figure out where you were. One field pretty much looked like every other field. And to the north, where the desert separated settlements from mountains, sand was, well, everywhere. Judging distances was nearly impossible without landmarks. By the time the sun poked its head over the horizon, Jon and Greg had given up. They headed back to the castle and flew straight into Prince Judas' room. When they arrived, Judas was asleep in his bed. They thought about heading home for a few minutes, but then realized that they couldn't possibly go back until Annie was with them. They decided to wake the prince.

"Prince Judas," Greg whispered, gently shaking the prince. "Wake up. We're back."

The prince groggily rolled over, slowly coming to life. "Oh, you're back. Sorry. I waited up most of the night, but I must have drifted off. What time is it?"

"Maybe an hour after dawn. Still very early," Jon answered. "We didn't have any luck. We looked everywhere. How about you?"

"Nothing. I did uncover an attempt to poison the whole castle. Unfortunately, Ella and my father were victims of the attack," Judas sleepily explained.

Greg gasped, "Did you get to them in time? Are they okay?"

"They're very sick, but they'll be fine. It will take a while, though." Judas was now out of bed, wrapping himself in a robe of scarlet trimmed in white fur. He jumped back up onto the bed. "I'm worried about Ephraim and Annie. We can't afford to be without a mage at a time like this. There must be some way we can find them."

"How do you get news to the people of the kingdom? Do you have a system of heralds or couriers who could get a message to the general population quickly?" Greg inquired.

"Yes, we have royal heralds," Judas explained. "There is a network of town squares in which they announce important news. Usually we can cover all the towns in the kingdom within one day. We don't use them often, so when they get used, people know the information is important."

Greg slowly began to spin out a plan. "Ephraim was known to the folks in the kitchen, probably to most folks in the palace. Perhaps someone could draw a reasonable picture of his face. If we could make several copies, we could offer a reward for information leading to his capture. We know that there are at least three people traveling together. If we supplied all the details we had, we could turn the whole kingdom into an investigative unit."

"We know that the kidnapper was the priest, Jeremias," Judas added. "Even though he has only been here a short time, he was well enough known for the artists to draw him competently."

"How did you figure out the priest did it?" Jon wanted to know, impressed with this bit of news. Judas then told the full story of Sam without an appetite, the sparkweed, the search, the dagger case and the empty room. "Father figures that it was Jeremias who stole the staff from his room. Only someone with an object of power like a royal dagger could have gotten the armory open."

"What's a royal dagger?" Greg asked in a disinterested, offhanded kind of way.

"I don't know exactly," said Judas. "I don't think I've ever seen one. My Father said he thought that this one probably had obsidian on each side of the handle, and that the dagger was some sort of key."

"Oh, interesting," Greg muttered, trying not to act too curious about the nature of the dagger. But his mind was racing. He knew the dagger he possessed was an amazing instrument. Could he also be the holder of a royal dagger? He wondered how many such daggers existed.

"What did your Father say when he found out that Ephraim had been kidnapped?" Jon finally asked, somewhat afraid to hear the report of what he expected was an angry outburst.

"He doesn't know, yet," Judas admitted. "By the time I got the chance to tell him, he had already eaten some of the tainted stew. He had to swallow the antidote immediately, and that made him really sick. I haven't seen him since. Ella said he would be sick all day today, and maybe even into tomorrow. I thought I had until tomorrow to get Ephraim back. I'd sort of rather wait until he is back to break the news." Judas lowered his eyes, embarrassed at his fear in facing his own father.

Jon walked over to the bed and sat down beside Judas. "I can understand why you feel that way. It must be hard to have a king for a father."

"He's a good king, I think. It's just that...." Tears were flowing freely down Judas' face. All this talk about his father had reminded him again that his father was now the only parent he had. He was used to spending most of his time in the company of the palace staff. It wasn't infrequent for him to go for many days without seeing either parent. Still, the thought of being motherless bothered him deeply. And knowing that his father had enemies willing to poison him was deeply unsettling. Judas wasn't ready to be king any more than he was ready to be alone. And for the moment, the fatigue, the loneliness, the grief and the fear were all ganging up on him.

"Don't worry, Prince Judas," Greg spoke comfortingly, as he approached the bed. "We'll go with you to tell your father. I don't think we will be in any danger if we go in prepared."

It took a moment for Judas to compose himself so that he could speak. A faint grin crossed his lips, and through his tears he reminded Greg why that wasn't such a good idea. "You remember the last time you guys were together, things got pretty rough. I'm not sure you want to get too close to my father when he learns Ephraim is gone. He will want you bound to this kingdom more than ever."

The room was silent while Greg pondered that thought. The king was dangerous, no question about it. And he really didn't want to get within an arm's reach of that man ever again.

"If only Eli were here to help us. He would know what to…" Judas stopped. "Eli," he slowly repeated the name, words slowly oozing from his mouth like honey from a jar. "Eli knows." Then he spoke so rapidly that he was barely intelligible. "How long would it take you to get back to the world you are from?"

'Uh, between 30 and 45 minutes, I guess," Jon stuttered. "But we can't go back. Not without Annie. How would we explain what happened to her? We couldn't…"

Judas cut him off. "You must! Only for a few minutes. Don't you see, Eli knows where they are! He must know! He can talk to Ephraim, in his head. Surely by now Eli knows exactly where they both are, and he will be able to tell you."

That Ephraim and Eli were in contact with one another was news to Jon and Greg. They knew Eli had a contact, but they hadn't guessed who it was. This really was excellent news!

Judas continued spinning his plan. "If you two will head back to your home to get the information, I will begin to assemble the helpers we need to get Ephraim and Annie back. I think this operation will probably rely on stealth, but a little bit of brawny back-up might be very welcome. And I know exactly who I need to invite on a mission like this."

"We can make it back home easily enough," Greg spoke up, "but we haven't slept all night. We really need to go to bed! And since time moves differently in our world than it does here, we really need to sleep here."

"Greg," Jon injected, "why don't we head home, get the information, and then return as quickly as possible. Prince Judas, if you would find a secure place in the palace for us to sleep when we return, we will be able to deliver the information, then sleep while you formulate the rescue plan."

"Excellent!" Judas clapped his hands. "Let's do it! Everything will be ready when you return. If I am not waiting for you in this room when you get back, know that I will be here shortly. And if no other beds have appeared, sleep in mine. I'm off to see Zarak." Judas stood, took two quick steps toward the door, then stopped abruptly, dropping his head. He turned back to the boys, speaking softly and slowly. "Forgive me. I am so anxious to do my part that I forget myself. Sir Jonathan, Sir Gregory, how can I ever thank you?" He reached for Greg's hand and then embraced him heartily, hugging him to his chest. Turning to Jon, he continued, "Where would I be without you?" Another embrace. "I will see you soon. Good providence, my friends," and he turned and left the room. By the time Judas started down the steps to the main entrance of the castle, Jon and Greg were already in the air, speeding toward home.

Jon stepped through the back of the cave into the trunk that was safely sequestered in the rock room. The house in Newport was quiet.

"I thought you might come," a voice spoke softly, urgently. "Actually, I hoped you would come." Eli was sitting on the rock, waiting for them.

"Do you know where Ephraim and Annie are?" Greg blurted out.

"Are they okay?" Jon added hastily.

"Yes, I do. I've been talking with Ephraim very recently. And Annie. Both are fine, though a little bruised and a little tired. I'll tell you what I know.

"They are being held captive in an abandoned ruby mine north of the city. This particular mine is located under the first major mountain they came to, so it is in the first tier of mines, one of the earliest ones. It is entered from the far side of the mountain, a fact which is very important. The main shaft of the mine divides into two smaller tunnels; Annie and Ephraim are chained to the wall in one of them."

"Can you tell us which mountain the mine is in?" Jon asked.

"I can't tell you exactly which mountain we want. But there are maps of all the mining shafts kept in the royal archives. I do know that only two or three first tier mines were entered on the north side of the mountain. You will be able to locate them on the maps. You will have to investigate all of them."

"Is there anything more you can tell us to help?" Greg asked, hopefully.

"Once you rescue Ephraim and Annie, get Ephraim's staff into his hands as quickly as possible. He will be much more valuable to you armed," Eli suggested. "There are only four men guarding your friends, but be careful. You are involved in a war and there may be casualties. Don't take unnecessary risks. Let the king and his men protect you."

"We've got to get back. They can't begin to plan without our information," Jon wearily observed.

Eli stopped him as he started to turn away. "Before you go, write your parents a quick note. 'We went for a walk,' I suggest. That will be true, if not complete. In case they return before you are done, that will explain your absence. Also, make sure you take the silver swords this time. They are more than keys, they are magical weapons. You may have reason to use them, if things get really serious."

"Thanks," Greg mumbled, while Jon scribbled the note. "We'll be back soon."

A second later they had disappeared through the chest once more.

## CHAPTER 36

# Conspiracy to Rescue

Judas decided to check in on his father before pursuing his other plans. He knocked on the door of the king's apartments and was admitted by a servant. The servant quickly explained that the king was far too ill to receive anyone today. When Judas asked whether his father would be all right, he was quickly reassured that by tomorrow, everything would be fine. Judas left best wishes for his father, with an invitation to call him, if his father needed anything from him. After that, he skipped down the stairs and headed for the barracks.

Protocol demanded that a guard accompany him, and so it was with a one man escort that Judas pounded on the wooden doors where the soldiers were still sleeping. He was forced to pound several times, and might have gone on pounding had not his escort lost patience.

"Open up. It's the prince!" he shouted. Things came to life in a hurry, and in less than fifteen seconds, a half dressed soldier opened the door and stood at attention while Judas and his guard entered.

"I need to speak with Captain Anthony. The rest of you may go back to sleep," Judas announced in a loud voice.

A door in the back of the room swung open, and the officer stepped through. "What's all the racket? I...," he paused when he spied Judas, "I'm sorry, Your Highness. We did not expect a royal visitor at this hour."

"Nor should you, Captain. I am sorry to come unannounced. But I must speak with you privately. May we use your room?" Judas asked politely.

"If you are certain that is best," Anthony replied, stepping back to hold the door open for Judas. Judas stepped through, dispatching his guard to wait outside the room.

"Please, "Judas began, "Make yourself comfortable, Captain Anthony."

"Thank you, Your Majesty. I am surprised that you know my name. I was not aware that we had ever met," Anthony asserted, truly surprised.

"We have not, to my knowledge. But you are the son of our most trusted general, and I know the high esteem in which he holds you. I have seen you spar and I know of your reputation. And frankly, I need you desperately right now," Judas admitted. "There has been a kidnapping. Ephraim, a serving boy, is missing, along with a young girl. I am afraid for their safety."

"A serving boy and a young girl seem hardly cause for this much concern. Surely they will turn up in a few days," Anthony grinned slightly.

"Captain, are you loyal to the Ruby Throne?" Judas asked in an accusatory, stern manner.

All traces of the smile vanished from Anthony's lips. He snapped to attention, stared straight into Judas' face, and barked, "Of course, Your Majesty!" then bowed his head.

The room was silent. Anthony may have heard Judas say, "Truth," but he didn't acknowledge it if he did.

"Anthony, everyone is important in the kingdom. But a serving boy who also happens to be the first mage is especially important," Judas spoke evenly.

Anthony's head snapped up and his eyes grew large. "The first mage has been kidnapped?"

"Yes, he has. Anthony, no one knows, not even the king, and we cannot afford to let anyone find out. We must find him and rescue him before it is discovered that he is missing. You already know about last night's events in the palace, I am sure. We cannot allow panic to spread through the kingdom."

"But why has the king not been told?" Anthony wondered aloud.

"The king is too ill. He will be fine in a few days, but today he is unable to help anyone. I need you to join me in the castle. There we will meet two other friends who are going to help us in this adventure. You will serve as our advisor, and if we need additional support, you will provide it. Providing you are willing," Judas added at the last minute.

"I am willing, Your Majesty, but I think your trust would be better placed in my father, the general. He would know more of..."

"Forgive me for interrupting, Anthony, but there are several reasons I have chosen you. Unless I miss my guess, the kidnapping of a first mage is the same thing as declaring war. And if the kingdom is attacked while we are away, I would want your father to be here. You may be right, to the extent that we should invite him to be a party to our plans. But then, again, if it should come to war, the less he knew of our whereabouts, the less an enemy could learn from him."

Anthony was stunned. This sounded almost like the speech his father had given him just a few days before. Apparently the time for action had come. "Of course, Your Majesty. I am at your service."

"Then I will go immediately to the castle to begin making our plans. Tell your men to make special preparations for training maneuvers. We want them to be battle ready at a moment's notice. I would ask you to prepare for a journey. Once you are prepared, come to the castle and ask to be admitted to the rooms of Prince Judas. I will inform the guards that you are expected. And Captain, tell no one where we are going or what we have discussed."

As Judas departed, Anthony was surprised at what he had just seen. The little princeling that he had seen so many times at play within the palace was surprisingly insightful—and more than a little courageous. Anthony still didn't know if he would follow through with the plan. A kidnapped first mage was more serious than Judas might imagine. But it wouldn't hurt for him to find out all that he could, before he decided whether to let his father in on the secret. Packing his gear, Anthony prepared for a journey, and then headed for the palace.

***

The Obsidian Prince was surprised that his brother had not

contacted him. Even though he did not expect the job to be completed yet, he thought Jeremias would have at least let him know if he had a plan...or at least good prospects. If he, rather than Jeremias, had been planted in the castle, he would have spent the evening working on a plan, and then at first light, when the spell would work again, he would have communicated his plan to his brother. Well, he had no choice but to wait.

The army of the Obsidian Kingdom was camped inside the western edge of the Primeval Forest, west by northwest of their homeland. The trees covered their presence, and they were careful about camp fires and anything else that might give away their location. The western edge of the forest was about a day's march from the Ruby city walls, and there were several settlements between the wall and the forest's beginnings. When the time came to attack, they could be at the city very quickly, indeed. All they needed now was the signal that the first mage had been neutralized.

Prince Stefan, properly called king now that his father had met his demise on the Great Board, still seethed with anger. Grief mixed with rage blinded him to any course of action other than war. He no longer cared about what was right for his nation or his people. What he wanted was revenge! There was a certain justice to seeking revenge on people who were greedy and self-righteous, he told himself. Cheaters deserved punishment; it just felt right!

King Stefan had been on the Great Board in the Grove. He was one of three pawns who survived the challenge. And the priest, Marfessol, who had led him home after the defeat, was at his side still. The bitterness of the priest bled constantly into the young king, until he was poisoned by its venom. Yes, he was ready to achieve justice! Justice and revenge!

But still, no word. He would have to be patient until his brother called.

## CHAPTER 37

# Ancient Archives

Anthony joined Judas forty-five minutes before Jon and Greg appeared. The boys were happy to find Judas waiting for them, and Jon was secretly pleased to see Anthony in the room. It had become habit for them to always fly invisibly, so once again, Judas and Anthony were startled when voices spoke to them out of thin air—Anthony, more so than Judas, of course.

"I'm glad you're here," Jon rang out, happily, but wearily. "Just clear off the bed!" As he spoke, the carpet landed and he clicked off the invisibility ring. Appearing from nowhere, Greg and Jon were now seated in the center of the bed. Jon just fell back with a sigh. "Boy, do I need to sleep!"

"Who are you?" Anthony trembled, the fear obvious on his face.

"Don't worry, they are friends. Captain Anthony, meet Sir Jonathan and Sir Gregory. You might remember that they are honorary Knights of the Ruby Kingdom and veterans of the Battle on the Great Board!" Judas proclaimed with great importance. Anthony's eyes were bright with excitement. "Most importantly, however, they are our very good friends." Judas smiled warmly at the both of them. "What have you learned?"

Greg relayed all the information Eli had given them while Jon listened from the bed. He was already half asleep, struggling to keep his eyes open until the report was complete. "I think it would be good for you two to do the research in the archives while we get some sleep. After lunch, we can create the plan and get to work, if that sounds okay to you," Greg suggested.

It did sound okay. Greg stretched out on the bed next to Jon and was asleep in minutes. Anthony and Judas moved toward the royal archives.

The official records of the kingdom were kept in the study of the king. But those were only records of current interest. Judas expected that records as old as ancient mining maps would have long since been removed to the storage vault under the grand ballroom. Moving rapidly through the southwest tower, down the steps toward the dungeon, Anthony and Judas found the door to the storage vault and quickly entered. The guards who were posted at the entrance to the castle cellars seemed surprised to have visitors, but they were quick to lend assistance to the prince they so rarely saw...especially when he was accompanied by their own captain. Judas noticed the way the guards worked to please this young captain. Zarak had been right; Anthony was an excellent officer who was both admired and respected by the men.

While the guards carried torches and lanterns to create light, Judas and Anthony searched the shelves that were lined with rolled parchments, old books, and various other artifacts that had once graced the tables and armoires of the apartments above. Things didn't seem to be very organized here. In actuality, books were rather rare. But there were more than enough carved candlesticks and wall sconces and unusual lighting fixtures to outfit another whole castle. Parchment rolls seems to be bundled according to event or purpose. Several old military campaigns were sketched on hand drawn maps of the island. Anthony was very interested in these and asked if he might borrow them to review them. Judas referred him to the king, at the same time suggesting that he would do everything possible to facilitate his request.

Old taxation ledgers were found, as well as accountant's books from the lands held by the royal family. Finally, after several discouraging hours, maps of the mountains to the north were unearthed. The Severus Mountains were a long chain that cut the island into two parts and then at its northern edge curved east along the coast of the island. The maps did not reveal what lay to the west of the mountains, but they did divide the mountains into mining parcels. Most of the mineral rights belonged to the Ruby Kingdom itself. After a time, however, private miners and mining companies had been allowed to superintend the plots for the royal government. For their efforts, a percentage of what was mined stayed in their own hands. Once the mines could no longer meet the production quota, they were either sold or given away as gifts to worthy citizens who warranted special reward.

There were more than fifty maps of the area. None of them seemed to be dated. Anthony and Judas knew they were looking for the oldest maps, and that they needed maps of the first tier mines. Map after map yielded information they did not need. Their frustration grew with each useless map they unrolled. As they got closer to the center of one bunch of maps that were rolled together, Judas noticed writing on the outside of the parchment. The inscription dated the map from 250 years ago, and referenced second tier mine closings.

"Anthony, check the writing on the outside of these maps," Judas instructed.

"Okay," Anthony sighed. But Judas noticed that he still kept unrolling every map.

"I think if you look for an inscription that references either second tier openings or first tier closings, you can avoid opening every map," Judas observed.

"I'm not the best reader, Prince Judas. I'd feel better if I looked, just to make sure I didn't miss anything," Anthony sheepishly explained.

"No problem, Captain. Whatever makes you comfortable is fine," Judas replied, trying to whisk Anthony's embarrassment away as quickly as possible. Now that there were inscriptions on several of the maps, Judas proceeded much more quickly. In a moment more, he had what he wanted. "I think this may be it. *Second tier openings.*"

Judas moved to a small desk near the shelves and unrolled the map. Anthony took a torch from one of the guards, and the two studied the drawings. The city and the mining parcels were clearly labeled

from an aerial view. Parcels were numbered, and several parcels were
"X"ed out. The first row of parcels had mining shafts and tunnels
drawn on them. The second row was much more uncluttered. Only a
few tunnels were indicated.

Judas studied the map. "Because elevations are impossible to
read, we are going to have a tough time finding our place on this map.
Our only chance is to find the old abandoned mine entrances and
compare them to this map. Once we find our bearings, it shouldn't
take us too long to track those scoundrels down."

Anthony was clearly puzzled. "How can you be so optimistic?
There are so many parcels, and it will take us a great deal of time to
travel between them. In fact, it could take weeks!"

Judas smiled, "It would take *us* weeks, but we are not alone in
this venture. We have the two things that will make this job possible.
One, we have Sir Jonathan and Sir Gregory to lend us their speed.
Two, we also have their perspective, a bird's eye perspective. And look
here at the map. Of all the mining parcels in the first row of land
tracts, only four have tunnels which begin in the upper half of the
property. And one of those is so clearly on the western side of the
parcel, that I doubt you could consider it a possibility. If we can find
any one of those openings, we should be able to figure out where the
rest are from the map."

Anthony was impressed. There was more to Judas than met the
eye. Perhaps his initial judgments had missed the mark. As they continued to study the map, other details became clearer. Judas noticed
that in two of the mines, tunnels from one site connected to tunnels
in another. And because they were drawn on the map in different
hands, it looked as if the completion of the tunnels was accomplished
at a later date. Maybe there was a back door to the place where the
prisoners were being held! And maybe their captors didn't know the
back door existed!

"I wonder what that means?" Anthony gestured to one of the
squares that was crossed out with a red X, underneath which was a
scripted "R". The other closed mines were indicated by black marks.
This parcel had no tunnels drawn on it, and the borders of the site

were inscribed with bold lines. There was a red tint to the paper here, as well.

"I don't know. There isn't any explanation, but it looks like that is reserved for royal use. But that doesn't make sense, because at this time, they were all owned by the royal government. Maybe we'll figure it out when we get there," Judas guessed.

"We probably should get back upstairs and make our plans. It must be past lunch time and we will want to get started as soon as possible on this journey. We will need the help of the sun if we are going to find those mine openings," Anthony reminded Judas.

Judas nodded, rolling the map back up and tucking it under his arm. "Lead the way, Captain," he sang out, and Anthony laughed. The guards scrambled to get the door open, holding high the torches that illuminated the corridor. As they passed through to the tower, Judas could see the barred door that led to the dungeons. Seeing the door reminded him that he really needed to explore this castle better. There was much he didn't know, and he hoped the castle would yield its secrets easily.

Anthony and Judas stopped by the kitchen to grab some food for lunch, and to give instructions for the preparation of their travel rations. Judas didn't give the reason he wanted certain foods packaged, but a first year cook could have figured out what was happening, if he were interested. Dried meats, cheeses, hard bread, water skins. Anthony carried a large tray of food back to the prince's room while Judas gave the kitchen strict instructions not to disturb his room.

"How long can we afford to let them sleep?" Anthony wondered aloud, whispering.

"A little longer, I expect. Leave the food there. After we finish all our preparations for travel, we'll come back and wake them," Judas instructed. "Now what do you think we will need?"

"Four horses at least, if we are all going," Anthony interjected. "The trip isn't more than a day, but extra water is a good idea. How long do you think this will take, I mean, considering all those special advantages you were talking about earlier?"

"I'm not sure. Sirs Jonathan and Gregory will not need horses.

They have other means of transportation." Anthony looked puzzled by this, but Judas continued. "I think we can locate the place by tonight. Then we will have to decide whether it is wiser to attack at night or during the daylight. If Providence favors us, we should be back home by tomorrow night. If not, it might take as many as three or four days."

"I'm sorry, Prince Judas, but how is it that our friends will not need horses? I know they have many powers, but can they also fly?" Anthony asked sarcastically.

"Yes, Anthony, after a fashion. While I have not seen them fly like the birds, I do know that they have a magical device that is able to fly. And when they are on it, they, too, move through the air at incredible speed. But please, guard this secret with your life."

Anthony could not speak. It was all more than he could imagine. Yesterday he felt superior to his weakling prince. Now he had encountered so many new things, things he had never dreamed of, that he felt very small, and very uninformed. The bewilderment shone on his face.

"Don't be alarmed, Anthony," Judas reassured him. "I know that this is a lot to digest. Just be glad that these two knights are on our side. Otherwise, we would have a great deal to fear!"

They left, then, making final preparations for their journey. Judas wrote a letter to his father, to be delivered by one of Anthony's soldiers 36 hours from then, in the event that they had not returned. It explained everything—Sir Jonathan and Sir Gregory were in league with them. Anthony and Judas would ride toward the mountains while the other two explored the mountains, looking for the mine entrances. Intelligence reports traced the movements of the criminals to the north. They would meet at the foot of a certain mountain to finalize their plans. They would steal the hostage (They only admitted that there was one) and hopefully escape before anyone knew they had come. If brute force were necessary, they would double back and call for reinforcements. But they would not return until they had "E" in their possession.

Judas pressed his signet pendant into the hot wax he had dripped on the back of the envelope. It was time to get going.

Having explained the plan to Jon and Greg, the quartet started out a few hours past noon. Jon and Greg held the map. Flying quickly and invisibly toward the mountains, they crossed the desert in just under an hour. It was hot! And the search itself would take place at a much slower speed. Greg read the map while Jon guided the carpet, and in another hour they had located their first mining tunnel entrance. It was one of the three mines that had northern entrances, and so they needed to find only one other mine entrance to establish exactly where they were on the map. They flew east to where the next entrance should be. Nothing. They recalculated, retracing their path. Assuming they were on the second site, they calculated where the mine entrance next to that site should be. Bingo! They knew exactly where they were on the map!

Jon and Greg were about four mines west of the spot marked with the Red X on the map. This was actually the center site of the three possible places the kidnappers might be. Since they were already at this place, they decided to check it out first. With invisibility cloaking their presence, they flew slowly into the mouth of the mine. It was very dark, and they could not afford to introduce any light. They did not speak. Neither could they proceed until their eyes had adjusted to the lack of light. After a few moments of tense, dark silence, they could begin to make out shadows in the cave. After disrupting a spider web with his face, Jon decided it would be best to turn on their shield as well. They would have to be careful not to give away their position by displacing a spider web.

Entering as far as light permitted, the boys saw no signs of current activity. They decided to check another location. They flew away silently, just in case they were mistaken. They didn't want to give away the element of surprise under any circumstance.

The eastern site was chosen next. It took only a few minutes to fly to the mountain, another thirty to locate the entrance. Following a similar procedure, the boys found nothing. Exhaling loudly, they now knew where Annie was being hidden. Or at least they were pretty sure they knew. They flew west and eventually found both mountain and mine entrance. Their hearts were beating wildly as they flew slowly toward the mine entrance. As they approached, they noticed the tracks of horses outside the cave, human footprints, also. Yes, this certainly was the place! Still, they couldn't see into the cave much past the entrance. The sun, starting to sink in the west, was casting long shadows past the mouth of the tunnel. The interior was shrouded in darkness. Just as they were about to cross the threshold of the tunnel, Greg spied a flickering torch in the recesses of the cavern. He lifted his hand to point it out to Jon, and at that moment, his hand and the front edge of the carpet crashed into some invisible barrier stretched across the mouth of the tunnel. Before he could stop himself, a cry of pain rang from Greg's mouth, which followed the noise created by the impact of hand and carpet.

Instantly the alarm was raised from inside. "What was that?" a voice shouted.

"I don't know. Don't see anything."

"Did you hear it?"

"I heard something. Be quiet a second. See if it happens again."

Silence followed this remark.

"Must have been a bird or something trying to fly into the cave."

"Must've."

"I'm going to start a fire for dinner. Get the…" the voices faded as the speakers drifted further away.

Jon inched the carpet slowly away and up into the sky. The entrance was guarded, magically sealed! How were they ever going to get through that? The sun was going down quickly, and they decided that they better get to the rendezvous point while they could still see. Once there, they could eat, think, and maybe even nap until their friends arrived.

The journey across the desert took about 10 hours by horseback. It would be nearly midnight by the time Anthony and Judas arrived. Jon and Greg set up camp at the agreed on location. Once the tent was assembled, they unrolled the carpet inside it. Having activated the necessary precautions, they drifted off to an invisible and well-shielded sleep.

CHAPTER 38

# Underground, Earlier

Jeremias woke with a start at dusk. He heard a noise, but having been asleep, he had no idea where it came from or what it might have been. When he looked outside the cave, he was surprised to see the sun sinking low in the West.

"Juvenal! Cyrus! Is it evening already? Why didn't you wake me?" he shouted.

"I'm sorry," Cyrus retorted, "we didn't know you wished to be waked."

"How are the prisoners?" he asked, standing to his feet and stretching out aching limbs.

"Good enough. We were just getting ready to start a fire for dinner. We have some dried meat for a stew, and some vegetables we must use today before they rot," Cyrus explained.

"Go to it, then," Jeremias ordered. "I have some things to which I must attend." He walked around the corner to where his prisoners lay. They appeared to be resting on their mats, unaware that he had joined them.

"Getting hungry?" Jeremias asked.

Ephraim rolled over on his mat to look at the speaker; Annie sat up. Annie spoke first. "Yes, as a matter of fact, I am quite hungry. I can't imagine that you had time to store anything very good in here, but I am hoping for the best."

Jeremias smiled, "A positive attitude is always best, my dear. And you young man?"

"I would like to eat. More than that, I would like something to drink," Ephraim spoke stiffly, the frustration evident in his voice.

"You must learn from the young lady, sir mage. Make the best of every situation. Dinner will be along in an hour or so. Your patience will be rewarded." Jeremias left.

Ephraim started to call out to the priest, but the words echoed in the cave without answer.

Jeremias walked from that tunnel into the other tunnel that branched out from the main cavern. When he was out of sight of everyone, he spoke the words he should have spoken sooner—"Sum familia obsidium."

"Brother, I am calling for you!"

There was silence for about 30 seconds. Then...*I am here. You may speak freely. What has happened?*

"We were successful in our enterprise. The first mage is in my custody. I also am in possession of his staff. As a result of the rapid execution of Operation Darkwing, the mage is chained to the inner wall of the mine our family bought some years ago."

*Who is with you?*

"I have Juvenal, a cousin of ours, as well as Cyrus and another called Crustus. I did end up taking a girl who was with the mage when we abducted him. She is just a common girl, but it was easier to bring her than leave her behind. I was afraid to do her harm, hoping for future cooperation from the first mage of the Ruby Kingdom."

*You have acted quickly, decisively, and efficiently. Brother, I am very impressed! Our troops are already amassed along the primeval forest, a day's march from the city walls. I will deploy our forces in the morning; the siege will begin at nightfall.*

"I have taken steps to assist you. Before I left the castle, I laced their food with sparkweed. You remember your encounter with that when you were a child, I suspect? Who could ever forget a sickness like that? I believe the palace will be very weak and vulnerable when you arrive."

*Excellent! I am amazed that you were able to accomplish so much in such a short period of time. You show great promise—I see a throne in your future!*

"Thank you, brother. I am concerned about one thing. That city has a never ending source of water. If they recover from the illness, which they will in a week or two, they may be able to hold out a very long time indeed. The castle has deep stores which I was not able to taint. I think it might be wiser to attack immediately while they are weak, rather than risk a long term campaign. Once they are well again, any advantage we have gained by the 'illness' will be lost."

*That is, of course, true, brother, but I am reluctant to expose our troops to any risks greater than necessary. I want this king deposed with as little loss of Obsidian life as possible. I would rather wait longer to protect our people, than rush ahead and sustain unnecessary casualties. No one else should die because a devil is on the red throne!*

"I understand, brother. I will keep the prisoner here until I hear further word from you. I will check in every evening to hear your reports and await your orders."

*Thank you, Jeremias. I expect a speedy campaign. I have 10 mages with me, as well as 40 acolytes. They have been training expressly for this campaign. Father ordered the training of this group when he first started his conquest for water, foreseeing the day when they would be needed. They are prepared, not only to assist us in the siege, but to bring down the walls, if necessary. Whatever you do, stay away until this whole ugly mess is over!*

"I will do exactly that, My King. I hope you rest well and travel with great speed tomorrow."

*Good night, brother.*

Jeremias grinned. Things were going exactly as planned. At least he thought they were.

❊❊❊

Anthony and Judas learned a great deal about one another on the trip to the mountains…without saying more than two dozen words. If Anthony expected Judas to need rest frequently, to need assistance with his mount, or to need any kind of indulgence at all, he was mistaken. Judas was strong, a competent rider, and not given to complaining. He was certainly not a royal brat!

And if Judas expected to ride with a rude, coarse, self-centered army officer, he was pleasantly disappointed. Anthony offered frequent stops for rest, shared provisions easily, and paid close attention to the needs of his prince. Given the rapid pace of the ride, it was as enjoyable as any ten hour journey on horseback could possibly be.

They saw the tent as they got close to the meeting place, and were relieved to make the reconnection so easily. Opening the flap to the tent, however, they were surprised to find it empty.

"I wonder where they could be," Judas thought aloud. "I would expect to find them waiting for us right here." He stood back up and strained his eyes toward the hills, looking for some sign of the missing duo.

The noise woke Greg, who nudged Jon. "They're here! Wake up," he whispered. Greg stepped out of the tent, directly in front of an astonished and perplexed captain.

Anthony jumped back! "I looked in there! The tent was empty! How did you get in there without me seeing it?"

"Captain Anthony, you should know by now that Sir Jonathan and I are capable of traveling invisibly," Greg explained, as Jon stepped out of the tent to join him. "But don't worry, we promise we will not purposely attempt to frighten you," Greg grinned broadly.

Judas, who had been studying the mountains for some sign of the boys, turned to join them as soon as the conversation began. "What have you learned, Sir Gregory?" he quickly asked.

"We know where they are. We also know that the entrance to the mine is magically guarded. We can't just fly in and grab them. We are going to need to develop a plan." Greg explained calmly. "Let's get settled in for the night, and then discuss our options."

After staking and tending the horses, they ate a simple meal and prepared the encampment. Jon was interested in their journey, and Anthony remarked about the smoothness of it. Once they had all settled into the tent, they began to discuss strategy.

No one in the tent had any idea how the magical barrier might work. Sooner or later, the people inside the cave would have to emerge. When they did, testing the barrier would be possible. Perhaps they could sneak through the entrance when the barrier was lowered to permit someone to leave the mine entrance. That would require a 24 hour watch on the entrance to the mine, and perpetual readiness to enter. Still, the kidnappers might not appear for several days.

Another approach, Jon suggested, would be to blast an opening through the side of the mountain around the entrance to the mine. Jon wasn't sure of the exact powers of the scepter, but there was always a chance it might be powerful enough. The unknown element was the position of the people inside. If Annie and Ephraim were on the other side of the wall they blasted, well, that would be a bad thing.

The foursome considered the possibility of luring their prey out of the cave. Some animal crossing in front of the cave might be an irresistible target for a hunting party. If they sent Jon and Greg to acquire an animal that could be released near the cave, perhaps those inside would go after the beast. But how could they force the beast to wander near the entrance to the cave?

"If only there was another entrance into this mine!" Jon exclaimed, exasperated.

"Wait a second," Greg paused, "how do we know that there isn't another way in?"

All heads turned toward Greg. "Eli said to look at the maps carefully. There are lots of tunnels sketched on them and who's to say that every tunnel actually got written down. Pull out that map and search for the other entrances to mines in the area."

It was dark in the tent, but Judas provided light for the map study. Anthony just stared at Judas' glowing finger. "Look here," Judas pointed, "There are three other mine entrances in the vicinity, but this one...it just looks like it might connect, don't you think?"

Jon did think, as did Greg and Anthony. But it was hard to tell from the map just how long those tunnels might be. Or more importantly, what their condition would be after years of disuse.

Anthony spoke up. "With the special abilities we have, it seems to me that the most reasonable approach is to explore the tunnels. I suggest that Prince Judas and either Sir Gregory or Sir Jonathan fly invisibly to explore the tunnels. I think it would also be wise for two of us to watch the front entrance. If, for some reason, they tried to move to a different location, we would be able to follow them from a distance."

The plan was quickly agreed upon, and after a little more discussion of possible next steps, the four decided to begin at dawn. Sleep came quickly.

CHAPTER 39

# Everywhere, at the Same Moment

Many things happened at once at the dawn of the next morning:

- General Zarak visited the barracks, looking for his son, Captain Anthony. Anthony, of course, was nowhere to be found. So intense was the General's questioning of the men, that the soldier holding the letter from Anthony broke down under the strain. Yielding up the letter, he explained that he had been instructed to deliver it 24 hours from the present time. Without a word further, the General tore open the missive, glanced over it quickly, turned, and departed quickly for the castle.
- A day's journey to the east, King Stefan gave the orders to break camp, form up and move west. The day of march had come.
- Inside the mine, Ephraim and Annie were served a crust of bread, a small wedge of cheese, a small cup of stew (leftovers from yesterday), and some musty tasting water. Ephraim had slept well, but only because Annie had refused to disturb him. By now, she was so homesick that it was hard for her to concentrate on anything else. Homesick and scared. She kept telling herself that this must all be a dream, and she expected to wake up any moment. But she knew she was deceiving herself. Still, she had enough presence of mind to realize that if they had any chance of escaping, they must be alert. And if she couldn't sleep, she had better do her best to make sure that at least one of them was well rested.
- Jeremias began to consider what he would say to his brother in his next report. He was pleased with himself. Everything had

gone very smoothly and they were safely hidden. His brother, King Stefan, was also pleased with him. He knew for certain that he would never take his final priestly vows, now. Hadn't his brother said it himself? There was a throne in his future!

• The sun woke Jonathan first, who roused Gregory and then Judas. Anthony was gone, probably out getting ready for the day. When they emerged from the tent, Anthony had breakfast well underway. Gregory tasted coffee for the very first time that morning, and decided that he would wait until college to try it again. Jonathan stuck to bread and cheese, and when the meal was finished, they were quickly under way.

Anthony and Gregory rode toward the mine entrance on horseback. They stopped far enough away from the entrance to safely stow their horses, approaching on foot. Crouching behind an outcropping of rocks, they settled down to watch the entrance.

Jon and Judas flew. They entered a mine shaft north and east of the place they knew Annie and Ephraim were captives. Once inside, Judas provided light for the expedition, Jon navigation. The trouble came when the tunnel divided. Knowing they wanted to go south and west helped them to choose, but they also decided to start marking the walls, just in case they got lost. As the tunnel narrowed, their progress slowed. Several times they found the tunnels partially blocked by fallen rock. The darkness seemed to close in around them and they could almost feel the weight of all the earth above them pressing them down.

After about three hours of relentless darkness, traversing tunnels that now all looked the same, Jonathan began to get discouraged. "Judas, it only took us about fifteen minutes to fly from the first mine entrance to this one. Don't you think we would have found something by now if we were on the right track?"

Judas thought a moment before he answered. "I am not certain I know what is best, Sir Jonathan. But this tunnel has only split twice so far. That means that if it is possible to get through this way, we have a 25% chance of being on the right trail. And given the general direction we have chosen, I think the percentage is higher than that.

I will agree that we need to allow time to follow other tunnels, and time to retrace our steps should this path prove fruitless. I am willing to gamble that we took the correct turn on the first fork in the path. I am much less sure about the second. I suggest that we travel about one more hour on this path, and, if we find nothing, we go back and search out the pathway we most recently bypassed. If that one also proves incorrect, we should return to camp and try the other two tomorrow."

Judas considered these words. The plan made sense, but what about Annie? Could she hold out for two more days? And how much time will have passed back in Newport? He guessed it didn't really matter, now. After being gone this long, he would have to explain the absence. And nothing short of the truth would do this time. But first, best to make sure everyone got home. Yes, the most important thing was getting Annie home safely.

"Sounds good to me," Jon agreed. "Let's keep moving."

It was only about fifteen minutes later when Judas motioned for Jon to stop. "Hold your breath. I thought I heard something," he whispered, and extinguished his glowing hand. Sure enough, there was the sound of some kind of pounding echoing down the tunnel ahead. It was faint, yet unmistakable. They were on the right trail! Judas restricted the light to the tip of his index finger, and they moved ahead, more slowly. At every turn in the corridor, they stopped, extinguished the light, listened intently, then moved around the corner. If the darkness continued, Judas relit finger, and they moved forward. Gradually, other sounds filtered down the cave, and pretty soon they noticed a faint increase in the amount of light in the shaft. They were getting closer. It was time to go completely dark. Flying invisibly, they moved up the tunnel until they arrived in a corridor where they could hear voices plainly. They stopped to listen, and Judas was able to make out the voice of the priest from the castle. That was no surprise. They could not figure out how many people were actually in the cavern ahead, but they knew there was more than one or two. The only way to find out for sure was to peek in and see.

The light entering the mining shaft from the main entrance was painful to their eyes. Gesturing to one another, they decided to wait a few moments until their eyes had adjusted to this new level of light. Once comfortable, they moved slowly to the edge of the main corridor. They noticed that an additional corridor stretched off to their left, but the action was taking place directly in front of them.

There were four men in the cave. Two older men were playing some sort of game off to the right side of the open area. A third person, much younger, was watching them, a few paces away. On the other side of the room, the priest was seated on some wadded up blankets. He was actually facing them, but reading some parchments. No doubt his position was designed to allow the sunlight streaming in from the entrance to illuminate his reading.

Without a sound, Jonathan gestured questioningly to Judas, mouthing the words, "Annie? Ephraim?" Judas shook his head, indicating his confusion. The entire entryway and main staging area was visible from their vantage point. Judas pointed toward the second corridor, and motioned for Jonathan to move them into it. There was a small glow of light coming from around the corner. As they got closer, they realized they had found the ones for whom they had been searching. Annie and Ephraim were huddled together, and it looked like they were reading. When they were about ten feet away from them, the confusion of the moment hit them. They didn't know what to do next. If they stepped off the carpet, they risked being heard. Annie and Ephraim were chained and they had no tools. If they startled Annie and Ephraim by appearing, the two might cry out in fear and give them away. Judas gestured back towards the tunnel by which they had entered, and Jon quickly understood. They retreated to a place where they could whisper without fear of being overheard.

After discussing several different options, they realized they were in trouble. Since Annie and Ephraim were chained, there was no way to free them without making noise. Any noise they made would alert the guards and they would be quickly surrounded. They weren't sure the carpet could carry four people; that had never been tried before. Three was a real squeeze! Worst of all, they didn't know what powers the priest might have. There didn't seem to be any way to make a silent exit. In the end, they decided to settle for illusion, illusion and a prayer.

Jon maneuvered the carpet directly in front of Ephraim and Annie. At exactly the same moment, Jon and Judas reached out from the carpet and clapped hands across the mouths of their friends. A second later, Jon switched off the invisibility. The eyes of Annie and Ephraim were wide with terror. To them, hands had appeared out of thin air to attack them. But before they had a chance to resist, recognition dawned and they realized who it was that was flying eighteen inches off the ground, directly before them. Judas gestured for them to remain silent, as he stepped off the carpet. Jon took the carpet about ten feet down the corridor, away from the main entrance, and brought it gently to the floor. He waited there while Judas explained, using gestures, what he intended to do.

Annie and Ephraim got quietly to their feet, extending the chain that held them to the wall to it's full length. They extended their legs to minimize their exposure to danger, and Judas stepped away. When they were all ready, Jonathan took the staff in his hands and two fire bolts exploded toward the wall where the chains were attached. Rocks crumbled and shouts erupted simultaneously. The ground shook with the force of the blast.

Jeremias was on his feet in a second, racing around the corner. He was greeted by dust and the smell of brimstone. The others were right behind him, yelling in bewilderment. But beyond the dust and the smoke, there was nothing else to see—only the corner of a sleeping mat extending past a small pile of rubble.

"Move the stones," Jeremias shouted to Cyrus and Crustus. He didn't expect to find anything. The pile was too small to be hiding anything as large as a body. But what he didn't find did surprise him. The chains were gone!

Anthony and Greg heard the blast and felt the tremor rippling from inside the mountain. Well, the element of surprise was certainly lost now! They ran to the entrance of the mine, hoping that by chance the magical shield had collapsed with the explosion. It hadn't. The men that had previously paced at the mouth of the tunnel were nowhere to be seen now. The cavern was empty, and Anthony drew his sword, expecting—no, hoping—to need it. Greg and Anthony could see the dust billowing out from the tunnel at the back of the cavern. They assumed that Jon and Judas were in there—probably Annie and Ephraim, too. But what should they do? Had their friends been able to escape? Were they all trapped inside? The feeling of helplessness was incredible! They could watch the scene unfold, but were powerless to influence the outcome of events.

A moment later, Jeremias, stepped back around the corner into the main cavern. He stared directly at the two men on the other side of the barrier. Seeing their frustration, he grinned. No one had escaped that way, he realized! Grabbing something from his sleeping mat, he stepped out of sight once again.

The only thing Greg had at hand was the silver sword tucked inside his belt. In frustration, he drew it, and using the hilt guard to protect his knuckles, he punched the magical barrier as hard as he could!

Jeremias pulled a small pouch of crushed obsidian from his tunic, and after having drawn a line in the dirt across the mouth of the first tunnel through which Judas and Jon had entered, he sprinkled the dust into it. Then he sang words strange and unfamiliar, musical and lyrical. When he was done, he ran his hand over his handiwork. A transparent barrier now covered the entrance to that tunnel!

He then explained his plan to his lackeys. There had not been time for anyone to get past them into the tunnel that was now guarded. No one could have escaped through the main entrance, for the barrier was intact. The prisoners must then still be in the same tunnel they were in previously. They could be deeper in the tunnel, and they might be magically hidden. But if they were present, and Jeremias stressed this point, they would find them, and he could master them. Of that he was certain. They would search this passageway inch by inch if they had to.

Jeremias explained to his men that things that were invisible were still actually present, so it was important not to trust one's eyes. Using a sword, Jeremias demonstrated how to sweep an entire area to make sure that nothing was present, seen or unseen.

It was now obvious to Judas that they would be found. But Sir Jonathan had explained the power of the shield, and he had seen the power of the staff! If he had to use deadly force, he would do so, but he hoped Jeremias could be made to surrender without violence. A moment later, Juvenal's sword struck the carpet's protective shield.

"Father, I think something is here," he stepped back quickly, pointing with the sword. Jeremias crossed the corridor quickly and explored the dimensions of the invisible, but obviously present, bubble in space. He stepped back five paces.

"Friends, get behind me quickly," he said. "Now stay back." He now directed his voice toward the bubble. "There is no doubt that you are watching me, but I am not altogether certain who you are. Of course, two of you I know rather well, isn't that right Ephraim and Annie?"

Judas shook his head, forbidding them to speak.

"Why don't you show yourself, now that we know you are here. At least that way we can look at each other while we speak," Jeremias continued.

"I don't think that would be wise," Judas responded. "Now why don't you move aside and let us leave peacefully."

"Ah, Prince Judas! You are truly the last person I would have expected to find on a mission of this sort. But surely you must know that there is no way I can let you escape. By now, our army is approaching your city. No, you must remain here, along with your first mage, until the battle has been won.

"Unfortunately, I must insist that you allow us to leave." Judas' voice was stern, and he spoke slowly, measuring his words. "If you do not, the same weapon that destroyed the chains will be focused on you. I do not wish to harm you. But if you force me to do so, I will do my duty."

Jeremias paused, staring through the space where the four stood invisibly huddled together on the carpet. He muttered something, and Ephraim and Annie slumped to the ground. Instantly, Judas knew what Jeremias had done.

"That won't work on me, Father. The same gem that empowers that spell also protects from that spell, if one is conscious of the threat. And trust me, Father Jeremias, I am very conscious of the threat you pose to me!" Judas warned.

"Quickly, men, grab the two we can see!" Jeremias shouted.

Judas looked down and realized that when his friends had fallen, they had not remained completely on the carpet. They were partially visible, and whatever was visible was not protected by the shield, either. But Jonathan, seeing the rapid approach, quickly launched a fire bolt at the floor in front of the group. When the smoke cleared, the mob had regrouped behind Jeremias about ten paces away. And Jeremias was grinning!

"That is an amazing weapon you have there!" Jeremias allowed. "I would hate to feel the bite of that. Look at the hole in the floor of the tunnel. Powerful." But the grin had not faded from his lips.

Judas was confused. "Yes, it is powerful. And that is why you will have to allow us to leave. If you detain us any longer, I will be forced to..."

"You will be forced to do what?" Jeremias sneered. "You get a powerful weapon in your hand, and you think that all the world must bow down to you. You Red Demons have always believed that might makes right! Well it doesn't always work that way, little boy." Jeremias was shouting loudly now. "Every once in a while, brain triumphs over brawn. But I am afraid that wisdom is lost on you." Jeremias seemed to regain his composure somewhat. Breathing deeply he extended his right arm. "Do you know what this is? Look very closely."

A sinking feeling came over Judas. Of course he knew what it was.

"This is the staff, the one in which the power of your first mage resides. There lies your first mage, asleep on the floor. Notice how powerless he is without his staff. And remember how powerful your fire-bolt is, how easily it destroys iron and rock. How do you expect to kill me without destroying the staff?" He stopped momentarily, relishing his victory.

"Now, I think it is time you began to listen to me. Without this staff, there is no reason to rescue the first mage. He is useless without it. As long as I have the staff, I control this situation. I would rather not destroy the staff, for it is an object of great power and deserves reverence. But if I must destroy this staff to assure the victory of my brother's armies, I will gladly do so, even if it costs me my life. You should have thought of that before you burst in here, Mighty Ruby Princeling."

Judas knew he had been beaten. How could he have forgotten about the staff?! His father had told him how important it was! Without the power of a first mage, the kingdom would likely be lost, and it would be his fault. What an idiot he was!

Jeremias began to speak again. "I think that you should…"

"Don't move…," came a voice from behind Jeremias. The bone-crunching sound of fist connecting to flesh was quickly followed by the bodies of Cyrus and Crustus crashing into the tunnel walls. "… unless you wish to die," the voice finished.

Jeremias froze, his fingers clenched around the staff. Gregory reached passed him and gripped the staff, but the priest would not let go.

Anthony pressed the steel of the blade more firmly against the neck of the priest. "It is too late to destroy the staff," Anthony slowly instructed. "Breaking the handle will not harm the gem, and you would be dead before you could do any harm to the power source."

Jeremias, knowing he was defeated, released his grip, letting Gregory remove the staff. Juvenal stood beside Jeremias, quiet before the point of Gregory's dagger. Jonathan and Judas quickly appeared and assisted Anthony in the clean up process. In a matter of moments, the priest was bound, his henchmen were sleeping soundly, and Annie and Ephraim were wrestled back to consciousness.

"Anthony, you saved us all! How did you get through the barrier?" Judas asked, amazed at the miraculous turn of events.

"Well, actually, I'm not the one who got us through. You'll have to ask Sir Gregory how he managed that trick," Anthony winked at Greg.

"Sir Gregory, then, tell us how you did it," the prince persisted.

Gregory hesitated before answering. "I wish I could say I figured out a clever way to undo the spell, or get around the barrier. The truth is, I was so frustrated—when I thought you were in danger and I couldn't get to you—that I punched the barrier."

Jon laughed out loud! "You punched it? Did you break your fist?"

"That's the strange part. I knew I would hurt my hand if I just punched the wall, so I drew my sword first, thinking the hilt guard would protect my knuckles. When I punched the barrier, my hand tore right through it, like a knife tearing through heavy fabric. I pulled my hand back, and realized that the silver sword was able to slice through the barrier somehow. I simply cut away the magic and opened a door!"

Ephraim seemed to be holding a conversation of his own at the same time as everyone else. It took a moment before anyone noticed how distracted he was, but Annie hushed them when she realized that Ephraim must be talking to Eli.

Ephraim paused to address the group. "Eli suggests that Judas, Jon and I return to the castle at once. The king needs to know that the prince and first mage are safe. And we must take special precautions concerning the priest. He must be thoroughly searched, and he should be gagged so that he is unable to speak. He has magical abilities and he is very dangerous. Oh, yes," he paused as if listening, "and give me the staff."

When they turned back toward where the priest lay, they realized he was speaking, but to whom, they could not tell. Judas walked directly toward Jeremias, listening as he walked..."I failed, brother. They have friends who can move invisibly and..." When Judas realized that Jeremias was somehow giving a report, he grabbed a scarf and quickly gagged the priest, who was already bound hand and foot. Jeremias managed to relate that the barrier had been penetrated, before Judas silenced him.

The search of the priest turned up several pouches of unknown substances. These were entrusted to Ephraim. They also found the royal obsidian hanging around Jeremias' neck. When Anthony reached out to take it, Judas told him not to bother.

Judas explained. "Anthony, this stone is a royal insignia, but it is also magically charged and linked to this person. It cannot be forcibly taken from him. If you try, you may succeed in removing it for a minute or so, but it will soon disintegrate and reappear around his neck." Before Anthony could ask any questions, Judas went on.

"There is more you must know. I also wear a similar stone. It gives me several special abilities. For one thing, I know my father is very agitated. He has been signaling me since late this morning. I have felt the stone grow warm at least four different times. That is how he alerts me to the fact that he wants me to contact him. At present, I have no way to make that contact, but we will rush home to see him. You, unfortunately, must conduct the prisoners, as well as Annie and Sir Gregory back to the castle. You will need some extra protection if you are going to be successful."

Judas slipped the royal ruby from around his neck and handed it to his captain. "Captain Anthony, this is the most precious possession I have. I am loaning it to you for the duration of this journey. It will protect you from the spells of the priest, and give you several other abilities. I will collect it again when we are all safely home."

Ephraim was running his fingers over his new staff, and as Judas led Anthony off to explain about the abilities of the royal stone, Annie cornered Jon. "We have got to get back home! We have been gone for two days. My parents are going to be hysterical! There is no way I am going to stay here any longer while you go running off to…" Jon interrupted her.

"I'm sorry things turned out the way they did. But we can't go back until we have delivered Judas and Ephraim. It will only take…"

"But you said you would take me right home if I wanted. And I want to get out of here now!" Annie shouted, stomping her foot.

Jon, trying to be patient, sighed heavily, then tried to explain. "Annie, I can fly to the castle and back in about two hours at top speed. That won't make a difference of more than ten minutes or so back in Newport. After I drop off the prince and mage, I will get you and Greg and we'll be out of here. Please understand, we can't think just of ourselves, here."

Annie thought for a moment. She had to admit that at this point, ten minutes wouldn't make much difference at home. The only question was whether or not she would still be free to return two hours from now, if she remained here! Strange things happened in this place!

Grudgingly, Annie agreed to stay behind. Judas, Ephraim and Jon would fly to the castle and Jon would return with two soldiers to reinforce Anthony. Greg and Annie would start the trip home on horse back with Anthony. Jon better not be late, she told him!

After reviewing the plan once more with the group, Ephraim, Jon and Judas departed. They walked around the mountain until they were out of sight of the mine entrance, making certain that none of the prisoners actually saw them engage the carpet. Jeremias had already reported far too much information. They couldn't afford to divulge any more important secrets!

One hour later, Jonathan was dropping off the prince and the mage. Judas instructed Jon to go find the soldier who had been given the letter, and to take him and a comrade back to Anthony. Jonathan did just that. Two hours and five minutes after Jon left his friends in the desert, he returned. Replacing Annie and Greg with two well-trained soldiers, Jon left Anthony behind as the carpet raced at eagle speed back toward the mountain entrance to Newport, back towards home.

## CHAPTER 40

# Magic Coerced

General Zarak pushed past the guards at the door to the king's apartments and walked into the empty study. A nurse was just leaving the king's bedchamber, and she scowled at the General as if she did not approve of his presence.

"Your Majesty!" Zarak shouted out. "May I come in?" He waited silently for a response. Eventually the king's valet opened the door that separated the study from the king's private lounge

"Is it urgent?" the valet asked, his tone pleading for the general to wait until a later time.

"I am afraid it is most urgent. This really cannot wait." Zarak sympathized with the king, knowing how sick he must be. But the note he had just acquired from one of his soldiers needed to be brought to the king's immediate attention.

The king was lying on a large sofa in his lounge. His face was pale, his eyes sunken with dark circles around them. When Zarak entered, the king did not turn to greet him.

"Your Majesty," Zarak offered a small bow.

"Yes, Zarak? What is it?" the king muttered, obviously completely exhausted, drained of all strength.

"I am deeply sorry to bother you, Your Majesty, but I have just gotten news that is very grave," the general explained. "I felt you should know, and I believe you will want to give me instructions."

"Please, continue," the king gestured.

"Apparently," Zarak stumbled along, "Ephraim has been kidnapped. The prince discovered this the evening of the poisoning, I suspect. He has recruited a team to recover Ephraim, and this team includes not only my son, Anthony, but the two wizards we met previously in the Grove on the Great Board. The prince believes that they will return by tonight. In the event of an unfortunate outcome, the prince left this letter with one of Anthony's men, to be delivered tomorrow morning to you through me. When I was unable to locate Anthony this morning, I pressed the men hard. That's how I found the letter early."

The fact that the king did not bellow in rage was an indication of just how sick he really was. But he was furious, nevertheless. "Idiot! How could he expect to deal with treachery of this magnitude by himself? He should have come to me immediately!"

"In all fairness, Your Majesty, you were not in any condition that night to…"

"Shut up, Zarak! I know what condition I was in!" the king shouted, then groaned at the pain the shout had caused him. "The prince is a stupid, little boy, hardly old enough to understand matters of espionage and warfare. He hasn't even begun his training with the regular troops, yet! How can we trust something this important to a mere child?"

"Your Majesty, this matter isn't just in the hands of a child," Zarak cautiously reminded the king. "Remember, Anthony is also along. I can't tell you that I understand why he went along with this plan without telling me, but I trust my son. He wouldn't jump into something that wasn't well reasoned with a good chance of success. The prince may not have a great deal of experience, but Anthony is neither naïve nor impulsive. And somehow, your son did manage to enlist the aid of some formidable magicians!"

The king sighed deeply. He held his head in his hands, his frustration obvious. "Then what do you suggest we do, send the cavalry after them?"

"Maybe," Zarak replied, "but perhaps not yet. The note was supposed to be delivered tomorrow morning, but only if things went wrong. That means they expected to be back sometime today. Why not wait until tonight to see if their plan works?"

"You want me to sit and do nothing, knowing my first mage has been kidnapped and my foolish son is trying to rescue him single-handedly?" barked the king, incredulously.

The general thought for a moment, then replied. "You are correct, Your Majesty. We should do something. If they do not arrive home on schedule, we are ten to twelve hours away from the place where we can be of help. We should send reinforcements right now, so that if there is a need, we can be nearby to offer assistance."

"So, what should we do?" the king asked, still perturbed.

"Send about 20 men north to the mountains to search for the group. If the men left shortly, they could be in the vicinity just after nightfall. In the event of catastrophe, they would be just what the prince would need."

The king considered Zarak's suggestion, then nodded his head slowly. "That's good. I would normally send General Artezes on a mission that involved the cavalry, but I am afraid that this situation may require some negotiation and subtlety. Zarak, those are your strengths. Please lead the men personally. Leave as soon as you are ready."

"Yes, Your Majesty," Zarak nodded. He and his men were gone within the hour.

✿✿✿

Just after noon, the commotion began. A rider stormed up to the city gates, demanding to see the king. Because he was a part of the system of heralds, he was quickly admitted to the castle and brought before General Artezes, who received him in his private quarters on the third floor. Panting, the courier guzzled down the water he was offered and gasped out his message. "General, we are under attack! The army of the Obsidian Kingdom is headed this way. Any who resist them are being cut down, though they don't seem to be stopping to pillage or steal. I think they are coming here!"

The aging general questioned the man intensely, then sent him to the kitchens to be fed and cared for. Artezes went directly to the king's rooms.

"Your Majesty, a courier has just arrived claiming that we are under attack by the Obsidian Kingdom. The army has..."

"We are what!?!" the king shouted. "How can they possibly be attacking us? We just resolved this thing in the Grove! They lost! Their king and queen are dead! Their mages no longer live! They can't possibly be attacking us!"

Artezes bowed his head. "Perhaps the courier is mistaken, Your Majesty. It does, however, seem like an unusual thing to make up. He says that the courier from Eastdown rode swiftly through the countryside, locating him just an hour ago in Trentonille. He claims that the first courier was also a royal herald and saw the army himself."

"Get me Zarak, General," the king started, then remembered that Zarak was already gone. "God help us, it's all beginning to make sense! The first mage kidnapped, the food poisoned, all preludes to the attack."

"The first mage has been kidnapped?" Artezes repeated, astounded.

"Yes, General, he has indeed. And just an hour or so ago I sent Zarak after him. I didn't even have a chance to let you know what was going on, and now everything seems to have broken loose! Quickly, mobilize the troops! We will have to do our best to ward off these invaders. And we will have to do it on our own, without the benefit of any magical protection. Sound the alarm, then return here to discuss our defenses."

Though General Artezes knew the condition of his own troops, he was surprised at the overall level of readiness evidenced by the army at large. The soldiers reported, armed and ready, in record time. They were awaiting his instructions when he returned from the king.

It had been decided to divide the troops into two sections. The cavalry would hide behind the western wall of the city, while the infantry would camp in front of the city on the western side of the small stream that flowed from the city wall. It was hoped that the enemy troops would be lured toward the infantry. Once they committed in that direction, the cavalry would sweep around from the north and push them from behind into the stream, where they would be on uneven footing. Perhaps that would give the Ruby soldiers an advantage against what looked like superior numbers. The soldiers were quickly deployed.

When Ephraim and Prince Judas returned to the castle, things were in a high state of panic. People were rushing through the gates to get into the city, bringing carts piled high with vegetables and grain. Messengers were running in every direction. The kitchen was in high gear, taking in stores, preparing for the possibility of a long siege. It wasn't until he got to his father's apartments that he finally learned what was going on. The guard at his father's door quickly admitted the prince and his friend to the king's study. The king, still weak from his illness, was seated at the table in the center of the room, sipping soup slowly. He looked up when the door opened.

"Judas, I can't believe...." He stopped for a moment when he saw Ephraim enter the room behind Judas. The expression on his face changed from rage to disbelief. "...I can't believe...you did it! Ephraim, you're safe! What happened?"

Judas began to tell the story of the kidnapping, the treasonous priest, the trip across the desert, but the king could not endure the entire story.

"We will have to have the details at another time. We have a great emergency before us. The army of the Obsidian Kingdom will arrive very shortly. We are under attack. What can you do to assist our armies?" the king asked Ephraim, pointedly.

"I do not know, my king," said Ephraim, with his head bowed low. "I only touched my staff for the first time a few hours ago. I have never tried it, not even once. I have only just begun my studies."

"There must be something you can do! Can you create darkness to buy us time? Can you shoot flames at the enemies? Can you turn their general into stone?" the king shouted, grasping at straws.

"I am sorry, Your Majesty. I do not know how to do any of those things," Ephraim whimpered, almost in tears.

"What good is a first mage if he is powerless?" yelled the king, angrily.

Ephraim stood in silence, shocked and embarrassed. What could he say? It wasn't his fault he was inexperienced. Power only came with training and time. It was unfair to expect anything more.

He couldn't decide if the king was waiting for an answer, or if he was trying to think of what else to say. But into that silence, another voice spoke.

*Ephraim, I will try to help you.*

"Eli!, I mean, Your Majesty, Eli will help me!" Ephraim squealed.

"What? Eli? Is he here?" the king asked.

"He's inside my head! Give me a little time, and I will see what I can learn. When I understand more, I will come back to report."

"Well, hurry! There isn't much time. The safety of the entire kingdom may well be in your hands," the king said, his voice filled with disgust. General Artezes entered the study at just that moment, allowing Judas to make his escape along with Ephraim. They ran back to the prince's room.

Once inside the room, the conversation inside Ephraim's head continued. Eli took Ephraim to sections of the book that gave secrets concerning the use of power. Eli reminded Ephraim of the primary principles.

*Because the Creator loves all people, no matter what side of a dispute they are on, it will be difficult, if not impossible, to use magic to destroy folks, especially in large numbers. You will do best if you can think of ways to manipulate the environment to prevent the conflict from taking place. If that doesn't work, concentrate your efforts against one or two key leaders. When all else fails, use your power to defend your friends. These will be the best, and most successful, uses of your power.*

"But Eli, how do I know I will be able to do it when the time comes?" Ephraim implored.

*We need to practice. I think it would be best if you went some place private, someplace protected. Ask Judi to take you down to the crypt. Once there, ask him to leave you alone so that we can begin to work with your staff.*

Judas was glad to have something to do and willingly took Ephraim down to the crypt. He wasn't as glad when Ephraim asked him to leave.

"I will place two guards on this door, and when you are finished, come to my room first. I want to accompany you when you return to my father," Prince Judas instructed. Leaving Ephraim to his own task, Judas headed to the fletcher's shop outside of the castle, within the walls of the city. The shop was empty, empty of arrows, that is. But the fletcher was still at work, along with two assistants, producing as quickly as his nimble hands could work. When he saw the prince, he bowed low.

"Your Majesty, I had not expected to see you today. Forgive my inattention, but the times are grim, and our hands must be about doing what they can to make a difference," the fletcher said.

"I would not take you from your work, kind sir. But I would ask that you begin to prepare a quiver full of my special arrows. I plan to make a difference, as well, and I hope I can put your work to good use," Judas spoke kindly. He decided to wait for the arrows. There really wasn't anything else he could do inside the castle. After a few moments, he realized that he could save the fletcher a few steps here and there by helping to gather supplies and materials. He quickly pitched in to help. The fletcher grinned. "Nothing like a royal apprentice," he teased.

"If this is the best contribution I can make at the moment, I am happy to make it!" Judas said, smiling. It was pleasant work, and Judas soon found more and more he could do to help. The hour passed quickly.

Judas collected his arrows and ran back to the castle. He dispatched a messenger to make one last attempt to secure more supplies for the fletcher's shop. Then he went searching for Ephraim. When he arrived at the crypt, the door was shut and the guards still in place. When he knocked at the door, no one answered. A few seconds later, a loud crash erupted from the inside, followed by the sounds of things breaking and falling to the floor.

"Are you okay, Ephraim?" Judas shouted.

"I'm fine," Ephraim replied. "Don't worry about me. But don't come in. It's not quite safe in here. I'll be up when I am ready." There was a pause. "I'm afraid one of your ancestors has a chipped nose," he added.

Judas headed back to his room. Halfway up the main stairs, he heard a trumpet sound, and he knew something important was happening. He figured it was time to take his position, so he retrieved his weapons and armor from his room, and moved toward the tower. He had decided many years ago that if the castle was ever attacked, he would work with the archers. He knew his father would never allow him out of the castle, so long as he was the only heir to the throne. But with good armor for protection, how could his father object to his plan to shoot? He was an excellent archer, and from the third floor, he had an excellent vantage point. Moving through the chapel and the priests' quarters, Judas prepared to make a difference from the third floor tower room. When he finally arrived, he saw the reason for the trumpet.

Below him, the armies of the Obsidian kingdom were moving into position. The numbers were impressive; a sense of foreboding filled Judas. The stream that issued forth from the eastern side of the city wall was the dividing line between the forces. Obsidians were on the eastern side facing west, gathered behind the houses that were built all along the stream. The Rubyites faced east. The front lines were disciplined, frozen into place. For an hour, men moved into place, positions were fortified, equipment inspected and adjusted. Finally, another trumpet sounded from behind Obsidian lines. A knight in full armor rode forward, a white cloth flying from the pinnacle of his lance. Next to him was a small herald. They wove through the houses, then stopped 100 feet short of the stream. Unrolling a parchment, the herald began to read in a loud voice, "King Stefan of Obsidia accuses the Ruby King of treachery on the Great Board. That treachery followed attacks on our property and resulted in the murder of the sovereign Lord of Obsidia and his Lady. This diabolical behavior will now be punished, unless apologies are made. The only acceptable apologies are the immediate surrender of water rights east of the Great Tirades, along with the surrender of the person of the Ruby King, to be judged and punished under Obsidian law. We wait one hour for your response." The knight and the messenger turned and rode back to their ranks.

The king, who had listened from the second floor tower on the south eastern side of the castle, was furious. Because there was no window large enough from which to issue orders nearby, he struggled into the secret passage and made his way upstairs to the third floor, then further up and onto the open roof of the tower. From there he shouted at the enemy:

"You ignorant fools! This quarrel was decided fairly in the Grove. Everyone knows the Great Board enforces its own rules. Your child king has deceived you and now uses you to get his own twisted revenge. Do not waste your lives following him. You have ten minutes to turn and leave, or you will be destroyed where you stand. The Creator will see to it!"

There was a rumble among the enemy troops. But a strong, clear voice rang from the center of the army. "He lies! And he breaks the law! If the land is the Creator's gift to the people, why does he hoard the land and its resources? No, we must take what is ours. Move out!" A trumpet sounded the attack.

Although the army began to move, it didn't exactly attack. Rather than charging forward, it began to divide. One section moved north, while a second drew closer to the stream. Rows of houses stood on either side of the stream, long empty of inhabitants. When the Obsidian army was within 100 yards of the houses, another trumpet rang out and arrows filled the sky! Flaming arrows! The target was not the opposing army, however, but the houses that stood between them. In another moment, the flames engulfed the wooden houses and the land between the armies was a blazing inferno.

At the same moment that the arrows flew, the northern half of the army attacked. Led by cavalry, they rode to the north of the castle, attempting to attack at the rear of the army and push them toward the fires. The king, seeing their plan, shouted, "Attack!" and the battle was engaged. Arrows flew from archers on the city walls.

The Obsidian cavalry, racing across the area behind the city, was surprised to find their Ruby counterparts waiting for them as they rounded the north western corner of the city wall. The two forces crashed into one another. The carnage was terrifying, horses screaming, men howling in pain, the clash of steel and the smell of smoke everywhere.

The din of the fighting was so loud that no one heard the singing. From somewhere behind the front lines of the obsidian infantry, a song was rising. The words were unintelligible, but the very sound struck fear into the heart of the king. It was the song of magic; something was afoot. The Ruby King yelled for his aide to find Ephraim and bring him immediately. They were in grave danger!

By the time Ephraim had been found and delivered to the king, the deadly spell had done its work! The cavalry was engaged behind the Ruby army. The fires along the stream prevented a forward advance for a short while longer. That left the infantry momentarily trapped between horses and fires. And into the gap came the snakes! Up from the banks of the stream, poison-fanged vipers writhed through the grass toward the red soldiers. The men in the front lines hacked away at them, but there were too many, and soon the screams of the soldiers in front of the city were added to the noise of the battle behind it. Panic swept through the troops and the red soldiers retreated into the city. A trumpet fanfare sounded retreat for the cavalry, who quickly disengaged and fled for the safety of the walls. The Obsidian cavalry did not pursue the red riders past the south western tower of the city wall, for fear of becoming targets for the snakes themselves.

The field in front of the city gates was a writhing mass of black. Guards posted just inside the gates hacked at any serpents unlucky enough to slide under the gate. But inside the gates was chaos! Men who had been bitten were wailing in pain. The moans of the injured filled the plaza in front of the castle. Surgeons attended to the wounded, while the officers sorted out their troops. Archers on the city walls continued to fire at the Obsidian cavalry.

The infantry was still out of range of the arrows. But now the fires were beginning to burn low. All at once, the singing stopped. And the snakes simply vanished! One moment they were there and the next they were gone! And into the void created by the disappearance of the snakes, the Obsidian army began to flow. Slowly, through the charred remains of the houses, across the stream, they came, taking up their position in front of the city.

The king was frantic! His troops had been embarrassed! The homes of his subjects had been burned to the ground, within sight of the city walls! His army had retreated and was now stuck inside the city. He needed magic, and he needed it now!

"Ephraim, do something!" he shouted. "We need to wipe these fools off the face of the earth! Hasn't Eli taught you anything yet?"

Ephraim was shaking. He raised his voice timidly to speak: "Your Majesty, we are making good progress, but I am still very uncertain. I'm not sure what I can do, and I'm not even sure if I will..."

"Ephraim, try anything!" the king roared. "But do something big! Do as much damage as you can, and as quickly as you can. A major magical attack of any nature will show them that you are present. And that might be enough!"

"I'll do my best, Your Majesty. Excuse me, Your Highness," the first mage said, and turned to leave the room.

"Where do you think you are going?" the king barked.

"I am going to the edge of the water. I suggest you stay away from the windows, far inside the castle." And with that, Ephraim departed.

Four guards accompanied Ephraim through the front doors of the castle, out across the yard, to the place where the moat drained under the city wall to form the stream that divided the plain in front of the castle. No one in the courtyard even noticed what was happening next to the wall.

Ephraim dispatched his guards to inform the officers to move their soldiers to the other side of the castle. When the space around him was clear, Ephraim planted his right foot in the waters of the stream that drained the moat, keeping his left foot on dry ground. He stirred the waters in front of him with the tip of his staff. Then he began to sing:

*"Fires burn and serpents slither,*
*Waters deep, I call thee hither.*
*Wind and rain, the time has come*
*To blow away Obsidian scum!"*

## SpellSong to Defend Against the Obsidian Kingdom

Ephraim repeated the song, all the while stirring the waters with the staff. By the time he reached the end of the second repetition, the waters of the stream began to bubble. The volume of water in the stream increased rapidly, and the bubbling proceeded out from where Ephraim stood and traveled under the wall. Where the stream bubbled, water began to rise at an incredible rate! A torrent of water burst out from under the city wall. In no time at all, the burned houses that surrounded the stream were swept away and a flash flood raced downward across the plain. Troops that were attempting to cross the stream lost their footing and were washed downstream, along with any on either side of the once small creek.

Black clouds that had begun to gather with the first strains of the song now dumped gallons of water on an already flooded plain. Great winds swept out of the north and lightening and thunder terrified horses and soldiers alike.

For an hour, Ephraim sang his song, and for an hour, the elements obeyed him. Finally, unable to endure the strain of concentration for another second, Ephraim slumped to the ground. Tender hands carried him back to the castle. He never heard the cheers of the people.

The magnitude of what Ephraim had done was not immediately apparent. As soon as the clouds cleared, it was obvious that over half of the Obsidian Army was no longer outside the city walls. The other half, seeing their ranks devastated, was retreating to the east. The mood inside the city walls was euphoric! The pendulum had swung from defeat to victory so quickly, that the soldiers and townsfolk were giddy! But the mood didn't last very long.

It took about an hour for the first reports of the price of the victory to come in. The flood that raced down the plain had wiped out seven entire villages. Without any warning, many had perished. If most of those villages hadn't been evacuated because of the invading army, casualties would have been in the hundreds. The flooding had spread so widely that many crops were destroyed. And those whose lives had been spared due to the evacuation, now had no homes to which they could return.

It wasn't until the next morning that scouts were able to determine the extent of the injury to the enemy invaders. While some had been swept away by the waters, the flooding was less severe closest to the city where the soldiers were, and more severe in the south where the waters had gathered momentum. Essentially, a large majority of the soldiers had been able to swim to safety. The greatest brunt of the water attack was borne by the people of the Ruby Kingdom! Fully seven-eighths of the Obsidian army had survived, and were even now regrouping off to the east!

The king's fury was uncontrollable! His first mage had destroyed his own kingdom and barely injured the enemy! He stormed around his room, shouting at servants and generals alike. Ephraim was forbidden to enter his sight and was placed under house arrest in a guest room on the third floor of the castle.

General Zarak and Captain Anthony had arrived during the night, with the traitor Jeremias in tow. Because Jonathan had already delivered Ephraim and Prince Judas to the castle, they assumed that the king already knew their situation, and that an immediate report was unnecessary. Unfortunately, Zarak chose to wait until late morning to visit the king, thinking the king needed extra rest to recover from his illness. He entered the king's chambers and instantly realized that everything was definitely not all right.. When he reported that Jeremias was safely chained in the dungeons below, the king ignored the news about the traitor and asked him where the two mages were who had assisted them. Zarak, of course, didn't know. The king flew into a rage and banished everyone from his sight! The palace quickly became a quiet place, with everyone actively engaged in leaving the king alone.

CHAPTER 41

# Obsidian Camp

To the East, King Stefan was regrouping. He had assumed that, given the time of his last communication with Jeremias, it was impossible for the first mage to be present in the city yet. The large scale magical attack was a complete surprise! He had not even bothered with defensive magic, for he assumed that he wouldn't need it for another twenty-four hours. But he would not be fooled again.

Marfessol seized the opportunity of this most recent defeat to further embitter the new young king against his opponents. He told Stefan that any king worthy to lead would not allow the deaths of his soldiers to go unavenged. He told him how embarrassing it would be to return to Obsidia, defeated by water instead of real soldiers. He reminded him of the selfishness of the Ruby King, and of his perceived treachery on the Board. And every reminder stoked the fire that burned in Stefan's breast.

Near mid day he was distracted from his troop inspection by a familiar voice. Jeremias was calling!

*I am chained in the dungeons of the Ruby castle. General Zarak escorted me back here personally. I was gagged until they brought me lunch, but now I am able to speak, thanks to the foolishness of a soft-hearted guard.*

"Why would those villains be so cruel as to gag you?" Stefan asked.

*They know of my magical abilities, and they also suspect that I can contact you. Judas heard me speaking to you after my capture, and put two and two together. At the time, I thought it worth the risk to speak to you.*

"You were correct to do so. But what actually happened? You were so sure of success! How could everything come crashing down so quickly?"

285

*There are mages in this group I have never seen before. Their names are Sir Jonathan and Sir Gregory, and they have amazing powers. One of them was able to get Judas and himself into the mine invisibly. I do not know how, but I think they came in through a back entrance we did not know existed. The other mage was able to break through a magical barrier I erected at the mouth of the cave. I have no idea how he did it, for at one time I saw him standing frustrated in front of the barrier, unable to pass through. He must have figured out a way to destroy it.*

*I had uncovered one half of the rescue attempt and had neutralized it, but before the situation was stable, I was blind-sided by the other half who came through the front barrier! The party left in two groups. Sir Jonathan, the prince and the First Mage walked away first, and the rest of us proceeded by horseback or on foot. About two hours later, we heard a shout behind us. There, standing in the desert, was Sir Jonathan, leaning on a golden staff! He had two soldiers with him. After speaking quietly with a Captain who had accompanied them, he left the soldiers with us and took the girl and Sir Gregory with him. Then they blindfolded us. I think they didn't want us to see the trio disappear. When they removed the blindfolds, the mages and the girl were gone! I only suspect that was the reason for the blindfold, because I saw four of them appear out of nowhere earlier.*

*It was only a few hours later that we ran into a group of soldiers in the middle of the desert, led by General Zarak. They seemed to know exactly where we would be!*

"These two mages must be the same two who appeared in the Grove. They killed our father; they must be assassins. We have got to find a way to get rid of them, permanently."

*I agree. Without them, our plan would have worked perfectly. I am not sure what help I can be from where I am. I will, of course, try to escape. I still have a few tricks up my sleeve, as you know. If the guards get close enough, I will use them. If anything helpful happens, I will let you know.*

"Thank you, brother. I look forward to seeing you. Either you will come to me, or I will personally unlock the door to your cell. Until that day, be well."

*And you, also.*

CHAPTER 42

# There and Back Again

The ride back to Newport was fast, too fast to really talk. But as soon as the three arrived in the cave, they all started to speak at once. It was as if the trip home was an incubation time for their thoughts, and the landing of the carpet cracked open all three eggs at once. Annie was worried about what her parents would say. The same thought was foremost in the minds of the boys. But there were subtle twists. What would Annie's parents think of boys who took their daughter away without permission? What would the Curtises do to their sons for damaging their relationship with the new neighbors? Basically, it all came down to this. They had to find out how things had progressed. If others had been called in to assist in the search, they would get their parents alone and explain everything. But if, by some stroke of luck—Greg was more inclined now to say Providence—the search was still contained within the family, an excuse like "time got away from us" might be enough.

In either event, they needed to get out of the house. No story would work if it didn't agree with the note they had left. Getting out of the house might be a problem, so they decided to use the carpet for cover, rather than leaving it in the cave. They flew into the basement, rounded corners, moved up the stairs, and slowly reached out to open the door to the living room. This was the moment of truth. Jon silently turned the knob and pushed the door open a crack. The room was dark. He pushed it further, and listened. No noise. Slowly he pushed the door open and they flew into the living room, snail speed. Everything was quiet in the house. Moving toward the back door, Greg spied the kitchen clock and whispered, "It's only nine o'clock. It's not that late. But where is everybody?"

Because the back door was more hidden from view than the front, they proceeded out that way, being careful to close the door behind them. They weren't afraid of anyone seeing them, but doors didn't usually open and close by themselves.

"Jon," Greg suggested, "let's get a bird's eye view very quickly. That way we can see if anyone is nearby or if anything unusual is happening." Jon took the carpet up three times higher than his house. On the way up they noticed that, although no lights were on inside the Curtis home, there were two or three lights on at the Monagul's. They could see First beach from their vantage point, as well as lights from many other houses.

"Fly over there. Let's check out what's going on in my house," Annie directed. "Maybe they are still unpacking boxes or something!"

Jon angled the carpet up against the house, just outside a window that was lighted. Inside, Mrs. Monagul was rocking the little one, singing softly. She seemed relaxed, yet anxious for the child to sleep. Tommy wasn't quite ready to sleep, however. He was squirmy and chatty, and seemed to want a great many things. Mrs. Monagul managed to find a stuffed bear in a nearby box, and began to settle back into the chair with the toddler, when Tommy decided he wanted "Da-Da."

"Da-Da will be back in just a few minutes. He went down to the beach to look for the kids. They'll be back soon. Now go to sleep," she whispered, as she stroked his curly blonde hair.

Jon instinctively took the carpet up high. "Let's find them," he said, "and see what's going on." It only took them a few minutes to spot the three parents, walking down the beach, shoes in hand. They stopped to talk to a few people as they walked toward the merry-go-round.

"I think," Jon suggested, "that if we got home right away and reported in to your mom, we could say that time got away from us. If we came up from the south, our paths would have never crossed. Then we could go catch up to our parents on the beach."

"It's worth a try," Annie agreed. "But I don't like lying to my parents."

"I won't exactly lie," Jon explained. "I'll say we checked out the beach, that we ended up going further than we planned and time got away from us. We came home up the boulevard. All of that is true. I just won't tell everything that happened."

Annie was still clearly uncomfortable, but decided to go along. She knew in her heart the deceit was wrong, but she had never had a night like this in her life. The kids snuck in the back door of the house and stowed the carpet downstairs inside the trunk. Then, slipping out the back door, they ran down the hedgerow, past Annie's house, and approached from the south. The front door was unlocked, so they went right in.

"Mom! Dad! We're home!" Annie hollered out. "Mom! Are you in…"

"Annie! Where have you been?" Annie's Mom came to the head of the stairs. "It's past dark! You should know to be home by dark!" Mrs. Monagul scolded. Although Mrs. Monagul was clearly displeased, she wasn't 'out of control' angry, and as soon as she saw the boys, she softened her tone. "Wait there a second," she said. Mrs. Monagul stepped back into Tommy's room for a moment, then re-emerged, something small in her hand. An odd, electronic chime sounded, and Mrs. Monagul began to speak again, but not to them.

"They're here, guys. Come on home. Everyone's fine."

The sound of static filled the air, then, "Thanks, Helen. We'll be there in about ten minutes. Bye," a voice came back

"Where did you guys go?" Helen Monagul asked, stuffing the walkie-talkie into a pocket. "We got your note, but we were worried when you were gone so long."

Jon tried his pre-planned line. "We checked out the beach and ended up going further than we planned. It took us longer to get back than we expected. We're sorry we were out so late."

"That's okay, boys," Annie's mom softened, her lips twisting into a small grin. "We're just happy you all are okay and apparently had a good time. Your folks will be back in a moment. Have you had anything to eat?"

"Nothing!" Annie shouted. "And am I starving!"

"Well, the microwave is somewhere in the kitchen, but it isn't hooked up yet. I'm afraid all I have in the house is the cold pizza left over from dinner. If you don't mind eating it the way it is, you're welcome to it," Mrs. Monagul offered.

The kids filed into the kitchen and grabbed cold slices. Paper cups were by the kitchen sink and tap water was the only option on the menu. They were in the kitchen, finishing their slices, when the front door opened and three more adults entered the house.

"Where have you guys been?" Mrs. Curtis asked. "We've been worried about you!" Mrs. Monagul had rerouted her husband up the stairs to say goodnight to Tommy, after which she joined the others in the kitchen.

Greg answered this time. "We checked out First beach, and ended up going a lot further than we had planned. It took us much longer to get home than we expected. We were afraid it would get dark before we got back. We came up the Boulevard way."

"Next time, head for home earlier," Dad warned. "You know you must always be home before dark. And now it will start getting darker sooner at night, so you will have to start back earlier. I'm glad you left us a note, or we would have been really worried."

"Sorry, Dad," Jon schmoozed. Greg chimed in, "Yeah, sorry, Dad." And although the story had been deceitful, they really were sorry. Sorry to have worried their parents, sorry to have stretched the truth, and sorry they couldn't just tell them everything that had happened. Annie hugged her dad, and Greg heard her say, "We sure saw a lot of sand!" He grinned. Now that was certainly the truth!

Ten minutes did not pass from the moment they stepped out of the Monagul's house, to the moment they were both in bed.

"We can't keep doing this, Jon," Greg whispered. "Sooner or later something is going to happen. We won't get back in time, or one of us will get injured. This isn't fair to Mom and Dad. I don't like hiding things from them."

"I don't either," Jon answered back. "But how can we tell them? They will never believe us!"

"Of course they will. All we have to do is show them the stuff.

How can you not believe the story when you are three hundred feet up in the sky soaring on a magic carpet?" Greg replied.

"But they will never let us go back again," Jon asserted.

"Are you sure you really want to go back again? We nearly got ourselves killed this last time," Greg reminded him. "And besides, they should be able to take care of themselves, now. Ephraim is back at the castle with Prince Judas. The Kingdom has its First Mage, the king must finally be happy!"

"But, Greg, think about what we haven't seen yet. We have spent all our time there involved with one little kingdom. If that world is as big as ours, there must be tons of other things to see! We could avoid the people there, and keep this new world as our private playground. We can travel invisibly anywhere we want. We will never be bored again! Think of it," Jon insisted.

Greg sighed. "You're right. But I'm right too. Let's talk about it tomorrow. I'm beat."

"Okay. G'nite, Greg."

"G'nmnmn."

At one o'clock that morning, Eli repeated his previous performance. He managed to terrify both boys, waking them up from deep slumber. Of course, he did it in a way that allowed the remainder of the house to stay asleep.

"Eli! We really need to sleep! Don't bother us right now," Jon pleaded. Greg didn't even sit up. After the initial fright was over, he just laid his head back down on his pillow, hoping to go quickly back to the dream he had been enjoying.

"I wouldn't interrupt your sleep if it weren't urgent," Eli frowned. "Ephraim is under house arrest. The Obsidian Army is attacking. A horn has been sounded, which means at least one Guardian will eventually arrive on the scene. This is exactly what I feared. If you do not balance the conflict with the Objects of Power, I am afraid my entire world will collapse."

"Who are the Guardians?" Greg asked out loud.

"The Guardians are the monsters given by the Creator to each kingdom as the final defense against destruction. They look like dragons, but they are much more. Creatures of magic, they are the only beings in our country that possess magic in themselves," Eli explained.

"Why must *we* balance the conflict? And *how* are *we* supposed to do that?" Jon asked, with great emphasis in his voice.

"I don't know exactly," Eli admitted. "I simply know that things are out of balance right now. There is only one mage in the Ruby Kingdom, and he is a child. The Obsidian Kingdom prepared for this attack by training a whole college of mages. They provoked this crisis when they were ready for open conflict. They will completely destroy the Ruby Kingdom if you do not intervene. The Guardians of each kingdom will fight to a standstill, but in the meantime, the Ruby Kingdom will cease to exist. The Obsidian King will appoint an Obsidian subject to rule on the Ruby Throne. Once the Obsidian Dynasty controls half of the Gemstone Island, they will proceed to eliminate the other two kingdoms, one at a time. In the process, the Objects of Power still present on the world will become warped by the evil done through them. The Creator will be patient only so long. When it becomes obvious that there is no desire on the part of our race to truly seek justice, he will lose patience altogether. Rufus believed that if that ever happened, creation would cease to exist."

"Oh," was all that Jon could think to say. The room was silent for a few seconds while the boys considered what had been said. Eli broke the silence.

"Not only do I need to have you go back, I need to have you go back right away. A minute or two here might make a difference of hours there. And we really can't afford that. Will you wake Annie and take her back with you? Please, Sirs Jonathan and Gregory?" Eli pleaded. "Your friends desperately need you."

Without speaking, Jon nodded and Greg got out of bed. They managed to pull on black sweats, but decided to carry their sneakers to the basement. They left the doors open as they went, knowing they still had to get Annie, somehow. Retrieving the carpet, they simply carried it up and out the back door, unrolling it in the backyard. Once again, they were thankful that there were no attic windows facing the back of the house. They decided to fly to Annie's window, feeling fortunate that they knew which window was hers. They had no idea how they would convince her to join them.

It turned out to be easier than they expected. When they arrived at Annie's window, a small reading light shone from the room. And there, standing by the window, was Annie, waiting for them! They couldn't believe it! She slid the window open and motioned for them to come in.

"How did...." Greg began to whisper.

Annie clapped a hand over his mouth, and pointed outside. The boys quickly understood her meaning. No more talking until they were out of the house. They paused a moment to shut the window from the outside. Then they flew back to their own house. Eli was holding the back door open for them when they arrived. In they flew, negotiating the openings to the lowest basement.

Again, Greg tried to ask questions, but was hushed. Better to talk inside, Annie gestured.

As they were about to step through the chest, Eli spoke from behind them. "My children, be very careful. Remember, the silver swords are defense and offense against magic."

Greg turned, one last question burning in his mind. "Eli, the necklaces. You've never told us about them. What are they for?"

"Ah, yes, I had forgotten about them. You and Jonathan each have one?"

They nodded their heads up and down.

"These necklaces are mostly defenses. The golden beads are just that, gold. They each weigh as much as one royal gold coin. The colored beads are tied to the elements of the earth, and protect one who swallows them from attacks linked to a certain force of nature. For example, the red bead protects a person from fire, the blue from water attacks, and so on. Only the black bead is offensive. Anyone or anything that tastes that bead will surely die. It is a magical poison, and is triggered both by the intent of the one who uses it and the contact with the intended victim. It will never kill accidentally. It is a weapon of last resort," Eli gravely explained.

"Now, go. The first horn has just been sounded. Please, my friends, save our world!"

CHAPTER 43

# Dilemma

Ephraim languished in his new quarters. He was tormented by what he had done. Even though Ella told him that he had done as well as could be expected, he couldn't get over the idea that he had destroyed so many homes and villages. What had he been thinking? Why couldn't he foresee the consequences of his spell? Why didn't Eli stop him?

Eli had tried to reassure him briefly, but then Eli had to leave. He said he had pressing business where he was. It was Ella who stayed with Ephraim. Ella continued to push him, questioning, instructing. All Ephraim really wanted to do was to sleep—anything to help forget what he had done. But Ella wasn't about to let that happen. There was too much to do, too much to learn, and too little time in which to do it.

As evening approached, Prince Judas came looking for Ephraim, and he brought a visitor. Sam had been very ill for two days and had hardly moved. Now he was starting to eat a little, but was still too weak to walk around. He needed special care, and Judas thought that perhaps Ephraim could help. Ephraim needed something to take his mind off his troubles, and Sam needed some tender loving care. It was a perfect match. Sam snuggled up on the bed on which Ephraim was lying, and Ephraim rubbed his belly while Ella went right on teaching.

After a full day of pushing, Ella finally told Ephraim the whole truth. "Ephraim, ya need ta work harder, and there is an important reason why."

"Why?" Ephraim asked, dejectedly. "I can't do anything right.

I get myself kidnapped, I flood the villages of my countrymen, I destroy their crops. What possible use am I?"

"The Obsidian army is goin' ta strike again. While yer first attack may have been ineffective, it did, at least, buy us some time. And right now, time is very important. I don't think ya can appreciate how important it really is," she added.

"It's not like I can become a great experienced mage overnight, you know. Pumping my head full of axioms and maxims, and expecting that to educate me isn't going to help me defeat armies that have swords and spears and powerful mages," Ephraim complained. Judas sat in the corner, listening to the debate.

"Ephraim! I'm thinkin' that maybe ya shouldn't act like ya know everythin'. After all, I'm a little older and wiser than ya are. Perhaps ya should try listenin' more and talkin' less," Ella scolded, her voice firm. The directness in Ella's voice caught Ephraim's attention—Judas', too.

"I'm sorry, Ella. I didn't mean to..."

"Enough, Ephraim. Please be quiet, and listen. Prince Judas, what ya are goin' ta hear is a secret. Neither o' ya will ever breathe a word, right?" Ella looked at both of them for their agreement. Getting it, she continued. "I am more than just a kitchen cook. I am a trained mage, though not from this kingdom. Eli and I have been married all these years, and we have worked tagether fer the good o' the land. I understand the subtleties o' the use o' power, and ya are correct, Ephraim, ya are young and inexperienced. Ya are far too young ta wield a staff!"

"Then why did..." Ephraim started in again.

"Quiet, young man. Not another word till I'm done," Ella rebuked him. "Ya are far too young ta wield a staff *offensively*. But ya might be able ta use one *defensively*. Usin' the power ta damage the earth or injure people is very difficult ta do, because, remember, ya are channelin' the power deposited by a benevolent Creator. And ya remember from yer readin' how much the Creator loves people. In order ta effectively use power aggressively, ya must believe that what ya are doin' will benefit people in a significant way. If ya are unsure that what ya are doin' will help, or if ya allow anger ta invade yer thoughts, ya are likely ta get unexpected results.

"That's why defensive magic is so much easier. Protectin' is almost always innocent. The need ta protect tends ta focus yer thoughts. Ephraim, ya are not ready ta use a staff ta inflict damage, but I do think ya are ready ta protect and defend those ya love." Ella stopped and gave him time to think. What she said made sense. He knew from his reading that motivation for an action was a very important part of using power. Magical acts could be tainted by bad intentions, which sometimes made results unpredictable. Of course, that made Ephraim wonder how his evil opponents could use magic at all.

"Ella, if intentions are so important to the use of power, why are the Obsidian mages able to use it so well?" questioned Ephraim. "Their intentions are destructive and evil. They are attacking us, after losing fair and square in the Grove. It doesn't make any sense."

"I understand yer question. It is a good one. But ya need ta be able ta look at something from two different sides if ya are ever goin' ta understand this. Think about it, my son. One man prays fer rain so that his crops won't die. His neighbor prays fer sun so that he has time ta reap an early harvest. Both men sincerely wish fer the good, but it cannot rain and be sunny at the same time.

"One kingdom needs water desperately. They resort ta dangerous behavior ta get what they think they need. Another kingdom responds ta the dangerous behavior by callin' fer justice. Mages on one side use power ta defend justice. Mages on the other side might use power ta attack those who selfishly deny others the things they need. All the mages involved feel like they are working fer good.

"But it may be that none o' them are really doing that! The kingdom attackin' ta get what they need may simply be jealous. They may not actually need what they want as badly as they believe they need it. They may just be deceivin' themselves in order ta feel good about their selfish behavior. And the kingdom who is defendin' their position may actually be usin' the rule o' law ta cover up their selfishness. It maybe that everyone is a little bit right and a little bit wrong," Ella explained.

The room grew quiet while everyone thought about what Ella had said. After a few moments, Ephraim spoke up. "I think we should spend some time discussing defensive uses of power."

Prince Judas slipped out of the room as the two mages began to talk rapidly. In his head, Judas wondered which kingdom had trained Ella in the magely arts. Could it have been Obsidia? Judas doubted it, but after discovering that Jeremias, his priest, was a traitor, it was hard to take anyone at face value.

Judas decided to check in on his father to see if there was anything he could do to help prepare for the invasion he now knew must come. As he approached his father's quarters, he could hear the king bellowing inside. Perhaps he would wait for another time to step in on his father. Judas decided to visit the fletcher's shop outside the castle walls. He remembered the fletcher kindly, and figured he could at least spend his time making certain he had all the arrows he would need.

King Stefan gathered his troops and reorganized his divisions. It took the better part of the day to dry everything out. By evening, the Obsidian army had established a temporary camp, and the king gathered his officers for instructions. The next morning, the attack would begin again. This time, they would prepare more carefully. They would move in under cover of darkness. They would have significant magical attacks. The city wall would be breached very early in the battle, trapping the Ruby army between the city walls and the castle walls. They would rush in and destroy the enemy. Then, they would storm the castle and remove the royal family. "Take them alive," he instructed. "I want to bring them to judgment myself. And don't forget to rescue my brother in the dungeon!"

The officers were shocked to learn that a member of the Obsidian Royal Family smoldered in the Ruby dungeons. This would enflame an angry mob even more. After carefully reviewing the trumpet calls that would be used in the darkness the next day, the officers were dispatched to relay the orders to the troops. The mages gathered to quietly rehearse their plans for the next day.

At midnight, King Stefan lifted a silver horn tied with a black rope to his lips. Three times he sounded the horn; the notes issuing from it chilled his bones—but not just his. Mages around the world, perhaps throughout the universe, heard the sound. And the one for whom the horn was especially created awakened from his slumber.

*\*\**

The first night he was captured, Jeremias slept fitfully, worrying about his fate. But by lunch time of the next day, he had settled on a plan that he thought would insure his freedom. All Jeremias needed was to see the face of the guard serving his meal, and he could put him to sleep. Unfortunately, the door was solid, and the guards rarely looked through the small barred square that served as a peep hole.

Two guards were at the door now, one holding his meal while the other barked out the rules. Dinner would be shoved under the door, and no additional meals brought unless the tin plate was returned under the door when the meal was finished, or so they told him. He would be given an hour or two to finish his meal, according to what was convenient for the guard. Jeremias had to act quickly. By stomping his feet, and then making wild gestures, Jeremias managed to communicate to the guard giving the instructions that he couldn't eat while gagged.

The guards conferred. The prisoner was supposed to stay gagged. But they also had orders to feed him. They couldn't obey both orders...and if they didn't feed the prisoner, he would eventually die. Ordering Jeremias to stand back, they unlocked the door after drawing swords, and entered the cell. Jeremias' heart fell. One of the guards was wearing a visored helmet which he closed before entering the cell. His face was completely covered. Jeremias would have to wait. While one guard placed his sword on Jeremias' neck, the other removed the gag. A moment later they were gone, the door locked behind them.

Jeremias contacted his brother, ate his meal—some thin soup barren of meat—and waited for the return of the guard. When he heard the foot steps returning, he started to cough, coughing with greater and greater intensity. When the guard got close enough, he started to bang his tin plate on the wall. His eyes were glued to the small square in the door, the place where he hoped his captor's face would appear.

"What's the matter? Cut out all that racket!" the guard shouted angrily.

Jeremias increased the coughing and the banging. Just as he suspected, the guard drew close to the door and looked in to see what was happening. "Sleep," Jeremias said. And the guard slept. Jeremias quickly got to his hands and knees, his face pressed against the cold stone floor, eyes searching the guard through the slot under the door. The torch that the guard had carried lay sputtering on the ground. Jeremias cursed his bad luck. The guard carried no keys! He would have to keep the game going.

Disguising his voice, he began to yell for help. Jeremias hoped that the guard, in his haste, would leave the helmet behind. When the footsteps got closer, he stopped yelling to prevent the approaching guard from discovering the ruse.

The second guard saw his fallen comrade and quickly came to his assistance. Taking a quick peek into the cell to make sure the prisoner was still secure, he felt himself falling, although he wasn't sure why. This time the torch fell right in front of the door, and Jeremias was able to reach it under the door. It took a few moments to extinguish, but once out, it served as an excellent tool for exploring. By setting his own hand aglow, Jeremias had enough light to prod the second guard, hoping for the jingle of keys. Elated to find exactly what he hoped for, Jeremias looped the small end of the torch under the leather strap that hung around the guard's neck. In about fifteen minutes, he had the keys.

Sliding them under the door, he began to search for a sword. Surely one of the guards had brought a sword! He would need the sword to pry off the back cover of the lock on the door. Once that cover was off, he could operate the lock in reverse and escape easily. He looked under the door carefully, from every angle. He tried looking through the small square. But no sword! How could these guards be so inept?! How was he going to get the metal plate off the back of this lock? "Ah," he said to himself, "If only I had a dagger or...." Before he could finish his sentence, a knife flashed in his hand. He was startled, but immediately recognized it as the dagger his father had given him, the one that had magically opened the armory in the Ruby king's private quarters!

He turned the dagger over and over in his hands. He knew there was some kind of power here that he didn't understand, but decided that it was best to figure that out later. Carefully using the dagger to pry off the back plate of the lock, Jeremias inserted the key and was out in a moment. A quick search of the guards revealed a sword on the ground behind the second guard. Jeremias snatched it up and headed down the dark hall. When he got to the top of the steps, he realized that he had difficult choices to make. If he was seen in the palace, he would be immediately attacked. But on this end of the castle, he didn't know where the secret passages might be. It might be smart for him to hide until his brother attacked. If he hid, however, he could never hide this close to the dungeons. As soon as they discovered he was gone, they would search every crevice until he was found.

Jeremias decided that the area of the castle he knew best, and the place they would be least likely to look for him, was in his old quarters. He wouldn't go into his old room, however, but there were some secret passages that ran along the outside wall of the chapel. Perhaps he could see what was going on from there, and who knows, maybe even lend his brother a hand. Slowly, Jeremias entered the crypt, crossed the room, and began to look for an exit on the opposite wall. In short order, he found one.

## CHAPTER 44

# Attack!

General Zarak woke at the same time he woke every morning. He was accustomed to seeing the sky slowly brighten as the sun struggled to break across the horizon. But the dawn did not come. There was no moon shining. Stars were absent. The world was dark. Very dark. Unnaturally dark. A shiver ran through the general's skin. He quickly sounded an alarm which woke servants and soldiers alike.

The first thing Ephraim heard was Eli shouting in his mind.

*Ephraim wake up! Quickly, wake up! You must get to the king!*

Confused and startled, Ephraim took a moment to catch his breath. "Eli, what are you talking about? I can't just go wake up the king. I'm under house arrest. I'm not..."

*Be quiet, Ephraim! Listen. The king must sound the horn, the silver horn. The Guardian must be awakened! Your lives depend on it!*

"I don't understand, Eli, tell me again what I must do."

*You must get the king to sound the silver horn. The Guardian must be called.*

Ephraim ran to the door of his room and tried the handle. Locked. "Guards, help me. I need help!"

"What is it you want, sir?" a guard asked coldly, but with respect.

"Open the door. I have an important message for the king." Ephraim shouted, urgently.

"I'm sorry, sir, you are not permitted to leave this room. You may have guests with royal permission, but they must come here. You are not allowed to go anywhere else in the palace. I am sorry, sir," the guard finished.

"Please listen carefully. The safety of the kingdom depends on my news. If you won't take me to the king, bring Prince Judas here. He will be able to help me!" Ephraim insisted. 'But do it now, to save your own life!"

The guard, uncertain what to do, decided that waking a prince was much less risky than waking an angry king. Whistling for a guard from the main hallway to assist him, he sent a messenger to bring Prince Judas to the room of the first mage. Ephraim was forced to wait for Judas to come, and in that time, Eli explained their predicament.

*The Guardians are creatures of great magic that enforce the balance of power in the Gemstone Islands. Each kingdom has one, though they are rarely seen and prefer to stay out of the affairs of men and women. A king may call the Guardian to assist only once during his reign, and then only in the time of greatest crisis. The Guardian will loyally defend his kingdom, or the interests of his kingdom, against all attackers. The Guardians cannot be made to initiate any attack, but once a kingdom's armies have been attacked or suffered casualties, the Guardian may be called to help. King Stefan called upon the Guardian of His kingdom in the night. The Ruby King must do the same in order to survive. You must instruct Judi, er...Prince Judas, to tell his father to sound the horn. Tell him the instruction is from me.*

Judas arrived as Eli was finishing, and asked the guard to open the door. As soon as the door was opened, Ephraim rushed to explain all that Eli had told him. "There's no time to waste. The horn must be sounded. The attack is coming right now!"

The prince ran down the hall, taking the steps between the third and second floor in groups of three and four. Crashing through the doors at the bottom of the steps, he ran straight into General Artezes, who was headed for the king's chambers. The general caught the prince, surprised by his sudden appearance, and stood Judas back on his feet. Muttering a quick apology, Judas spun away from the general and ran into his father's study. Zarak was already present, as were several other officers from the army. Anthony stood in one corner of the room. The king looked up as Judas entered, and was about to gesture him away, but Judas spoke out quickly.

"Your Majesty, I have an urgent message from Eli," he spoke

sternly and loudly, mustering up al his courage. The king looked back at him, confusion written on his face.

"How can you..." the king started. Judas interrupted him, speaking loudly to cover the king's words.

"Father, you must sound the silver horn. There is no time for questions. Eli says that it must be done. Now."

"The horn! How can you know it is time to sound that accursed instrument? The enemy is not in sight. Don't you know that if...." Judas didn't let him finish.

"I know exactly what it will do. Do not delay. The Guardian must be awakened. It may already be too late. Another horn was sounded hours ago." Judas spoke clearly, with authority. And the king was visibly shaken.

"Another horn? Already sounded? How do you know? I didn't hear anything." The king shook his head in disbelief.

"Eli heard it, from the other side of the world. There really is no time! Please, Father, get the horn and sound it!" Judas shouted.

The king paused for a moment and mentally regrouped. Then he rose, staring hard into Judas' face. "How dare you try to give me commands!" he accused, his voice burning with rage. "You have no right to..."

At that moment, a messenger burst through the door to the study. "They are here!" He shouted. "We are under attack, Your Majesty."

The king whirled around and ran through his quarters to the tower room at the southeastern corner of the castle. At the same moment, Anthony slipped something into Judas' hand, whispering in his ear, "I need to return something that is yours." Judas quickly slipped the ruby around his neck and followed his father. But rather than proceeding through the bedroom and into the tower, he stopped in the king's room and searched for that spot on the wall, the trigger to the king's armory. With one hand on his royal gem, and the other on the wall, he watched the doorway through which his father had disappeared. It only took a moment for the armory door to gently slide open. The horn was hanging just where it had been previously. Judas brought the horn to his lips, inhaled, just as his father returned into the room.

"No!" his father shouted, too late. Three short blasts burst from the horn, and even though they were in the interior of the castle, there was no doubt that the sounds were heard around the world. They seemed to cut through everything!

"What have you done?" His father screamed. "I told you not to call the Guardian! He is just as likely to destroy us as destroy our enemy! You have made your last mistake, Judas. Guards! Take the prince to the dungeon. Lock him there and do not feed him until tomorrow." Two guards came alongside Judas, each grabbing one arm. Silently, they moved him out of the king's quarters.

As they moved down the corridor, a voice spoke behind them. "Halt! A moment, men." The guards turned to see their Captain, Anthony, approaching. He walked up to Judas and spoke softly.

"I do not understand everything that is happening. But after our adventure in the north, I do not believe you would ever betray us. And it may be that you have just saved us all." He paused for a moment, struggling to keep in balance his frustration with the king and his loyalty to the kingdom. "Fare well, my Prince," he said, before turning and heading back to the king's chambers.

The guards continued down the main stairs, through the ballroom corridor, into the southwestern tower, and down the stairs into the basement. Judas trembled as they led him away. He was humiliated by his father's words, but he knew that he had done the right thing. Why was his father so arrogant? Couldn't he listen to anyone? Judas was relieved to have been able to sound the horn, but angry at his father's foolish reaction. So many conflicting emotions jangled around inside Judas' head that it was hard to pay attention to where he was going.

CHAPTER 45

# Renegade Priest

Outside, the city was surrounded. Black soldiers stained the landscape in every direction. The red armies were amassed inside the city walls, patrols posted on top of the wall that surrounded the city. The castle itself was taller than the city wall, but it was difficult to see all of the enemy troops because the city wall hid many of them from view. The number of enemy soldiers was also difficult to calculate. The dark, dense cloud made visibility very difficult. In fact, the back ranks of the enemy army were obscured in the black mist. Archers from both armies began to fire on one another, although only the first ranks of the enemy forces were in range of the arrows.

General Zarak ordered his soldiers to stop shooting until the enemy was in better range. Wasting arrows would be a serious mistake, one they could not afford. But the Obsidian army held its position, and did not advance. It was almost as if they were waiting for something or someone—which was exactly what they were doing.

For half an hour they stood in position, waiting. General Zarak began to wonder if the Ruby armies ought to attack. He was, however, reluctant to open the front door with invaders on the door step. It was very possible that this was the beginning of a long siege. They would know soon enough.

When Judas and his escorts reached the level of the dungeons, they were immediately surprised that the regular guard was not present to meet them. Passing the guard station, they approached the first cell with torches held high. As they reached the door of the cell, the torch cast its light further down the hallway, revealing the missing guards lying on the floor. Judas and the soldiers ran to give assistance, only to discover that they were only asleep. When they had been revived, the soldiers from upstairs began to abuse the guards for sleeping on the job. One look into the cell where Jeremias had once been a prisoner made it clear to Judas what had happened.

"Don't harass these men. I think I know what happened. The prisoner cast a spell on them that put them to sleep. Look in the cell; he has escaped. We must find him!" Judas insisted.

"I'm sorry, Prince Judas," one of the soldiers began.

Judas cut him off quickly. "Let me show you what happened," he gestured toward the guards who had been previously asleep. With a word, the two soldiers who had escorted Judas down the hallway were now asleep, slumping toward the floor. The guards were astonished.

"Think nothing of it. It is a simple spell, and the priest knew its use well. In fact, he used it on me once. But we must find that traitor right away. Men, if you will help me, we will begin the search immediately!" Judas explained to the guards that the two soldiers would be asleep for about an hour and that it would be necessary to leave them behind. They would gather reinforcements from upstairs. In the mean time, to protect the soldiers from the traitor while they slept, Judas thought it best to lock these soldiers into cell one.

Choosing to separate to cover more area, Judas sent each guard upstairs to recruit a partner to assist in the search. Each was assigned a floor of the castle, and each was warned to hit first, ask questions later. Gagging the prisoner would be necessary. Judas himself would start in the basement after finding a suitable assistant. Judas hid in the archives until the guards were out of sight.

Judas was troubled by the turn of events that placed him in this situation. Why hadn't his father wanted to sound the horn? And why had his father thrown him in the dungeon? He hadn't disobeyed his father directly. He simply did what Eli told him was necessary. Why couldn't his father see that? Judas was very confused. And he was angry.

After waiting a few more minutes for the guards to disappear, Judas climbed the tower stairs, and entered a secret passageway in the ballroom wall. He worked his way toward the king's quarters. He felt sure that the traitor would try to injure his father. After all, that would be the most effective way to assist the enemy troops. Judas worked his way north along the wall, to the passageways that would eventually lead him to the second floor. He made his way along the throne room and over to the passageway that ran along the outside of the king's rooms. He could see messengers in the king's study, along with one minor officer and General Artezes. The general sat at the table, his back to the wall. The king was not there.

Continuing south down the passageway, Judas paused outside the king's personal lounge. As he listened very quietly, he heard footsteps overhead. That puzzled him. Who would be in the chapel area right now? Perhaps servants worried about the invasion? Or maybe, but wait! The chapel wasn't directly over his head! Directly above him was a secret passageway, just like the one in which he was standing. Someone was in there, and it could only be one of two people. Either the king was moving from one place to another secretly, or it was the priest! There was no time to waste!

Running down the passageway, he turned the corner and climbed the stairway to the third floor tower opening. Pushing the door open, Judas saw his father staring out at his army from the opening in the wall.

"Father," he shouted, as he ran toward him, "Jeremias has escaped! He is near here and you are in...." At that moment, the door from the priest's third floor secret passage sprang open, and Jeremias pushed into the room. He grinned.

"Dagger!" he said, and with one quick motion launched his knife end over end at the king. Judas shoved his father hard, pushing him out of the way of the blade. Unfortunately, the blade that was intended for his father ripped through the flesh of his own forearm. The wound was superficial, but bloody nonetheless. By the time Judas looked back at the door where Jeremias had stood, the priest was gone.

Judas tore the cloth from his sleeve and wrapped it around the wound. The king was silent, staring at Judas. He had a confused look on his face. When finally he spoke, he stumbled at first, then managed a short, "Thank you. You saved my life. I'm sorry."

The conversation might have continued then, except it was cut short by screams of terror coming from the soldiers inside the courtyard. When the king and Judas turned to look outside, they couldn't believe their eyes. Flying out of the mist, directly toward the city, was a giant, black, evil thing. It could only be a dragon! The Guardian of the Obsidian Kingdom had come! They were doomed! Judas grabbed the bow and arrows he had previously stowed on the third floor and ran for the main hall. The king began to shout orders to his soldiers below.

Attacking directly at the city gates, the Guardian roared hideously and simultaneously sprayed a deadly black acid over everything in his path. The city gates burst into flames, and the metal bands that reinforced the wooden planks melted. Even the stone of the walls began to smoke. In moments, the entryway into the city was cleared and the black soldiers began to attack through the main gates.

While the front lines repelled the attack, the rest of the troops began to retreat back into the castle. The king, afraid that the attackers might gain entrance to the castle itself, began to shout to the guard at the main door of the castle to close the door. Judas arrived in the main hall just as the doors were being shut against a stream of Ruby soldiers.

"What are you doing?" Judas yelled. "They'll all be killed by that dragon!"

"King's orders!" the guard replied, and continued to loosen the bolt that anchored the left door to the ground. Judas put his head down and charged, driving the man backwards, across the pathway, onto, then beyond the small drawbridge and directly into the moat. Spying Captain Anthony just beyond the bridge, Judas ran to him, shouting his instructions. "Anthony, draw back and keep this bridge and door open until every soldier is safely inside. Then, raise the bridge and shut the doors." Judas returned to the castle. He had a traitor to find.

The king, however, seeing the door still open, screamed for it to be shut. He yelled curses at the soldiers who were retreating, order-ing them to turn and fight. The roar of the battle was so loud in the courtyard, however, no one below could hear his voice. But there was one who could.

The great black dragon wheeled in the sky when it heard the king's violent speech. Diving from high above the tower, the dragon targeted the opening at which the king stood. Once again, a reptilian screech was followed by a fiery blast of corrosive spray that covered the southeastern tower, flooding into every open window. The king screamed in anguish! Judas heard the dragon's scream and ran to the tower room where he had just left his father. By the time he arrived, General Artezes was already at his father's side. The general moved away, letting Prince Judas get as close to his father as possible. Gri-macing in pain, with his teeth clenched against it, he managed to say, "Judas, don't let them win." Then he passed out, and was still.

"Call for Ella and the healer. General, help me move my father to his room and then stay with him until help arrives." Judas spat out orders as if he had been born to do it. "And you," he pointed to a nearby soldier, "get Ephraim from his room. Bring him at once to the study."

The battle would have been very short if reinforcements hadn't arrived at exactly that time. Flying from the west, Jon, Greg and An-nie saw the black dragon circling above the castle, above the black mist. For some reason, it did not see them. Perhaps it was too preoc-cupied with its own affairs. Jon guided the carpet down into the black mist, into the castle, and into the prince's room. There they dropped off Annie.

"See what you can find out, Annie. Check on Ephraim first. We're going to distract this dragon, maybe do a little damage. We'll be back as soon as we can!" Jon ordered, speaking as rapidly as pos-sible. Annie nearly had to jump off the carpet, the boys were in such a hurry.

Flying back out the window, the boys proceeded slowly through the dark mist. Visibility was only a few hundred feet, and they couldn't see the dragon anywhere. Because the armies of the Obsidian Kingdom were in close proximity to their Ruby counterparts, the dragon could not spray the enemy without destroying his own soldiers. And so the dragon repeatedly attacked individual soldiers behind the enemy lines, and sprayed his deadly acid on the castle itself, hoping to wreak havoc as the wet mist entered through windows and openings.

Gregory spied the dragon swooping down from above toward the south western tower. "There he is, Jon! Blast him!" Greg shouted.

Without a moment's hesitation, Jon unleashed a fire bolt directly at the dragon. The first fire bolt flew right over the dragon's head, getting his immediate attention. The second shot was right on the money, completely enveloping the dragon's face!

The dragon stopped in mid flight, hovering at the point where he had been hit. He slowly scanned the sky for his attackers, and though Jon and Greg were invisible to everyone else present that day, the dragon was not fooled. Spying the flying twosome, the dragon laughed, then hissed, "Prepare to die!"

Jon didn't waste any time. Jerking the staff as hard as he could, he sent the carpet straight north as fast as it would go. Greg placed his hands on the eagles on the carpet, trying to coax as much speed out of the tapestry as possible. The dragon was in hot pursuit.

CHAPTER 46

# Counterpoint in Spellsong

Back at the castle, the last of the red soldiers had retreated behind the walls and Captain Anthony managed to get the main doors shut. Archers from atop the castle walls began pelting the enemy soldiers with arrows, inflicting as many casualties as possible. Quickly, the Obsidian soldiers interlocked their shields, creating a protective umbrella above their heads. General Zarak supervised the archers as they continuously sought for targets. From his vantage point on the castle wall, he coordinated the entire defensive effort. Anthony brought order from chaos in the halls below. He organized the remaining foot soldiers into three companies, and stationed each company in one of the main rooms on the first floor of the castle. When it was time for the raiding to begin, he wanted them ready for action and easy to mobilize!

Annie was just leaving Judas' room when she saw Ephraim being escorted through the doors into the king's study. She shouted to him, 'Ephraim! What's happening?"

He turned, as did the guards who were leading him, to see who had called. Recognizing her instantly, he shouted back, "Annie, you're here! Is everyone here?"

"Yes, all present and accounted for! What is going on?" she questioned as she ran to where he was. Judas, hearing the noise, met them at the study door and brought them all inside.

"Where are Sir Jonathan and Sir Gregory?" he implored, desperately. "Tell me they are here!"

"They're here, Prince Judas. Don't worry. They are out fighting the dragon." She shivered when she thought about it. Judas relaxed a moment. Maybe all was not lost, then.

He quickly explained their situation. The king was mortally injured, the army trapped in the castle. The city gates had been destroyed by the Obsidian Guardian. He had summoned the Ruby Guardian, but had done so very late. There was no guarantee help would come in time to save them. They would have to do the best they could on their own. As he was speaking, Ella entered the room, on her way to see the king. She stopped at the table in the center of the study.

"Ephraim, I told ya that ya are not ready ta use a staff yet. But the situation is dire. We are goin' ta have ta take some risks if we are goin' ta survive. I want ta give you somethin', but on yer word, ya must return it ta me when the battle is over. Do ya agree?"

Ephraim looked first at Judas, then at Ella. There was confusion on his face. "I agree, Ella. What do you have for me?" he asked, unable to imagine what Ella might have.

Strapped to her leg, under her long dress, Ella had a staff. She removed it and presented it to Ephraim in exchange for the staff he had held since his return from the mine. "This is the First Mage's Staff. Friends returned it ta me after the incident in the Grove. I have had it ever since. The staff ya had belongs ta the second mage."

An expression of wonder stretched across Ephraim's face. Ella had the staff all this time? Why hadn't she given it to Ephraim? There would be time for questions later, perhaps. Now he would...he never finished the thought, as Ella began again to speak.

"Remember, First Mage Ephraim, you will be most effective defensively. Please don't forget." With that, she passed out of the study toward the room where the king lay dying.

Judas asked his friends to wait for one moment, while he checked on his father. He followed Ella into the king's personal chambers, and found his father lying on his bed unconscious. Ella took a brief look, whispered a question to the healer kneeling beside the bed, heard the response, then shook her head. She motioned for Judas to come close to her. When he did, she drew him in to her and wrapped her arms around him.

"My Prince, yer father will die very shortly. He has been given every medicine we have, and they have eased his pain as much as they can without killin' him. It will not be enough. There are no magical solutions ta this.

"I can sense the tension that still exists in him. And I think it is time ya say goodbye. Think well on yer last words. They will be the last he ever hears from ya in this life, maybe ever."

Judas knew his father was near death, but he had secretly hoped that the healers would be able to do something. If not the healers, then the mages. He was out of options; there was no room left for dreams.

He thought of the last twenty four hours he had spent with his father. They had been the worst of his life. He had seen his father's selfishness and cowardice. He had known his father's rebuke. He had been arrested by his father. But he also remembered those moments in the tower. The "thank you." The apology.

He walked over to the bed on which his father lay, badly burned and heavily drugged against the pain. Kneeling beside it, he drew close to his father's face. Yes, he could sense the tension, too. His father was holding on, holding on for something. He wondered what it was. He spoke softly, directly into his father's ear.

"Father, this is Judas. Everything will be okay. I love you. I will care for our people. You can rest in peace."

The king's body immediately relaxed. He breathed twice more and was gone. Judas felt the ruby on his chest grow suddenly cold. He had forgotten that it was there.

Judas stood to his feet and received Ella's embrace. As he stood there, a tear slipping down his cheek, he heard singing from outside the castle. The melody was eerie and haunting, like music from a funeral. He lifted his head from Ella's shoulder to listen.

"Ella, how do they know so quickly that he is gone?" he asked, his voice shaking.

"Yer Majesty, they do not know. This song is not a song fer the king. This song is designed ta destroy yer castle. We must get ta work immediately, before it is too late." Ella strode from the room, calling for Ephraim as she went. "Ephraim, call fer Eli. Let him see what is happenin'. Tell him the words o' their song. Then get down ta the main entry way. It is time ta fight back!"

The only opening in the front wall of the castle was the circular opening, five stories above the main doors. Any window lower than that would have been a huge security risk. In order to see what was happening outside, the small party moved to the southwestern tower. What they saw was chilling!

Standing just outside the charred remains of the city wall, a line of ten men, all wearing black cloaks, stood in an ordered row. Behind them, another 30 to 40 others stood. The second group was clothed in dark gray. The men in black were singing.

*"Crush selfishness,*
*Grind greed to gravel,*
*Render Red recalcitrance to*
*Rubble for the rabble."*

SpellSong for Primary Attack on Ruby Kingdom

The words floated over the mist, and slowly, very slowly, the mist started to gather. At first it was impossible to understand what was happening. General visibility improved, as the mist collected into a great black circle that surrounded the castle walls.

Before their eyes, the black circle became more and more concentrated, until it was not more than a band of black about a foot thick. Then the others began to sing.

> *"Infuse our words with life,*
> *May power follow right,*
> *Till all the deeds of night*
> *End, vanquished, in this strife."*

This song was a perfect counterpoint to the first, weaving musical strands of support into the first spell. As they sang, the black band, which now resembled a thick black rope, began to constrict, slowly closing on the walls of the castle.

Ella shouted first, finally understanding what was happening. "Ephraim, get ta the main entrance. They are tryin' ta crush the castle walls magically. Ya must strengthen them."

*Yes,* Eli added his voice, *Ella is right. You must anchor your staff on the floor of the palace. Begin to sing strength into the castle walls. Unless you resist this magic, the castle will be destroyed and many lives will be lost.*

As Ephraim ran from the tower to the main entrance, Eli made several suggestions about the wording of the song-spell. Still, the final wording would have to be Ephraim's alone. It was almost impossible to sing a spell another had written. It just wasn't in the nature of the use of power. Power use was too personal, too influenced by the internal mindset of the mage. Although hard to explain, Eli knew better than to tell Ephraim exactly what to sing.

Once Ephraim arrived in the center of the main corridor, he anchored his new staff to the floor and began to sing. Both his hands were on top of the staff, covering the gem. He could feel the ruby growing warm under his fingers. All around him, the soldiers that were stationed in the center corridor stared at him. They were very quiet. The singing from outside the castle had grown louder. Now another voice challenged the external magic:

*"Truth and kindness, eternally strong,*
*Lend your virtue, flow through my song.*
*May walls of stone and structures of wood*
*Remain invincible, magic withstood."*

### Ephraim's SpellSong to Reinforce the Castle

Ephraim FMR

Truth and kind-ness, e- ter- nal- ly strong,

Lend your vir- tue, flow through my song. May

walls of stone and struc-tures of wood re-

main in- vinc- i - ble, ma- gic with- stood.

Unfortunately, Ephraim had to work blindly. He could not see if his song was having any effect at all, and he could not stop the song to ask if it was working. In a few moments, Annie voiced to Ella the question that was in Ephraim's mind, "Is it working?"

"It's workin'," Ella replied. "But will it be enough? That's the question. Whatever ya do, Ephraim, don't stop singin' now!" She turned to the prince, "Judas, bring a few o' your best archers and come with me. We need ta learn some things."

Selecting three men from among the soldiers, Judas followed Ella back to the tower they had just abandoned. The soldiers below were still protected by the umbrella of shields. But Ella had another target in mind.

"Do ya think ya can reach those mages with yer arrows?" She asked the men.

"Yes, Ma'am," the first archer replied. "I'm certain we can. It will be a long shot, but I am sure we can reach the ones in front."

"Then please try ta do so. We need ta stop this song." As the archers stepped up to the tower opening, Ella stared at the effects of the Obsidian mages' spell. The castle walls were completely encircled by a black, writhing, snake of a rope. The rope appeared to be about five inches in diameter, but was not yet tightly constricted around the walls.

The first archer drew his bow and launched an arrow high into the sky toward the singers. It curved through the air, and within 20 feet of its target, seemed to shatter and disappear. There didn't seem to be any reason for the arrow to disintegrate.

"Try another, please," Ella asked. A second archer stepped forward, this time shooting more directly at the target. Again, just feet before hitting the singers, the arrow crashed and fell directly to the earth. "All o' ya, try again," Ella instructed. The results were similar.

"I was afraid o' this," Ella explained. "They have defended themselves magically. We will not be able ta disrupt the spell by distractin' the mages. We must think o' somethin'." Then an unsettling thought occurred to her.

"Judas, we also must protect our mage! If they are able ta disrupt Ephraim, all will be lost. We will have no defenses left. Go! Quickly! Set up a guard around him with strong orders ta keep him from bein' disturbed or distracted!"

Judas and the three archers raced back through the ballroom to the main corridor. As Judas stepped through the door into the room full of soldiers, movement on the stairs caught his eye. Coming down from the second floor was a figure in a white robe. It was an acolyte's robe, hood drawn so that the face inside the robe could not be seen. Judas grabbed the bow from the man next to him, quickly nocking an arrow. There wasn't time to explain. In one fluid motion, Judas raised the bow, aimed and let the shaft fly! The arrow buried itself in the arm of the figure, while Judas shouted, pointing at the steps, "Protect the mage!"

It took a moment for the soldiers in the room to understand what was happening. Some heads turned to look at Ephraim, while a few followed Judas' hand to where the white figure stood, clutching his arm. Reacting quickly, two soldiers leaped toward the steps and bounded up them, but Jeremias was quicker still. Before the soldiers could reach him, Jeremias called for his dagger, twisted, and threw, straight at Ephraim on the floor below. Jeremias was tackled by the soldiers in the next instant, but the dagger was already on its way.

Judas held his breath. Time seemed to come to a standstill, as thoughts raced through his head at lightening speed. If Ephraim was struck, it was very likely that his castle walls would collapse in a shower of stone and mortar. Death and destruction would follow very quickly. He couldn't believe what he was seeing, but there was nothing he could do to prevent it. He was too far from the mage to get there in time. He looked away, afraid to see his friend savaged by the dagger.

Fortunately, Anthony never looked away. Ever vigilant, he had been waiting for the prince to reenter the room, expecting to receive orders. When Judas had entered, Anthony saw the raised bow, the flying arrow, and understood. He ran toward Ephraim, all the time watching the figure on the steps. And when the dagger was thrown, Anthony leaped into the air, thrust his shield forward, and intercepted the blade!

Judas heard a great crash, and felt the whole castle shudder. But when he looked back again, Ephraim was still singing, and his captain was picking himself up off the floor. Judas couldn't believe his eyes! Anthony did it! Ephraim had stumbled slightly when he saw Anthony racing toward him, but, knowing he could not stop, he quickly recovered.

The struggle on the stairs was over the moment the soldiers hit the wounded priest. Judas ordered Jeremias gagged and bound, then tied to the banister of the main stairway. Whatever happened to the castle would happen to him as well.

"Captain Anthony, well done!" the prince praised him loudly, in front of the men. "We all owe you our lives!" Anthony had no response, his head lowered in humility.

"Now, what next?" Judas inquired.

"My Prince," Anthony looked up, "We must do something! Waiting inside these walls with nothing to do will kill us. We are fighting men; we should be fighting!" The men grunted their agreement, but Anthony quickly silenced them.

Judas selected several nearby soldiers to serve as messengers, and then began to give orders. "Send the Generals to me in the southwestern tower. Anthony, select ten of your finest men to protect the mage. Then join us there." Judas turned and strode quickly past the soldiers, soldiers that were now his. No one would know until after the battle that their king was dead. It was a secret best kept for now.

CHAPTER 47

# Grim Guardians

A few miles past the city, the black dragon suddenly, surprisingly, disappeared from behind them and reappeared in front of them. Jon yanked the staff to keep from flying straight into him. The dragon watched, as if playing with them. Jonathan continued to fly away from the beast, but in another moment or so, the dragon was in front of them again. This time they simply stopped. It was clear that the Guardian could fly much faster than they could. Why he had allowed them to get this far was a mystery. Perhaps he had been curious to figure out who or what they were. Or maybe he needed a few moments time to figure out what to do with them. Whatever the reason, they now knew one thing for sure. They weren't going to outrun this monster.

After a few moments of staring, the dragon spoke, in a hissing, raspy voice. "Who are you? What are you doing in this kingdom?"

At first, the boys were too frightened to respond. But the dragon continued to stare, waiting for their answer. Gregory spoke first. "I am Sir Gregory of Newport, and this is my brother, Sir Jonathan of Newport."

"Why do you say that you are Knights of Newport? You are clearly in league with the Ruby Kingdom!" the dragon accused.

"Well, we do support the Ruby Kingdom because we have friends in that Kingdom, but we are not bound to any one kingdom," Jon answered truthfully.

The Guardian seemed to be able to verify the truth of the statement, pausing for a moment to consider. "Alas, that does not matter. Aligning yourself with the Ruby Kingdom was your fatal mistake.

I will..." he paused, cocking his head to the side, as if listening to something far away. "It is a good day to die," he rasped, as he drew his head back and arched his neck to strike. As the Guardian's head raced forward, a deafening roar filled the heavens and Jon and Greg were completely engulfed in a dense cloud of black, acidic spray. The Guardian simply turned and flew rapidly back to the castle, not even bothering to check to see if he had vanquished his opponents.

Shaken, but not injured, Jon and Greg watched the dragon depart. The defensive shield of the carpet had protected them from any physical injury. It took a moment for them to gather their wits, but they quickly realized that they could not afford to let this dragon ravage the troops. They had to distract it, at least until help arrived. Back towards the castle they flew. Arriving in front of the castle, they saw the ranks of mages lined up outside the city walls. They heard the music, and saw the black rope strangling the walls of the castle. They fired an incendiary blast at the corps of mages, but the blast was deflected. Magical defenses! They fired again, but as they did so, the black dragon dropped out of the sky, high above them, spraying them again with his vile acid. Screams erupted from the soldiers in the courtyard below, as acid from their own Guardian dropped down onto several of them.

When the dragon saw that his breath attack was ineffective against the intruders, he charged them with fang and claw. Biting at his enemy, he was surprised to encounter a magical shield. He stopped his attack, shaking his head. What was this? He had never experienced anything that could survive his attacks before! Still, he was not worried. Flying a quick circle, the dragon came at them again. This time, as he approached the boys, he began to veer sideways, so that at the last minute he was able to spin and strike the invisible shield with the full weight of his body.

Jonathan was already gripping the staff with all of his strength when the impact came. Gregory, bracing himself for impact, had grabbed Jonathan around the waist. Otherwise, they might easily have been thrown off the carpet. As it was, the carpet careened backwards under the impact of the enormous Guardian, but it stayed in the air.

The dragon was no longer over-confident. Looking back over his shoulder, he spied the carpet still aloft. Rushing in with both claws before him, he grabbed at the invisible shield with his small but deadly arms, and pushed the carpet toward the earth. The bubble hit the ground with all the force of the dragon that was on top of it. Bones crunched. Darkness closed in around Jon, as he lost consciousness. Greg was cushioned by Jon's body, and although momentarily dazed, was quick enough to notice that Jon's leg now stuck out through the edge of the protective bubble. The dragon snapped at the leg, but Gregory pulled it back to safety in the nick of time. Just then, the dragon screamed!

CHAPTER 48

# Spell Shearing

Annie watched the events in the courtyard while Prince Judas and the others ran back to the main corridor. She and Ella became more concerned by the moment. The rope was getting tighter and tighter and seemed to be gaining strength. At one point, it seemed that the whole castle shook, and then began to fight back again. But this was clearly a losing battle. Ephraim would not be able to last forever, especially against forty mages. Just then, a fire bolt erupted out of nowhere, bouncing off the defensive shield that surrounded the obsidian mages. She had seen that kind of fire bolt before. Even though she couldn't see them, she knew that Jon and Greg were back! She heaved a sigh of relief, but just then the dragon came roaring into view. It was obvious that another battle was in process, only half of which was visible to her.

Seeing the fire-bolt, however, took her mind back to their escape from the mine. Something Greg had said after the rescue came back to her in that moment. It concerned the silver swords. Greg had said that after he realized his sword was a magical weapon, he had used it to cut his way through the magical barrier that sealed off the entrance to the cave. A sword that cut through magic! That was it! Now she knew exactly what she had to do!

"I'll be back," Annie shouted at Ella, and was down the tower stairs in a flash. Reaching the bottom, she yelled at a group of soldiers, "You, get the longest and strongest rope you have, and get it to the top of this tower as fast as you possibly can. The king needs it!"

Annie ran back up the stairs that she had just come down, this time heading all the way to the top. She could see the dragon chasing something, but she didn't have time to pay attention. The soldiers were already running up the stairs after her, ropes in hand. As soon as they got to her, she began shouting the orders. "Tie the longest rope here. You, give me your gauntlets!" The gloves were hopelessly big, but she didn't mind. She needed protection for her hands. There was no time to waste.

Annie tied the other end of the long rope around her waist. Instructing the soldiers to hold tightly, she grabbed onto the rope they were holding, stepped over the top of the wall, and began to lower herself down the other side. Rappelling was not something she had done very often, so she moved very slowly. The gauntlets protected her hands, but the sword at her waist was troublesome. Creeping down the face of the wall, inch by inch, she slowly made progress toward the rope that was strangling the life out of the castle walls. She could feel the pressure building within the structure under her feet. She had to hurry; this thing was going to collapse any minute! And if the walls fell, well, she didn't want to think about that!

She stepped over the rope, and paused to readjust her grip so that she could draw the sword. As she did, a great shadow passed over her. She looked up, horrified, to see another great dragon, blood red, fly in front of the castle. The black dragon was now on the ground, holding something down, it seemed. The red dragon screamed as it flew straight at him, covering him in flame. The black dragon screamed in rage.

Annie forced herself to look away. Sliding the tip of the silver sword between the castle and the shimmering black rope, she slowly began to draw the sword back and forth, back and forth.

At first, she was unable to twist the blade enough to get it to bite into the rope, but eventually it seemed as if strands of magic began to fray away from the whole where the silver touched it. Pulling and pushing with all her might, Annie began to make progress. Sweat beaded up on her forehead, as she clenched her teeth against the strain of her labor. She was about half way through the fully constricted cord, when, in the next moment, the entire rope seemed to melt away, as the sword slipped directly through the heart of where the rope once was. There was a collective gasp, almost a shriek, as the disruption of the spell fed back onto those who were casting it. Many of the Obsidian mages lapsed immediately into unconsciousness. Some lay moaning, writhing in agony. The song had evaporated. The spell was destroyed.

King Stefan was devastated. He had seen Annie the moment she had stepped over the wall. He had yelled for the Guardian to intercept her, but the Guardian was preoccupied with his own prey, and distracted by the appearance of another of his kind. The king's men outside the castle had their shields raised to protect themselves from the downpour of arrows. They never saw Annie. Everyone else was simply too far away to do anything in time. Stefan couldn't believe his plan was coming apart! But the battle was far from over. Even the appearance of a second Guardian couldn't deter him from trying to satisfy his need for revenge.

"Send our Guardian to distract their Guardian, Your Majesty," Marfessol suggested. "Then ram the front door. Attack while they are celebrating the demise of our spell!"

Pleased, the king shouted to his Guardian: "Obsidian Guardian, drive off the Ruby Guardian so that we can attack."

But the great dragon only looked back at the king and hissed, "Quiet, you fool." The king froze in his tracks.

After the Ruby Dragon had bathed his counterpart with flames, he whirled back to the castle wall, just beneath the place where Annie still hung. "Cut your rope. Climb up and hang on," he ordered, hissing the words through his teeth. Annie did exactly that, scared senseless. She crawled slowly up the neck of the dragon, hanging just behind his ears, as he flew back to accost his adversary.

"I see you have captured a prize today," he hissed at the black dragon.

"What is that to you? This is pointless," the black dragon answered angrily.

"I don't think this is pointless. You seem to be attacking my family. That is a mistake," the red dragon responded, obviously greatly irritated as well.

"This is pointless, because you know that you cannot harm me and I cannot harm you. We are equally matched, by the Creator's will. Why waste all this energy fighting?" the Black Guardian asked.

"Correct, but if you destroy my kingdom, I will destroy your kingdom. Where will that leave us?" the red dragon reasoned.

"Ah, but these insects I have caught here are not of your kingdom! They are from another place and do not merit your protection. These I will destroy!" he growled, venomously, looking back at the boys beneath his feet.

"Now! Silver sword!" the red dragon hissed to Annie. The dragon suddenly lurched forward, bringing his head right next to the black dragon's head. Annie swung the sword, nipping the dragon's long ear.

The dragon's scream split the sky, as he ducked away from the red dragon, still holding his position on top of the carpet. That scream was a terrifying and yet somehow transfixing thing. Every soldier in view of the exchange immediately turned to watch the drama unfold between the two behemoths, unable to look away.

"What was *that*?!" the black guardian painfully cried.

"I think you know," the red dragon grinned in reply, moving quickly out of range of the black dragon. "And now you know that things are not as balanced as you thought. In fact..." The black dragon hissed loudly.

"A Silver Sword of Power!?! You fool! You will destroy us all! You know I will not allow you a second chance to use that dragon-killing sword on me. I have seen your little lackey now, and one blast of my breath will melt her from your back. And I will destroy any other you convince to wield that sword."

Unfortunately, in his obsessive attention to the small girl perched behind his opponent's ears, the Obsidian Guardian forgot about the two "insects" under his foot, on whose protective shield he now leaned. Greg, of course, had not missed a word that had passed between the two giants. Drawing his own silver sword, he gripped the hilt with two hands, and plunged the blade directly into the side of the great beast. The Guardian howled in pain, pushed away from his attackers, and rolled onto his side. The drops of black blood that fell from his wound burnt the ground where they landed. Within moments, the dragon lifted off, still crying in pain, and flew unsteadily back toward the West.

Someone, far beneath Mt. Kyd-juum, heard the sound made by the unleashing of the power of a silver sword against the indestructible Guardian. He paused in his work to listen carefully. When he heard the sound a second time, he knew he had not been wrong. "Ah, they are back. Soon it will be time to craft the weapon that will defeat those swords, that will bend them to my will," he thought to himself.

CHAPTER 49

# Victory!

Judas, who was now in the Southwestern tower with his generals and others, watched the whole thing unfold. All the soldiers outside the city walls stared hypnotically as the limping black dragon fled the battle field. General Artezes knew the time to loosen the counterattack had arrived. "Anthony, now!" he shouted. The herald relayed the orders and Anthony attacked.

The castle doors burst open, unleashing a charge of cavalry into the courtyard aimed straight for the city gates. Directly on their heels, flowing into the vacuum created by the horses, the remaining two squads of ruby soldiers poured.

Once the cavalry had cleared the city walls, the two other squads of soldiers clustered back to back at the city gates. In a quick maneuver, half of the obsidian army was trapped inside the thick walls of the city, without any possible means of reinforcement. In a matter of minutes the whole tide of this conflict had changed. The cavalry was nipping at the heels of the forces surrounding Stefan, and Anthony, directing this assault, was right in the center of two squads of red soldiers, standing exactly where the city gates had stood a few hours earlier.

When Stefan saw the cavalry charge, he quickly turned to flee, sounding retreat as he went. All the Black Army outside the city walls fled with their king, but there was no escape for those inside. Reading the writing on the wall, the soldiers trapped inside the city walls began to lay down their weapons. Shouts of "Mercy! Mercy!" rose from the beaten men, and mercy was given.

"Lay down your weapons!" Anthony's voice roared out. "Down

on your knees, and you will not be further harmed!" The Ruby soldiers inside the walls quickly gathered weapons and organized the prisoners. Their comrades outside the walls remained vigilant against the possibility of a return of the black army.

But inside the castle Judas was frantic. "This cannot end this way! It will never be over! General Artezes, I must speak with Stefan."

"It's too late for that, I think," the general sputtered, surprised at Judas' words. "You'll never catch him now."

"But I must! Get me Ephraim, get me my fastest horse, get me some way of getting to Stefan before he gets away!" Judas shouted, clearly despondent. "General, call back the cavalry. Stop chasing them!"

Ephraim, watching the clean up operation from the main entryway to the castle, was whisked up the steps to Judas. Artezes, clearly confused, gave orders to the trumpeters to sound the calls that would cancel the attack. "Your Majesty, I don't understand. This is exactly where we want...."

Judas cut him off. "Ephraim. How can I get to Stefan? I must talk with him if this is ever going to end."

"Send the guardian. He's the only one who can stop him in time," Ephraim replied.

"Can you manage it, Ephraim?" Judas asked, tentatively.

"I'll try." Ephraim began to sing a soft tune. It was almost inaudible, but the effect was immediate. The red guardian, who had been circling the field with Annie mounted behind, turned directly back toward the castle, stopping outside the tower window where Judas and the others stood watching.

"My friend," Judas nervously began, "we must have peace. Can you, will you, stop that king long enough for me to catch up with him and speak with him?"

A smile slowly spread across the reptilian face. "Annie. Best you stay here. My king, mount your horse." The moment Annie was off his back, the dragon twisted and shot straight toward the retreating army.

By this time, Artezes had two mounts at the front door of the castle. He jumped on one and held the reins while Judas mounted the other. His next words astonished Artezes. "Wait here, general. Ephraim, cover us with something to deflect arrows, if you can!"

Artezes protested as he scrambled off the back of his horse. "But Your Majesty, you cannot go alone; it is far too dangerous!" Zarak, just behind the horses, rushed forward to reinforce Artezes' objections. "Judas, uhmmm, Your Highness. Please reconsider. This is..."

Grabbing the reins of Artezes horse, Judas spurred the horses into action, breaking free from the press of his advisors. "Sorry, gentlemen. For this, I need Anthony. Ephraim, get to work!"

Whether Ephraim was able to provide any protection or not, no one ever knew. In moments, Judas was beside Anthony at the city gates. "Quickly, Anthony, ride with me. We must catch Stefan and end this conflict." Anthony was astride his horse in an instant, joining Judas in a mad dash toward Stefan.

The dragon had done his job. Quickly outpacing the retreating army, the red dragon situated himself directly in their flight path. Starting a few fires in the field around him, he was able to create a burning barrier. In order not to provoke a fight, he kept the fire between the soldiers and himself. Once the retreat had stalled, he hissed with a crackling voice like thunder: "Stop! Wait! For the next few minutes you are under my protection. Be still, and you will not be harmed. Attempt to fight or flee, and I will withdraw my protection."

"What treachery is this?" Stefan shouted. "Why should we wait for...."

"Enough!" shrieked the dragon. "Wait and be quiet. One comes who would speak with you."

Stefan ordered *halt* to be sounded. Confusion reigned on the battle field. The Obsidian army realized, for the first time, that they we no longer being pursued. A good "tenth of a mile" separated their last rank from the red cavalry, which now stood motionless on the plain behind them.

And now into that space rode two men on horseback, galloping at full speed. They slowed as they reached the first soldiers at the rear of the army.

"We must see the king," Judas announced, with as much regality as he could muster. Soldiers stepped in to intercept the two, blocking their path, protecting their monarch. Anthony reached for Judas' arm, stopping him. Then he spoke directly to the soldier standing in the front of the blockade, as if giving orders. "You, there. Serve your king. This one," he gestured toward Judas, "is completely unarmed. And now, here is my sword, as well." Sword and belt fell unceremoniously to the ground as Anthony lifted his empty hands into the air. "We go completely unarmed," Anthony finished and was silent.

"Unarmed" was something the soldiers understood. The soldier Anthony had addressed stepped forward and picked up the captain's sword. He took the reins of both horses in his hand, then turned and shouted, "Make way! Make way!"

A pathway appeared through the center of the army, opening directly to King Stefan himself. Judas was within 50 feet of the king before Stefan saw him. Stefan's attention had been completely absorbed by the dragon in front of him. But now fear was replaced with confusion. Turning his mount, he slowly made his way toward Judas, Marfessol at his side. He stopped ten paces in front of his ruby counterpart

Judas mustered his deepest voice to shout across the distance that divided the two kings, making certain his voice would travel to as many other ears as possible. "A new day has dawned. As the new king of the Ruby Kingdom, I would hear your complaints before you depart. The justice of the future need not imitate the justice of the past. Please, speak freely, King Stefan. I need to hear your truth," Judas requested calmly.

Stefan looked at Judas, then turned back to look at the red guardian. Judas read both terror and confusion on his face. Stefan's eyes narrowed as the fear was replaced by anger and hatred. "You killed my parents, mother and father. You cheated on the Great Board, dishonoring yourself by using outsiders in defense of your kingdom. You destroyed the dam we built to get water for our crops. My people need this water, if they are to thrive, but you will not relent nor bargain fairly. You deserve to be destroyed." He stopped abruptly.

Judas began calmly. "You have also killed my mother and father. The dams we destroyed were built across streams that fed our farms. Those dams were stealing our water, and no negotiations were requested before they were built. We did not cheat on the Board. The rules clearly state that anything in the Grove may take the place of a converted pawn. It was the Creator who placed outsiders in the Grove at that moment. Stefan, if we had cheated, the Great Board itself would have protested, destroying our forces. You know that this is true!" By the time Judas was finished he was greatly agitated.

Stefan considered the words of Judas. The part about the Great Board was confusing. What Judas said made sense. But the water, they needed the water. Without it, they would never grow strong as a nation. Water was wealth, prosperity. He had to have water! "Judas, we must have water! You hoard all the water supply coming down out of the mountains. We must..."

"You shall have water." Judas interrupted. Stefan stopped, straining to make sure he had heard correctly.

"What did you say, Judas?" Stefan responded.

"You shall have water. I will not give you all the water, for we also have need of it. But I promise you, we will find a way to share the water. Perhaps we can begin by diverting a fourth of the water from the Great Tirades as soon as the dams can be rebuilt. Then, over three or four years, we can increase the amount until we are sharing it equally. Will that buy us a truce?" Judas asked, hopefully.

There was a long silence. Finally, thoughtfully, Stefan spoke. "Yes, Your Majesty, it certainly will."

"Before you go, I would like to seal our deal," Judas added. "I have your brother just inside the doors of the castle. I am afraid he is wounded, and that by my hand. I would return him to you, in exchange for a token of your promise."

"What token would you have?" Stefan asked, wondering what Judas might want.

"Your brother has a dagger. It is an object of power that he used to violate the sanctity of my father's apartments. I understand that he was only operating in what he thought were the best interests of his kingdom, but the feelings of vulnerability linger. I would like to have that dagger. I cannot take it from him. He must freely give it."

"You shall have it," Stefan replied, jubilantly. He was still having trouble believing that he had actually won with words the water rights he had come to fight for.

Marfessol was silent. Judas closed the distance between himself and Stefan and placed a hand on Stefan's arm. "May today mark the beginning of a new way among us—cooperation before competition, compassion in place of contempt." Stefan smiled; Marfessol melted away, out of sight. The battle really was over.

## CHAPTER 50

# Epilogue

The celebration inside the city was spectacular! The old king had been buried in a solemn ceremony, the Royal Remembrance Ritual observed in every detail. Now, seven days later, most traces of the battle were gone from the city.

Ephraim, now well rested, had returned the staff of the first mage to Ella the moment the battle was ended. Smiling, Ella handed it back to him, after getting his promise to limit himself to defensive uses of power for at least another year.

Judas half-heartedly supervised the moving of his things from his old room around the balcony to his new apartments. He felt too young to be king. But Providence had already made the decision. He would do his best to earn the trust of his people.

The coronation was planned for noon. The palace was packed, people filling the main entryway all the way up the stairs to the throne room. To the left of the Ruby Throne, General Zarak stood, polished red armor gleaming. On the right of the throne, newly promoted General Anthony stood. A fanfare of trumpets announced the approaching royal procession, as Prince Judas followed the new Chamberlain to the dais. Judas had appointed a chamberlain to help him oversee the kingdom and to compensate for his youthful inexperience. The appointment had been very popular, and Artezes climbed the steps to the throne, carrying the crown before him. At the top of the stairs he turned. Judas now stood directly before him, though on a lower level.

"Hear ye, Hear ye, people of every village and town, high and low, noble and common. I now crown Prince Judas as king, King of the Ruby Kingdom, Sovereign of the Nation, Arbiter of Justice, Commander in Chief, and Prophet of Providence. Long Live King Judas!"

"Long live the king!" the people cheered back, repeating the refrain. As Artezes placed the crown on his head, Judas thought of his friends who had helped to save his kingdom, wishing they could be here to see this moment.

***

When Jonathan woke up, his head throbbed and his leg ached. He didn't recognize his surroundings, but he knew the people around his bed. And he figured he must be in a hospital somewhere. Somewhere near home.

Mom was sitting on the foot of his bed, opposite from the leg that hurt. Dad was in a chair right next to his head, and Eli was standing off in the corner of the room.

"Hey, looks like he is coming around," Mom announced softly. "How do you feel, honey?" she asked gently.

"My head is killing me. What happened?" Jonathan asked.

"Well," Mom glared at his father for a moment, then continued, "Greg and your father have been trying to explain that to me. But I would surely like to hear what you have to say."

It was only then that the significance of Eli's presence struck him. Oh, no! They must know everything, he thought.

"I really have a bad headache," Jon stalled. "Where's Greg?"

"He's fine," Dad answered. "And don't worry. We know the whole story. Annie's parents do, too."

Jon relaxed, feeling like a thousand pound weight had been lifted from his shoulders. "But what happened? I can't remember coming home or how I got here. And where is here?"

"You're in the hospital, honey. You have a concussion and a fractured leg." Mom knocked on the cast, then continued. "You're really lucky you weren't more seriously injured. Greg and Annie got you home, along with some help from those friends of yours that I have never met."

"Jon," Greg nearly shouted, entering the room from the hallway. "I'm glad you're all right!" He ran up close to the bed to get a better look.

"Thanks for getting me back home," Jon whispered to Greg.

"No problem. We had lots of help!" Greg smiled. "I'm just glad everything is all right, right Dad?"

"Right, Greg," Dad said. "Right, Dad?" his father looked toward Eli.

"Right, son," Eli replied, and then grinned at Jon.

"Son?" Jon questioned, puzzled. "Did you say 'son'?"

"Yes." Eli smiled broadly. "You may call me Granddad."

"Granddad! You're kidding!" Jon squealed. "That's impossible! How can my father be your son if you are from the Ruby Kingdom? I thought..."

"Don't get too excited, Jonathan. There's plenty of time to figure everything out," Eli reassured him.

And so the story slowly unwound. Years ago, when Capt. Curtis, then Daniel Rocquefist, was a child of about Jon's age, the Gemstone Islands were threatened by a great evil. A twisted mage managed to find out where the Creator had hidden most of the Objects of Power. Once they were in his possession, he was able to establish himself as sovereign of all the land. A cruel tyrant he was.

Eli, second mage at the time, married, with one child, recovered the items that had been stolen and gathered several others that had not yet been found. The trouble was finding a place to hide them where the tyrant couldn't eventually regain them. It was then that Eli discovered that another world existed, and that it could only be reached under unusual circumstances.

Eli and his son were inseparable companions, and Daniel was already an advanced apprentice mage. Together they planned to transfer the Objects of Power out of their world. The problem was—whoever took the Objects out could never return home again. All along, Eli had planned to be the one to leave his kingdom, but Daniel knew that if Eli left, the world would be defenseless against the powerful tyrant.

When the time to act finally came, Daniel wasn't left with much of a choice.

One night, when the plans were nearly completed, soldiers broke into their home. Eli was detained at the castle; Daniel fled into the night. He gathered the Objects, raced to the Sacred Grove and invoked the spell. It was the brutal attack of the sorcerous king that actually shed the drop of blood needed to complete the spell that transferred Daniel to a different world. There he meticulously carried out the plans that he and his father had made. Objects had to be hidden, tracks covered, histories erased. All of that, Daniel had done.

Once his work was completed, he traveled to a new town and took the name Curtis, claiming to be abandoned by his parents. He was placed in foster care in Middletown, RI until he left for college, where he met and married the woman who was now Mrs. Curtis. Mom knew that Dad had once lived in Middletown, but had always believed that he was an orphan. Of course, Dad sort of believed that he was an orphan, too, since he knew he would never see his real parents again.

"I can't believe I never figured out that you had found the Objects," Capt. Curtis exclaimed to the boys. "I knew sooner or later someone would show up to recover them, and I secretly hoped I would be able to see it happen. I thought that maybe there was a chance that someday I could go back. I never expected to see my father again!" There was a tear in the Captain's eye as he spoke.

Suddenly, Jonathan remembered Annie. "What do Annie's parents think about all of this?"

A sheepish look crossed Capt. Curtis' face. "Frankly, they don't know what to think. I don't think they would have ever believed the story, if Annie hadn't called her dagger."

"Her dagger?" Jon asked.

Greg piped up. "King Judas gave her Jeremias' dagger as a special gift."

"King Judas? When did he become king?" Jon asked, full of disbelief.

Greg chuckled. "I guess there are lots of details we'll have to catch you up on. We'll get it all straightened out before we go back."

"IF you go back," Mom corrected. She glanced around the room, first at Dad, than at Eli. Both quickly averted their eyes.

Jon was glad that the secret was out, at least to his parents. But he could tell that the future was still very much up in the air. For a second, he wondered how much Mom really knew. How much did they really tell her? Maybe it was best to just keep his mouth shut for a while. Maybe he needed to be quiet and listen. Maybe he had better...he was growing confused.

"I think I need to get some more sleep," Jon observed, weakly. "I'm feeling really tired."

"That's something I can help you with," Eli offered, smiling, the ruby on his right hand glowing brightly.

"Don't you dare, old man," Mom warned. Jon closed his eyes. Before he could figure out what his mother meant, he was asleep.

\*\*\*

Cover design by Jeff Bretsch / Chess match by Ray Whitney

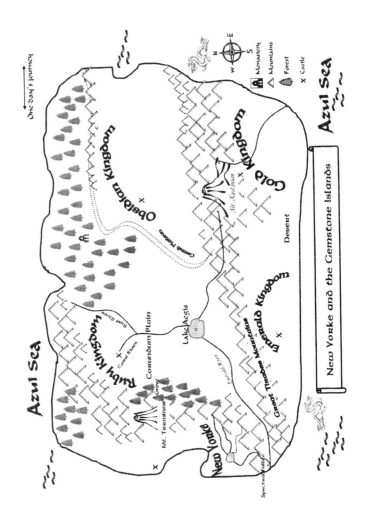

New Yorke and the Gemstone Islands

321412